A Salzburg Sunrise

by

Liz Ringrose

First Edition

Print Edition

ISBN 978-0-9933689-1-2

For Nigel

Chapter One

Out there somewhere was the real Natalie Grey, thirty years old and raising children. She would also be forging a nice career and living with a husband who didn't find her boring and who hadn't left her for a quantity surveyor called Sigourney. The unreal Natalie, also thirty but feeling much older, was standing in front of a bendy bus, in central Europe, hoping the driver wouldn't mow her down.

Her friend Glenda hurried along with their suitcases. 'No fear of him driving off,' she told Natalie, 'they have an integrated transport system. He waits for the train passengers to disembark. Isn't that great?'

Glenda rarely needed a reply so Natalie didn't offer one.

'Wherever there are umlauts things work efficiently. Have you noticed that? And handshaking is very big in this country. So civilised. I've noted all my observations down.'

On the bus Natalie stared out of the bus window. For a week she'd allowed Glenda to guide her round some beautiful scenery in an Austrian lakeside town. Now they were moving to stage two of Glenda's itinerary: a week in Salzburg soaking up culture.

'I hope you're not daydreaming about you-know-who.' Glenda dug her in the ribs.

'No. I'm just taking in the view.' To the left the wide valley was bordered by mountains, to the right the hills were shallower, deeply wooded and dotted with homesteads.

'You don't fool me,' Glenda said. 'All thoughts of home, work and particularly *men*,' she spat out the word, 'are forbidden. We agreed, right?'

Natalie nodded, inclined her head to the countryside. 'But I thought we were coming to a city for our second week.'

Glenda tapped the side of her nose and turned away.

It had been the feeling of unreality that led Natalie to accept Glenda's invitation to go on holiday. She might as well live this strange, detached life somewhere nice for a couple of weeks. It was true that one's boss wasn't the obvious holiday companion but Natalie rather liked her; they were the same age, had a love of dramatic scenery in common, and Glenda took the lead, booking the flights, choosing hotels, printing out reams of information from the Internet and arranging every microscopic detail.

Glenda, Natalie suspected, had problems of her own.

She noticed her friend's hair was escaping from its elastic band but thought better than to mention it. Glenda was pretty but dragged her hair into the same tight ponytail every day and wore no make-up. Not that Natalie would win any beauty contests herself at the moment. Her bobbed haircut had grown out and now brushed her shoulders. She hadn't bothered to bring her straighteners so it kinked in a succession of question marks around her face. So she'd been surprised when the receptionist at work had suggested that she and Glenda might go out *on the pull.* 'Nice looking pair of girls like you could easily bag a couple of ski instructors,' she'd said.

Natalie remembered holding her breath while Glenda composed her crushing reply. There had been ample sarcasm about ski instructors not working in September and sundry disparaging remarks about men who were, certainly for herself and apparently for Glenda, right off the itinerary.

Hotel Friesen was a short walk from the bus stop in a quiet village street. Horse chestnut trees shaded a terrace at the front where a couple of people were eating a late lunch.

'We've got the best of both worlds here,' Glenda explained. 'Ten minutes on the bus into Salzburg but lovely surroundings on our doorstep.' She gestured to the traditional houses, balconies overflowing with geraniums, the lane curving away into fields; then she stopped outside the hotel door and began to riffle through her papers.

A family unloading luggage from a taxi navigated around Glenda's suitcase.

Natalie gave the family an embarrassed smile as they edged past; their small daughter wheeling a tiny case of her own in fluorescent pink.

Glenda muttered to herself, 'The hotel booking sheet is here somewhere. Ah, got it.' She drew a page to the top of the pile and moved forward. Before Natalie could warn her Glenda fell over the child's case, sprawling onto the path. Her sheaf of print-outs flew up and A4 paper descended in all directions.

Startled, the child howled. Glenda leapt up and grabbed for the papers. A passing delivery van wafted them in its wake and they slid across the road, curling up against neighbouring fences and the wheels of a parked bicycle. She ran to and fro, snatching at the sheets. The child was still wailing. Glenda shouted, 'Don't just stand there, Natalie, why aren't you helping me?'

But then a woman came out of the hotel. She wore a sprigged cotton dirndl dress and had orange Crocs on her feet; a plait hung down her back. She stood beside Natalie watching Glenda on her hands and knees in the road. 'Mein Gott, what is happening?'

Natalie held out her hand. 'I believe we have a reservation,' she said, 'but we're having trouble locating the confirmation.'

Chapter Two

'Are you going up *and* down?' The man behind the Perspex window raised his eyebrows.

'Just up,' Glenda said, handing over some coins. 'We'll walk down.' She scooped up the tickets and steered Natalie towards the queue. 'Have you ever been on a funicular before?'

'I've never even heard the word before.' Natalie shuffled towards the turnstile.

Glenda had planned their city itinerary with precision. They were two days into their visit and first call today was the great white fortress sitting on its rock high above the city. Following her fall she was sporting a bruise on her arm which might have been worse if the woman with the plait, who was one of the hotel owners, had not insisted on packing ice round her arm. Her name was Karin, a year or two older than Natalie and Glenda, and she oozed capability. Under Glenda's supervision she had printed off more tourist information to replace the lost sheets. Once or twice Natalie thought she saw mischief in Karin's expression.

A low roar beyond the turnstile grew louder as the funicular train approached. Then they were filing along a tiny platform where the single carriage stood, its compartments staggered to accommodate the slope of the hill. A couple of children darted through the first door.

'Go to the last one.' Glenda jabbed Natalie in the small of her back. 'We'll be able to see over their heads.'

They held on to straps as the carriage filled and the doors hissed to a close. The funicular glided backwards up the slope and the old town was laid before them, ancient churches, Baroque domes and towers all set against the dense green backdrop of the hill across the river.

'I left my stomach at the bottom,' a woman said and a few tourists nodded in agreement. But Natalie's stomach was very much where it should be and she was astonished to feel a tremor of something that felt like excitement. No surely not; anticipation maybe.

At the top, as the crowd spilled out of the funicular station, it was as though they'd been transported back to the middle ages. Buildings enclosed within the fortress walls were older and plainer than those in the town below. Sun gleamed off the white-washed towers, Natalie shaded her eyes and wondered how many people, over the centuries had stood on this spot and done the same. The rustle of internet printouts brought her back to the present.

'We'll look at the view over the city first,' Glenda said, striding towards the battlements.

There it was again, that strange sensation nudging her tummy as Natalie looked down at the old town and allowed a, 'Wow' to escape her lips. She picked out landmarks; the cathedral and the bridge over the river they had crossed in the bus. Glenda was reading out information but it was difficult to listen when all she wanted to do was breathe in the view and hold it inside her.

She posed for a photograph beside a canon; then took one of Glenda looking out over the southern walls, the mountains giving her a dramatic backdrop. Natalie hadn't brought her camera; wasn't even sure where it was. It probably still had pictures on the memory card of herself and Adam with Toby at Alton Towers. She wasn't ready to see things like that. It was a pity you couldn't erase your own memory card.

'Will we have time to go up there again?' she asked Glenda as they took the shady path back down to the city.

'We'll see if time allows later in the week.' Glenda was shuffling her papers. 'Mozart's house next,' she said, 'the one across the river.'

On the footbridge they paused for photos and stood aside for a tour group to pass by. A young woman in a dirndl and apron led the way, holding a folded umbrella aloft. A straggling group of American tourists followed her, taking quick snaps of the view as they hurried to keep up.

'I'm glad we're independent travellers,' Glenda said. 'I couldn't bear to be in a group like that, all following like sheep.' She quickened her pace and called over her shoulder. 'Come on, we've lots to see.'

'Baaah,' Natalie said under her breath.

The Mozart house was tranquil. Natalie held the information recorder to her ear and wandered through rooms of portraits and musical instruments. She knew nothing about Mozart but imagined the small boy playing piano and enthralling his audiences. That made her think of Toby and his tears when she last saw him so she blotted out the image and listened to the music.

There was a café next door and they ordered cake. A waitress in traditional dress brought their drinks to the table.

'I like the clothes the locals wear.' Natalie stirred sugar into her Cappuccino.

Glenda gave a coy smile. 'I'm going to buy myself a dirndl. They cost a fortune but they're very well made.'

'Why do you want one?' She imagined Glenda wearing it for work at the vet's when they got home.

'For the Sound of Music tour. I watched the film again just before we left. I've learned all the words to the songs.'

'I'm not sure I'd want to do that, I …'

'Oh, it'll be great fun.' Glenda bit into her cake ending the discussion. Natalie felt the stirrings of mutiny. Sitting on a bus with avid movie fans didn't appeal at all.

'Are you sending any postcards?' Glenda straightened the place mat under her cup of Earl Grey tea.

Frowning, Natalie imagined signing a card with just her name instead of the usual *N and A*. 'I'll definitely send one to Toby, my little brother.'

'*Little* brother? How young is he?'

Natalie pressed her finger onto the last crumbs of her cake and felt herself tensing.

'He was nine last month.'

'Nine? good grief he could be your son not your brother.'

'I suppose so.' She licked the crumbs from her finger then clutched at her napkin, wiping her hands, screwing the paper into a ball.

'Your mother must be very young. How old was she when she had you?'

'Hey,' Natalie injected a light hearted tone to her voice, 'I thought we weren't going to talk about home.'

Glenda sipped her tea and dabbed her lips with her napkin. 'Sorry, you're right, and I have a problem. I keep seeing this word, 'Mozarteum' written on things and I don't know what it is.'

Natalie leaned back in her chair. 'Where have you seen it?'

'It was on something in the Mozart gift shop, but I couldn't understand the rest of the sentence.'

Glenda took out her purse, summoned the waitress and asked for the bill.

'I'll sort it,' she said. 'Pay me back later. I'm keeping a tally of everything we spend.'

Natalie avoided the waitress's eye. She felt ridiculous not carrying any money. Like the Queen, Glenda had said when they were staying by the lake. But her head had been all over the place when they first came away and Glenda became impatient if she rummaged for the right coins. She'd taken charge and Natalie allowed her to do so; except now she was beginning to feel … better? No, she didn't feel better; she still wasn't *the real Natalie*

Grey but maybe an *alternative* Natalie was emerging and it was something to do with this city.

With the help of the phrase book Glenda asked the waitress about the Mozarteum but couldn't make much sense of her reply. They did glean directions to it and after an hour walking in Mirabelgarten and photographing the palace, the flowers and statues from every angle, they made their way to a wide street running parallel to the river.

'It sounds like a cross between 'Mozart' and 'museum' Natalie said as they approached the grey stone building, not as grand as the baroque houses across the river but still beautiful with statues set into niches in the walls. 'Perhaps that's what it is, a dedicated museum.'

Glenda waved a dismissive hand. 'I've a list of the museums. This isn't on it.'

Steps led up to huge wooden doors. Glenda hesitated, pulling out her wad of printouts and taking a last flick through them.

'Look, we're here now.' Natalie tried the door handle. 'It's open. Are we going in?'

A foyer led to more steps then corridors leading left and right. There was a reception booth but nobody was manning it. After a few seconds a tall, thin man walked down a corridor towards them. He carried a briefcase. Glenda cleared her throat.

'Do you speak English?'

He looked at her with no interest but replied politely, 'Yes, I do.'

'Could you tell us what the Mozarteum is?'

His attention slid to Natalie who met his gaze but tried not to stare. There was barely any flesh on his pale cheeks; his expression impossible to read but she recognised eyes full of sorrow. Then she really *was* staring and he stared back.

For a second he touched long fingers to his forehead then ran a hand through his shoulder-length hair which might have been blonde or grey.

'I don't work here,' he said. 'Please excuse me.'

He made to go out of the doors but Glenda raised a hand. Natalie held her breath.

'Well there's nobody at reception so could you at least tell us what goes on here?'

'Maybe he's in a hurry.' Natalie moved forward, caught his eye once more, this time seeing a spark of gratitude; he turned to Glenda.

'Your friend is correct. I don't have time to help you. Someone will be here soon, I'm sure.' He opened the door and stepped out into dazzling sunshine. Natalie had the insane idea he might shrivel up like Dracula.

'You weren't very helpful,' Glenda called after him. 'What a creep,' she whispered, looking ruffled. She kept glancing at the door in case he came back in.

'I think he was ill,' Natalie said. 'His clothes were hanging off him and he looked sad.'

A woman hurried along apologising in English for keeping them waiting. She quickly explained that the building was a musical institute. 'We have a wonderful library,' she said, 'if you'd like to view it.'

But Glenda seemed less enthusiastic now and said they would return another day. She was silent as they walked back across the footbridge into the heart of the old town.

They ate a late lunch in an Italian restaurant in a pretty square, the windows flung wide open. Natalie felt her emotions churning. She'd been numb for so long it was strange to feel interest stirring. There was no denying this city was working some kind of charm. She watched pigeons rising to the rooftops and groups of tourists photographing each other by a fountain; but she still steered her gaze away from couples or women with pushchairs.

The number seven bus was crowded on the way back to the hotel. Glenda took a seat near the driver. She had a shopping bag on her knee in which a pale green dirndl, lacy blouse and an apron were swathed in tissue paper. Natalie sat towards the back, gazing out of the window at the now familiar landmarks; the low building of the ice stadium, the area of open grassland where she could see across the valley to the high mountains, some now darkened with the sun behind them. A synthesized voice announced each destination and she pronounced the names in her head.

The bus pulled up at a row of shops where a window displayed dog beds, cat baskets and brightly coloured leads. Someone got onto the rear of the bus carrying a paper sack of puppy food.

It was the man from the Mozarteum.

Natalie put her head down not daring to look but he faced away from her, the sack on his knee, his briefcase balanced on top. Now feeling safe to study him she noticed his hands resting on the case were long and slim, the nails neatly trimmed and clean. It seemed strange his hands were cared for but the rest of him was unkempt. His hair was blond, sitting jaggedly on his collar. His age might be anything from forty to sixty. She imagined when he was younger or healthier he must have been good looking.

At the next stop an elderly woman got up to leave. She paused by the man and rested a hand on his shoulder, whispering to him. He looked up, placing his hand over hers. Natalie strained to hear his voice but the hiss of brakes drowned it out.

The moment was soon over; the old lady said something about the puppy food; patted the sack and smiled, then she was off the bus and the man's head went down again; sadness reclaiming his features. Natalie tried to pull her cloak of numbness around her but found she'd left it behind somewhere in the city.

A couple of stops from their hotel he got off, gauntness

off some music for a student. 'And I met that dreadful American woman,' he told Max, 'or was she English?' He stroked the dog's silky ears when he came to sit beside him. 'Yes, English and she had a friend who wasn't dreadful and who had large, worried eyes, the colour of which I can't remember. No, wait. They were grey and she was pretty.'

Opening the fridge he took out packs of ham and cheese and peeled off slices. He ate them from the packets, not bothering to use a plate. 'I can't give you stuff like this,' he said as Max's gaze swivelled from the ham to Leo's face and back again.

'Just this once, then.'

A slice of ham slid down Max's throat and he wagged his tail for more.

In the bathroom Leo's razor dragged but he persevered, wincing at the tiny cuts. It was eleven o'clock already, where had that hour gone? He dressed quickly then pulled off his shirt again and found a clean one. There was just enough time to open the shutters in the small music room, wipe over the piano keys, throw music onto the stand and move a photograph frame two centimetres to the left.

'Morning, Herr Meier.' Lucy Weber's mother steered her daughter through the door. The girl ran to the kitchen to make a fuss of Max while her mother, wafting perfume and something resembling garden mint, went to drag her back.

Leo preferred it when Lucy's father accompanied her to her lessons. He at least paid attention as the child played, offering encouragements, praising her when she succeeded with a difficult passage. But his wife spent the entire hour tapping and scrolling her iPad while her daughter sat rigid, her eyes never fully on the music. The woman would invariably excuse herself and go to the toilet. Leo imagined her scanning his house for evidence of a new female presence.

When the lesson was over he told Lucy she'd done so well she could take a dip into the treats jar. After stuffing a kinder egg into her rucksack she gave Max one last hug.

'School starts next week. We must rearrange your lessons.' Leo picked up the diary.

'We'd like to come at three o'clock if that suits you, Herr Meier?'

'Is that OK with you, Lucy?' The girl nodded so he wrote it into the book then opened the door, wanting them to be gone.

'We're having some friends to dinner on Friday evening.' Frau Weber hovered on the doorstep. 'We wondered if you'd like to join us.'

She smiled and Leo noticed she'd touched up her lipstick, a smear of it on her teeth.

'So kind, but my father and sister are coming from Vienna and we have plans.' He closed the door blowing a long slow breath of relief through his lips.

When the phone rang he was carving a chunk of bread from a stale loaf. With one hand he squeezed it into the toaster and lifted the phone with the other.

'Hello Leo.'

Her voice was quiet but he knew her instantly, pictured the sensual mouth, the hair that fell below her shoulders. The image gave him no pleasure. 'Britte, is something wrong? Is he okay?'

'He's fine and nothing's wrong. How are you?'

Leo felt impatient. 'What can I do for you?'

'He wants to see you.'

He let the words settle into his mind; heard her take a breath.

'Leo?'

'Yes. It's just … a surprise … why now?'

The bread was burning, too thick to be expelled by the toaster. He pulled it out and tossed it across the kitchen. Max approached it warily.

'There's a lot going on and … he wants you to be a part of it.'

'Is he getting married?' A quick mental calculation … twenty-one, twenty-two?

'Always the romantic, Leo. No, he's not getting married. He's coming to Salzburg next week. Can I tell him you'll see him?'

'You have to ask? '

'I heard things are bad for you right now and …'

'Everything's fine. Ask him to call me. Tell him … tell him I look forward to it.'

She hung up. Only Max chewing burnt toast broke the silence.

Reception was quiet at Hotel Friesen. Leo assumed guests were in the city, pouring into Mozarts Geburtshaus or slogging their way up to the fortress. Karin was planning her own holiday; Googling riding schools in South Africa. Max bounded through to the garden in search of Otto, the hotel Dachshund.

'Lucy Weber's mother asked me to dinner. I told her we had plans so I'd better book a table.'

Karin pulled up the restaurant bookings on her computer. 'Maybe you'd like Frau Weber's cooking better than ours?'

Her grin was infectious. Thank goodness for friends like her who never commented on his appearance or asked, *how are things?*

'She will have a nice single friend for you to sit next to. Are you sure you don't want to go?' She winked but was already tapping into the computer. 'How is your Papa?'

'Remarkably well. He spends a lot of time with my nephew, it must keep him young.'

'Okay, seven-thirty, your usual table.'

They went outside to watch the dogs racing in and out of the fruit trees, Max more eager to play than Otto. Leo wanted to tell Karin about the telephone call but no matter how he rehearsed the words in his head he couldn't give them a voice. Maybe he wanted to savour them for a while before he shared them.

He bought a beer and sat in the garden long after Karin was called back to reception. He watched the changing shadows on the mountain, the lone paraglider circling the summit. Day two hundred and fifty-seven was now notable, but it was still another long day to be endured; another day trying to function as the man he used to be.

Chapter Four

The world, or the city at least, is my oyster, Natalie thought as she strode across Residenzplatz the following morning. Today she was free. She had seen Glenda onto her Sound of Music minibus and, with an exaggerated wink from Karin in reception, had set off for the bus stop unencumbered by plans, itineraries or Internet printouts. She'd even drawn some money out of a cash machine.

'Whatever will you do on your own?' Glenda had asked and without waiting for an answer insisted Natalie should ring her or Karin if she got into difficulties.

So far she'd made it into town on the bus, bought a bottle of water and watched a guy playing a guitar on the steps of the cathedral. All without incident. There had been a few moments when she'd considered crossing the river to the Mozarteum in the hope of catching sight of that man again. But what would she say if confronted by him? *Sorry my friend was rude. Why do you look so sad?* And then she remembered he didn't work there anyway. Put him out of your mind, she thought. Put everything but this city out of your head.

In Mozartplatz she decided to sign up for a walking tour and joined the long queue in the tourist office. To her relief the staff spoke English, and when she finally reached the counter the transaction was painless.

'Can you make that *two* tickets for the walking tour please?' The voice was American and male. Natalie turned and found herself staring at a checked shirt. She followed the pattern up to see a man in his twenties with very dark, curly hair and a short, well-trimmed moustache and beard through which he was grinning.

'Sorry to butt in like this but it saves her putting the tickets away.'

He held out his hand. 'Connor Selby. You must think I'm very rude. I apologise.'

Natalie shook the proffered hand, gave a polite smile, pushed the ticket into her bag and walked out into the sunshine.

There was half an hour before the tour began so she crossed the square to the courtyard cafe of a museum, chose a table in the shade and ordered tea.

'Perhaps you'd let me buy you that.' Mr Selby was there again.

'No thank you.' She attempted to study her information brochure, but added, 'It's not necessary, really.'

'I didn't catch your name,' he pulled out a chair to sit down, hooking a small rucksack over the arm. Natalie didn't know whether to laugh or be annoyed. Laughing would be a novelty; she hadn't tried it in a while. A waitress came over and he ordered coffee.

'It's no wonder we Yanks aren't popular here in Europe.' The illuminated grin was back.

'I'm sure that's not true.' Natalie stirred the teabag round in her glass.

'No it is. We're given instructions when we leave US airports. Don't speak too loudly. Don't complain the beds are small. Don't butt into queues for tickets.'

She did laugh then. He seemed harmless if a little pushy but all the same she was pleased she'd chosen a shady spot so that she wasn't screwing up her eyes against the sun, or sweating like the tourists at a neighbouring table who were peeling off cardigans.

When Adam left, Natalie thought, he took all my self-confidence with him. She knew she looked OK, wearing a new, cherry red T-shirt and cropped jeans that even her mother said showed off her slim legs; but searching for something interesting to say still proved impossible. She settled on asking if he was looking forward to the tour.

'I am. I never seem to get enough time just to hang around the city.'

Natalie leaned forward. 'How long are you here for?'

He sipped his coffee, elbows resting on the table. 'I've been touring Europe for a while now, with friends. We came to Salzburg and I liked it so much when they moved on to Milan, I stayed. Been here a couple months.'

Natalie's questions tumbled out. 'Do you plan to stay? What job do you do or are you incredibly rich, like all Americans?'

He matched her mischievous smile. 'I wait tables in a restaurant. Today's my day off.'

Natalie had forgotten her tea.

He glanced at his watch. 'We'd better head back across the square.'

With a self-assured wave he beckoned the waitress and insisted on paying for the tea. Natalie drank a little more before grabbing her bag. As they crossed the road a taxi moved away from the kerb and Connor placed a protective hand on her arm. His fingers felt cool and dry against her skin.

She enjoyed the camaraderie of the guided tour. The day had taken a strange but interesting turn. She was in a group of twenty or so people, following Regina, a local guide. There were several more Americans, some Germans and a group of French nuns who chattered and laughed as they made their way from place to place. What an uncomplicated life they lead without men, Natalie thought. Perhaps I should hold it in mind as an option.

Although Connor spoke to everyone he often fell into step beside Natalie. In the cathedral they sat together, heads thrown back admiring the vast, painted domes of the ceiling. Along the side walls were wrought iron racks where people lit candles and dropped coins into a box. Connor fished a couple of Euros from his pocket and lit a candle from one already burning. Natalie moved away, respecting his private moment but he called her back.

'My grandma died last Christmas,' he said.

Mumbling her sympathy Natalie felt a sudden need to get out into the sunshine although Connor seemed in no hurry. 'Is there someone you could light one for?'

She shook her head. 'I'm not really religious,'

'Me either. I just thought it might be nice to remember her in an amazing place like this.'

'My real Dad died when I was very little,' she continued edging away. 'I don't actually remember him at all.'

'Oh. OK.' He smiled and walked over to join her but then she changed her mind.

'I think I will light one.' She pulled out her purse. 'I'll catch you up.'

Once he was gone she dropped several coins into the box, lit a candle and placed it next to Connor's, then with trembling fingers selected another. Biting hard into her lip she stared at the three flames burning side by side until her vision blurred and she turned away.

At the end of the tour the group stayed together chatting, some exchanging restaurant recommendations. Connor spoke to a couple from Munich in slow but impressive German. Natalie felt superfluous. It had been a lovely morning and she'd met some nice people but it was time to move away. She said goodbye to the American family who were rushing off to a midday concert; but then he was there, his large hand in the small of her back. 'Wanna grab some lunch?'

She felt relieved and panicked all in one go. 'Oh, I don't know, I …'

He extended the invitation to the German couple but they

already had plans. He turned back to Natalie, eyebrows raised.

She felt a delicious bolt of courage run through her. 'OK then. Do you know somewhere nice?'

'I know just the place. You're going to love it.' He grabbed her hand and steered her across the road, past the ancient horse fountain, and into the wide expanse of Kapitelplatz. She wondered should she pull her hand away, but it was nice. She hadn't felt like this for a long time.

Market stalls lined one side of the square, there might have been something nice to buy for Toby, but Connor led her past them and up a steep, cobbled street below the fortress. He stopped at a very old building. 'After you,' he said, finally letting go of her hand.

Inside they climbed a wide marble staircase to a corridor with cavernous dining rooms leading off it. The hum and chatter of the diners rose and fell as they passed each doorway. A waiter approached and they followed him outside to a terrace with trees and vines shading the tables. The old city was spread out before them. They were almost level with the roof of the cathedral; other domes and towers pushed up between the buildings and beyond these the river wound through the town disappearing into the distance.

Over pork schnitzel and half litres of beer Connor asked how long she would be in the city. Natalie explained she had three more full days, making a point of mentioning she was travelling with a friend.

'So where is she today?'

'She's on the Sound of Music tour.'

'Why didn't you go too?'

'My dress made from curtains is in the wash.'

He smiled, reached across and took hold of her left hand.

'So, you're married?'

She pulled her hand away. 'I … I was married. It ended this

summer at least I think it's ended. I don't know why I keep wearing ...' she glanced down at her ring.

'I'm sorry.' He took a swig of beer leaving froth on his moustache. 'Change of subject then?'

He told her of his travels in Europe and how he'd taken time away from his work in IT to make the trip. Then he asked about her job and there was no way to make it sound interesting.

'I work at a vet's surgery.'

'A what?'

'I do clerical work at a veterinary practice. Glenda and I work in the offices. She's the practice manager.'

'Glenda is the friend you're vacationing with? So she's your boss?'

'She is.'

Natalie thought of the day after Adam left; dragging herself into work, Glenda taking charge and looking after her. They'd barely had a conversation that wasn't about work before that.

Connor speared a piece of buttered potato. 'Have you been to Hellbrunn palace yet?

Frowning, Natalie tried to remember Glenda's itinerary for the remaining days. 'I think we plan to. Why?'

'It's beautiful, very old. We could go there this afternoon.'

'Oh. I don't think so. I should get back to the hotel. But thanks anyway.'

He smiled. 'No worries. But make sure you go see it while you're here.'

When they'd ordered coffee, Natalie went in search of the loo. She descended marble stairs into the depths of the ancient building. In front of the mirror she splashed cold water onto her cheeks. The warm day and a nice American had given her a glow. She tried to rearrange her hair into more of a style. Glenda would say she should be wearing a hat in this heat.

Rummaging in her bag for a tissue she noticed several text

messages waiting on her phone, all from Glenda.

Where are you? Why isn't your phone on? Please let me know where you are.

Wondering if her friend was back from her excursion and wanting to meet up she listened to the voice mail.

Natalie, is something wrong? Why aren't you answering? Please ring the minute you get this. She looked again at her shining face in the mirror. Maybe it was Connor's attention, maybe it was the beer, but she felt emboldened as she pressed Glenda's number. She answered immediately but Natalie jumped in first.

'Sorry you couldn't reach me. I turned off my phone in the cathedral'

'Well I've been worried about you, that's all. Where are you now?'

'I took a guided tour,' Natalie watched a bead of moisture sliding down the mirror. 'And I've met a nice man called Connor. We're having lunch.' She held her breath.

'I see.'

What, no telling off? No urging her not to speak to strange men? She asked if the Sound of Music tour was living up to expectation.

She heard Glenda's long intake of breath. 'It is, thank you, although the Sound of Music gazebo looks like something you'd see at B&Q.'

There was a pause. Natalie decided to fill it. 'Please don't worry about me; I'm having a nice relaxing day. I'll see you later at the hotel.'

She ended the call and walked back to the table. Connor was paying the bill and she thrust a number of notes into his hand, not allowing him to protest. As they rose to leave she asked if the offer of a trip to Hellbrunn was still open.

They caught the bus by the river. Natalie felt shivers of

anticipation as they travelled south from the city. With her knee pressed up against Connor's leg she was somewhat disappointed when the bus ride ended.

Hellbrunn palace sat in an oval courtyard with parkland stretching away to the side. Neat parterres of bay trees and curved paths were punctuated by statues. Ducks and swans crowded the edges of the lake where families fed them crusts of bread. Beyond the park a single, steep hill rose from the valley floor

Connor draped his arm around her shoulders. 'Maybe we should give the palace a miss and you can do that with your friend. What say we head to the Italian garden and take the tour?'

The ornate pools and grottoes were dotted with trick fountains that sent jets of water shooting from statues, innocuous looking benches and stone animals. Children shrieked with excitement as they got wet.

'Stay near to the guide,' Connor said, drawing Natalie close, 'she operates the mechanism.' Sure enough they remained dry until one last path must be negotiated. He took her hand and they ran. Water sprayed from dozens of tiny holes in the paving stones forming an arc over their heads. At the end of the path a photographer was stationed to catch the action.

'Thanks for bringing me here,' Natalie said, laughing and wiping droplets from her hair and face.

He kissed her forehead. 'Pleasure's mine. Believe me.'

She didn't have time to be embarrassed; they were joined by other tourists who arrived, soggy but happy, to wait by a table where the snapshots were soon displayed. Connor fished around and found their picture. Natalie stared at her happy face, pressed against his. This is what I could be like, she thought, if things were different.

After that it seemed natural for Connor's arm to be round

her shoulders. They climbed the hill to see the folk museum but finding it closed walked to the edge of the outcrop. Across the valley the mountains rose to snowy heights.

'That's Bavaria,' he said, 'we're close to the border here.' He drew her down to sit on a bench beside him and they leaned back enjoying the sun on their faces.

Natalie let her shoulders relax. 'Today has been so,' she hesitated, 'unexpected. And I'm not even carrying printouts.'

'Printouts?'

She closed her eyes. 'It's a long story. I won't bore you with it.'

Her face became shaded as he leaned over to kiss her. The brush of his beard against her chin was silky, his lips warm and gentle and she allowed herself to kiss him back.

She barely noticed the sun slipping behind the mountains as the kissing continued. Connor stroked her hair, drew her closer but made no attempt at anything more intimate. As the shadows lengthened he whispered into her neck.

'I should get you back to your hotel.'

Feeling a thud of disappointment Natalie searched for his mouth with hers, not wanting this to end. Finally he drew away. 'Unless you'd let me buy you dinner.'

She looked at her watch, it was after six. For a few moments she was undecided, but then nodded. 'Dinner would be lovely.'

As they walked through the darkening gardens she checked her phone; five more texts from Glenda. She sent one in return. *We're going for dinner. Don't worry. I'm fine.*

When Connor pulled her into his arms again any guilt she might have harboured melted away.

Back in the city they ate in the garden of a restaurant on a hillside. As it grew dark fireflies darted among the trees. Natalie watched them then became aware that Connor was talking.

'You're adorable, Natalie.'

'Did you say I'm boring?'

He laughed. 'What? No. Why would you think that?'

Embarrassed, she stared into her wine; wouldn't look at her watch again; didn't want to see the counting down of their time together. Silently cursing the efficient service of the waiter she lingered over her coffee and nibbled microscopic pieces from her after dinner mint. Adam's face tried to creep into her mind but she pushed it away.

Finally Connor reached for her hand, stroking her fingers. She looked up into his eyes, reading the question they held then lowered her gaze, hoping he would understand. She wasn't ready for anything more.

She barely remembered the taxi ride. Connor gave the hotel address and some Euros to the driver. He kissed her lingeringly before she got into the cab, slipping a piece of paper with his hastily scribbled email address, into her hand. She turned and watched him waving until the corner hid him from view.

At the hotel Karin was about to close reception. Natalie saw their key was hanging on its hook by the desk.

'Your friend is in the pool,' Karin said. The mischievous smile tugged at the woman's lips. 'She has also been in the fitness room.'

Natalie shuffled uncomfortably. 'I've been out all day. I think she might be angry with me.'

Karin glanced at the door through which Glenda might appear. 'I think it's not been the best day for her.' She grinned. 'The Sound of Music wedding church was being renovated.'

Chapter Five

Leo turned into his road and saw his nephew Florian waving from an upstairs window.

'They're here then,' he said to his dog and felt a frisson of anxiety in his stomach. What might be expected of him? Would the family want to *talk*?

The front door was ajar; the aroma of coffee mingled with that of Marina's famous apricot strudel. His sister had reclaimed the family home and he was glad.

She didn't rush to hug him but gave him her broad smile and inclined her head toward the coffee maker. 'Wait till you try this.'

Florian thundered down the stairs and threw his arms around a startled Max, then straightened to his full height and held out his hand to Leo.

'Welcome, young man.' He held his nephew's hand with both of his; not mentioning how much he'd grown. He remembered himself at eight years old, above average height. He wondered if Florian received the same kind of teasing at school.

'May I take Max for a walk?'

'He's just had a long trek on the mountain, but you can give him his dinner if you like.' He opened a cupboard and showed him the level to which he should fill the measuring cup.

'Papa's taking a nap,' Marina said, placing a cappuccino and a slice of strudel on the table. Another incline of her head suggested, sit; eat. 'Well, he was asleep until my noisy son made that racket coming downstairs.' She went to the freezer and drew out a tub of ice cream. 'Florien's favourite,' she said, scooping out a huge spoonful and placing it on Leo's plate beside the strudel.

He watched it begin to melt against the hot pastry, pooling

like cream and thought he should mention the phone call from Britte but then he heard the creak of the floor above and his father's footsteps on the stairs.

Leo stood to greet him, feeling the familiar comforting bulk as he hugged him.

'Eat that strudel before you disappear altogether,' the older man said then headed for the coffee maker.

The food was delicious and now, with Marina pouring her father's drink, telling Florian not to excite the dog just after his dinner, he felt his appetite leap into life. It was when he was alone he forgot to eat, didn't make any meal an occasion but a swift necessity when the hunger pangs progressed to light-headedness.

'I don't suppose you have many students now.' Leo's father sat opposite him at the table, sipping coffee, closing his eyes with satisfaction.

'I do. I have at least three every day. I saw two girls for piano this morning and I have a boy for a guitar lesson in an hour.' He tried to keep impatience from his tone. Why did people think he wasn't working? Work was the one comforting constant in his life. And maybe he did sleep in now and again but he had never been late for a pupil.

'It looks like you have a lot of apples this year.' Marina joined them at the table.

Leo flashed her a grateful look. 'Luisa at the Friesen is going to take some.'

'Ahh. The only woman who makes desserts as good as mine. I'm looking forward to our meal tonight.'

'You should learn to cook,' his father said. 'Make a few apple pastries of your own. Goodness knows you could do with eating them.'

'I've been cooking for years, Papa, and pastries are alright but in moderation.' He prayed Florian would come in from the garden and break the tension. Sweat was trickling down Leo's back, the coffee, though delicious, was making him hotter. 'I'll just go for a shower before my student arrives.'

Day two hundred and sixty one and he was still having the same conversations with his father. In the shower he thought about Frau Weber's invitation to dinner. Would it kill him to accept someone's offer of company now and then? Maybe he was losing his social skills. He'd been so dismissive of those English women in the Mozarteum. He thought of the pretty one who had understood he needed to get away. He could have been friendlier but instead he'd retreated into his dark tunnel.

He was glad of the lesson which kept him in the music room and afterwards brought out his own guitar and taught Florian a few chords. The boy was a quick learner and Leo was surprised when Marina told him it was time to get ready for dinner. He liked it when time passed without him noticing the minutes.

Florian took Max's lead and walked ahead with his grandfather. Marina linked her arm through Leo's as they passed the church and followed the path between fields which had become parched in the dry weather. Leo gathered his thoughts and took a deep breath. 'Britte rang this week.'

'My God, what did she want? Is … is he all right?' Marina stopped walking, her hand slipped from his arm.

Leo laughed. 'Yes he's fine. I can't quite believe it but he wants to see me.'

She folded her arms across her chest. 'Why would he not want to see his father?'

'Because we're strangers. How many years has it been?'

'So he's a man now, able to make up his own mind.' Her hand flew up to her cheek, a gesture he'd seen all his life. 'She's not coming with him?'

Leo felt his stomach lurch either from hunger or dread, he

wasn't sure. 'No. At least I don't think so. Why would she?'

Marina took his arm again. 'I could think of a few reasons but I don't even want to say them out loud.'

'Do you think I should tell Papa?'

'No. Wait until you know what he wants.'

'Don't be cynical, he may not *want* anything.'

'They know your circumstances, Leo.' Her grip tightened on his arm.

The restaurant was busy. A storm was rumbling in the distance and diners from the terrace came indoors. Karin had been drafted in to help and Leo saw her dash past the door, dividing her time between reception and the kitchen. He'd eaten his venison, which was delicious but couldn't face dessert, his stomach churning again when he thought of Marina's words. Might Britte want to accompany Andreas? He prayed not.

As the diners thinned out Karin, Luisa and their brother Lukas all found time to come and say hello to Marina and his father. Thunder cracked overhead, rain pelted against the window. Luisa brought Florian some home-made biscuits, one of which he fed to Max under the table.

'You should ask Karin to your house for dinner,' his father said, none too quietly, as she carried their plates to the kitchen.

'Don't wish a miserable wretch like me on a live wire like Karin.'

'Maybe some of her electricity might rub off on you.'

Otto appeared at the door and Max scrambled to his feet, barging through their legs to greet his friend. Otto's loud, hound bark reverberated round the restaurant. Leo stood up but Karin was already bringing Max back to their table, and then, over her shoulder, he looked straight into the eyes of the girl from the Mozarteum; the one who wasn't dreadful; the one who was prettier than he'd remembered. She gave him a half smile of recognition but he was too taken aback to return it. He saw her rake damp hair back from her face, a hand with long slim fingers and a wedding ring. Then Karin barred his view, laughing with Marina and his father about the dogs.

Leo craned to see round her but the doorway was empty and for no reason he could explain his dark tunnel yawned open.

Chapter Six

On their last evening Natalie and Glenda took a taxi into town. Glenda went into raptures when Karin made a phone call and the car arrived within three minutes.

Natalie would like to have stayed in the hotel; she enjoyed eating outside under the horse chestnut trees and it had been nice helping Rosina, the young waitress, to practice her English. After a tense few hours they'd put the matter of Natalie's day with Connor behind them. They were on holiday after all. Glenda had said they shouldn't spend it in disagreement.

She had booked a dinner concert and they both dressed up for the occasion. Natalie wore smart black trousers and a floaty mauve top; Glenda had gone all out and put on a dress which showed off her very long legs. She'd even left her hair down although she kept pushing it behind her ears. 'This has been a good break,' she said as they sped along Aignerstrasse into town. 'It's been nice to travel round a country where everything runs on time. But I think we both need to start making plans as soon as we get home, don't you?'

Natalie felt her stomach tighten. 'Plans?'

'Yes. You've been on your own for a few months now. You must have some thoughts about the future.'

'Not really. Not yet.' She wanted to lose herself in this unreal life for a few hours longer.

'Well, I wasn't going to mention this until we got home,' Glenda's smile was conspiratorial, 'but after Christmas there's a practice manager's position coming vacant at the Bowling Road branch. I'm certain you could get it.'

'Oh … I … Do you think so?' Natalie was flattered but the feeling mingled with rising panic at the thought of holding such a position.

'We won't talk about it now,' Glenda said, pulling Euros from her purse to pay their fare.

The taxi drew up in a square close to the Mönchsberg hill that bordered one side of the old city. Swallows screeched and swooped around the buildings. Natalie recognised St Peter's Church with its ancient cemetery from the tour she had taken with Connor. To the right of the cemetery the restaurant nestled against the hill, its cavern-like courtyard hewn into the base of the rock. Diners sat at tables in the open air but Natalie and Glenda followed others inside and up a staircase festooned with elaborate flower displays.

'They've been serving food since 803,' Glenda whispered. Natalie glanced at her watch; it wasn't yet eight o'clock. Glenda hooted with laughter. 'Oh do wake up. I mean the *year* 803. This is the oldest restaurant in Europe. Didn't you read any of the info sheets I gave you?' She took Natalie's arm as if to soften the reproach; then they were greeted by the Maître d', who took their tickets.

Natalie caught her breath when they walked through double doors into the hall. It was large and ornately decorated in Baroque style. Three tall, stained-glass windows gave a blurry view of the square. Above dozens of candle-lit tables, the frescoed ceiling rose high, echoing the gentle hum of conversation.

The Maître d' led them to a table at the front, close to the tiny stage, and pulled out velvet covered chairs for them. Glenda looked smug.

'See what forward planning gets you?'

The table was set for eight and four people were already seated. An Australian man, perhaps in his forties, introduced himself, his wife and his two younger brothers who both stared at Glenda's legs. Seemingly oblivious she engaged them in conversation about the merits of on-line ticket booking. They were soon joined by an elderly French couple, Manu and Helene, who sat to Natalie's left. Manu asked her if she was a big fan of Mozart.

'I'm new to his music.' She felt embarrassed and glanced at the programme. 'I don't know any of these.'

He put on spectacles. 'Ah, they will sing from three operas. All very different,' he said. His accent was strong and romantic. He paused for a moment to help Helene slip off her jacket then turned back to the programme.

'Above all Mozart knew what it was to be a fragile human being and this he showed in his music, especially the opera. You will hear it and feel it in your heart.'

He clutched the front of his shirt for emphasis. Pointing to the arias he explained a little about each one.

'Don Giovanni,' he said, 'was a scoundrel; an abuser of women. He loved them and left them. He was cruel, merciless.'

Natalie thought of Adam. Yes, he'd been cruel and merciless that terrible night. She was pleased when Manu moved on to describe another aria.

'Now here,' he said, 'Papageno has been longing for love and at last his little Papagena finds him. You see,' he patted the back of her hand; 'there is love for everyone. You just have to seek it out.'

She bit her lip. 'But what about this first aria?'

'The *Marriage of Figaro* is complex. It has betrayal, sorrow, lots of jokes and of course the Contessa forgives the Count for his infidelity.'

The musicians, in 18th century costume, walked in and took up their instruments. Natalie, joining in with the applause, still thought about the opera and wondered, if Adam were truly sorry, whether she could forgive him.

The music was played and sung between courses and they chatted to the other diners. Manu was attentive to his wife, pouring her wine, adjusting the stole around her shoulders. One of the Australian brothers was deep in conversation with Glenda. Natalie spoke to the other three. They had only been in the city for twenty-four hours so she recommended a few tourist sights and restaurants. 'Order the pork schnitzels at Stieglkeller,' she said.

The soprano was beautiful and very young. As she sang Natalie felt the fine hairs on her arms lifting. In character the tenor, slightly older, tried to lead her away but the girl was reticent, injecting a breathy confusion into her voice. Manu leaned close and spoke into Natalie's ear. 'If she takes Don Giovanni's hand she is lost. They both know this.'

Natalie's throat tightened, her own breath caught as she watched Zerlina struggling to resist the Don. At the end, when the applause thundered round the room she saw even Glenda was wiping away a tear.

'Does she escape him in the end?' Natalie asked Manu, as their dessert was served.

'Oh yes. A woman comes to her rescue. And then she marries her young sweetheart.'

He touched Helene's arm and Natalie wanted to cry all over again.

In the final aria the singers strutted around flapping imaginary wings. The little bird man and his true love together at last. Natalie glanced across to smile at Glenda just in time to see her striding away from the table towards the door.

The Australian woman leaned forward. 'Is your friend alright? She was bawling all through the last song and that was supposed to be the happy one.'

A storm of applause erupted and people were beginning to push back their chairs. Natalie grabbed her bag then scooped up Glenda's jacket. She bid a hasty goodbye and rushed out to the corridor. No Glenda. Pushing open the door to the cloakroom she saw her sitting on a gilt-edged chair, her face in her hands, ignoring the bemused attendant who gently patted her shoulder and proffered tissues.

'What on earth's happened?' Natalie crouched in front of her. Glenda blew her nose, stood up and went to the hand basin, splashing water over her face washing away streaks of mascara.

'I'll be alright in a minute.' She patted her face dry and thanked the girl who seemed relieved that a happier group of women were now pouring into the room.

Outside the air was warm. 'Do you want to walk for a while?' Natalie asked. 'We can always get a taxi later on.'

Glenda nodded, seeming happy to follow Natalie as she led the way out of the square and along to Kapitelplatz where the floodlit bulk of the Fortress crouched on its hill above them.

'Sorry about all that,' Glenda said. 'It was that stuff about finding true love. It just got to me.' She still dabbed at her eyes.

'Do you feel as though you want to talk? I mean, I don't like to pry but …'

Glenda stopped walking and stared up at the cathedral for a few moments as if looking for inspiration. 'I could do with a drink, actually. Where would you suggest?'

Flattered that she was to decide Natalie took a narrow lane below the fortress and onto a street where she had walked with Connor. A bar on the corner had tables outside.

They ordered a carafe of red wine. Glenda took a sip then folded her hands on the table.

'We have something in common,' she said. 'My husband dumped me too; last Christmas.'

'Why have you never said anything?' Natalie's hand shot forward almost toppling her wine. She touched Glenda's arm for a second.

'Only the senior partner at work knew. Even my mother didn't hear about it for nearly a month.' She fished a tissue from her pocket. 'I've always been such a joke. I know I'm fussy and hard to live with but …' she stared into the brooding sky. 'I thought Martin was different. We were very happy at the start. You'll never guess where we met. A cat show.' She gave a sad little laugh. 'Our eyes met over the colourpoint Persians. I'd only gone into the show because it was raining. We were going to have one; a Persian. Never got round to it though.'

Natalie struggled for something to say. 'You could have one now,' she said finally.'

Glenda shook her head. 'It was something we planned together. Just wouldn't be the same.'

'So is your husband … with another woman?'

'He didn't leave me for anyone. He went back to live at home; that's really insulting, don't you think? But then just before we came away my mother took delight in telling me he was seeing someone now. He's a teacher. I think she's another member of staff.'

'I'm so sorry.'

'You know, I was jealous of you the other day, hooking up with that guy. I've thought about finding someone. Trouble is I still find myself comparing everyone to Martin.'

'Do you still love him?'

'I don't know. Maybe he's just another habit I can't break.'

For a while they sipped their wine in silence. Natalie realised that within half an hour the basis of their friendship had shifted. No longer the lamb trailing behind the bossy sheep she now felt the stronger of the two. This city really was working some kind of magic.

They resisted the temptation to order more wine and instead walked on through the old town to the footbridge. Lights from either side of the city reflected in the fast flowing Salzach. They could hear the rush of water over rocks but then came another sound, a long rumble of thunder, far off, echoing around the mountains.

'Okay, tour guide, we could be in trouble here; where to now?' Glenda hugged her jacket closer to her body.

Natalie knew they could turn back to the taxi rank but she longed for one last ride on the bus. 'This way.'

More thunder rolled around the hills. The stop was just ahead and they only waited a minute or two before the number seven came into view. Sitting by the window Natalie watched lightning illuminate the peaks of the mountains, edging them in silver, giving them shape in the darkness. She turned to her friend.

'Are you feeling any better?'

Glenda had pulled her hair back into a scrunchie and resumed the habit of tucking away imaginary wisps. 'I'll be alright. Once we're home I'll be back into my routine, making lists, being organised. There's a lot of comfort in … you know … doing stuff.'

'I do admire you being so together. I just feel numb most of the time.' Natalie felt her cheeks grow warm. 'At least I did until we came here. I don't mean meeting up with … Connor … it's just that I've begun to feel a bit better this week, as though there is more to life …' she trailed off.

'I've always been organised,' Glenda said. 'Our house was chaos when I was a child. I spent hours alone in my room and they didn't seem to miss me. My dad's okay but I think my mother hated me from the day I was born. Why else would she call me this stupid name? At school girls were called Lisa or Emma or Kirsty. I told everyone she named me after Glenda Jackson. Actually it was after some warty old aunt who'd left her a few quid.'

When the bus arrived at Valkenauerstrasse the first huge drops of rain splashed onto the pavement. Natalie and Glenda ran along the quiet street to the hotel, the rain falling heavily now, their clothes beginning to hold the wet. Pushing open the front door of the hotel they rushed inside. Karin, walking into reception, flashed Natalie a wicked grin as she saw the state of them. Delicious aromas wafted from the dining room and Rosina hurried by with a tray of drinks. On the rug the Dachshund sat, raindrops spangling his coat. It felt so much like coming home Natalie could have wept.

Glenda lifted the key from the hook then said. 'Shall we swim? Our hair's already soaking wet so it won't matter. What do you say?'

Tired as she was Natalie was pleased to see Glenda's mood lightening.

'Alright. I'll go up and pull our swimsuits out of the cases; I'll meet you by the pool.'

She walked through the bar, Otto following at her heels. When she passed the door to the restaurant a young Labrador bounded out, nudging at the Dachshund wanting to play.

Karin rushed forward. 'Max always wants to play and poor old Otto can't keep up.'

She wrapped her arms around the young dog's body and guided him back into the restaurant. His owner left his table and came forward. He was laughing, sharing a joke with Karin, clipping the lead onto his dog.

Natalie stared at the man and she found she couldn't move. The warm light from the restaurant lamps played on his hair, making it shine when a few days ago it had been lifeless and dull. He met her gaze and this time his eyes were bright. A boy around Toby's age came forward taking the lead and steering the dog away. Natalie saw an elderly man sitting beside a dark haired younger woman. The boy squeezed in between them, the dog at his feet.

'He has people who love him.' Natalie told Otto as she climbed the stairs to their room. 'If he can look so ill and be happy then surely, somehow, I can get through this.'

Chapter Seven

It was raining in Coventry and the world looked grey and flat as they drove towards the city. Natalie tried to imagine the clouds were mountains but couldn't sustain the image. A cold wind buffeted the car and leaves were already falling from trees lining the dual carriageway.

As Glenda turned the car into her road Natalie grasped at the tiniest hope that Adam's car would be on the drive but the house looked lifeless as she dragged her suitcase from the boot.

'Don't be alone tomorrow,' Glenda said. 'Go and see that little brother of yours.'

The thought of seeing him made Natalie smile. Whatever else happened there was always her precious Toby.

A pile of envelopes lay behind the door but some had been moved and were lying on the stairs. The house was cold and silent. The breath she had drawn in to call Adam's name escaped soundlessly.

Walking through to the kitchen she saw a dirty coffee cup on the draining board; some junk mail addressed to him was open and lying on the worktop. Upstairs nothing seemed different at first but then she found the toilet seat up and a crumpled towel hanging over the bath. In the bedroom she dared herself to hope there might be a note on the pillow; instead she saw her bedside drawer was open and a couple of CDs lay on the bed. She closed her eyes for a moment then forced herself to look further. In the spare bedroom the exercise bike was gone. Two years ago they both struggled to get it upstairs. He must have had help to move it. She opened the wardrobe, some of Toby's clothes hung on the rail for when he came to stay. Below them his spare trainers sat in isolation where Adam's hand weights and exercise mat used to be.

She opened more cupboards and drawers but couldn't pull her thoughts together enough to remember what should be in them. In the living room there were gaps in the CD rack.

The tears came when she'd made tea and sat on the sofa. They ran down her face, dripping off her chin and into the Beauty and the Beast mug that Toby had bought her. I must have been dreaming for the last two weeks, she thought, all those lovely mountains and Connor. She had difficulty forming pictures of them in her mind. But the man from the Mozarteum seemed real enough and she shed a few tears for him too.

The telephone rang and she snatched it up.

'Nat, you're back. Can I tell you something that happened on Dr Who?'

'Yes of course, Sweetheart.' She held the phone to her ear as Toby related the plot of an entire episode. She blew her nose and finished drinking her tea. After five minutes she heard her mother's voice.

'Natalie, I didn't realised he'd phoned you. How are you?'

Why did her mother always sound business-like?

'Adam's been here,' her voice was a croak, 'looks like he's been … getting more of his stuff.'

'Oh, well did you at least enjoy your holiday?'

It didn't seem right to say that she wished she were back there now; that the heartless raiding of the CD rack made her long to be on the hill at Hellbrunn being kissed by someone who thought her adorable. Instead she described the hotel they'd stayed in at Zell am See that first week. She wanted to keep Salzburg to herself for a little longer.

'Why don't you come round, Natalie? Your dad could drive over and get you. Toby, get that Dalek off the coffee table.'

'No. No… thanks, I'm tired.' Much as she longed to see Toby she couldn't face small talk just yet.

'So what are your plans now, darling?'

Plans? What was this obsession with plans?

'I don't have any.'

She heard her mother draw in a long breath. 'You know, Natalie you can sit back and let life happen to you, or you can grab it and make it work for you. That's what I've always done. You mustn't let that,' she lowered her voice, 'arrogant bastard destroy you. Look what a nice time you've just had without him.'

'But it wasn't real life, Mum. It was just a holiday. Look I'll have to go, I need something to eat.'

'But you'll have nothing in. Come and eat with us.'

'No. Thanks anyway. I'll come tomorrow if that's OK.'

Toby came on the line to say goodbye. 'When you come for dinner I promise you won't be exterminated,' he said.

Her mother was right; there was nothing in the fridge but some tomato ketchup, a fossilised onion and some flat Coca Cola. She rang and ordered a pizza then picked up the post. Separating junk mail from bills and card statements, she saw there was nothing that couldn't wait until Monday so she propped the envelopes against the bread bin and gathered up the junk mail to put in the recycling box. *It's never too late to learn.* The sentence caught her eye. It was a prospectus for local evening classes. She scanned the list of courses. Could she really see herself going line-dancing or making table decorations for Christmas?

Christmas. She didn't want to think about that.

Then she noticed a beginner's German class on Wednesday evenings. She thought of the synthesized voice on the bus and the chatter of Salzburg schoolchildren; the lengthy words on road signs and billboards. But what would be the point of learning a language? Maybe she'd be better off improving her computer skills if she was going to apply for practice manager. Sooner or later Adam would stop paying the mortgage and she'd need to be self-sufficient. She slid the prospectus into the recycling box and poured herself a glass of the flat coke.

The pizza arrived. With the box on her knee to warm her legs she flicked through the TV channels but nothing appealed. Her eyes were sore and it was tempting to curl up and sleep but she forced herself to open the pizza box. The dry crust stuck to the roof of her mouth and after a couple of slices she gave up. She thought of the meals they'd had at The Friesen, the light-as-a-feather dumplings, perfectly cooked meats and desserts with names they couldn't pronounce even though Karin had tried to coach them.

Taking the box through to the kitchen she abandoned it on the worktop and rummaged through the recycling until she found the college prospectus again. *Never too late* … Was it too late to hope Adam would come home? She prayed not.

Chapter Eight

Leo watched his shirt swirling around in the machine, willing the quick wash cycle to come to an end. 'I should have done this yesterday,' he told Max who was sitting in his basket, ears drooping, thumping his tail a couple of times when Leo spoke.

He'd chosen such a high spin speed that when eventually he opened the machine he had to peel the shirt from the drum. It was creased beyond recognition.

He plugged in the iron and tried to smooth out the creases while the shirt was still wet.

There would be no time for the planned leisurely stroll into town along the river, gathering his thoughts. He'd need to sprint to catch the bus.

His collar was still damp as he stepped off at Mozartsteg footbridge and crossed the river. The day had started sunny but now grey clouds gathered behind the fortress and a strong breeze made the flags outside the museum ripple, their cords, beating a rhythm against the poles.

At the courtyard café only two tables were occupied, neither by a young man. Now Leo had time to breathe a little. He smoothed his hair back, knowing he should have had it cut but this length was easy to deal with. Karin told him it made him look like an absent-minded professor, which was fine by him.

A waitress came over and he ordered a double espresso, needing to sharpen his wits. He drank it quickly, clattering the cup back into the saucer. A glance at his watch told him the boy was late. Maybe he'd changed his mind; maybe Britte had told him not to come; maybe this day would not be notable after all. What day was it? Leo's mind went blank for a second. Two hundred and eighty … three no four. Scheiß! He felt in his pocket for his diary but it wasn't there. It must be two hundred and eighty-three because … he stood up to check his trouser pockets and then he was there; the boy; the man; tall as he was himself, slim, standing beside him, holding out his hand for his father to grasp it.

'Sorry for being late. I got lost in those narrow streets.'

His voice was deep, his accent *hoch Deutsch,* far removed from Leo's Salzburg dialect.

In those first flustered moments, ordering more coffee, asking to see the lunch menu, he couldn't take his eyes off his son. His hair was short, barely reaching the collar of his dark blue linen jacket. He saw his own sister's eyes but the sensual mouth was Britte's. Even after all these years he recognised it, but he pushed her face from his mind; concentrated on Andreas's hesitant smile.

'Where are you staying?' He knew he should think of something more meaningful to say but before Andreas could answer the waitress returned with their drinks and they took a few moments to read the menu.

They chose club sandwiches; sipped their coffee as an awkward silence lengthened.

'I'm staying at the Elefant,' Andreas said. 'I'm here for two nights then I'm catching the train to Munich. I have friends there.'

His words came out in a rush and Leo saw, from the way the boy clasped his hands together, he was nervous too.

'It's great that you came. I mean it's great to see you. You were … ' Leo smiled, 'you were very little when we last met.'

'I don't remember it.' Andreas looked down at his coffee.

'Britte … your mother said there was much going on in your life.'

'Yes.' He looked up, met Leo's eye and a grin lit up his face. 'I have a place in our Gwandhaus orchestra. Next year we'll be going on tour.'

Leo felt real happiness surge through him. 'What do you play?'

Andreas's coffee cup stopped on its way to his mouth. 'You don't know I play viola?'

'No. No … I'm sorry.'

'I've played since I was seven years old. First violin, then a few years ago I …'

Leo was grateful for the arrival of their food. 'It's a great achievement to get into the orchestra.'

Andreas unfolded his napkin, pulled the cocktail stick from his club sandwich. 'I know you sent money … for my birthdays. It paid for so many of my lessons.'

Leo's happiness was replaced by a churning sense of regret. A cheque once a year; he could have done much more. 'So have you already joined the orchestra or …?'

'I'll take up my place in two weeks. I still can't believe it.'

'Maybe we'll see you here at the festival one day.' Leo knew this sounded trite but he couldn't put shape to his feelings let alone express them.

'I was … um … sorry to hear about your wife.' This time Andreas didn't meet his eye.

'Thank you. Life has been … a challenge. But your news is wonderful. Perhaps you'd let me buy you dinner while you're here in Salzburg; if you don't have plans already?'

They arranged to meet later at his hotel. Leo fought down the urge to ask him to the house. Too soon, he told himself and besides except for the music room the place was a mess. He wasn't even sure he'd turned off the iron.

They walked across Residenzplatz, the sun had reappeared sending shafts of light through the waters of the horse fountain, turning them to rainbows. Andreas stopped to watch the fiaker horses feeding, nose bags in place, tourists taking photos.

Leo was suddenly assailed by the idea that his son might cancel their date; find an excuse, have found him lacking.

'I wanted to do more … when you were growing up. It's just that …' He didn't want to bad mouth Britte or her husband, they'd raised this fine, talented young man. 'We all decided it would be better … less confusing for you.'

Andreas stopped walking. Tourists detoured round them. 'I could have lived with the confusion.'

His throat tightening, Leo wanted to say it wasn't his decision; that his whole family had grieved over it. 'We can't go back, but you're here now and I hope very much to stay in touch.'

'That's what I want. It's why I came.'

Mustering good manners Leo said, 'I hope your mother and … father are well.'

For the first time his son's mouth set into a tense line. 'They're healthy yes, but they're getting divorced,' he said.

Chapter Nine

Natalie was greeted at the door by Toby wearing a silver cyber man's head, his words distorted by a voice altering mechanism. He pulled her inside; issuing a garbled warning to any alien life form that might be patrolling the cluster of modern, executive homes. Her mother was in the hall, a striped apron over her T-shirt and leggings; there was a dusting of flour on her cheek. There were red highlights in her blonde hair.

'Ten more minutes with that, Toby, then it goes into the cupboard; and I don't want you boring your sister with Dr Who today.'

Natalie stepped forward to kiss her. 'Can I help?'

'No, just making the gravy. You could go and drag your dad out of his shed though.'

She walked up the garden with Toby chattering incoherently through his mask. The *shed* was in fact a summer house kitted out with heating, Internet access and a burglar alarm. Her step-father sat in his leather chair, reading an Italian property magazine.

'Hello, Love.' He slid the magazine into a drawer and stood up to peck her cheek. She sank onto the spare chair. Toby, pulling the helmet from his head, placed it on the floor and draped his arms around her neck. She pretended to nibble his hands.

'Mum says to bring you in for dinner but I wanted a quick word if that's OK.'

'Of course it is. Son, do you want to go and tell your mum we'll just be couple of minutes?'

'No, he can stay.' Natalie held on to Toby's arms noting he had written T.I.M.E on the fingers of his left hand and L.O.R.D on his right, in mauve felt pen.

'There are a couple of things actually. First I wondered if you knew a good solicitor, and second if you have a spare laptop I can borrow.'

Her dad came round the desk and perched on the end of it. 'Laptop's no problem. You've obviously been doing some thinking about the other matter though.'

She stared at the floor for a moment; the sightless eyes of the cyber helmet stared back. 'I should find out what my options are. I can't keep ignoring the situation.'

'So you've accepted he'll not be back?'

'No. I can't let myself believe it yet. But Glenda said I should think about the future and if he never comes back well …'

'But would you want him after what he's done?'

Toby wriggled free from her grasp and lay down on the tiles. He rubbed at the lettering on his fingers, smudging the ink.

'I don't know. It's hard to think about. When we were in Salzburg we went to a music institute and Glenda asked this man a question. He looked terrible, as though he was very ill. He seemed … I don't know … without hope.'

Natalie conjured up the image of the man on the bus, a sack of puppy food on his lap. 'But I saw him again on our last day. He was with his family, smiling and having a good time and I thought … I don't know, maybe I should pull myself together a bit. There are folks worse off, as Auntie Maureen would say.'

Her father leaned forward to stroke her hair. 'You'll be smiling again soon, Lovie. I promise. Tell you what, my old car's doing nothing in the garage right now and your Mum's always on at me to shift it. You can borrow it if you like.'

'Really? Dad that would be fantastic. Thanks.'

'Give me a week to get it serviced and add you to the insurance and you can nip round and get it.'

Natalie hugged him, then they sat in silence for a moment;

she looked at a picture of a Dalek on the wall. It seemed to be eating a bag of crisps. Pinned to a cork board above her father's head was a yellowing newspaper cutting of a prisoner's mug-shot.

'Why is that still there, Dad? You've been retired for months.'

He didn't turn to look at it but clicked his biro on and off a few times. 'I know I should take it down but it was … you know … my finest hour getting him behind bars. Sometimes I can't believe I'll never sit behind that desk again, get a call, race off in an unmarked car.

'That's quite a speech, Dad. I didn't know you missed the job that much.

He glanced at Toby now back in his cyber helmet. 'Nip and tell your mum we're on our way, Son.'

Natalie watched him trot down the path, detouring across the lawn to threaten the recycling bins. Her dad tapped his pen against the edge of the desk.

'I need to find something to do, Nat. Don't get me wrong, I love your mum and Toby to bits, but I'm used to doing stuff. I'm getting more stressed doing nothing than I was getting up at four in the morning and going on stake out.' He tossed the biro into the drawer. 'We'd better get in before she comes looking.'

'But you get to spend much more time with Toby now, Dad.'

'Yep. That's true. But in the week when he's at school and your mum's at work the hours drag.'

Natalie saw her mum lean out of the back door and beckon them in. 'Her apron's off, dinner really must be ready now,' she said.

The familiarity of her mother's dinner table was comforting. Slices of hot roast beef lay on her plate and she helped herself to vegetables. Toby sat beside her, his napkin tucked into the top of his sweatshirt and fanned out across his chest. Natalie felt a wave of love for him wash through her. She poured gravy over his dinner.

'So are two you thinking of buying a place in Italy?'

There was the swiftest exchange of glances between her parents.

'Don't worry, Toby and I don't mind you spending our inheritance, do we Sweetie?

Toby, his mouth bulging with food, shook his head. Her mother cut into a roast potato. 'We thought we'd just see what's available out there. You know how much we love Firenze.'

Natalie remembered hot summer afternoons playing ping-pong with her dad while her mother lay bronzing by the pool.

'We've fallen in love with a little place a few miles from Prato; it would be nice to have an apartment to use in the winter. You should come with us.'

'I'm not really one for scorching sun holidays.' She squeezed Toby's hand when he pulled a face. 'Dad's lending me a laptop, by the way, so you can email me.'

Her mother mumbled through the potato. 'You need to get out and meet people, not sit indoors in front of a computer screen. You can become reclusive. I read about it in the Sunday supplement.'

'You sell software, Mum.'

'I sell to businesses. Why don't you come to Salsa dancing with me? There are lots of unattached men, you might meet someone.'

'They're all gay,' her dad said. 'Don't try to push her into anything, Christine'

'Dr Who isn't gay,' Toby said, wiping gravy from his chin.'

'Actually I'm going to join a German class.'

Her mother stopped chewing for a few seconds. If she was going to comment she seemed to think better of it.

'Why's that then, Lovie? Her dad raised his eyebrows. 'Want to go back to Austria some time?

'I'd love to go back. I like the language. It was frustrating not being able to ask for stuff in the shops and cafes. It's lucky they all spoke English.'

'There's a German boy in my class,' Toby said, 'he's from a place called Monster. How cool is that?'

'Were there any nice people in the hotel?' Her mother squashed another potato with the back of her fork and poured gravy on to it.

'Lots, but if you're going to ask about single men I did have a date while I was there, with an American called Connor. He lives in Salzburg.' Natalie couldn't help smiling when she mentioned his name.

'You'll have to invite him over. What job does he do?'

'For crying out loud, Chris, give her time to catch her breath.'

'I'm sorry.' She reached across the table and touched Natalie's arm for a second. 'I'm just longing for a glimpse of the old Natalie. She's been missing for too long and now *he's* out of the way…'

'Let's drop it for now.' Her dad's voice was gentle but firm.

'Who's the old Natalie?' Toby asked his mother.

'What I mean is your big sister used to do lots of lively stuff like running and swimming and sports.'

'And lots of things you didn't like, if I remember correctly.' Natalie thought of the trees she climbed in the park, the thrill of being so far from the ground.

'Is there an old Toby?' he asked, his straight eyebrows moving closer together.

Natalie slid an arm around him. 'There's only one Toby, just like there's only one TARDIS.' She smiled, wanting to change the subject but not daring to mention the practice manager position in case her mother started asking about unmarried vets.

'How's grandma doing? Are we nipping over the see her later?

'Not today. The carers have taken them out for lunch. I hope she doesn't wander off. Her mind might be going but her legs are still strong. We'll have to go one night in the week and pray Auntie Maureen isn't there. That woman can talk you into a stupor.'

Back at Natalie's house her dad squeezed himself behind the desk in the spare bedroom. He took a laptop from its case and opened it up. 'This should do you for a bit but you might want to think about getting a new one.'

'Don't worry; I'm sure this is fine. I just want to be able to surf the net and get emails.'

'Fish me something out with your Broadband details on and I'll get cracking then. You could put the kettle on if you like.'

Natalie sifted through a file of old phone bills then went downstairs. She made tea and brought up a packet of biscuits that she knew Dad wasn't allowed at home.

'I've been threatened by villains and knocked senseless on the rugby pitch but she's convinced these will kill me,' he said. 'She means well.' He turned the tiny chair round to face her. 'This American, is it him you're wanting to email?'

'Always the detective, eh? I'm not harbouring hopes or anything. He was nice to be with, that's all.'

'I was never that struck on Adam, Love.'

'I know, Dad.'

'And you should have let me break his legs when I offered.'

'I hope you're joking!'

'Maybe, but he wouldn't half get a mouthful if I came across him.' He took two biscuits from the pack and dunked them in his tea. 'All you went through together. I don't know how he could do it to you, I really don't. Oh bugger.' He picked up his spoon to fish out the soggy biscuits.

Just before bedtime, Natalie made a mug of hot chocolate and sat down at the laptop. She'd found a brochure from the hotel in Salzburg. The photos of the restaurant and garden made her long for warm evenings eating beneath the canopy of horse chestnut trees. Carefully inserting the address she began a message thanking Karin and the family for their hospitality and saying how much she had enjoyed her stay. After sending it she began another email.

Hi Connor, how are things in wonderful Salzburg? She drank some chocolate and stared at the curtains. Wind was rattling the rotary clothes drier in the back garden. Summer was over. *I'll never forget our day together …* No. Erase that, it sounded clingy. *It seems a long time since Hellbrunn and those hilarious fountains.* She told him about the German class then put two kisses after her name. Hesitating, she deleted the kisses and sent the message.

Sitting back in the chair, finishing her drink and noticing how shabby the room had become, she pondered on ways to brighten it up. But then the laptop bleeped and there was an email in her inbox. A tingle of anticipation shot through her as she saw Connor's name.

Chapter Ten

Just before seven o'clock on Wednesday evening Natalie wandered along a corridor inhaling wafts of polish and disinfectant. A queue had formed outside room twelve and she tagged on to the end.

'Are you joining us for German?' A man in his sixties asked.

'I'm just going to sit in this week and see how I get on.'

His name was Joe and he introduced her to the dozen or so other students. They were mostly retirement age but there was a couple in their forties and a younger girl called Ellie who said she was moving to Munich to live with her German boyfriend. 'I should at least be able to order a beer,' she said.

The teacher arrived in a flurry of apologies for her lateness and unlocked the door. She was young with blonde, spiky hair. Out of her bag she drew books and an array of printouts. Glenda would definitely approve. She welcomed Natalie to the group.

'I've just been on holiday to Salzburg,' she said. 'I'd love to go back some time and it would be nice to be to speak a little German in shops and restaurants.'

There were nods of approval from the other students. Will I ever go back, she wondered. When Connor had pressed his email address into her hand she'd wondered how serious he was about keeping in touch. But he'd answered her email in the same flirty vein that he'd spoken to her in Salzburg and said she could stay with him if she ever returned.

'We have had two sessions already, but I think that's no problem.' The teacher explained. Her name was Gabi, short for Gabrielle and said she was from Cologne, pronouncing it the German way, Köln. Natalie tried shaping the word with her lips.

The class members went through their homework. They'd had

to write a few simple words about what they'd been doing at the weekend. Joe had been out to dinner. Gabi corrected any errors and wrote his phrases on the board. Natalie put the date on the first page of her new notebook and wrote the sentences down.

Ellie groaned when it was her turn. 'I can't say it in German,' she said. 'It's too complicated.'

Gabi's pen was poised at the whiteboard. 'OK. Tell us in English and we'll see if you can work it out.'

'Well, my dad's laying a new patio so I helped him break up the old concrete with a pick axe. Then the axe handle split and we went to B&Q to get a new one.'

Joining in with the laughter Natalie felt her tension sliding away. Gabi wrote vocabulary on the board and they all tried to say the words.

'You never know when you might need the German word for concrete,' Joe said.

One word, meaning "excellent" was hard to pronounce. They broke it down to its four syllables – aus-ge-zeich-net and Natalie discovered she could mimic Gabi's accent almost perfectly.

Joe nudged her arm. 'Are you sure you're a beginner?'

At coffee break they trooped down to the refectory. Joe told her he'd been to Salzburg a few years ago. It was nice to talk to someone who knew the city.

'The best time to go,' he said, 'is when they have the Christmas markets, especially if it's snowing. Now that is a treat.'

By nine o'clock Natalie had filled two pages of her notebook and made a list of books she would need to buy. In the carpark Ellie was walking alongside Joe.

'Natalie, I'm sure I've seen you on our estate. I live on Weston.' she said.

'Oh. I'm just round the corner from you, then.'

'Joe's giving me a lift. Do you want to come with us?'

Natalie looked at Joe who nodded. 'More the merrier.'

In the car they giggled over their pronunciation; practicing a few of the phrases they'd learned. Natalie was dropped off first, 'Tschüs,' she called to them as the car pulled away.

Once inside she made tea and put bread in the toaster. 'Ich heiße Natalie,' she repeated aloud. 'Ich wohne in Coventry. Mein Bruder heißt Toby.'

She liked the way her tongue rolled around the consonants and the unfamiliar, whispered "ch" sound. Reading the notes she'd made she realised she would have to buy the text book pretty quickly if she were to catch up with the others. But it's been a good day, she thought. I've arranged to have the locks changed and I've made some new friends.

Honey dripped from the toast onto her fingers. Licking it off, she picked up the telephone. No messages. Well, that was OK, she wasn't expecting any.

Tentatively she thought about Adam. Changing the locks would be a good move, it gave her a tiny feeling of power but despite everything, if he were to knock on the door now and want to see her, she knew she would let him in.

Chapter Eleven

If the party had been anywhere but at the Friesen Leo would have made an excuse not to go. In front of the mirror in the hotel toilets he smoothed back his hair. He'd finally had it cut because his neighbour said he had enough for a pony tail; but it was still all one length and reached his collar. He took a deep breath, let it out very slowly then went back to the dining room.

You'll meet lots of interesting people, Lucy Weber's mother had told him. So far he'd been introduced to several thirty-something couples intent on talking about work and their cars. There was an elderly aunt of Herr Weber's who, he was told, had been quite a famous photographer in her younger days, but she'd been positioned at the opposite end of the table making conversation with her impossible.

He was seated between a friend of Frau Weber called Helena and the husband of the photographer. It seemed rude to ask him about his wife's former career and for a moment Leo was tongue-tied, unable to think of a suitable topic.

The older man cleared his throat and said, 'I hear you're a widower.'

Leo forked up some of his '*bauernsalat*' and nodded.

'My brother lost his wife in a car accident years ago,' the man went on. 'Shocking, only thirty-four. Two young children.'

'A terrible loss.' Leo said, concentrating on spearing salad leaves.

Helena turned to him. 'Do you have children, Leo?'

Leo. She's very familiar considering we've just met, he thought; then chided himself for being starchy. Few people in Salzburg knew about Andreas. He'd told. Karin years ago and recently shared the news of his visit to Salzburg, but how could he now admit to a son without explaining he'd fathered him years before his marriage to Sofia? That afternoon he'd had a text from Andreas asking if he'd like to meet up in Wurzburg in December and hear him play. He was so proud of the boy but these were not the people to share secrets with.

He was about to say no, to Helena when he realised he'd spent so long in thought she had turned away to the man on her other side and was discussing the merits of Lanzarote as a winter holiday destination.

The photographer's husband placed a brown-spotted hand on Leo's coat sleeve. 'The sun comes out again, eventually. Believe me, it does. One morning you'll wake up and it won't be the first thing you think about.'

He was so sincere that it was easy to chat to the man who introduced himself as Peter.

The main course came and a few moments were spent talking about the food.

'How long have you taught piano?' Peter asked.

'I taught music in school for many years and then … my wife needed care and …'

'So now you teach from home?'

Before he could say *yes* Leo felt pressure on his instep. He pulled his foot away. Having long legs he often needed to apologise for accidently touching someone's foot under a dinner table. Opposite him Frau Weber, wine glass in hand, was deep in conversation with a friend.

'Yes, I have many students now; mostly children but a few adults too.'

There it was again, this time on the side of his ankle. Leo tucked both feet under his chair.

'Do you think I'd be too old to learn?' Peter asked. 'I've often thought about it.'

'Not at all; you're never too old to …' Glancing up he saw

Frau Weber had stopped talking and was staring at him.

'Never too old to what, Leo?' she said, raising her eyebrows.

'To learn an instrument.' He directed his reply to Peter then jumped as he felt a stockinged toe touch his knee. He braced one foot under the table and eased his chair back as far as he dare.

'Maybe I'll book some lessons myself,' she whispered, raising her glass.

At the other end of the table her husband got to his feet and even though most people were still eating he gave a little speech thanking everyone for coming. Leo had entirely forgotten the party was to celebrate the man's fortieth birthday and wondered if he should have brought a gift. Herr Weber rambled on for a few minutes while Leo wished he could finish his venison before it became completely cold.

Somewhere between day two hundred and ninety and two hundred and ninety-five he'd fully regained his appetite. It had crept up on him and was, he supposed a positive sign although cooking was still a lonely chore.

When they'd all toasted Herr Weber's health and finished their main course, Leo escaped into the hotel garden to get some air. What on earth was that woman thinking of touching his knee like that? Too much wine, of course, that had to be it.

He walked across the terrace, past the swimming pool now covered for the winter and stood in the shadow of a balcony. Beyond the garden he could hear Karin calling to Otto as they set out for their evening walk. He envied her the peaceful solitude of strolling at the foot of the mountain, breathing in the scent of pines and listening to the rush of water coursing down into the stream. Sofia had loved to walk…

'There you are.'

A warm blast of garlic breath made him jump.

'Why are you hiding out here, Leo?'

Frau Weber had a lighted cigarette in one hand. She tried

to stroke his cheek with the other but he jerked his head away. Smoke drifted up into his eyes. 'Frau Weber I think we should …'

'Call me Julia.' She pressed against him, trapping him against the wall.

'I know you must be lonely, Leo. Why don't we meet up sometime for coffee?'

'Please.' He took hold of her shoulders and forced her away from his body. 'We should return to your husband's party.'

'I've come out for a smoke. He won't expect me back just yet.'

Leo edged along the terrace but she took hold of his sleeve. Now in the light of the hotel windows he saw she'd undone the buttons of her blouse, her bra on show. She followed his gaze down and smiled. He tugged his sleeve from her grasp, turned back to the hotel and saw Karin's brother standing at the door to the wine cellar.

'Leo,' Lukas called. 'Just the man. Come and give me your opinion.'

He opened the door and Leo strode towards it. Julia Weber had shrunk into the shadows.

'*Mein Gott.*' He leaned against the cellar wall while Lukas selected two bottles of wine.

'Frau Weber strikes again?' Lukas rolled his eyes.

'What is wrong with her? Coming on to me at her husband's party?' Leo was shaking, angry with himself for glancing at her blouse; the thought bringing heat to his face.

'She has tried it with me and …' he shook his head and looked away for a second, 'and my Papa who is old enough to be her father.'

Leo groaned. 'Now what shall I do? I can't go back to the table.' He gave a nervous laugh. 'I was looking forward to sampling Luisa's '*Bayerische Crème*' dessert.'

'No problem. Follow me.' Lukas locked the cellar door and

led him through the gate. They re-entered the hotel through the kitchen door. Tucked away in a corner was the table where the family ate their own meals.

'She won't find you here,' Lukas said without any trace of amusement. 'The woman is a menace.'

'Could you let her husband know I've had to leave?'

Lukas nodded and headed for the restaurant. A few moments later Luisa came and put the dessert, a napkin and cutlery in front of him.

'Lukas said you were feeling a little over heated in the restaurant,' she said.

Leo smiled. 'Something like that yes.'

Later, leaving by the kitchen door and hurrying down the lane he met Karin returning from her walk. He made a fuss of Otto.

'How was the party?'

He thought about trying to make light of it, to tell her about Julia Weber and be comforted by her undoubted outrage, but then he thought of Lucy, and wondered what he would do if Julia brought her along for her lesson next week. 'The food of course was wonderful,' he said.

Back at home he let Max into the garden. Pouring himself a Schnapps he stood at the door while the dog snuffled round the lawn. He and Sofia had never had a large number of friends, just a few very good ones with whom they'd sometimes share a meal or go to a concert. They were still there, those friends, supportive but in the background. He'd refused so many invitations since her death, not wanting to cast a shadow over their evening or be the odd one at the table. Perhaps he should ring them, make contact again.

In the night he woke, sweating, restless and in a state of semi arousal. He went into the bathroom, ran himself a glass of water and drank it all. Surely to God he hadn't been dreaming about Julia Weber. The woman repelled him. Back in bed he straightened his pillows, wriggled across the sheet to where it was cooler. He pictured Sofia, her halo of dark hair, the joy of her smile and drifted back to sleep.

Hours later he stirred again, but was still floating on the fragments of a dream. He was in the city and the sun was bright. He was taking hold of her hand, turning to kiss her. But it wasn't Sofia. The eyes were as bright and lively as hers but the hair was lighter, the woman taller, younger. She gazed up at him and contentment spread through him. Her smile was wide but her words, as she began to speak, were English.

Chapter Twelve

Her mother swung the car through the care home gates so sharply Natalie's head banged against the passenger window. When she'd turned off the engine she made no move to get out of the car, sitting rigid, still grasping the steering wheel until Natalie asked what was wrong and the floodgates burst open.

'Your dad is driving me bonkers and he's not doing himself any favours.'

Without waiting for Natalie to comment she continued. 'After years on the bloody force you'd think he'd be happy to relax but he's bored out of his wits.'

'Maybe he should get a part time job or something.' Natalie thought back to the conversation she'd had with her dad.

'I've suggested he come dancing with me but he's not interested.'

Natalie turned away to hide a smile. 'He's only been out of the job a few months, Mum. I'm sure it'll all recede into the background eventually.'

'Well it's not receding fast enough for me.' She gathered her bag and coat and a fruit cake she'd bought along the way. 'Oh that's all we need.'

Natalie saw Grandma's sister, Auntie Maureen walk through the gates, her ancient poodle wedged under her arm.

In the day room Grandma looked tiny in the high-backed chair. Natalie kissed her forehead and sat beside her.

'Is Toby not with you?' Grandma craned her skinny neck towards the door.

'Dad's taken him to a birthday party, Gran. They've gone to the bowling alley.'

'Bowling alley? Whatever do you mean?'

'They have parties in places like that now. It saves messing the house up.'

The old lady didn't reply but fished a piece of cardboard from the side of her chair, folded it neatly and stuffed it up the sleeve of her cardigan. She was watching her daughter who had collared one of the care workers and was talking in a low voice. Natalie tried to distract her. 'I hear you went out for lunch the other day, Gran, was it somewhere nice?'

Grandma frowned as if trying to remember then her face went blank and she looked out of the window. Auntie Maureen was stalking her dog round the lawn, a blue plastic bag in her hand.

Her mother sat down busying herself unwrapping the cake and taking a small knife from her handbag.

'Does Dad know you carry that?' Natalie felt laughter welling. 'Does he ever do a *stop and search* at home?' Her mother's withering glance stemmed further teasing.

Auntie Maureen arrived, chattering to another visitor, the blue plastic bag not in evidence.

'Everyone here loves Candy,' Maureen was saying. 'She gets lots of fuss, don't you Candy. Ooh, here's our Natalie. Look, Florrie, it's our Natalie come to see you.'

'I can see her. I'm not daft.'

'No. Well, are we in time for tea? I think I heard Janine with the trolley. Is it time for tea, Florrie? I'm spitting feathers.'

Natalie met her mother's gaze and saw a nerve jumping below her eye.

'Did I tell you I'm learning German, Gran?' Natalie passed her a piece of cake on a serviette. For a second all chatter stopped. Grandma narrowed her eyes, took the cake and balanced it on the arm of her chair. 'You're going to *Sprechen Sie Deutsch* are you?

'I fancied having a go. I've only had one lesson so far but …'

'Natalie's learning German,' the old lady said to Maureen.

Her great aunt looked at Natalie but passed no comment. For Auntie Maureen this was a first.

'Seems a funny thing to be doing.' Grandma continued. She broke off a corner of cake but didn't eat it.

'I went to Austria. Do you remember I told you about it?'

Natalie took the proffered cup of tea from the care worker. She'd asked for it without milk, a habit she picked up in Salzburg. Looking up she saw Grandma exchange glances with Maureen who launched into an anecdote about the fish man's van breaking down and him asking to use her fridge until the relief van arrived.

'Do you have any cardboard?' Grandma asked Janine.

'Not today, Darlin'. Drink your tea and I'll look for some tomorrow.'

Natalie's mother whispered, 'Don't talk to her about German lessons.'

'Why not?'

'You know how confused she gets?'

'And that would make her worse would it?' Natalie took a swig of tea and felt a flush of irritation rise to her face.

'And the bag split,' Auntie Maureen was saying. 'Frozen prawns everywhere. I was sweeping them up for days. Candy found one under the washing machine, didn't you Candy?'

'We should talk to her about everyday things that she doesn't have to struggle with.'

'She's not struggling and I should think everyday things get a bit boring round here.'

'OK, well I'm not particularly interested in hearing about it either. Can't imagine why you'd want to learn that language.'

'What do you mean *that* language? You're sounding like a racist now.'

'I won't qualify that remark with a reply.' Her mother turned away.

Natalie wondered whether to mention the Bowling Road job but for the last few days she'd found her own thoughts steering away from the possible promotion and settling on the far more enticing images of Salzburg and Connor who emailed her most evenings now. And what's the problem with learning a foreign language, she wondered. Thousands of people do it. She asked how Toby was getting on at school.

'He's fine, though he doesn't seem to have a special friend. He jogs along with the rest but doesn't talk about any in particular. Do you think I should talk to his teacher?

'Not unless you think he's lonely and he doesn't seem to be. Does he ever mention Adam?'

'He talked about him soon after … he went. Wanted to know when he was coming back. I told him he mustn't ask you about it though.' She leaned forward to brush some crumbs from the front of Grandma's cardigan. Candy shuffled forward to lick them off the carpet.

'I wish you'd consider coming to Italy in December.'

Natalie shook her head.

'But if you came along we could stay for Christmas. We'd all be together.'

'What about Grandma? She wouldn't be there.'

Her mother's teacup clattered down and she leaned in to whisper. 'She hardly knows what day it is so we could bring her present before we go. But if you don't go none of us will; we're not leaving you on your own for Christmas.' She reached out and pushed Natalie's fringe to one side. 'Are you growing your hair?'

'I thought I might.'

'But the in between stages are so untidy. All the curliness is coming back.'

'Natalie has lovely hair,' Grandma said, interrupting Maureen's steady stream of chat. 'It's all springy. Just like … just like …

Maureen, what was his name?'

'It'll take more looking after,' her mother said loudly. 'That nice bob suited you best.'

'No. He wasn't called Bob,' Grandma said. 'It was something …'

'See. I told you she was confused.' Her mother stood up. 'I'm just popping into her room, make sure everything's OK.' She collected plates, cups and saucers and took them over to the trolley.

'We went out for dinner to the Horse and Trumpet,' Grandma said to Natalie. 'I had beef and Peggy over there had lamb. It was lovely.

'Is beef your favourite, Gran?'

Grandma's face took on a dreamy look. 'I like it with dumplings.'

'Hang on, Florrie.' Maureen chided. 'You don't have dumplings with beef. You have Yorkshire pudding.'

Grandma looked mutinous. 'Natalie knows you do. You'll have seen beef and dumplings while you were in Germany.'

'It was Austria; remember I told you about Salzburg?' Her mother was right; Gran's confusion was getting worse.

Through the steamy windows she could see there was snow in the rain. She dreaded Christmas and felt guilty declining the invitation to Italy.

Her mother reappeared. 'She's got loads of cardboard under her mattress. I've been talking to the manager and she says they keep removing it a little at a time. Do you think it's a fire hazard?

'Well, she doesn't smoke so I shouldn't think so. Why not let her collect it if she wants to?'

Her mother sat in the chair next to Grandma and gently slid the folded card from up her sleeve. 'Let's tuck this down the side of your chair, Mum,' she said, 'it's too bulky up your cardi.'

'Natalie's learning German,' Grandma said. 'German of all

things.'

When they were preparing to leave the old lady became tearful and that set her mother off. Natalie suggested Auntie Maureen stay a bit longer and she was more than happy to agree. They'd been joined by another visitor who introduced himself as Bernard and said he'd always loved poodles, so both owner and dog were basking in his attention.

'We'll pop by again on Sunday, Grandma,' Natalie said, kissing the old lady's cheek.

In the corridor her mother snuffled into a tissue. 'I hate the way she's going but there's bugger all we can do about it.' Grandma's voice drifted after them.

'What did she say?'

Natalie frowned. 'I'm not sure but it sounded like *Bis bald*.'

Her mother fished in her bag for the car keys. 'Sorry?'

'I must have misheard her. *Bis bald* is German for *see you soon*.

Chapter Thirteen

Natalie had been to Glenda's house before, when they were planning the holiday. It was a traditional semi in a tree-lined street. The place was as she'd expected, immaculately clean and tidy. The wall between the two downstairs living rooms was removed to create what Natalie's mother would call a 'through lounge.' An extended kitchen with a conservatory attached, reached out into the mature back garden.

Her previous visit had been on a hot summer evening and they'd sat in the garden poring over brochures and maps. This evening it was chilly and wind whipped round Natalie's ankles as she got off the bus.

This second invitation had come, late on Friday. Glenda had taken the afternoon off, giving no explanation. Her colleague, Clare was certain she was going for an interview. 'How else would she have the nerve to take time off just after your Austrian holiday?'

Feeling her heart sink Natalie had to admit it was the likeliest explanation; so she was nervous when Glenda rang asking, in an excited voice, if Natalie would like to go for dinner the following evening.

'It'll only be lasagne or something, would that be OK?'

'Sounds lovely.' Natalie lowered her voice. 'You haven't got yourself a new job have you?'

'Whatever gave you that idea? Come round about seven if that's not too early.'

Now, at Glenda's front door Natalie placed a carrier bag between her feet and rang the bell. She had brought a bottle of red wine and a tub of cherries.

Fearing Glenda might be wearing her Austrian dirndl she was

relieved to see her friend in jeans and T-shirt with an apron over the top. Her hair scraped up into the usual ponytail.

'Sorry about the casual look,' she said, leading Natalie through to the kitchen. 'I can't dress up when I'm cooking.'

Natalie, in the trousers and blouse she wore in Austria tried not to stare at the gleaming appliances. A laptop sat open on the scrubbed pine table.

'I've uploaded all my photographs. We can have a look after dinner. Oh, and I've bought you this. Don't get excited it wasn't terribly expensive.' Glenda handed her a CD. It was a compilation of Mozart pieces.

'Oh, that's really nice of you.' Natalie was happy to see that it included one of the arias they heard at the dinner concert.

Glenda poured them both some wine. 'Come with me, she said. 'Leave your glass there a minute.'

Natalie followed her out into the hall and up the stairs. Opening the door of the back bedroom Glenda gestured Natalie to go in, then stood at the door, eyebrows raised.

Natalie looked at the double bed with a heap of fluffy cushions in the middle of it but then the pale cushion on the top began to move. She edged closer and saw a downy head lift up. The kitten blinked and opened pale blue eyes. It was the cutest thing she had ever seen.

'Oh, can I touch it? Is it a boy or a girl?'

Glenda walked in and scooped the fuzzy bundle up in her hands. It was a large kitten but most of its bulk was fur. The muzzle, ears, feet and tail were a blue- grey; its body and legs almost white.

'He's a darling little blue-point boy. I fetched him from York this afternoon,' Glenda said, her voice rising to an almost inaudible squeak. She held the kitten to her face and emitted a series of indecipherable phrases, all of which sent him into an ecstasy of purring; then she handed him to Natalie.

His fur was so soft she could barely feel it under her fingers.

'What's his name?'

'Well, that's another story. Pop him back down. I'll tell you about it as we eat.'

Glenda had set the table in the kitchen. It was like one of those rooms that couples rave over in TV programmes, all shiny surfaces and flawless tiles. She declined Natalie's offer of help. The salad was freshly tossed, the lasagne bubbling perfectly through the clean, glass of the oven door. Natalie sat down and sipped her wine.

'The CD is really to thank you,' Glenda said, when the food was served. 'You were right; there was no reason for me not to get the kitten. I've got to move on; can't keep harking back to the past. And neither must you.' She shook out her napkin with a thwack. 'So that's my news. What have you been up to since we got back?'

Natalie balanced strips of pasta on the back of her fork and explained about the missing exercise bike and CDs. Seeing her friend's face grow red with indignation she blundered on. 'I changed the locks on the house and I've joined a German class.'

Glenda's eyes widened over the rim of her wine glass. 'Good move about the locks but German? Whatever for? No sorry, that sounded rude.' She waved her fork in a kind of apologetic gesture. 'I know you enjoyed using the phrasebook on holiday but I didn't realise you fancied learning the language.'

'I didn't know I did either. It was an impulse.'

With a conspiratorial smile, Glenda asked, 'You're not thinking of flying back to the man with the beard, are you?'

Natalie's mind focussed on Connor's face for a second. She now kept the Hellbrunn photograph beside her bed so that his smile was the first thing she saw each morning.

'No.' But as she chewed a perfectly cooked piece of courgette she fantasized about waking every morning beside Connor and going to work in Salzburg.

'I suppose I'd better tell you the name of the kitten,' Glenda said. 'When you buy a pedigree the breeder has a continuing interest.'

'To make sure you're looking after him OK?'

'Partly, but it's more for the show bench.' Glenda balanced her knife and fork on the edge of her plate. 'You see he's a fine example of a Persian so she'll want me to show him, and although I've no intention of dragging him all over the country at weekends I've told her I might. I feel a bit bad about fibbing so that's why I agreed to the name.'

Natalie waited to hear it but Glenda toyed with a bit of pasta. 'You see they have a pedigree name. There's nothing you can do about that and he comes from a long line of champions so,' she paused again, 'he's called, Barbaradear Sheridan Wicky Woo.'

'What?'

'For pity's sake, Natalie, that's the first and last time I'm going to utter those words!'

Trying to stifle laughter Natalie brought her napkin up to her face but then she saw Glenda's lips were twitching too. After swigs of wine they dissolved into giggles.

'So which part of that are you going to call him?'

'I've decided on *Mr Woo*. I thought that sounded the least ridiculous. The rest is a hideous amalgam of their family names. Pretentious or what?'

'Well, you wouldn't want to stand at the back door calling him by his full name.'

Glenda's eyes flashed. 'Oh, he's not going out.' She gave an exaggerated shudder. 'He'll be a house cat. I might have a run built for him in the garden but he's not going to wander the neighbourhood.' She speared a piece of broccoli. 'Anything could happen to him.'

They talked about work, Glenda urging her to think seriously about the Bowling Road job. 'Have you always done office work?" she asked. "What I mean is did you go to business college?"

Natalie paused mid-chew. This was beginning to sound like an interview and with sinking spirits wondered if it was the reason for the invitation.

'I did go to college,' she might as well be truthful, 'but my course was physical education.'

'You wanted to be a PE teacher?'

A bubble of anxiety rose in Natalie's chest and the question lay between them for several seconds. She reached for her wine and took a gulp. 'I did, yes.'

'So what happened, how did you come to be …?' As if sensing her discomfort Glenda trailed off. 'Obviously you can tell me to shut up if you like.'

Natalie was in dangerous territory; the past, appearing like a dot on the horizon, threatened to speed towards her. Part of her wanted to talk about it, tell Glenda everything, but the silence became embarrassingly long and her courage failed. 'There weren't many jobs locally when I left college and then I met Adam and I didn't want to work away from home.'

'So you gave up your dream for him.' Glenda's voice was flat.

'Well, it wasn't *quite* as straightforward as that, but in a way I did.'

'Would you go back to it now he's gone?'

Involuntarily Natalie flexed her calf muscles. Walking at Zell am See had toned them up. Adam always loved her shapely legs; she wondered when he stopped admiring them.

'There's no chance of that.' She attacked the remainder of her food, hoping the subject might be dropped but Glenda stopped eating.

'Can I ask you a personal question?'

This time all Natalie's muscles tensed. 'Okay.'

'You must have been married for about ten years but you still seem awfully involved with your parents. Is it because they've given you support since Adam left or …'

'We've always been close, they've been … there for me and … I adore Toby.' She spoke quickly, loading her fork with pasta; concentrating on not letting it slide off.

'Sorry, I shouldn't be so blunt. I don't know what it's like for family to rally round.' She drew a deep breath. 'Anyway, what this trip has shown me is that you have bags of energy for the things you enjoy. It would do you a power of good to go for practice manager, think of it as a whole new start, and of course I'd give you an excellent reference.'

Natalie's mood sagged further. She'd hoped for an evening of holiday reminiscences but even Mr Woo waddling into the room with a toy mouse in his jaws didn't distract Glenda from relating the job description for Bowling Road point by point. It seemed easiest to go along with her and she promised to give it serious thought.

When Glenda was lifting a Marks and Spencer trifle out of the fridge Natalie glanced at the laptop, still open and showing a photograph of Hellbrunn palace. She thought about sunlight on her closed eyelids and Connor's lips whispering across her cheek.

'We haven't looked at the holiday pictures yet."

Glenda slid the dessert onto the worktop. 'Goodness me, I completely forgot and there's something I want to show you. Talk about bad pennies turning up.'

She scrolled through the photos and stopped at one she had taken of Natalie when they were en-route to the Mozart house. She was smiling into the lens and leaning on the rail of the footbridge.

'What do you think of that then? Isn't that a bizarre coincidence?' Glenda tapped the screen and Natalie leaned closer. Where the footbridge met the bank of the river she saw the profiles of tourists and Salzburgers hurrying by, but on his own, behind the crowd was a tall, thin man, shoulders hunched; head down, carrying a briefcase.

'It's that odious man from the Mozarteum,' Glenda said, turning her attention back to the trifle. 'I've a good mind to delete that one.'

'No don't do that.' Natalie had never mentioned that he'd been on their bus that day, the old lady stopping to talk to him. It wasn't a happy memory of the trip but now she felt the pull of the city she'd fallen in love with and for a moment it lightened her mood. 'You will let me have copies of them all won't you?' she said.

Chapter Fourteen

Leo's hotel room faced the river Main. On the far bank floodlights played on the mellow stone of a fortress high on a promontory. Long cargo barges slid by causing barely a ripple and before darkness fell he'd watched a holiday cruiser approach, adorned with Christmas lights. Passengers, muffled into coats and hats gathered on deck taking photographs. From the volume of laughter drifting over the water he imagined they were drinking Gluhwein too.

A shiver of anticipation ran through him. Tomorrow night he would hear Andreas play and this evening they would meet for dinner. He hadn't visited this part of Germany before. It reminded him of childhood storybooks: narrow medieval houses with steeply-sloping rooves cramped around cobbled squares.

Lying on his bed he closed his eyes, his dog curled up beside him, but he was unable to settle so he flicked through the TV channels then showered and dressed. At seven-thirty he clipped the lead to Max's collar and they walked to the ancient bridge against a tide of tourists heading into town for the Christmas market. Here the river thundered through sluice gates, the reflected lights from the fortress fragmented and churned into the black torrent.

Altemainmuhle restaurant still had the old water wheel attached to its wall but inside it was stylish with pale oak tables, beams from the old mill workings and exposed brickwork. Subtle white lights twinkled against the windows. Leo hung up his overcoat and scanned the tables. He saw Andreas stand up and beckon him. They shook hands.

'I'm glad you're here, Papa. How was your journey?'

'Fine, fine.' *Papa.* How good that sounded.

They ordered beer and settled Max under the table. Leo began to say how busy the autobahn had been but he saw Andreas was distracted.

'Papa, I hope you won't mind. That is … I wondered how you felt about …' He ran a finger down the outside of his beer stein. 'My mother decided to come after all.'

A prickling sensation crept over Leo's scalp. 'She's …?'

'It was a last minute thing and …'

'Is she joining us for dinner?'

'If you have no objection.'

Andreas was sitting forward now and Leo, sensing the boy's anxiety, tried to keep his own voice even. 'No, that would be … I mean it would be nice to see her.'

He felt heat rush to his face. Was she watching close by and waiting for the signal to join them? He ran a hand through his hair, shifted in his seat causing Max to raise his head.

'I'll text her, then.' Andreas drew a phone from his pocket.

Leo was facing away from the door; he felt vulnerable and unprepared. Twenty years had elapsed since he'd seen her and now at any moment she'd be there, wanting to talk, asking him about his life. He took a clumsy swig of beer and splashed some over his shirt front. Grabbing a napkin he dabbed at it, praying he had a few moments to gather his thoughts.

'She's here.' Andreas beckoned and Leo stood, made a slow turn; brought up a hand to cover the damp patch on his shirt.

Britte was taking off her coat. Her legs were just as fabulous as Leo remembered, the hem of her dress touching her knees. The material clung to her still slim waist but her breasts were larger, the cut of the dress accentuating their fullness.

It seemed she was in no hurry to face them as she took time to slide a scarf from her neck, tucking it into the sleeve of her coat. She's every bit as scared as I am, Leo thought and a long-forgotten ache of affection for her caught in his throat. Finally she looked up, met his gaze and walked towards them. The years didn't roll away for Leo, the leggy teenager in tiny shorts and halter top had vanished. Britte was a woman and beautiful.

She held out a hand and he curled his fingers around hers feeling a tremor. He wasn't sure if it came from her or him. Andreas pulled out a chair for her to sit and there was a breaking of tension as she realised Max was under the table. Leo guided the dog away from her legs. The waiter arrived with menus and while the other two seemed to study the list of dishes intently Leo stared at the page unseeing and tried to think of something witty or interesting to say.

In the end Britte spoke first, asking about his journey, the weather in Salzburg and telling him how anxious Andreas was about the forthcoming concert. Leo found it hard to meet her eye, then, worried she'd think he was staring at her chest, directed most of his replies to Andreas. But when the boy excused himself a few moments later they were left, less than a metre apart and there was no avoiding her gaze.

'It's so good of you to come all this way, Leo, especially at this time of year.'

'I wouldn't have missed it.' He stopped himself saying that the time of year had no significance for him; that Heiligenacht would pass un-marked unless his sister renewed her pleas for him to go to Vienna. 'You're looking very well, Britte.'

In fact she looked tired. Close to he saw that her make-up fell short of disguising dark circles beneath her eyes. She's going through a divorce, he thought, a bereavement of sorts.

'You too,' she said. 'Are you coming out of the darkness now?'

He wondered if she'd rehearsed the phrase. '

'Not really … but I …'

A look of embarrassment flushed her face.

He smiled. 'Maybe I can see the exit but can't quite reach it.'

'Like at IKEA?'

He laughed and her face broke into the smile he remembered.

She clamped a hand over her mouth then said, 'Oh God, I'm sorry. I'm just so nervous.'

'Me too.'

Before they could say more Andreas was back and conversation turned to the concert and their son's ambitions for the future. Amid his pride Leo felt a tinge of something else – regret? He wouldn't analyse the feeling; it might take him to a path he didn't want his thoughts to follow.

He ordered a local wine. The squat bottle with the long neck had a glass stopper, the first he'd ever seen. The wine slipped down well and he'd almost demolished his steak before remembering to have some wrapped in foil for Max.

Britte, it seemed, was vegetarian and maybe a reluctant one, he thought, as she pushed baked mushrooms around her plate but ate very little.

After dinner they walked towards the main square. The Christmas market had closed and Leo said he must take Max along the river bank before they returned to the hotel. As the Rathaus clock chimed ten he shook hands with Andreas. Britte came close, the subtle scent of her enveloping him.

'See you at the concert.' She kissed his cheek, a simple token of friendship and then she was gone, taking their son's arm, not looking back.

Leo followed the path by the river, the water still thrashing through the sluices. He knew there'd been a time when he might have slid from the bank himself, let the current take him. How clever his sister had been buying him a puppy.

In bed he didn't want to think about Britte but images came anyway, pushing aside Sofia's gentle smile and the English girl whose worried eyes and sweet face often visited him at night.

Britte is the reason I didn't see my son grow up, he thought, trying to muster resentment, even anger, but instead he thought of the place where a locket had lain at her throat, the way her dress swished, revealing the hollow behind her knee as she walked to collect her coat; and later, as sleep began to claim him, the years did slip away and he saw her lying naked at the lakeside all those years ago.

Chapter Fifteen

'How sad are we?' Ellie said. 'Two gorgeous women with the weekend at our feet and we're staying in doing German homework.'

'We could go for a drink afterwards and practice our personal pronouns if you like.' Natalie walked out of the spare room onto the landing and turned up the thermostat on the central heating. December had blown in with gales and freezing temperatures.

With Glenda coaching her almost daily on the responsibilities of a veterinary practice manager, she was thankful for her new friendship with Ellie with whom, so far, she had only the vagaries of German grammar in common. They were both progressing well in the class and the teacher had recommended they do some extra work from an on-line tutor site.

'We need Joe here,' Natalie said, her brow furrowing as she struggled with the answer to a question on the screen. 'He's good at explaining this stuff.'

'Did you know his wife has Alzheimer's? Ellie said. 'He's so sweet, he never complains but it must be hard for him, they're only in their sixties.'

'I didn't know. Poor woman. Poor Joe.'

'I think the reason he's in the class is because he likes the company.'

'We ought to ask him out for a meal one evening.' Natalie liked the idea of adding a date to her empty social calendar.

'We've got the class Christmas party to arrange,' Ellie said. 'We haven't agreed whose house to have it at yet.'

'We could have it here. Do you think Gabi would be okay with that?'

'I think she'd be pleased. I dropped a glass of red wine on her carpet last year.'

'Talking of wine,' Natalie said. 'I've a bottle somewhere my mother gave me. Shall we open it?'

'We might not get much German done if we do.'

Downstairs she opened the bottle of Shiraz then rummaged in the food cupboard for some crisps. To remember the German names of furniture and appliances she'd put Post-it notes all over the house. Toby thought it was great fun and she'd let him help. She remembered him sticking the label to the fridge and trying to pronounce, *Kühlschrank* .

'Natalie,' Ellie called downstairs with a smile in her voice. 'A message has just flashed up on the screen and I'm sure I saw the word, *adorable* in it before it disappeared.'

Connor, she thought. It was nice to have some male attention but … it wasn't Adam. She took the bottle and glasses upstairs, the bag of crisps tucked under her arm. While Ellie poured the wine Natalie clicked open the message.

'Do you want to read it?' Natalie found herself smiling.

Ellie read aloud, '*Hi, Adorable Natalie, are you ready for me to write in German yet?* Wow, who is this from?'

'His name's Connor. I spent a day with him in Salzburg. Nothing … really happened except … there was rather a lot of kissing.' She stared into her wine. 'We've been instant messaging on and off for a few weeks.'

Her friend's smile widened. 'Reply then, I won't look.' Ellie turned her chair around so that she was facing the door.

'I'll do it later.'

'Do it now.'

Natalie took a sip of wine then typed, '*My German is still very basic. Maybe I need some private lessons.*'

Yes, come over here right now, it's my night off and I'm all alone. Do you love snow? We had some today. The city is romantic. The speed of his reply made her laugh out loud.

She navigated away to the webcam link he had sent a few days earlier. Sure enough a thin blanket of snow covered the rooftops and church domes. When she switched to the webcam in Residenzplatz the Christmas market was in full swing; crowds huddled round the brightly lit stalls and at the centre a tree as high as those in the garden of the hotel, was bedecked in lights.

She typed, '*It's beautiful. Wish I was there.*'

'*Catch the next plane and I'll take you there; buy you a mug of Gluhwein and watch the snowflakes melting on your hair.*'

'I'm nipping to the loo,' Ellie said. 'Give you some privacy.'

Natalie sat back in her chair and took her hands off the keyboard. It was so long since she'd played the flirting game, she needed a moment to think.

The telephone rang. She picked up the handset. Adam's number was on the display

'Natalie?'

Her heart drummed. She stood up and sat down again. It was Adam except that his voice wasn't right. He'd assumed a refined kind of accent, like he used on the phone to house buyers. He didn't sound like her Adam at all.

'My solicitor has heard from yours,' he said. 'They suggested we talk.'

Ellie flushed the loo and came out of the bathroom. Natalie mouthed Adam's name. Her friend picked up her wine glass, gave Natalie's shoulder a supportive squeeze then went downstairs.

A message came in from Connor. *Are you still there or have I scared you off?*

She tried to pull her thoughts into order. Dad's friend, Irene, had been kind and offered her legal services whenever Natalie was ready to take things forward. 'Adam I changed the locks but then found |out I'm not supposed to do that without telling you,' she gathered her courage, 'but I didn't appreciate coming home from holiday and finding things missing.'

'No. I'm sorry about that. It was wrong of me to go to the house while you were away.'

The house. He didn't say *home*. She felt wrong-footed. An angry, irritable Adam was someone she could deal with. She could muster her own anger and feel strong. A conciliatory Adam was a different matter.

'About the mortgage …' she said.

'Oh, don't worry I'll keep paying it for now.'

Again his tone was soothing but remote. She didn't ask how long "for now" was.

Another message on screen: *Natalie, speak to me, I'm lonely. I need you to fly over and cheer me up.*

She typed: '*Still here, just on the phone.*'

'Is there anything else I can help you with?' Adam sounded like a kindly librarian talking to a customer. What should she say? Yes, please come home and stitch my life back together? On the screen, Connor: *They're singing carols on the cathedral steps tonight; bring snow boots and warm gloves and I'll look after you.*

Natalie wanted to cry - about Adam's remoteness and Connor's silly sweet words, but she fought away the tears and sent a reply: '*I've missed the last flight.*'

'Are you typing? It sounds like you are?' Adam's strange new voice in her ear.

'I'm on my laptop.'

'Oh. Right.' Now *he* sounded wrong footed. Boring old Natalie was sitting at a computer in the evening instead of on the sofa watching his choice of TV programme.

'*If I had my own wings I'd fly there right now,*' she tapped out quickly.

'So what are you typing?'

Mind your own business. 'I'm doing a German tutorial.'

'Oh. That's weird.'

She wanted to say, weirder than you and your stupid new

voice? Instead she looked at the screen: *Or we could go to Hellbrunn, find our bench on the hill and take up where we left off…*

'I've met someone in Austria. It's only sensible to learn the language.' Now I'm telling stupid lies, she thought.

'I see.'

He sounded annoyed now and if they'd had this conversation a few weeks ago she'd have felt a surge of hope that he might be jealous; that the thought of her moving on might have panicked him into coming home. But sometime between then and now she'd come to accept her situation without even realising it.

'I really need to get back to this, Adam.' She was cutting him short when surely she should have been clinging on to this fragment of contact, but no, her voice was strong and firm.

She heard him clear his throat. 'Should I make a note of your new email address then, in case I need to …'

'No. I think it's best to say everything through our solicitors now.'

He began to speak but she held the phone out in front of her and pressed the button to end the call. She called downstairs, 'He's gone. Adam that is.'

As Ellie came back into the room she typed: '*Got to go now, a girlfriend is here and we're drinking wine.*' She added a smiley face at the end of the sentence but her own lips refused to mirror it.

Chapter Sixteen

She didn't want to think about the night Adam left but talking to him dragged the whole traumatic scene to the forefront of her mind. The larger it loomed the further sleep retreated. In the end she got up and made herself some tea, sat by the fire and let the pain engulf her.

He'd brought flowers and it was the flowers Natalie remembered long after the shock and anguish receded into numbness. Carnations, a single gaillardia and some baby's breath. He'd kissed her too, on the forehead, and said the food smelled good. As she dropped poppadoms into hot fat she told him about her day. Glenda had asked her to cover for a girl going on maternity leave. He made noncommittal noises. She heaped rice onto his plate and thought that at one time the mention of maternity would have led him to touch her arm, a gesture that would tell her he understood the subject was painful to her.

'Will it be more money?' He poured very large glasses of wine and pushed one across the table to her.

'Clare's senior to me so I guess it will. That would come in handy wouldn't it?' She took a long drink, desperate to unwind. 'Of course it won't be for a while yet. Do you think it's a good idea?'

Adam tore off a chunk of naan bread. 'If you think you can do it, go for it.'

He looked at his watch. Natalie had hoped for reassurance, encouragement.

'Is there something you want to watch on TV?'

'No. I've got to call Barry about the houses near the park. I might have sold one today.'

She never understood why estate agents needed to talk to each other quite so much, in the evenings, but Adam often rang his boss at home. He said it showed commitment. That brought her back to the matter of Clare's job.

'I might have to stay a bit later in the evenings,' she said. 'There'll be a lot more work if ...'

'Fine. Go for it. I'm sure you'll be great.'

Biting her lip Natalie couldn't think why he was so impatient. She ate in silence for a while then took a deep breath. 'We haven't planned a holiday yet, have we?'

'Work's hectic at the moment.' Adam drained his glass and refilled it.

'I mean for later in the year; August or September maybe. I could pick up some brochures or something.'

'I'd leave it a while.'

'But it wouldn't hurt to look, would it, just see what there is available?'

'Okay. Okay. Pick up some brochures.'

She thought tonight might be different; a meal at the table instead of on their knees, a nice bottle of wine. But it was turning into just any other night – Adam distant; she bewildered and unsure what to say. Years ago she'd have grabbed her coat and bag and said, 'Let's go out, have a drink, get an embarrassing tattoo,' and Adam would have laughed, threatening to divorce her if she was serious about the tattoo, and they would end up in bed, whatever tensions there'd been between them forgotten. But it wasn't like that anymore.

Adam stood up. He hadn't eaten much. Taking his mobile from his jacket pocket he made for the stairs. 'I'll just make that call.'

'Did you want me to put your dinner in the oven?'

'No, I'm not that fussed about it.'

Her own appetite waning Natalie sipped her wine and pushed a piece of chicken round her plate, forcing herself to eat it.

Above her head she could hear Adam's voice, muffled by the bedroom carpet. The call was lengthy. She finished eating, putting her knife and fork together neatly; pouring herself more wine. After fifteen minutes she heard him moving around in the bedroom. She took the plates out to the kitchen and put the kettle on for coffee.

'Adam, do you want some ice cream?'

No reply.

She went upstairs. Adam came out of the bedroom with a fistful of underwear.

'What are you doing with those?'

'I'm sorry, Natalie.' He squeezed past her and went into the spare bedroom. The holdall they used when they went to the gym lay open on the floor. He thrust the underwear into it.

'What do you mean, sorry? Sorry for what? She looked at the holdall as he walked back to the bedroom opening the wardrobe doors and lifting down the blue linen jacket she'd chosen for him last Christmas.

'What are you doing?' Acid surged into her stomach, she felt the thump of her heartbeat in her ears. 'Adam?'

The jacket was on the bed, he was tucking the sleeves in, folding the whole thing in two. Natalie grabbed at it, tugging it from his hands and threw it down.

'What, Adam? Tell me.'

'I can't stay, Natalie.' He picked up the jacket, rolling it into a ball.

Her head pounded, she reached to touch him but he turned, went back onto the landing then she heard him in the bathroom, clattering the door of the cabinet. She found her voice, and shouted, 'What's going on? What did Barry say? Are you … are you in trouble?

He came to the door, a can of deodorant in his hand; his face was white. She'd only seen it like that once, a long time ago.

'I've met someone, Natalie. I didn't want to hurt you but I can't do this anymore.'

'Can't do ... do what? …' She sank onto the bed, trembling. Her head wouldn't stay still, her feet twitched against the divan. 'Met someone?'

Adam crouched down, leaning his back against the airing cupboard door. 'I met this woman. We were selling the riverside flats, she's a surveyor. We've been … together.'

She concentrated her gaze on the legs of the dressing table. The varnish was coming off and it would all be alright in a minute because Adam would laugh and say he was joking, like she did about getting tattoos. The legs of the table blurred, merged together and she closed her eyes. She tried to sob but all the breath caught in her throat. Stumbling out of the room she sat down beside him, pulled at his hands. The deodorant rolled away, her fingers tried to grasp his but he curled his hands into fists in his lap and turned his face away.

'Adam. Adam no, no please…' She leaned towards him but he slid himself back up the door and she fell against his legs. He moved away, retrieving the can; went back to his packing, throwing things into the holdall.

In a moment he could be gone.

Natalie ran downstairs, yanked the car keys from the hook and threw them into the back of a cupboard. The debris of the meal lay on the worktop, ice cream melting in its tub, the flowers in the sink. Walking upstairs again she sat on the top step.

'Adam, tell me what's wrong. This is mad.' She tried to laugh, make it sound silly, but her voice was thick and unrecognisable. Finally he sat back down on the landing and put his head in his hands.

'You and me, we've not been right for ages. I'm bored. I want more. This is my chance.'

She processed the words; words that someone else might say,

but not Adam. Words you'd hear in a TV drama or a film.

'You said, you said you'd met …'

'Sigourney. She bought one of the flats.'

The pain took shape. It had a name. It was real. She started to sob but it turned into something like a scream. She banged her fists against the carpet. 'Please, Adam, no.'

But he was in the spare room again. She heard the zip slide shut on the holdall. He tried to get past her, pushing the bag forward but she clung to it.

'Natalie. Just leave it. I've got to get out of here.' He struggled down the stairs; still she hung on to the holdall straps, crashing against the banisters, falling in a heap at the front door.

'Where are the keys?' He barged through the house, throwing things aside, cushions, magazines. Grabbing her handbag he emptied it onto the floor scattering purse, hairbrush, tampons. 'Tell me, Natalie, or I'll call her and get her to pick me up.'

Worse than a slap.

She dragged herself up and retrieved the keys from the cupboard. Her nose was running; she searched for kitchen roll while Adam went back to the door.

'What have I done, Adam? Talk to me please.'

'I'm done talking to you, Natalie.' The door closed behind him.

In the kitchen she unwrapped the flowers, pulled open the little sachet of crystals and emptied them into a vase. The carnations sat well with the baby's breath but the gaillardia lolled from side to side, turning its head away.

Chapter Seventeen

Leo felt guilty driving the short distance to the Residenz building, but he didn't want to leave Max in the hotel. He pushed two heat pads under the dog's blanket and hoped they'd stay warm all evening.

The interior of the Residenz was ornate and lavish, but there wasn't time to admire Baroque stucco and statues, he was running late and followed a straggle of concert goers into the Kaisersaal. Most of the audience was seated and he was embarrassed as he took his place in the second row between two young women.

There was no sign of Britte.

Less than two minutes later, as Leo scanned the programme, members of the orchestra filed onto the dais.

Seeing Andreas he felt the ludicrous impulse to wave like a parent at a school play. Instead he gripped the programme and watched his son share a smile with another musician; settle into his chair and move the music stand back a little to accommodate his long legs. He watched his fingers fold around the neck of the viola; saw him tighten the bow hairs, place his chin on the rest before pulling it away and settling it more comfortably; movements that must be second nature to the boy that Leo had only known for a few months.

The tuning ended and the lights dimmed. Leo drew in a breath as Andreas' bow touched the strings and he was sure it was only his son's rich deep notes he could hear as the Mendelssohn piece began. He forgot the women either side of him, forgot about Britte, even Sofia was absent from his thoughts as he watched Andreas play. Pride welled inside him but there was an unwelcome stab of envy too. At that age he'd have loved to perform in concert. Whether or not he was good enough he would never know.

At the interval he wandered towards the bar, joined the queue and bought Alkoholfreiesbier. Standing against the wall, a distance from the crowd, he saw Britte striding towards him wearing the dress she'd worn the night before. When she smiled his stomach did a back flip. She had a large glass of white wine in one hand and an evening bag in the other.

'Wasn't it lovely? Did you see how confident he looked?' She reached up and kissed his cheek.

'It was …' The kiss flustered him. 'He looked very relaxed.'

'There's Haydn in the second part,' she said… 'Do you remember I always loved Haydn?'

Leo didn't remember but he nodded all the same and took a sip of his beer.

'I'm in a dreadful seat,' she said, 'almost in the foyer. Are there any spare places near you at the front?'

So she *had* seen him. 'I'm afraid not, I'm surrounded by his friends.'

Britte sipped her wine leaving a pink imprint of her lips on the glass. Leo tried not to stare at it. 'I suppose Andreas will be busy after the performance?'

'Yes, they usually go for a meal together.'

'Do you want to … I mean we could … have supper.'

She looked surprised but her smile told him she was pleased he'd asked. 'That would be nice.'

They finished their drinks in awkwardness and little bursts of small talk. It was a relief for Leo when the bell rang.

At the end of the concert Andreas met them in the foyer, hugged his mother and shook Leo's hand. 'We're heading off to eat.' He looked apologetic. 'But I'll see you before you leave in the morning?'

Leo began to wish he'd booked another night, but snow was

forecast and he'd a long way to travel.

Britte sat in the car while he walked Max by the stripped out flower beds. When he returned he passed her one of the heated pads which she wrapped her hands around. She wore no gloves and her nails were painted red. For a horrible moment they made him think of Julia Weber.

They found a restaurant just off the main square where they could park outside. Max gave a whine of discontent as he settled back down on his bed. Britte ordered white wine and Leo risked a beer. He wasn't hungry but he ordered plaice with fried bacon and Britte said she'd have the same but without the bacon. She had almost finished her wine when the food arrived.

'I'll have another,' she told the waiter, 'just a small one this time.' She looked into Leo's eyes. 'You'll have heard I'm getting divorced?'

Leo noticed that she was pronouncing her words carefully. 'Yes. I'm so sorry. It must be very difficult for both of you.'

'Not difficult for him. He has a … replacement.'

'Oh.' He cut into a potato, finding he was hungry after all.

Britte scraped sauce away from her fish, her red nails splayed along the handle of her knife.

Leo felt unease creep over him. Last night he'd found her attractive, beguiling. He'd decided early in the day that he would ask her out for supper but without any clear idea of how the evening might end. He'd taken so long getting ready, changing shirts, forgetting deodorant and having to undress again to apply it. It was like preparing for a date although once the concert began all his attention had been on Andreas. What on earth was he doing here with Britte? Already he found himself stealing a glance at his watch. Suddenly an old memory rose to the surface. 'Do you still play?' he asked. She'd been a flautist and yes, she did love Haydn. He remembered a summer morning at music camp, hearing her play the tripping melody of a flute trio. She wore shorts and her hair reached to her waist.

She looked incredulous and took a long sip of wine. 'Of course not, why ever would I still do that?'

Unable to think of a reply Leo stared at his plate.

'Andreas put paid to my music career. Babies and orchestras don't mix, you know.'

Leo felt guilty by association. 'Would you not think of taking it up again?'

'Who would want a forty year-old flautist?' Her lovely lips curled into a sneer. Before he could reply she leaned across the table and lowered her voice.

'She's much younger than him; some kind of therapist. Oils or herbs or something. God knows how they met.'

'Oh. I …'

'Must have been going on for ages.' She drained her glass. 'I just didn't see the signs.'

'Does he still … see Andreas?'

'I bet you were never unfaithful were you, Leo?' This time she didn't lower her voice. A woman at the next table gave him a sideways glance.

'Britte, we should talk about something else. Tell me where the orchestra is playing next and …'

He was horrified to see tears roll down her cheeks. Her face grew red. Nothing of the lovely woman from the previous evening remained; even so Leo felt sorry for her.

'Britte …'

'Oh don't look at me. Don't say anything.' She dabbed at her eyes with a tissue then got up and headed for the toilets. Most of her food was uneaten.

Returning she was more composed and said no more about her divorce. When Leo turned the conversation to Andreas' career she was enthusiastic. 'They're hoping to perform abroad next year. That will be so exciting for him.'

He drove her to her hotel. Max, loose on the back seat, leaned over and licked the side of Britte's face. She recoiled, wiped her cheek, pushed him away.

'Do you want to come in?' she asked.

'No. I'm sorry.' He chose not to make excuses.

She turned to him; put her hand on his arm. 'Please, Leo.'

Another memory came. He felt his throat tighten and he stared ahead, avoiding her eye. *Please, Britte. Please. Let my papa kiss him goodbye.* He remembered the sneer that time too; three year old Andreas crying in her arms. The last time Leo's father had seen his grandchild.

'Goodnight, Britte.' He leaned across her to open the door and caught the stale alcohol smell of her breath. She got out, left the door open and walked up the steps into the hotel.

Leo drove to the end of the street and stopped, took out his phone and texted an apology to Andreas, mentioned the snow. He found his sister's number and began another text: *If the offer of Heiligenacht is still open …*

At the hotel he threw clothes into his case and was grateful he'd paid his bill in advance. He left twenty Euros for water and biscuits from the minibar.

In the car he set his satnav for Vienna. Max stretched and sighed on the seat beside him. The snow was falling heavier now and Leo needed to be on his way. He needed normality. He needed his family.

Chapter Eighteen

Joe arrived first. He came to Natalie's door laden with foil covered trays of Bratwurst.

'Thought we'd come and see if you needed a hand,' he said. 'Ellie's just getting her stuff out of the boot. I'm not kidding, she's bringing so much beer and wine you might need to apply for a drinks licence.' He placed the sausages on the worktop. 'And, she's a little worse for wear. It was her office party today too, so I'm not sure whether she'll be a help or hindrance, bless her heart.'

Natalie felt a surge of excitement; tonight the house would be full of people and not one of them acquainted with Adam. This was *her* territory now. She'd made an effort to make the house look festive. She and Toby had chosen a small tree which he helped her decorate. He drew pictures of Dr Who, a dragon and his remote controlled car. Then he cut out the shapes, plastered glue round the edges and sprinkled them with glitter. Dr Who looked so good she put him on top of the tree instead of a fairy.

'We're supposed to be talking German all evening,' Ellie said walking into the kitchen, bottles clanking. Do you think that means now or when everyone gets here?'

'Definitely when they get here,' Joe said. 'I don't know how to say, 'shove that lot in the fridge' even though the German names are stuck on everything.'

'Still emailing the lovely Connor?' Ellie whispered.

'Not heard from him today.' She'd checked her emails a dozen times.

'Maybe he'll fly over and surprise you.'

Natalie took a swig of wine and felt herself blush. 'Don't be silly. He's probably going home for Christmas.' But just for a second she imagined herself greeting him at the door and then when the bell *did* ring she jumped, almost spilling her drink.

'So nice of you to let us hold the party here, Natalie.' It was the married couple Sandra and Graham who had brought sauerkraut, noodles and a huge bowl of potato salad. Then Gabi arrived with a beef dish with dumplings. Pity Grandma's not here, Natalie thought.

It was strange having them all in her living room and at first conversation was a little stilted. But then Ellie spotted Dr Who on the Christmas tree and began a loud rendition of the theme tune, 'Da da da dum da da da dum …' and a few joined in to humour her. Soon they all had a drink and were exchanging cards and reading out their greetings. Joe had brought a CD of German carols and Natalie found a lump in her throat as Gabi sang along.

The table filled up with food and bottles of wine. Natalie piled plates and cutlery at one end. It was lovely seeing them all tuck in. She remembered another time when she'd brought out all her best tableware, a time so sad she pushed the thought away.

'What's that gorgeous smell?' Ellie sniffed the air as she picked up a pile of serviettes from the kitchen worktop.

'It's Kaiserschmarrn,' Natalie said, peeping into the oven where the Austrian dessert was keeping warm. 'I found it on the Internet. It's caramel pancakes all chopped up with cinnamon and icing sugar. Schmarrn means "mish-mash" which is just as well. She stopped Ellie pushing a finger into the hot plum sauce she'd made to go with it.

Nipping up to the bathroom she couldn't resist ducking into the spare room to check her emails. She smiled as she saw Connor's name in her inbox and her heart did a bit of a flip.

'Hey, Miss Adorable. Are you up for some instant messages tonight?

His email had come in half an hour ago but she sent a quick

note back.

'Sorry, German class here for a party. Maybe later?'

'Sure. I'll be waiting. Till then I'll be thinking about that hill at Hellbrunn.'

She remembered those lingering kisses and typed quickly. 'I'll think about that night too. Speak later xx.' Her heart flipped a little more as she went downstairs.

Gabi had brought a quiz for them to play and encouraged them to answer in German. Everyone laughed when Sandra spoke pidgin German in one of her responses.

'Did Gabi ask how many countries border Germany?' Ellie's stage whisper made everyone laugh.

'I think so,' Joe hissed back.

They began counting them on their fingers. Natalie thought it was a good moment to serve the dessert. In the kitchen she smiled as she listened to them debating.

'Oh I'd forgotten Luxembourg.' She heard Ellie say and then repeat it in German when Gabi insisted.

'And you forgot the Czech Republic,' Joe said.

Natalie didn't hear his next comment but there was a roar of laughter and somewhere, amid the hilarity, was the sound of the doorbell.

'I'll get it,' Joe called.

'Probably carol shingers,' Ellie said. 'Don't forget to greet them *auf Deutsch.*'

Natalie spooned plum sauce into bowls and piled the chopped pancake over the top. She was just wiping her hands on a tea towel when Joe pushed open the kitchen door. 'Natalie there's someone asking for you. I …'

His puzzled expression made Natalie drop the tea towel. Could Ellie be right? She hurried to see.

Adam was at the front door.

Her head jerked back in amazement. Thoughts of Connor

slid from her mind as she saw he was holding a Christmas card and a bottle of wine. He gave her a shy smile.

'Adam … I have friends here. We … we're in the middle of our party.'

'Well, I want to talk to you, Natalie. It's important.'

Her voice felt wobbly but she took a deep breath, 'Could you come back later?'

'I'd rather talk now.'

He followed her into the kitchen. Joe picked up two dessert dishes. 'Let me start taking these through.'

Adam stared at the paper German flag that Toby had coloured in. It had come away from its sticky tape and was hanging by one corner. Natalie heard Gabi begin asking questions again. 'On which river does Hamburg …'

Picking up the tea towel and winding it round her fingers Natalie looked again at the card in Adam's hand. 'Is that for me?'

He put the card and wine down on the worktop. 'Can we talk upstairs?'

Heart drumming now, she put down the tea towel and clattered the remaining dessert dishes onto a tray. 'Give me a minute.'

In the living room Ellie threw her a worried glance. 'Is everything alright?'

'I hope so. I'll just be a while; can you all help yourselves to dessert and more drinks?'

Adam followed her upstairs. She walked into the spare bedroom trying not to think of the last time she'd seen him there, throwing clothes into a holdall.

Sitting down at the desk she closed her laptop.

'I like your hair longer,' he said. 'Really suits you.' Then he frowned at the Post-it note bunting of German names. 'You're still doing that course then?'

'I am.'

He raised his eyebrows and smiled again but it was a tight smile this time with no warmth in it. His hair was slightly different too, brushed forward and held with wax or mousse.

'Is that your dad's old car on the drive?'

'Why are you here, Adam?'

'You said, that time on the phone, that you'd met someone in Austria is that still …?'

She glanced at the laptop. 'Why are you asking?'

'I just wondered if you were thinking of going out there … what with you learning the language and everything.'

'Well …' She clasped her hands together to stop them from shaking. 'I'm not sure yet, but …'

Adam peeled a Post-it off a cupboard, looked at it then smoothed it back on.

'We need to talk about the house.'

Her tiny flame of hope began to gutter. 'What about it?'

'I'd like to think about putting it on the market.'

'Oh.' Her face grew hot. '*You'd* like to think about it?'

'Not without discussing it with you, obviously.'

'Why now?'

'Well. I can't see any point in waiting much longer.'

'What if I don't want to move?'

'If you were going abroad ...' He sat down on the spare bed. She'd seen the impatient set of his shoulders a million times.

She faltered. 'What if … my plans don't work out? I'll have nowhere to live.'

'You could buy me out. Your dad would lend you the money.'

Now there was no concealing her shaking hands. He had the good grace to look away.

'Adam, please … please don't do this. Not yet. I'll … I'll take over paying the mortgage.'

'It's not the mortgage that's the problem.' He stood up, walked to the window and looked out into the darkness. 'You've never liked this house. I thought you'd be glad to see the back of it.'

'But it's … it's all I've got left. All there is of …' She couldn't end the sentence. Tears slid down her face. 'I don't understand. You have her apartment.'

He continued to stare out of the window. She felt in the desk drawer for tissues, trying to gather her wits. 'I'll need to talk to my solicitor. I'm not saying anything about it till then.'

'I want to sell, Natalie. I'm entitled to the money.'

'And what am I entitled to, Adam? Not a husband or a family, that's for sure. And no proper explanation for why you just went that night.'

'Don't start this again.' He pushed his hands into his pockets.

'Why shouldn't I?' She stood at the door, barring his way. 'Why shouldn't I ask why you upped and left me in the middle of dinner?'

'Don't make me say this.'

'Just tell me, Adam. It can't be worse than not knowing?'

He spread his arms wide. He was angry now. 'You wonder why I went. Okay. Look at yourself. Sitting here with ridiculous bits of paper stuck to furniture; a bunch of losers and misfits for friends. Everything about you is … boring.'

Had he struck her in the chest? It felt like he had. She slumped against the door, her breath coming in short bursts. 'You don't … don't mean that, Adam. Why would you say …?'

'I never meant to come and upset you, Natalie. I thought we'd be able to talk by now, but if you want to do it through solicitors, that's fine.'

'You're not taking my home from me.' She put her face in her hands.'

'I've got to. I want the money.' He pushed past her and opened the door. His familiar scent agonisingly close. 'We need a bigger place.'

'Adam …' She reached out a hand towards his chest but it froze on the way.

'Sigourney's pregnant,' he said.

Her tears dried as shock engulfed her. The front door slammed. On trembling legs she went downstairs to where an awkward silence gripped the room. Gabi broke it, valiantly trying to get the quiz back on course.

'We'll have to be going, actually,' Sandra said. 'We've an early start in the morning.'

One or two others nodded and hauled themselves off the sofa. Natalie was holding onto the banister. Ellie went into the kitchen returning with a large measure of Schnapps which Natalie drank, the glass clattering against her teeth. Joe carried plates and glasses out to the kitchen, helping the others find the dishes they'd brought their food in.

At the front door they were solicitous, touching her arm as they stepped out into the frosty night, wishing her a nice Christmas. Somehow she found her voice to return their greetings.

'I'm sorry I've got to dash too.' Ellie gave Natalie a hug. 'I'm leaving for the airport at five.'

'I'll just walk her round the corner, Joe said. 'Make sure she doesn't fall over.'

The cold air made Natalie's head swim.

In the kitchen Adam's card and wine were still on the worktop. She pushed the bottle to the back and propped the card up in front of it.

By the time Joe returned she had stacked the pots in the dishwasher. Everything else could wait till morning.

'I'll help you clear up,' he said but Natalie shook her head.

'Joe, I really want to be on my own. I'm ever so grateful but …'

He didn't look convinced but took his jacket from the hook in the hall and stood at the kitchen door. 'Ring me, Natalie, if you need anything. Drink lots of water. It'll help.'

She promised she would.

When he'd gone her dizziness advance to nausea. She clamped a hand over her mouth and ran upstairs to the bathroom.

For ten minutes she retched into the toilet, wishing she could purge herself of Adam's words. A line had been crossed now and she had to live with it. When the vomiting subsided she washed her face, went downstairs and opened a bottle of mineral water.

Sitting on the sofa she saw a page of the quiz that Gabi had left behind. What the hell am I doing learning German, she thought, and flirting with Connor? I've been kidding myself. I'm not making a new life I'm drifting. She tried to think about Salzburg, the hotel, but even the man from the Mozarteum seemed like a character in a dream, the details blurred.

Before heading to bed she picked up Adam's card from the worktop and once she was settled in bed she slowly peeled open the envelope. It was a corporate card, the kind his firm sent to clients, a snow scene of a village and a frozen duck pond. Inside he'd written, *To Natalie and all the family, with best wishes from Adam and Sigourney.* There was a kiss beneath each of their names. For several minutes she stared in disbelief at his handwriting, the familiar biro lines, the point of the capital A and the rolling letter m. She had scores of cards bearing these pen strokes. Quietly she slipped out of bed, opened the wardrobe door, felt behind her shoes and lifted a box lid. She slipped the Christmas card in with the others. Then she lay back down, staring at nothing, not allowing her eyes to close in case she saw his angry face.

Chapter Nineteen

Christmas passed in an anxious blur. Toby, feverish with Tonsillitis, spent the festivities ensconced in his quilt on the sofa, alternately watching a cartoon channel and nodding off to sleep. His barely touched presents lay on the carpet close by.

Natalie had packed a bag and moved in with her parents over the holiday. She didn't take her laptop. After the night of Adam's visit she hadn't emailed Connor so often. There seemed little point in flirting with someone she'd never meet again? She didn't tell her parents about Sigourney's pregnancy, nor did she tell them she had an interview at the Bowling Road practice in case she blew it and didn't get the job.

The second week of January brought a heavy snowfall and although a thaw was beginning she chickened out of using the car for work. It was the day before her interview and she stood at the bus stop, hands crammed into her pockets for warmth, her shoulders hunched and aching.

Peering into the traffic to see if the bus was coming she saw her dad's car approaching. She waved and for a moment it was as though he hadn't seen her but then he pulled up and lowered the passenger window.

'Hop in, Lovie, I'll drive you home.'

She'd barely got in before he pulled away. 'Blimey, Dad are you being chased? Let me get my seatbelt on.'

She noticed an appointment card sitting in the drinks holder between the seats and picked it up. She was going to ask if it was for Toby then she saw her dad's name on it.'

'You off to the docs, Dad? Is something wrong?'

He grabbed for the card and stuffed it into his jacket pocket. 'No. Everything's fine. Let's just get you home out of this weather.'

'What's the appointment card?'

He stared ahead, turning onto her estate, manoeuvring over the piles of slush that had frozen. When he pulled up outside her house he leaned over to kiss her cheek. 'Shall we see you at the weekend?'

'Never mind the weekend, Dad. That card was for the hospital. What's the matter?'

'Nothing at all.' He glanced at his watch and drew in a deep breath. 'Look, Natalie, don't say anything to your mum but I've decided to see someone. It's a private appointment, that's why it's so late. I'll have to go.'

'See someone about what? Are you poorly?' A cold sensation washed over Natalie. Her dad was the strongest person she knew.

'No. I'm not ill. You know I told you I was … well, bored and a bit down about leaving the job? I'm hoping this chap can suggest something. Some happy pills maybe.' He winked and squeezed her hand. 'Anyway, if I don't go now I'll be late.'

She gave him an awkward hug and got out of the car.

Watching his car lights disappear along her road Natalie felt her stomach screwing into knots. Her dad wasn't the type to get depressed. She was sure he was holding something back, and how might this affect Toby?

As she slid the key into the door the phone was ringing. She dived to answer it. Glenda's voice was almost unrecognisable, breathless and pitched high with anxiety.

'Can you come round? Please, Natalie. I've lost Mr Woo.'

She rushed upstairs, pulled on thick socks and walking boots and was back out at the bus stop within ten minutes. The journey took an age. Freezing fog settled in and the traffic slowed to a crawl. Brake lights of the cars in front pierced the gloom and Natalie fretted to think of the little cat outside in all kinds of danger.

Glenda's front door was open and she stood on the drive tapping a saucer with a spoon. She was wearing Uggs and a fleece hat but no jacket. She looked enormously relieved to see Natalie.

'He got out of the house, I don't know how but I've searched everywhere.

Glenda's nose was bright red from crying and the biting cold. 'How will we ever find him in this?'

The fog had deadened the traffic noise giving the road an eerie atmosphere.

Tears rolled down Glenda's cheeks but she went on tapping the saucer. 'I've been knocking on doors to see if anyone's seen him but lots of people aren't home yet.'

'And you've searched the house?'

'For pity's sake, of course I have. Oh, I'm sorry, Natalie. I'm just so stressed.'

The saucer tapping reached a deafening crescendo.

'Glenda, come inside and we'll think what to do. You can leave the door open.'

On the worktop in the kitchen a single Christmas card remained, the message visible, *To Darling Little Woo, from Mummy.*

'When did you last see him?'

'I came home at four. He was asleep on his cushion in the sitting room. I fed him and we had a bit of a cuddle then he was playing in the kitchen. I changed the beds and took the linen down to the utility room.' Fresh tears started. 'I've even looked in the washing machine and the drier.'

'So did you go outside and leave the door open?'

'I never do. I'm fanatical about it.'

Natalie could believe that.

Glenda's brow furrowed. 'Someone came asking after a neighbour up the road, but I'm sure Woo wasn't anywhere near the door. The trouble is he's so quick. He might have slipped out, but surely I'd have seen him.'

'Were there any little tracks in the snow?'

'No, not at the front nor in the back garden.'

'Surely that's a good sign then?' Natalie felt hope rising. 'Might he have gone under the shed?'

They took a torch into the back garden. Natalie saw a half constructed wooden cat chalet in one corner. While Glenda got down on her knees to shine a beam under the shed Natalie began to call, 'Mr Woo-oo' and was ashamed to feel somewhat foolish.

Back in the house she checked rooms and cupboards, all the while calling his name. In the corner of the kitchen sat a ping-pong ball and a bit of blue wool he'd been shredding. Natalie longed to see his little flat face appear round the door or from under a sofa.

There was a shepherd's pie cooling on the worktop. Her stomach rumbled.

While Glenda continued calling and tapping Natalie made slow progress up the road asking neighbours if they'd seen him. People were kind but in a hurry to close their front doors against the bitter cold. Several invited her to go and look in their back gardens. Shining her torch around snow covered lawns she saw no tiny footprints.

At ten o'clock Glenda offered to drive her home.

'No. I'll stay with you and keep looking.' She was pushing away thoughts of him coming to grief on the main road or getting shut in someone's garage. How long could he survive in freezing temperatures?

'But you need to be fresh tomorrow for your interview.'

'Forget that now. My interview's at three o'clock anyway. I could take the morning off and sleep late.'

'Well at least go and have some of that shepherd's pie. You can heat it back up in the microwave.'

While Natalie tried to eat she could hear Glenda, sitting in the doorway alternately calling the cat's name and tapping the saucer. The pie was delicious but she only managed a few mouthfuls before putting her coat back on and taking another walk up and down the street. Once or twice she thought she heard a cat's cry but it might have been a baby somewhere behind closed curtains, snug and safe. She thought obliquely of Toby when he was tiny, whimpering in her arms while her mother sought an hour's precious sleep. For the first time she wondered if she'd neglected Adam when Toby was born. Maybe she'd channelled too much of her love into her little brother. It was all irrelevant now.

By midnight both she and Glenda were stiff with cold. She fielded Glenda's offers to call a taxi and said she'd stay to keep her company.

'I can't go to bed. I'd never sleep and I'd be shooting down here every time I heard a sound,' Glenda said. She had brought her quilt downstairs and wrapped herself in it. The calling was almost a whisper now and she'd abandoned the spoon and saucer. She insisted Natalie have a bath and get into the spare bed.

In a borrowed tee-shirt she took her phone from her bag and put it on the bedside table. There was a voicemail from her mother. *Wondered if you could give Toby a lift to school tomorrow. I've got an early meeting and your dad's got a dental appointment. I don't want him to miss it because …*' the message rambled on. She sent a quick text and lay back on the sweet-smelling pillow. Toby, she thought, was the one true spark of joy in her life.

Tossing from side to side in the unfamiliar bed Natalie prayed the little cat would come home. If he didn't how on earth would Glenda get over it?

She drifted in and out of a dream. Toby was in her spare room playing with a kitten. She could almost hear its little cry. As she rolled over and pressed her face into the pillow she heard it again. Coming fully awake she turned on the lamp and listened. There it was, a muffled cry. When she sat up she couldn't hear it. She lay back down and heard it again accompanied by a scratching sound. Leaping out of bed she flung open the wardrobe but there was nothing but neatly ironed clothes and shoe boxes. She turned back to the bed. It was a divan with sliding doors for storage.

She edged one door open and Mr Woo tumbled out, blinking.

Bursting into tears she gathered him up and went out onto the landing. Her friend was sitting on the doorstep, her head resting on her knees.

'Glenda, he's here.'

Leaping up she tossed the quilt aside and scrambled upstairs, grabbing the little cat, holding him to her face and sobbing.

Natalie made coffee while Mr Woo raked his litter tray. Seconds later he was eating fish and rice and purring like an engine. Glenda poured large measures of brandy into their mugs. Mortified she explained how she kept her spare linen in the divan. 'He must have crept in while I was sorting out clean sheets, and gone to sleep. I feel so awful, him being shut in all those hours and you up all night when you've a big day ahead.'

Natalie waived away her apologies. 'I'm just glad we found him.'

Once Glenda had checked that every door and window was secure they went back upstairs. 'I'll drive you home first thing,' Glenda said, 'and I'll never forget this, Natalie. You've really been here for me. I don't know how I'd have coped …'

'Don't worry. You were really kind to me last year, remember?'

'Take the whole day off tomorrow. I'll square it with the vets. Oh. I completely forgot to tell you in all the panic. Clare had her baby this morning; a little girl. Both fine, apparently. Her husband rang work just before I left.'

Natalie mustered a smile. 'How lovely for her.' A dull pain nudged her heart.

Glenda shrugged. 'OK if you like that sort of thing. I was going to say cats are a lot less trouble, but after today I'm not so sure.' She glanced down at Mr Woo who sat on the landing, washing his face with an oversized paw.

Sinking back down onto Glenda's spare bed Natalie fell asleep without turning off the lamp.

Chapter Twenty

The snow continued to thaw during the night. Back at home the next morning Natalie, eyes gritty from tiredness, squinted against the low sun.

She had a quick shower, pulled her hair into a clip at the nape of her neck; dragged on jeans and a jumper then put two slices of bread into the toaster. On the table her German books were spread out reminding her she hadn't done her homework. For the first time since she'd signed up for the class she thought she might give tonight a miss. She needed more sleep but, until the interview was over, there'd be no chance of that.

Snow slid in large melting chunks from her car but it started first time when she turned over the engine. Despite the thaw she drove slowly along her road, the wheels sliding on piles of slush.

Already at the door, Toby was grumpy. Her mother rolled her eyes and headed for her own car.

'There's two school trips in a few weeks,' Toby said. 'One to the zoo and one to a steam train but Mum says I can only go on one of them.'

He threw himself into his booster seat and gave a dramatic sigh as she secured him in.

'That seems fair to me, Tobes. You'll have a nice time whichever one you go on. Have you chosen yet?'

'No.'

They pulled away and drove out of the estate. In the rear view mirror she could see his little face set in a frown.

'You know, Toby you're a lucky boy. You have lots of nice things and you get to go to Italy a lot. I bet none of your friends have so many holidays.'

'In Italy they have hungry dogs and nobody looks after them

and Mum says we can't bring one home.'

'How's Markus? Have you said hello to him in German yet?'

'*He's* going on both trips.' Toby kicked the back of the passenger seat.

'Don't kick the seat, Toby. There's no need for that.'

The traffic was heavy and she turned down a side street to take a short cut. Emerging onto another road she saw traffic calming bollards and humps. There was a building site on the right and a string of parked vans and trucks. Toby began chanting a list of his friends who might be going on both school trips. Natalie's back was tense as oncoming vehicles swerved into her path as they avoided the parked vans. Toby gasped.

'There's Uncle Adam.'

She glanced to the side. He was on the pavement by the building site, his arm around the tall, willowy woman beside him. Even in a hard hat she looked good.

'Stop! I want to talk to Uncle Adam.'

'We're not stopping.'

'Yes.' Toby yelled and kicked the seat. 'I want to.'

Natalie glanced in the mirror, saw his tears; looked back at the road but too late. She ploughed into a bollard, jolted forward and felt the full smack of the airbag.

Toby was screaming. The bag deflated. There were people at the car. Natalie released the central locking and the rear door flew open. Adam leaned in to Toby who continued to yell. A man in a checked shirt opened the driver's door. 'Are you alright, Love?'

'My brother?' Natalie turned. Toby was out of the car, Adam stooping, holding him close but he wouldn't stop shrieking. The builder helped her out. She drew in long breaths. Her legs were wobbly. She reached out for Toby but Adam turned away and she looked into the face of Sigourney, tanned skin, expert make up. She'd discarded the hard hat.

The man still held Natalie's arm. 'He's fine, look. Don't worry.'

Then the unthinkable happened. Sigourney bent to fold Toby into her arms, crooning, stroking his hair.

Adam turned to Natalie. 'What the fuck were you doing?'

'Steady on, Lad.' The builder put a thickly muscled arm between her and Adam.

She couldn't speak. She stared past him at Toby, clinging to Sigourney's neck.

'We'll take him to A & E, get him checked over. He's my nephew,' Adam said when it looked as though the builder might object.

'You need his seat out of the back,' Natalie said.

Nobody spoke on the short journey to the hospital. Natalie stared at the back of Sigourney's sleek head. Behind Adam Toby, swollen eyed and whimpering, refused to hold her hand. At the hospital she let Adam do the talking while she stood outside and phoned her dad.

Adam and Sigourney stayed until he arrived, one side of his mouth numb from the dentist. Her mother, frantic and gibbering appeared a few minutes later. In a cubicle, as they waited for a paediatrician, her mother hissed at Natalie, 'How did it happen? Adam said no other car was involved.'

'I didn't see it. I …

'And what the Hell were those two doing there anyway?'

'I don't know. They were on the pavement.' Natalie's head ached. The doctor had said she was fine but she longed to lie down and sleep.

'Was that it? You were busy looking at them and not where you were going?'

'Christine, give her a break.' Her dad's voice muffled from the dental anaesthetic. 'She's had a shock too. And let's try and keep calm for him.' He stroked Toby's head. 'Natalie, let me call you a taxi. You don't need to wait.'

'No. I'll stay till the doctor's seen him.'

'I think you should go now,' her mother's voice rose. 'As if we haven't enough to worry about at the moment.' She started crying which set Toby off again.

'What … what do you mean?'

'Maybe you'd better get off, Lovie,' Dad said. 'I'll drop by when I've looked at the car.

'Oh God, I'd forgotten about it. What shall I do?

'Don't fret. I'll sort it.'

She kissed Toby's cheek, whispering how brave he was, holding her tears until she was in the taxi and on her way home.

She ran a bath and sank into it. Her head still ached and her chin was tender where the airbag had struck. The scene played itself over and over in her head and she couldn't stop shaking. What if it had been worse and she'd lost Toby? In the bedroom she lay down, the phone clutched in her hand.

Dozing and half dreaming, she saw Sigourney, concerned but aloof. Adam smug and taking charge.

At last her dad rang. 'Toby's fine. He can go back to school tomorrow, much to his disgust.' She could hear the smile in his voice. Now it was tears of relief that she wiped away.

'I've had the car towed to the garage, Lovie. You need a new wheel and quite a bit of bodywork done. The bollard's fine, by the way.'

'So I'm not in trouble with the police?'

'No. I'd come round but your mother's gone out to buy Calpol. Are you alright, Natalie? I know those airbags pack a punch.'

'My face is a bit sore but otherwise I'm fine. Thanks for everything and I'm so sorry.'

'Pay no attention to what your mum said. She was shocked that's all.'

But it wasn't over. A few minutes after she put the phone down Natalie heard the doorbell. Her mother began talking as she walked into the house.

'I don't want you taking him anywhere, ever again. You can't even be trusted to get him to school.' She threw her bag down on the sofa. 'I blame your dad for letting you use that bloody car. He has angina you know. He doesn't need this.'

'What? He has … is it serious?' So that's what the appointment was about.

'He's alright as long as he's careful.'

'Mum. I'm sorry about …'

'You're sorry? When are you going to get a grip?' She paced the room. 'What's happened to you? You never go out except to exercise or do those stupid German lessons. Who in their right mind has these things all over the house?' She pulled a post-it from the top of the TV and screwed it up. 'You've even got your grandmother speaking German, as if she isn't confused enough.' She drew a breath. 'I know you've had bad times but so have lots of people. I was much younger than you when I was widowed. You were three years old. I didn't hide away. I had to bloody get on with life and that's what you should do, not hark after the past.'

Avoiding her mother's angry stare Natalie's eyes fixed on the smart skirt and jacket she'd put out to wear at the interview. She'd completely forgotten about it. It was half past one, she could still make it.

'Life's passing you by but you just sit here night after night hoping he'll come home. Well after today I'd say it's pretty obvious that's not going to happen, wouldn't you? And if I'm honest I'm beginning to understand why …' She turned away.

'What, Mum? You're beginning to understand why he left?' Natalie's headache left her. The pain, the hurt, the anguish over losing Adam went too, leaving behind white hot anger.

A sensation of weightlessness coursed through her, her fingers curled into her palms and her sore chin jutted forward.

'You're right, Mum. Life's passing me by.' She set her lips into a bitter smile, 'but I've got an interview this afternoon for a promotion.'

'Oh. Well, you never told …'

'And with a bit of luck the extra money will help me buy a one bedroomed flat.'

'Why would you want a one …?'

'Because Adam wants me out of here.' She threw her arms wide. 'He told me just before Christmas. Wasn't that nice of him?' She snatched her mother's bag from the sofa and thrust it at her.

'He wants you out?'

Natalie walked to the front door and opened it. 'Yes, so that he and his girlfriend can buy a bigger place.' She gestured for her mother to leave. 'I need to get ready.'

Her mother stepped outside. 'Natalie, I'm sorry I …'

'And there's one more piece of good news, Mum. Sigourney's having Adam's baby.' She slammed the door closed.

Running upstairs to the bathroom she felt a bizarre elation. She ran cold water into the basin and bathed her hot face. Her mother was ringing the doorbell and knocking; then the letter box opened. 'Please let me back in.'

Natalie went to the bedroom and opened the window. 'My interview is at three o'clock. Can you leave me alone?' Once she heard the car start she dialled her parent's number and asked her dad if she could speak to Toby.

'I've got to go to school tomorrow, Nat. It's not fair because I've been in an accident. You should get a whole week off for that.'

'You should, Tobes and I'm so sorry about hitting the bollard. Are you feeling alright?'

'No, because the snow's all melting now.'

She pictured his frowning face and bit her lip. 'You know, Sweetheart, this might be a good time to ask Dad if you can go on both those school trips.'

He blew her some noisy kisses down the phone and hung up.

After a few more phone calls she hung up the skirt and jacket in the wardrobe. She put on her boots, still damp from the night before, her warmest coat and gloves and went out for a walk.

The sun was creeping low as she did circuits of the park. Schoolchildren were walking home, scooping up snow and hurling it at each other. Sitting down on a bench she took out her mobile and rang work.

'Glenda's not here.' The practice secretary sounded annoyed. 'She left at lunchtime. Are you ill or something, Natalie?'

'Not really, no. Is Glenda at home, do you know?'

'No idea. Nobody tells me anything.'

Glenda didn't answer the door. Natalie walked down the side of the house to see if she was in the garden. There was no sign of her. Through the kitchen window she could see Mr Woo on the tiles, attacking something. Putting her face to the glass she could see it was a whole cooked fish. He must have stolen it. Back at the front door she rang the bell again.

Still no answer.

An uneasy feeling crept over her. She looked through the front window. A lamp was on and items strewn on the floor, clothes and shoes. Feeling panicky now she lifted the letterbox and peered in. Glenda's briefcase lay on its side in the hall. Natalie put her mouth to the letterbox. 'Glenda. Are you there? Is everything okay?'

The sound of movement came from above. Standing back she looked up at the bedroom window but the blinds were closed. Seconds later the door opened. Glenda, bare-legged and wearing a short dressing gown, pulled her inside. Her hair was sticking up and she looked feverish.

'Natalie. How did you get on?' She glanced up the stairs.

'I'd love a chat if it's not a bad time. Were you in the bath?'

'Err no'

Further noise from the bedroom made it clear she wasn't alone.

'Oh God; I'm sorry Glenda. I'll go.'

'No stay a second. I must …'

A man's head appeared over the banister. He had dark, wavy hair and a friendly grin. 'Hello,' he said.

Natalie returned his greeting. Glenda moved into the kitchen, gesturing for her to follow. Mr Woo was well advanced into the fish now.

'He wants to come back, Natalie. He rang out of the blue this morning and begged me to see him.'

'This is Martin? Your husband?'

'Yes.' She looked as though she might jump up and down with excitement. 'He said he never stopped loving me and wants us to give it another go. Natalie I can't tell you how happy I am.' She began to cry but was still smiling.

'Oh, I'm so sorry I disturbed you,' Natalie whispered.

'Look. I want to hear all about the interview. Can I ring you later?'

'No. Just enjoy yourself.' She nodded towards the stairs. 'We'll talk tomorrow.'

'But I feel awful. You've come all this way.'

'Don't be silly. I'm so pleased for you. I'll see you soon.'

Checking her phone she saw messages from both her parents. She turned it off and thrust it into her pocket. At home the light was flashing on the answering machine too but she went upstairs to her laptop. There was one email from Ellie asking if she'd done her homework. She sent a quick message back.

Nothing from Connor.

In the bedroom she pulled clothes from the wardrobe and threw them onto the bed, selecting jeans, jumpers and leggings. She pushed as much as she could into her small suitcase then packed her camera, a photo of Toby, her notebook, and a German grammar book into her rucksack. The laptop fitted nicely into a compartment in the back; the power supply and leads she shoved in with her clothes.

From a box in the wardrobe she withdrew a large, brown envelope and laid it on her pillow. Also in the box were her wedding photos and pictures from holidays over the years. Her favourite photo of Adam, taken before they were married, was at the bottom. For months she hadn't been able to look at it but he stared out at her now, his hair spiky; his face thinner, that secret smile. She put it back into the box, pulled off her wedding ring and dropped that in too. After dragging a stool from the spare bedroom she climbed up and opened the loft hatch. She lifted the box through the opening and pushed it as far as she could into the darkness.

From the bathroom cabinet she retrieved her contraceptive pills and slid them into her handbag. She'd had no reason to take them for months; even before Adam left their lovemaking had become less and less frequent. But the pills were comforting somehow; they kept her in the realm of the childless. It was easier that way.

Last of all she picked up the large brown envelope from her pillow. She took it downstairs and put it on the dining table. In the kitchen she poured herself a measure of brandy left over from the German party. Sitting at the table she let the drink swirl around in her glass for a few minutes before taking a sip. The phone rang and she waited till the answering machine took the call before she opened the envelope.

A sheet of paper slid out, settling in front of her. She placed her lips against it, kept them there for several seconds then carefully pushed the sheet into the envelope. It fitted perfectly in the back of the rucksack where her laptop would keep it flat.

The phone was ringing again when the taxi driver came to the door.

'Aren't you going to answer that, Love?' His breath misted the cold air.

'Not this time.'

He carried her suitcase to the car and put it in the boot. Natalie locked the door then put the keys through the letterbox. She heaved the rucksack onto one shoulder and walked up the path.

'Are you going somewhere nice?' the driver asked as they headed out to the ring road.

'Salzburg,' she said.

Chapter Twenty-One

It was after eleven o'clock local time when the plane touched down in Salzburg. Natalie wound her watch forward an hour. She had tried to sleep during the flight but could only doze, jerking awake as the reality of what she'd done sank in. Was it only this morning she'd been driving Toby to school; and only yesterday she'd been searching the streets for Glenda's cat? She didn't allow her thoughts to rest on Toby's face for too long.

Her head ached and her legs felt weak as she crossed the tarmac. The cold was so intense each breath stung her nostrils and she clamped her gloved hand across her face until she was inside the terminal building.

A group of skiers waited in baggage reclaim, their excited chatter grinding on her nerves. She needed to sleep, needed to escape the memory of her mother's words but had no idea where or when she'd be able to rest. She had only a vague idea of where Connor's apartment was located. She watched the noisy group drag their ski sleeves from the luggage carousel and envied them their set itinerary. For a moment she wished Glenda was there to take charge as she retrieved her case and wheeled it through customs into the arrivals hall.

Across the road the bus into the city was still running and she handed some coins to the driver. 'Zentrum, bitte,' she said, hoping he wouldn't ask exactly where in the centre she wanted to go. It was an effort even to scoop up her change and ticket. She stowed her case and dropped into a seat.

Snow was heaped in piles along the roadside. It looked grimy and drab in the sodium lighting. The longed-for thrill of arriving in the city hadn't coursed through her as she'd hoped. The bus stops were unfamiliar and she wished more than anything she were on the number seven heading for the welcoming reception at Hotel Friesen.

Fresh snow fell as she walked up Linzergasse. There were youngsters standing at the door of a bar, hopelessly underdressed for the weather. Natalie felt old and ugly as she wheeled her case past them, scanning the ancient buildings for the restaurant where Connor worked, her legs feeling weaker with every step and yet her pulse drummed in her ears.

The place was shut but she could see lights beyond the bar and a moving shadow told her someone was still inside.

Stamping her feet to warm them she looked up and down the street. There was no alley leading to the back of the restaurant so she took a deep breath and knocked on the door. When no one appeared she banged louder and shouted, *Hallo.* She tried to conjure up a German phrase to ask about Connor or his apartment. Oh God, why hadn't she rehearsed this? Her strength just about gone she shouted again and there he was, walking towards her; lovely gentle Connor who would make everything alright.

He stood a few feet from the door, pointing to his watch. '*Wir sind bis Morgen Geschlossen*,' he said and turned away.

'Connor!' Natalie shouted.

He approached again.

Her teeth were chattering now, more from anxiety than the cold. 'Please open the door.'

He reached up to draw back a bolt then fiddled with the lock. When the door opened he stared at her, his brow creased into a frown. There wasn't the slightest spark of recognition in his eyes.

'Connor, it's me!'

He was closing the door but Natalie stepped forward to touch his arm. He jerked away for a second but then reached out to push back the hood of her Jacket.

'Oh my God, Natalie!'

He crushed her against his chest and the rest of his words were lost in her hair. Then he was drawing her into the restaurant, pulling her case in and closing the door.

'You're freezing; sit there.'

She sank into a chair while he went behind the bar. He pressed a switch and the hot drinks maker flickered into life. Natalie couldn't stop shaking. Now that he was taking charge the day's events pushed their way to the forefront of her mind: Toby's screams, her mother's anger and her own impulse to run away not only from home, but from her chance of promotion. She put her head down and sobbed and once the tears started they wouldn't stop. Connor sat beside her, pressing a paper napkin into her hand.

'Hey, Baby don't cry. Has something bad happened?' He put his arm around her, pulling her close. 'Did you come straight here from the airport? Where are you staying?'

She felt a bolt of panic and tried to smooth her hair from her face knowing she must look a sight. 'I was hope … hoping to stay with … I mean would it be okay if I …'

'You can stay with me, you know that. I wasn't sure if you were back here with your boss.'

She thought of Glenda, barefoot in her dressing gown, beaming like a lighthouse. 'No. I came alone and … I'm sorry to land on you but …'

'Drink this.'

He pushed a mug of hot chocolate towards her and she wrapped her cold hands around it. The distinctive aroma of rum rose with the steam.

'Don't try to say anything now, let's get you home and we'll take it from there.'

Home. So many times she'd wondered what it would be like to call this city home, but now it was entirely terrifying. Glenda had urged her to plan for her future but she didn't even know what the next hour would hold.

Connor called for a taxi and although his apartment wasn't far away Natalie was grateful just to lean against him and close her eyes. The shaking continued and as Connor helped her out of the car her teeth were chattering again. Her phone vibrated against her hip.

The apartment was neater than she'd expected of a young man living alone. It was in a block above a supermarket in an area of Salzburg she hadn't seen before. The sound of train wheels slowing told her it was close to the station.

Connor thoughtfully pointed out the tiny bathroom. She could hardly bear to look in the mirror; her face was a disaster, swollen red eyes and a runny nose. Poor Connor, she thought. He must wonder what he's done to deserve this.

'I know how you Brits love your tea,' he said, 'but I don't have a teapot. I've made it in the cup if that's okay.' He held out the mug with a teabag string dangling from it. 'Can I make you an omelette or something? I usually eat in the restaurant but I could rustle …'

'No. It's really nice of you but I couldn't eat now.

In the darkness of the restaurant she hadn't noticed Connor's curly hair was shorter than in September and he'd swapped his neat beard for fashionable stubble. But his gentle eyes were the same and his smile just as sincere as he sat beside her on the red IKEA sofa.

'I don't wanna pry Natalie, but has someone hurt you?'

'No.' *Sigourney's pregnant.* 'Well, not physically.'

'It's just that you have a bruise on your face and I wondered …'

'Oh.' She raised her fingers to her chin. 'I had a bit of a car accident this morning and … do you mind if I … could I tell you about it tomorrow?'

He lay back on the sofa and pulled her gently into his arms. 'You were in an accident? Hell, no wonder you're upset. Just take it easy.'

Natalie rested her head against his chest and let him stroke her hair. She felt his heart beating against her cheek. Only the incessant buzzing of her phone stopped her relaxing completely.

When she'd finished her tea Connor went into the bedroom reappearing a few minutes later with a duvet and pillow. While she took her cup into the kitchen he spread the quilt over the sofa, plumping up the pillow, placing it at one end. Nothing had ever looked so inviting to Natalie's aching head.

'That's great, thanks so much, Connor.'

'This is for me. You're in there.' He nodded towards the bedroom. 'I've changed the sheets and duvet cover.'

'I don't know what to say, you're so kind … I …'

'Don't say anything.' He folded her into a gentle hug. 'I'm glad you're here. I'm sorry I didn't know it was you at first, what with that hood up and your hair grown so long.' He kissed the top of her head. 'And I mean it; it's great to see you.'

Connor's bed took up most of the room with just a built in wardrobe to the side. His alarm clock, a German crime novel and a half eaten packet of biscuits were on the floor. Natalie turned her phone off completely and put it next to the biscuits.

Wearing a long t-shirt and a change of underwear she sank into bed. Despite the clean bedclothes she could still breathe in Connor's masculine scent.

He tapped on the door and asked if he could retrieve the clock. 'Don't want it going off in your ear in the morning.'

She daren't think about the morning, couldn't let her thoughts drift to what Connor might expect of her and what the consequences of leaving home would be. She closed her eyes, took long slow breaths and listened to the rumble of trains departing to far off places.

Chapter Twenty-Two

Never having made a New Year's resolution before Leo wondered why so many people found them difficult to stick to. Maybe they set their goals too high. He'd decided to get fit after eating too much of his sister's excellent food over the holiday and finding his trousers pinching at the waistband. He didn't want to slip back into not eating, so exercise was the logical alternative. Walking Max wasn't enough even on the mountain, with his dog's inability to pass a tree without stopping.

'Take up horse riding,' Karin suggested, one Sunday lunchtime at the Friesen.

'No. He should swim.' Luisa was adamant.

'Hang-gliding keeps me fit,' Lukas said, when he joined them briefly.

'I think I'll try running for a start.'

Leo bought expensive shoes, a tracksuit, shorts for when the weather grew warmer and a trendy water bottle. He loaded Mozart and jazz onto his iPhone, paid the earth for some earphones and was ready.

At first, dreading his neighbours, or worse still, his pupils seeing him jogging, sweating and gasping for breath, he went out late at night. But then he encountered Karin walking Otto at the end of her shift and while it was lovely to chat it didn't help his get-fit regime. Early mornings were dark, the paths still icy and hazardous so he ran before lunch, along the foot of the mountain, sometimes with Max. If the dog stopped to snuffle in the grass Leo jogged on the spot.

He also started playing the piano again. He crammed his students into the afternoons and spent the mornings tackling pieces he'd found difficult in the past. Once or twice his elderly neighbour, Gerde, came in to listen.

As Mozart Week approached his friends Erik and Christe arrived in the city to attend some of the concerts. They bought him a ticket for an orchestral performance at the Mozarteum and wouldn't let him pay for it despite his protests.

'I'll buy you dinner beforehand, then,' he said.

He booked a table at M32, the restaurant on the Mönchsberg that had panoramic views of the old town. He chose it because he and Sofia had never eaten there and hoped it lived up to its reputation. Although he'd booked for three there was still a fourth chair at the table. When Leo returned from hanging up his coat a waiter was removing it. He caught Christe's eye and smiled.

'What shall we drink to,' he said when the wine was poured, hoping nobody would say *absent friends*.

'The future.' Christe raised her glass. 'You know, Leo, you should come and stay with us in London for a couple of weeks. We even have some snow this year.'

'I'd love to but I have a dog now and he's still young. I wouldn't really want to leave him.' In fact he was enjoying his new routine, especially the running, and didn't want to interrupt it. There was a pattern to his days that felt like a comforting blanket.

'Talking of the future,' he said, when their starters arrived, 'I'm in touch with Andreas now.'

Christe was dipping an artichoke into mayonnaise but it stopped in mid-air for a second. 'You've contacted him? Oh, Leo how wonderful.'

'It was the other way round, actually. Britte called me.'

'After all this time?' Erik's voice was quiet. 'What did she want?'

'Nothing. Don't look so worried.' Leo smiled and they seemed to relax. It was a pleasure relating his first meeting with his son and he even went as far as to tell them he'd met Britte in Wurzburg.

'That must have been difficult for you,' Erik said.

They were waiting now for their main course. Leo was enjoying the wine and relaxing so little by little he described the night of the concert; Andreas' performance and then the disastrous meal with Britte.

'She wanted me to … go back to the hotel with her.'

'Oh my God, Leo. You weren't tempted surely?

'Christe! You can't ask him that.'

Leo laughed. It felt good to do so. 'No. Quite the opposite, in fact.' But was that entirely true? That first night in the restaurant with Andreas Britte had been different. Might he have succumbed then? He liked to think not.

'Erik tell me about your work. How many more years will it keep you away?'

Conversation settled into an easy flow and Leo felt soothed by the familiarity of old friends.

He hadn't planned to eat dessert but changed his mind when he saw a chocolate cake and kumquats being delivered to a neighbouring table. When they'd made their choices Christe caught his eye.

'Leo, I hope you know me well enough to realise I'm not trying to match-make …'

'But …' Erik said, and gave his wife the hint of a frown.

'No. I'm really not. It's just that a friend is coming tomorrow from Graz. She'll be staying at our hotel. She's recently divorced and feeling vulnerable.'

Leo watched his friend clasp her hands and then unclasp them, wrapping her fingers around the stem of her wine glass.

'She's not up for any match-making either but we're going out for dinner with her - after tonight we'll probably come here - I just thought you might like to come along and make it a …'

'An even number?' Leo raised his eyebrows.

'No. Not even that. It might be enjoyable for both of you to have a nice, no strings evening.'

'Yes. I'd love to.' He wasn't at all sure that he'd love to but he felt mellow enough right now to make Christe happy.

They had plenty of time to get to the concert so they walked down the Mönchsberg even though the paths were slippery. Their breath preceded them in the frosty air, turning orange in the glow of the lights that lined the way.

They crossed the footbridge where snow topped the pillars at either end and lights from the town were reflected in the rushing water below. Leo wondered how his friends could bear to be away from this wonderful city for so long.

Stepping into the foyer of the Mozarteum Leo felt the thud of memory. He'd often thought about the young English woman who had asked for his help. He'd been dismissive, he knew, and regretted what must have seemed like rudeness. But now, standing where the exchange had taken place, he thought of her friend, the one he'd seen at the Friesen the night of the thunderstorm, the one whose wide grey eyes had held his for a second or two. Was it simple attraction that caused him to think of her more than once over the last few months? What else could it be?

Christe was buying programmes. Leo tried to cling to the warm glow the food and wine had given him but it was fading away.

'Erik,' he said. 'About this meal with your friend. I don't …'

Erik touched Leo's shoulder. 'No problem. I'll tell her later.'

They joined the crowd heading for the stairs.

Chapter Twenty-Three

Natalie woke to the sound of Toby screaming. She sat up, head pounding, drenched in sweat. Throwing the quilt back she swung her legs out of bed.

Salzburg.

She was in Salzburg but could still hear him screaming. As she waited for her heart to slow down she heard another voice, a woman scolding, German words. From the window she saw a young mother on the opposite pavement, pushing a buggy. A boy who wouldn't hold her hand was crying now.

Suppressing a rising sense of panic she wrapped her arms tight around her body. She could get dressed and take a taxi to the airport, get on the next plane home and somehow apologise to Glenda for missing the interview. But then she thought of Adam wanting her out of the house and the prospect of staying with her parents until she could find a flat.

No. She couldn't go back. Not yet.

There were no aspirins in her sponge bag. Not only her head but her face ached where the airbag had struck. She pulled on joggers and opened the bedroom door.

'Connor?'

Silence. His duvet was folded at one end of the sofa; the pillow resting on top. He wasn't in the kitchen and when she tapped on the bathroom door it creaked open. She was alone. Everything seemed alien; Connor's toothbrush in a mug by the basin; a bottle of Hugo Boss cologne beside it. She opened the cabinet looking for painkillers and saw his razor, a brand of shampoo she'd never heard of; a packet of condoms. She stared at them. Did Connor have a girlfriend or was he just sensible? Might he expect her to sleep with him? There had been a time when she'd wanted to. She helped herself to two paracetomols and went into the kitchen.

Finding no kettle she boiled water in a pan, took a mug from a cupboard and teabags. It was only when she placed the mug on the worktop that she saw a tray with a cloth draped over it and a note from Connor on top.

I have an early start today. Help yourself to breakfast, xx. Call me when you wake up. Under the cloth she found croissants, a small box of eggs, a pack of bacon and a key on a Homer Simpson fob. There was still a hint of warmth in the croissants. He must have gone out to buy these for me, she thought. But the sensation of strangeness wouldn't let her go. She swallowed the tablets, buttered a croissant and tried to eat. It felt dry in her throat as she swallowed and after a few mouthfuls she gave up. An image of her breakfast table at home came to mind: she and Adam pretending they'd run out of Coco Pops when Toby stayed over, her little brother's grin when he saw they were joking. Things hadn't always been bad; she couldn't even guess when the unravelling had begun.

After a shower she felt better but her pulse was still thumping in her ears. Taking long deep breaths she tried to slow it down but once she picked up her phone it speeded up again. Twenty-six missed calls, a catalogue of texts and voicemails. She found Connor's note and keyed in his number. He answered immediately.

'Hi, Sweetie. Thought I should let you sleep this morning.'

His voice at least was familiar and warm.

'Connor, I'm so sorry to land on you without emailing or anything. Yesterday was … horrible and I just needed to get away.'

'Like I said it's okay. But I'm gonna be here till around two-thirty. We're prepping for a large party. Will you be alright there alone till I get home? We can talk then.'

It was just after eleven. 'I'll go for a walk, clear my head. See you later and … thanks for the food.'

She dressed, adding an extra layer to combat the cold, tucked her phone into her pocket, picked up the key and walked out onto the landing. There was a buggy by the lift and a child's glove on the floor. Natalie picked up the glove and draped it over the handle. At the last minute, before the lift doors closed, she remembered to make a note of the number on Connor's door.

The cold was sharp in her nostrils again and she pulled up her fleece scarf to cover her nose and mouth. Turning right she headed towards the train station and was pleased to find the main bus station adjacent to it. How thrilled Glenda would be to see that, she thought.

She caught a bus to the old town and there was the fortress standing guard; the curving hill of the Mönchsberg like a protective arm around the ancient buildings. Her unease lessened as she saw familiar sights, the alleyways with their smart shops connecting the narrow streets; the fiaker horses. Her phone buzzed against her hip and she knew she must soon face all the questions. Right now she didn't have any answers.

Putting her debit card into an ATM she was relieved when it churned out Euro notes. Across Residenzplatz she could see the café beneath the museum. It was where she'd sat waiting for the guided tour to start, where Connor had come to sit with her a lifetime ago. She pushed open the door, grateful for the rush of warm air and found a table in a quiet corner.

She ordered hot chocolate, in German. It came with a heap of cream on top. After a few sips she felt in her pocket for her phone. Four more missed calls, more texts.

Midday in Salzburg so eleven o'clock at home. If her mother had gone to work she would catch her father alone.

He answered on the first ring. 'Natalie. Thank God! We've been going frantic here.'

'Sorry, Dad. Is Toby alright?'

'He's at school. What's going on with you? Your mum said you had an interview but that strange girl you work with said you never made it.'

'No. I'm …'

'And I'm sorry but I used the spare key and went into your house. We thought you might … well, I don't want to say what we thought … you having had an airbag in your face.'

'Really, I'm fine. But what about you? Mum says you have angina. Why didn't you tell me the other day? I feel terrible giving you more stress.'

'That's no problem, Lovie. Trust me. Anyway, I saw you'd taken clothes with you. Where are you?'

'Salzburg.'

'You're … are you staying with the Yank?'

'I'm at Connor's, yes. And do you know what?' She looked up at the café ceiling, struggling to hold back tears and took a deep breath. 'It's really nice to be with someone who isn't telling me what to do or making me feel pathetic.' An elderly man at the next table turned to look at her.

'It was several seconds before her father spoke again.

'Okay. Do you need any money?'

Natalie took the phone from her ear and stared at it. 'Money?'

'You took off in a hurry. I thought you might need some.'

'I've just drawn some out. Mum said some horrible things to me, you know.'

'Oh, she told me, and you'll be pleased to hear she's feeling bloody terrible about it. And as for Adam, if I was to meet him right now he wouldn't father another child, I can tell you.'

'I don't want to think about him or Mum. Right now I don't want to think about anything.'

'Have you booked a flight back? I saw you'd put your keys through the letter box.'

'No, I'm not coming back just yet.'

'Lovie, I'd better ring off and let your mother know you're alright. You'll keep in touch?'

'I will.' Her tears were starting to win the struggle.

'And for Heaven's sake ring that boss of yours. She's been plaguing us all night and all morning for news. Is she on drugs or something?'

Natalie smiled for the first time since she'd been back in Salzburg. 'Love is the drug, Dad.'

She heard the smile in his voice too. 'I don't think Bryan Ferry had her in mind.'

'Kiss Toby for me, won't you?'

'If he'll let me.'

They were silent for a couple of heart beats.

'Natalie, do you know what you're doing?'

'No. Not at all.'

'Well, maybe your old dad shouldn't be saying this but try and have some fun. God knows you deserve it.'

As she ended the call Natalie turned her face away from the table, tried to wipe away tears with the back of her hand but they ran down to her chin. She felt gentle pressure on her shoulder and turned back. The elderly man handed her a clean paper napkin.

Chapter Twenty-Four

'Wake up, Sweetie, we're going skiing.'

Natalie heard the words but they made no sense. She opened her eyes and dragged herself up into a sitting position. Connor was crouching beside the bed, his broad grin in place, eyebrows raised for her reaction.

'Skiing? I don't ski, I …'

'A minor detail.' He blew her a kiss from the door. 'We need to be at Mirabel in an hour. Bring sunglasses.'

'I don't have any with me.'

What day was it? Saturday. She'd been in Salzburg for three weeks. Glenda had let her take unpaid leave but she knew pretty soon she'd have to book a flight home. She'd called her dad every day so that he didn't worry and stress his heart but so far she hadn't spoken to her mother.

Pulling the curtains back she saw clear blue sky and squinted as sunlight reflected off the snow piled at the side of the road.

Connor was singing in the kitchen. The now familiar clatter of plates and coffee mugs meant he was making her breakfast despite her many protests that they should take it in turns. It was a welcome novelty to be spoiled. He was still sleeping on the sofa too.

She pulled on leggings and a sweater and padded through to the kitchen. 'Connor, I can't go skiing. I'd break both my legs and I don't have the clothes.'

He pushed a croissant towards her. It was warm and chocolate-filled.

'Jo-jo has to work so she's lending you her jacket and goggles.' He licked chocolate from his fingers. 'You can do as much or as little skiing as you like and we hire all the stuff there.'

'But is it expensive?' She was beginning to panic about money and might have to take up her dad's offer of a loan.

'Not really and anyway I have this.' He wedged a croissant between his teeth and reached up to take an envelope from the shelf. He waved a cheque in her face. 'Birthday cash from my Mom.'

'When was your birthday?'

'Tomorrow. So you gotta come or you'll spoil it for me.'

For a second Natalie wondered just what Connor's age was. She'd always guessed he was late twenties. But shouldn't he be settled in a career rather than waiting at tables half a world away from home? She thought about Adam, he often worked weekends. Right now he'd be on his way to the office or meeting clients at a development. But then she remembered the time difference and knew he'd still be snuggled up to Sigourney and her thickening waistline.

Connor smeared a blob of chocolate onto her nose. 'So you're coming, right?'

In the bathroom she turned on the shower. What did it matter how old he was? Have fun, Dad said and why not, even if she did end up in plaster.

Half an hour later they were at the bus stop in Mirabelplatz, their breath streaming out onto the frozen air. Connor's friend Rachel greeted her like a long-lost sister and handed her a rucksack.

'Jo-jo said it should fit you and there are some gloves in the pocket.'

'It's really kind of her but I doubt I'll be skiing.'

'Yeah, right.'

Natalie had forgotten the names of the two men she'd met at the restaurant one evening, but they gave her a hug and said they were glad to have her along for the trip.

As the shuttle bus sped south out of the city Natalie was

in awe of the scenery. Snow covered the mountains from peak to valley and glistened in mesmerising blue patterns on the meadows. Removing his gloves Connor took hold of her hand and something of the old magic she remembered from September stole through her. Today she wouldn't think about home; wouldn't dwell on Toby's insistent texts that she should be there to watch him in a table tennis tournament. Much as she adored him she still refused to plan more than an hour ahead. It was enjoyable just being swept along by Connor and his friends. 'They're a bit full-on at times, I know,' Connor had said, 'But they're good guys really.'

It took an hour to reach their destination, the mountain peaks growing ever closer. As they emerged from a tree-lined road Natalie drew in her breath. The mountainside sparkled in the sun and teemed with people. A pretty village nestled in a hollow.

'Welcome to Flachau,' she heard someone say.

The bus eased its way into the village centre and as they clambered off, zipping up coats and pulling on gloves, Natalie saw the place was entirely given over to snow sports. Youngsters wandered by with snowboards under their arms, groups of children chattered and laughed as they pulled on boots and hats; the shops were crammed with ski-wear, their multi-coloured merchandise spilling onto the pavements. Everywhere people were gathered, eating and drinking outside restaurants or at temporary food and drink stands with umbrellas to shade them from the sun. The scent of roasting chestnuts wafted by.

Natalie had grown accustomed to the stinging cold but she was grateful for Jo-jo's snug jacket as Connor led her by the hand through the crowds to a ski-hire shop.

'I'm still not sure I want to do this,' she said, although her resolve wasn't quite so strong now she was letting the atmosphere of the resort surge through her.

'You'll be fine.' Connor gave her hand a squeeze. 'Wait here

I'll be back in a while.'

'But where are ...?'

He left her queuing outside the ski-hire with Rachel and the men whose names she now remembered were Robbie and Ross. She felt in her bag for her purse and hoped her credit card would withstand the day's onslaught.

On the slopes beyond the village scattered groups of skiers descended, now and then disappearing behind clumps of snow-jewelled trees. Rachel was right; now she was here she wanted to ski, however badly.

Connor reappeared and thrust a ticket into her hand. 'I've booked you a couple of hours tuition, is that okay?'

'Yes. Of course but,' she lowered her voice, 'how much does it cost?'

He waved a dismissive hand. 'Courtesy of Mom, remember?'

He handed the others tickets for the regular slopes. Natalie thanked him and zipped hers into her jacket pocket with the uneasy feeling that he'd blown all his birthday money in one go.

Within twenty minutes she looked like a skier and it hadn't cost nearly as much as she feared even after buying trendy new sunglasses and a warm hat with long ear flaps for Connor which she hid in Jo-Jo's rucksack.

The boots felt weird and heavy but now she couldn't wait to get onto the snow. She carried the skis and poles against her shoulder. Connor drew her to one side.

'Will you be OK on your own? We're going to head up on the lift but I'll have my cell switched on if you need to call. If you're not happy I'll stay here with you.'

'I'll be fine. Go and have fun.' She didn't want to make a fool of herself in front of him anyway.

He looked at his watch then cupped her face in his hands. 'If you're sure. We'll meet you back here at two o'clock and we'll all grab some food.' He kissed her lips fleetingly. 'Don't break a leg.'

Despite the cold Natalie's face burned as she made her way to the tuition meeting point. As sweet as Connor had been with hugs and stroking her hair when she got upset, he hadn't attempted to kiss her until now. Don't read too much into it, she told herself. This is just a fun day out to celebrate his birthday.

It took just a few minutes on the lift to arrive at the beginners' slopes. A middle-aged couple from London sat beside her, the woman nervous and good-humoured, berating her husband for suggesting they try skiing at their age. Natalie tagged along with them, comforted by their English humour.

The instructor was an American girl who looked about sixteen but in no time she had them in a straight line learning how to find their centre of balance. Natalie clutched her poles and ensured her skis were parallel. Think of them as two French fries, the instructor said.

Gradually finding the courage to move forward she fell immediately onto her backside followed swiftly by the lady from London. Laughing to cover her embarrassment Natalie gritted her teeth and began again.

'Don't let your knees come together,' the instructor said as Natalie ground to an ungainly stop and pitched forward, 'pretend there's a basketball between them.'

After forty minutes she could just about stay upright and had learned to slow herself down by bringing the tips of her skis together to form a wedge shape.

'Imagine a slice of pizza' she repeated to herself, 'narrow to go faster, wider to go slower.'

'All this talk of French fries and pizza's making me peckish,' the London chap said as he glided along beside Natalie.

Time and again she slithered down the slope, rigid, holding her breath; trying to remember all the instructions; then suddenly her knees relaxed and she allowed herself to breathe; to look ahead rather than at her feet. A rush of excitement caught her. The cold air slid past her warm face, she was skiing and she hadn't thought of Adam and Sigourney for hours.

Just before two she caught the gondola down to the village. Her legs felt wobbly and her arms were stiff but she was still on a high. She spotted Rachel, then Connor and the others waving to her from doorway of a restaurant.

'We're eating inside,' Rachel said, 'before my butt freezes and drops off.'

'Kaiserschmarrn all round?' Connor asked as the waiter approached. The others nodded so Natalie did too, even though the word brought instant memories of the night Adam came and spoiled the German class party.

They drank mugs of mulled wine and swapped skiing stories. Connor made everyone laugh describing Ross's attempt at a small ski jump. 'He was winding down the windows like crazy,' Connor said, miming the action with both hands. Ross hung his head in mock shame while they ordered more wine.

It seemed strange to eat a dessert dish as a main course.

'It gives skiers a huge boost of calories,' Connor said. Certainly the plates of chopped pancakes and plum sauce disappeared quickly.

'Just what my ass needs,' Rachel slapped her tiny behind, 'a huge boost of calories.'

She, Ross and Robbie went back up the mountain for another hour's skiing but despite Natalie's protests Connor said he'd stay behind with her and take a walk round the village. The wine had made her woozy so she was grateful when he took her hand to steady her on the snowy pavement. They found a cosy café and ordered hot chocolate laced with rum.

'You've got to let me give you something for my lunch,' Natalie said. 'You can't pay for everything today.'

Instead of answering he slid down the hood of her jacket and gently eased her hair out of her collar.

'Can't believe I didn't recognise you when you arrived,' he said.

'I suppose I do look a bit different. I've lost weight and …'

'Your hair is lovely. I like it longer.' He picked up a wavy strand, wrapping it round his fingers.

Natalie stared at her hands and then forced herself to look up at him, returned his smile. He might have leaned in for a kiss if their drinks hadn't arrived.

'You're really kind to let me stay with you.' Natalie spooned whipped cream into her mouth, letting it dissolve on her tongue. 'I'll give you some money before I go home. I suppose you really need to know when that will be. Problem is I can't seem to make decisions right now.'

'Like I said at the start, stay as long as you like. I can't believe you're here after … you know … I mean last year we did flirt a little and …'

'We flirted a *lot* and did quite a bit of kissing if I remember rightly.'

'You know, we really didn't do enough kissing.'

And then he did lean in and his mouth tasted of chocolate and rum and gentleness. Natalie felt her tension fall away and warmth spread through her body.

On the bus back to Salzburg she was suspended in an ecstasy of anticipation with Connor's arm around her and her cheek resting against his chest, the time ticking to the rhythm of his heart.

He didn't ask his friends back for coffee, they all hugged and said goodbye at Mirabel with a promise to meet up tomorrow.

The apartment was warm but still Natalie shivered as she took off her jacket. With her heartbeat in overdrive she took Connor's hand and led him into the bedroom. Fresh snow touched the window, sliding and melting on the sill as Connor lifted her hair to kiss her neck.

She heard a church bell chime midnight and then nothing more but her fractured breathing as Connor undressed her. He was gentle, considerate; almost reluctant until she clung to him, pulling him down to the bed, imprisoning him with her limbs.

Sometime in the dark of the early morning she slid from his embrace and tip-toed into the kitchen, turned on the light and poured herself a glass of water. Connor's cheque was still face up on the worktop and Natalie's pulse quickened as she saw it was for a thousand dollars. She snatched it up to make sure. On the back was a note from his mother. *Please use this to buy a plane ticket home.*

Sitting on the sofa, sipping the water, she felt guilty about reading the note. Would Connor return to the States now? Escape from all her worries might be over sooner than she thought.

Her phone hummed in the pocket of her jacket. Who on earth could be ringing in the middle of the night? Oh God, was Toby ill? She grabbed her coat and pulled out the phone. Her mother's voice was barely audible. '*Please come home. Grandma is dying …*'

Chapter Twenty-Five

Natalie was trapped in a window seat beside two boisterous children. She stared at the airport building as they thundered along the runway for take-off. Connor would be back at the apartment by now. What a way to start his birthday. He'd held her hand in the airport until she couldn't delay going through security any longer. They'd hardly spoken and she'd been grateful for that. He kissed her very softly and said he'd see her soon.

Her head felt as though it might burst; she'd been selfish and thoughtless and now her real life was reclaiming her. What had she been thinking of leaving everything behind like that? *She's had a massive stroke. If you want to say goodbye you'd better come soon,* her mother had said. Natalie was lucky to get a seat on the first flight of the day.

Her dad was waiting at Coventry. 'Are you coming to us or do you want the spare key to your house?'

'I'll stay with you if you don't mind, but can I go to see her right now? I'd never forgive myself if … well, you know.'

They headed for the ring road. 'You're mum's coping quite well but she was there all night so she'll be bushed by now. Maureen stayed too.' He swore at a cyclist and indicated to go round him. 'And talking of Maureen the old girl's courting. Can you believe it? She's seventy-eight. Remember that old poodle fancier who visits his old mum in the home? They seem to be an item.'

'Goodness! Never too old, then. Is Toby at school?'

'Yes and Markus' mother's taking him home with her for tea. He won't talk about your gran, poor little man.'

At the care home her mother folded her into a hug and all thoughts of their last meeting were put aside.

Gran was asleep, an oxygen mask over her nose and mouth. Her face, shrunken and slightly askew from the stroke, was grey. Her shallow breathing had a rasping sound to it. While her mum went to fetch tea Natalie stared at her grandmother. 'I should have spent more time with you,' she whispered.

Her mother, putting a mug of tea on the bedside table, looked more tired than Natalie had ever seen her.

'She hasn't eaten anything solid for days and she's been so confused, mumbling nonsense.' She reached forward and brushed a lock of hair from Gran's forehead.

Natalie fought back tears, then, feeling her phone vibrate against her hip she drew it out of her pocket and saw there was a text from Connor: *Thinking of you, Miss Adorable.*

'Is that your American?'

'Yes.' Natalie didn't want to talk about Connor or Salzburg. It all seemed a bit of a dream now. She put her phone away.

'Is he missing you?' Her mum sipped her tea then pulled a face. 'This is Earl Grey I think. Shall I go and change it?'

'No, it's alright. I often have it now.' Natalie was pleased to sidestep questions about Connor.

'I keep wondering if we should have looked after her at home instead of her coming here,' her mother said.

'But you work full-time and you have a nine year-old. That's a lot to deal with and you do see her several times a week.'

'She's been getting ever so forgetful. I don't think she remembers my visits anyway. She was calling for Maureen ten minutes after she'd left the other day and asked how Adam was, would you believe?' Rain started pelting against the windows. 'I bet you had snow over there, didn't you?'

'It was starting to melt today.'

'It was nice of you to text Toby every day. He'll be pleased to see you later.'

'I've missed him.'

'It should be you with a nine year-old, not me.' Her mother dissolved into tears.

This was the last thing Natalie expected to hear. 'Don't say that, Mum. Toby's wonderful; you wouldn't want to be without him?'

'You know what I mean.'

She did know and didn't want to talk about that either. Just for a second she would have given anything to be sitting with Connor and the others in a restaurant somewhere, worrying about nothing more than where they'd eat dinner.

'Maybe you could sleep now, Mum. Why don't you nip home for a bit? I'll stay here.'

'I mean it, Natalie. There isn't a day goes by without I think it …'

'Mum! Don't say any more and don't ask me to be someone I'm not.'

Gran was in such a deep sleep the nurse suggested they go home and rest for a while.

Her dad had made them a pasta bake and took two wine glasses from the cupboard.

'Don't pour me one, Dad.' Natalie felt woolly headed from tiredness.

'I'll not have one either,' he said, 'in case they … you know … call us back.'

Natalie dozed for a couple of hours but worry chased all chance of deep sleep away. She longed for the comfort of Connor's arm around her, the rhythm of his breathing.

When she heard the sound of a computer game she realised Toby was back.

He was staring at the game but the joystick was idle on his desk. When he turned to face her she saw his lashes were stuck together in clumps and there were tears on his cheeks.

She wanted to throw her arms round him but decided not to acknowledge that he'd been crying. He jumped up and hugged her but it was a swift embrace and he sat down again.

'Did you have something nice to eat at Markus's house, Tobes?'

'It was nice but I didn't want to eat it.'

'How about I buy you a McDonalds?

He shook his head then seemed to rethink the idea. 'Can I have a doughnut?'

'Anything you like. Find something warm to put on and I'll tell Mum and Dad.'

She slipped her jacket on and pinched one of her mother's scarves.

'Take my car,' her dad said. Yours is in the garage if I need it.'

Natalie's face became hot with embarrassment remembering the state she had left it in.

'And if you can cheer him up that would be great.'

Once they reached McDonald's drive-by window Toby said he might manage a burger. She asked for large Cokes and it suddenly felt strange ordering food in English. Not wanting to go straight home she drove to the edge of the estate where the landscaped back gardens and ornamental trees gave way to farmland. She made sure the doors were locked and thought that if this were Salzburg they could get out and walk and feel entirely safe.

Toby made inroads into his burger but dropped half of it back into the box and nibbled on the doughnut. Natalie, still hungry, shovelled fries into her mouth and drank most of her Coke.

'When Gran dies are you going away again?' Toby said.

'I haven't decided what I'm doing yet, Tobes. But even if I do you know we can talk on the phone and text. Maybe in the summer Mum and Dad could bring you to see me.'

His lower lip began to tremble. He pushed the box of food

from his knee. It fell against the paper mug of Coke and Natalie grabbed it before it spilled.

'But you might come home and you won't know where we live,' he said. 'I might not see you ever again.'

'What do you mean?' Bewildered she wriggled round and put both drinks behind her seat. She tried to take his hand but he pulled it away. 'What's the matter, Sweetheart? I know you're worried about Gran but …'

'Why did you have to go away? It's not fair and when Gran dies I'll never see you.'

His tears were flowing now. He turned in his seat to stare out of the window. A couple walked by, Natalie heard the murmur of their voices. She handed him a tissue.

'Toby, nobody will *ever* stop me seeing you. Why would you think that?' Her exhausted brain struggled to follow his logic.

Then his voice rose and he faced her. 'But you don't like Italy. You don't want to go there. You said so.'

'Italy? What does that have to do with …?'

'I don't want to go there either. I want to stay here. I want to stay here with you.'

A cold sensation crept up Natalie's back. 'But you enjoy your holidays and …'

'No!' He shouted, tugged his seatbelt away from his body, struggling to get out of it. Natalie pressed the button and released him. His face in the sodium lighting looked grey and contorted. 'No. You don't know. You don't know.'

She gripped his hands. 'Whatever it is *tell* me. We can sort it out.'

His head went down to his chest and he wept, his anger gone. Wiping his face Natalie spoke soothingly. 'Don't worry, Sweetheart. Everything will be alright.' She reached for his Coke and he drew on the straw for a few seconds.

'I heard Mum and Dad talking. I'd got told off and sent to

bed.'

'When was this?'

'Ages ago. I went downstairs again because Markus had given me some swap cards and I'd left them in the hall and I wanted to get them.'

Natalie stroked the hair from his hot forehead. 'So what did you hear?'

'You won't tell Mum I was listening?'

'Nobody's going to be cross with you.'

He gulped air. It was growing cold but she didn't want to interrupt him now.

'Mum said there was a school I could go to but I'd have to go on a bus. Dad said I wouldn't like it and he got cross with Mum.'

Natalie stared out of the window above his head, anxiety increasing. 'They were talking about Italy were they?'

'Yes and Dad said I don't make friends. I don't know what he means because Markus is my friend.'

'What did Mum say then, Tobes?' She felt guilty pumping him.

'She said I'd make friends in Italy when we lived there all the time. Then she said it didn't matter talking about it yet because we can't go while Grandma's still alive.'

Natalie sank back in her seat, head pounding, trying to keep her voice even.

'They're planning to move to …'

'I don't want to live in Italy, Nat. They won't make me will they?' He gripped the drinking straw in his fingers, bending it back and forth. 'I want to stay here and I want you to stay here as well.'

'Listen to me, Toby,' she put her hand on his shoulder. 'I promise you they won't force you to do anything you're not happy about.' Even as she said the words she knew it was wrong to promise but she couldn't bear the sight of his anguished face.

His eyes were huge and bright with tears. As they drove home he reached across and took hold of a piece of her jacket, clutching it in his grubby fingers. Natalie placed her hand over his and hoped he couldn't feel the tremors that ran through her body.

At home her mother was in tears on the sofa. Natalie gripped Toby's hand and looked at her father.

'Don't worry, Lovie, your mum's just overwrought.' He tilted his head, a hint to take Toby upstairs.

In the bathroom she bathed his face. 'Looks like Mum's very upset Toby but you're still not to worry. I promise you everything will be alright. Come down and have some hot chocolate when you're ready.'

'Maureen's doing another night shift,' her dad said. 'I reckon we should all turn in early and get some sleep. She said she'd call us if … you know.'

In bed Natalie couldn't get warm. Toby's revelation about her parent's plans, if he'd heard them correctly, was a shock but she couldn't bring up the subject now.

Other anxieties churned in her brain. Glenda would be expecting some idea of when she might return to work; Adam would be putting the house on the market. It struck her suddenly how little she'd thought of him in the last few weeks. His ability to hurt her was finally diminishing.

Chapter Twenty-Six

She was aware of movement. Someone patting her shoulder. It was still dark

'Wake up, Lovie.' A whisper close to her ear.

She sat up, disorientated and dry-mouthed. 'Dad. Is it Gran?' She tried to focus.

'She's had another stroke, Natalie. Your mum can't drive herself. I'll have to stay with Toby.'

'Is this … is this it, do you think?' She was out of bed, pulling on her dressing gown.

'Probably is. I'm so sorry. You'd better get your mum there quickly. Safely mind,' he added as he left her alone.

'She threw on the clothes she'd worn the night before and was down in the hall in ten minutes. Her mother was silent, her coat on, hands pushed up into the sleeves. Natalie hugged her, knew there was nothing she could say to make this better.

'I'll get there when I can, Chris,' her dad said as he walked them out to the car. There'd been a frost and he sprayed the windscreen while Natalie got in and started the engine.

'It's a miracle she's hanging on,' her mum said as they left the estate.

'They made them tough in those days.'

'Tougher than you could imagine. Oh, please let us make it in time.'

At the home there was an air of quiet concern. A carer greeted them at the door and attempted no small talk.

Gran's oxygen mask was still in place but her breathing was shallow and erratic. 'Can she hear us?' Natalie asked the nurse.

'She's going in and out of sleep but she's very weak now. She might well respond if you talk to her.'

She left them and they sat either side of the bed for almost an hour. Natalie's mother held Gran's hand, whispering to her and was rewarded by a faint return of pressure from her fingers.

Natalie stared at her grandmother's face trying to commit every eyelash and softly folding wrinkle to memory. She tried not to think how Toby might be feeling.

'I'll go and get us a drink,' her mother said standing up and stretching her back. Do you want me to see if there's anything to eat?

Natalie shook her head; wiped away her own tears. She stroked the old lady's cheek. 'I love you, Gran, and we'll all miss you.' She would have given anything for her to be in the day room now, hiding cardboard up her sleeve.

She was so intent on staring at the transparent skin of her grandmother's hand that it was a moment or two before she realised her eyes were open and she was struggling to say something behind the mask. Natalie moved it aside.

'You're b…back from … S…alzb…'

'From Salzburg. Yes.' She felt a surge of bittersweet happiness. At this late stage the old lady's confusion seemed to have cleared. 'I've been there for a few weeks. You'd love it.' She babbled on in almost a whisper, describing her attempts at skiing. 'I speak German a little better now and …'

She felt her grandmother's fingers move in hers, sliding from her hands then gripping her wrist with surprising strength, her mouth pursing. Natalie leaned closer.

'Course you can … speak … Germ … Your grandad … he …'

'Shhh… Don't make yourself out of breath,' she said, wanting to cry but keeping her smile in place.

'Ad … Adolf.' Gran's eyes bore into hers. 'Adolf.'

'Would you like a drink?' Maybe the confusion hadn't left her after all. She lifted the glass of water and steered the straw between Gran's pale lips.

She drank for a few seconds then, before the mask went back into place, she said, 'M … mein … Adolf.' The name was like a sigh.

Then her mother was back. 'She's awake. Oh, thank God,' She slid the cups onto the table and sank into the chair, kissing Gran's forehead, stroking her hand.

Natalie stood up and walked to the window, taking long breaths, trying to keep the tears back. It was light now. Outside clumps of daffodils leaned over in the wind, a plastic plant pot rolled in circles on the lawn.

'Natalie.' The faintest whisper.

Turning she saw her mother's face was a sea of tears.

'Has she …'

A tiny nod. She removed the oxygen mask. An aura of peace had replaced the laboured breath. Natalie and her mother stood in a fierce embrace, crying into each other's hair, moving apart when the nurse came in quickly exiting again to find the doctor. There were several minutes of comforting words, brave faces then they leaned over to kiss Gran one last time.

Matron made them tea in her sitting room. Natalie found herself staring at the green and red patterned carpet and thinking of scrubbed Austrian floorboards.

Her mother stirred her tea round and round. 'I've rung Maureen. She said Gran woke in the night while she was here but she didn't say anything. Did she try to speak to you?'

Natalie hesitated for a beat then shook her head. 'That mask thing … I don't think she could …'

Auntie Maureen walked in with Bernard. She hugged them both. Bernard stood, eyes cast down.

'Was she awake at the end?' Maureen mumbled through the tissue in her fingers.

'She had just woken,' Natalie said, 'and Mum walked in. It

was as though she was waiting for her.'

Maureen nodded several times. Bernard hovered at her side, placing an awkward hand on her arm.

The room felt too small. Natalie stood up. 'I need some air.'

In the garden she sheltered from the wind and rang Connor's number. He answered on the second ring.

'Hey Sweetie, how's it going?'

In the background a Salzburg church bell chimed the hour.

She burst into tears; her words a stream of gibberish. Connor kept up a soothing dialogue while she balanced the phone between shoulder and ear, pulling tissues from her pocket; blowing her nose.

'I'm so sorry I can't be there with you,' he said. 'And there's so much I want to say to you, Natalie, but I know this isn't the time.'

At home they made endless cups of tea. Her mother and Maureen reminisced over large glasses of whiskey. Her dad and Bernard joined forces to make dinner, their conversation stilted but friendly. Markus's mother had taken Toby to the park.

It wasn't until later when she was in the bath that Natalie thought about Connor's words, *so much I want to say.* Maybe he wanted to tell her he was going home. But he was so loving and sweet. What if his feelings were growing more serious?

She couldn't think about it now. The weight of her sorrow was sinking in and it wasn't just the loss of her lovely grandma. Toby was depending on her to make things right about Italy. She lay back and closed her eyes, wondering where on earth she would start.

Chapter Twenty-Seven

The funeral was three days later.

'Thank God they could do it so quickly.' Her mother had chosen Grandma's favourite hymns.

'Maybe they had a cancellation,' Auntie Maureen said.

Natalie was pleased to see a few of Grandma's former neighbours had turned up and joined in with *All things Bright and Beautiful* in reedy voices. Some of the staff from the nursing home were there too.

'Lord knows how many funerals they must go to in a year,' her dad whispered.

They'd decided Toby shouldn't attend and he was sleeping over at Markus's house. He'd made a card for Grandma and written *goodbye* in it. As an afterthought he'd drawn two angels on the envelope, one with go-faster stripes.

Despite Natalie's reassurances that all would be well his anxious face nearly broke her heart.

The following day, when she was the only one out of bed, Natalie took a call from Auntie Maureen.

'Is your mum there? The matron was asking when we want to collect your Gran's things. They're not rushing us or anything but I thought I'd head over there.'

'She's still asleep, Auntie. I'll give you a hand if you like.'

Maureen gently folded Grandma's dresses and put them into a suitcase.

'Oh, look at this.' Natalie pulled a shred of cereal box from the pocket of a skirt.

Maureen raised a smile. 'She wasn't always batty you know. She was such a strong one, far more so than me. And she could do a crossword puzzle in quarter of an hour. Mind like a steel trap her Edwin used to say.'

'I don't remember Grandpa ever so well. I was about twelve when he died.'

'Edwin was a smashing chap; worshipped your gran.' Maureen turned away to a chest of drawers and began to pull out petticoats and pairs of large, white pants.

A carer brought them a pot of tea and for a few moments they sat in armchairs, lost in their thoughts.

From the dressing table Natalie picked up a faded chocolate box which held a few pieces of jewellery: a gold locket on a chain, some old fashioned brooches, a string of pearls with a broken clasp. At the back of a drawer was a small box. Natalie lifted the lid. Wrapped in cotton wool was another brooch. 'Oh, look at this, Auntie. It's an edelweiss.'

The clasp and setting were silver, the petals of the flower she had come to know so well in Salzburg, were enamelled in green and white.

Turning she saw that Maureen had stopped folding petticoats and was staring at the brooch. 'I didn't know she still had that.'

'Now I'm intrigued because Gran knew a few words of German. Did she ever go to Austria on holiday? I mean it must have been years ago because I don't remember …'

'No. She never went abroad. She must have bought it here.' Maureen turned back to the clothes.

'Did … did she know someone called Adolf?'

This time Maureen's head snapped up but she kept her face turned away. 'Course not. Who do you know in Coventry called Adolf?'

'She said the name before she died. I didn't mention it before because I thought she was confused, but now… '

'I could drink another cup of tea, Natalie if you fancied bringing one.' Maureen's voice was trembling now.

'Okay, but is there something you're not …?'

'Lordy, Natalie, are you getting that tea?'

She came back with a tray. As well as the teapot and cups she had brought a glass of brandy, begged from the matron. 'You're looking pale, have a sip of this.'

Maureen dutifully swigged the drink then stared at Natalie. 'Are you going back to Salzburg?'

'I'm not sure … I'd like to see if things could work … you know, Connor and me, well it's early days and … but we're going off the point now, Auntie.'

Maureen knocked back the remainder of the brandy. 'If I tell you, Natalie, you'll have to promise me you'll never repeat it.'

'Alright. I promise.' Curiosity was pushing other emotions aside now.

Maureen carried her cup and saucer to the window. Sunlight had broken through grey clouds and slanted across the lawn. Natalie bit her lip and waited.

'During the war we were in the Land Army, Florrie and me. I lied about my age and they didn't even check-up. They sent us over the other side of Leicester. It was a lovely farm. Ashamed to say I really enjoyed the war.' She took a sip of tea. 'There was a camp with prisoners. Some were trusted and helped on the farm, supervised, of course.'

'Do you … you mean prisoners of war?'

Maureen nodded. 'Edwin was away, fighting. Royal Navy. It was ever so dangerous protecting those convoys. Florrie was always worried, but then …'

'She met Adolf? Was he a prisoner?'

'He was; one of the trusties. Poor lad, fancy having the same ruddy name as Hitler. Nobody spoke to him, only the farmer and his wife. He worked hard. Said he'd done farming before. He was good with the cows. He could cook too, that was a novelty. Sometimes he cooked dinner for all us girls.'

'So did she … were they … lovers?'

Maureen's cup clattered against the saucer so she put it on the table. 'She never said outright. It was strictly forbidden, you know, fraternisation. But he gave her that brooch, said it was his mother's.'

Natalie ran her fingers over the smooth petals of the flower. 'So he went home, then, at the end of the war?'

'He did. I can still see her … she was … more upset than I'd ever seen her. She gave him a photo of her and me. She didn't have one of her on her own.'

'Poor Gran. She's carried a torch for him all these years?'

'Must have.' Again Maureen turned away. Natalie knew she couldn't stop now.

'She never saw him again?'

'Well, how could she?'

'You tell me, Auntie. I'm sure there's something you're keeping back.'

Maureen held her hand out for the brooch and closed her fingers round it. 'Your mother can't ever know, Natalie. If I tell you …'

'Of course.'

'He came to England in the fifties. There was some sort of trade exchange thing. He'd built up a business; to do with farming equipment, I think. I don't know how he tracked her down but one day there he was at the door.'

'Oh my God. Was Grandpa there?' Natalie's hands were trembling. She wrapped them round her teacup.

'No. He must have watched him go to work and then knocked, bold as you like.'

'What? Did she let him in?'

'Lordy, No. The net curtains would have been twitching all down the street. I don't know how she held herself together on the doorstep but she said she'd meet him in town. Natalie, she nearly didn't go but … she just had to see him one last time.'

Maureen was crying now. Natalie went to her side; put an arm round her thin shoulders.

'She came to me; asked me what she should do. She said he'd hardly aged at all; still handsome.'

'Did he want her to go away with him?'

'No darling. He was married and had two boys. He showed her photos of them.'

'So she went then … to meet him?'

'They spent the afternoon together. That's all they had, just a couple of hours in a hotel room and then he was gone.'

'What year was this, Auntie? Had she already … I mean … was my mum born then?'

Very slowly Maureen looked up. She met her gaze and held it. Natalie felt her cheeks burning. 'You mean … he was …?'

'Had to be. Florrie and Edwin had been married for years. She thought she was barren. But then … well … she fell for Christine.'

Natalie covered her mouth with her hands. It was a few moments before she could speak. 'My mother is half German?' At any other time she'd have laughed out loud. 'So I'm part German too. How weird is that?'

'From the day Christine was born we never spoke of it but I'm certain if he'd got in touch again she'd have told me.'

'Do you think Grandpa knew? I mean if they'd tried for a baby all that time and …'

'If he suspected there'd been someone else he never said. He was a quiet, gentle man, Edwin. He worked hard and did his allotment. He thought the sun shone from your Gran. Perhaps it never entered his head. Perhaps he just thought they fell lucky.'

'Gran must have been heartbroken though. Losing him all over again and him never knowing he had a daughter.'

'She did her duty. She devoted herself to Edwin and Christine and she was beside herself when Edwin died. She did love him … the thing with … Adolf was just … one of those things I s'pose.'

Her mother, German. The irony of it. Natalie found herself thinking of Adolf, wondering if he were still alive. He'd be going on ninety.

'Did she ever write to him, do you think?'

'Can't imagine she did, them both being married and all. Too dangerous. Besides, she put it behind her.

'But she mentioned his name … just before …'

'Well, her mind must have been wandering over the past. I'm glad she remembered him.'

Natalie took photo frames from the chest of drawers and laid them on the bed. There were a few of herself at stages of growing up, Toby as a baby in her mother's arms. She stared at Gran's wedding photo searching for her mother's features in Edwin's face but could find none.

'Could I take these home, Auntie? See if Mum wants any of them.'

'Course, Darlin. You won't say anything though?'

Natalie shook her head, wrapped the pictures in newspaper and put them all in a carrier bag.

At home her father was emptying food from supermarket bags; her mother still in bed.

'I think the last week has caught up with her,' her dad said. 'Thought it best to let her sleep.

'I wouldn't mind a chat as we're on our own.'

'Need some more cash, Lovie?' His smile was teasing.

'No, but thanks for the offer.' Natalie filled the kettle, settled it on its stand and switched it on. 'Toby was crying the other night. He reckons he heard you discussing moving to Italy.'

For a second or two she saw surprise register on his face and he turned away, ran a hand across his forehead, a gesture she'd seen a million times.

'And he was upset was he?'

'Is that an admission that you are moving?'

'Hey, I'm the detective.'

'You *were* the detective.'

They both stared at the kettle.

'You pick your moments, Natalie. We've got a lot going on at the moment.'

She felt a surge of anger. 'We're talking about Toby's feelings here. He was almost hysterical the other night.

'Nothing's decided by any means. It might never happen.'

'But even if you're thinking about it you need to talk to Toby. He really doesn't want to go.' She remembered her brother's face and the way he'd clung to her jacket.

'Anyway,' he turned to face her. 'What about you? Have you decided what you're doing? Staying or going back to Salzburg?'

'I'd rather keep talking about Toby right now.'

'I can't tell you anything because I don't know. Natalie please let's drop this.'

'Will you at least let *me* know what you're planning?'

'I think you ought to set your own house in order before you criticize mine.'

Stung she turned way, took mugs from the cupboard, opened the fridge looking for milk.

'I'm sorry. I shouldn't have said that.' He touched her shoulder. 'There *are* things we need to talk about, Lovie. Toby … well, he doesn't make things easy for your mum.'

Natalie was wrong-footed. 'What has he done?'

Her father looked at her for several seconds then he stared down at the shopping on the worktop. 'He talks about you all the time. When he brings something home from school you're the one he wants to show it to. He's forever asking when you're coming back so that he can stay over with you. Nothing we do is ever … oh, I don't know.'

She heard the toilet flush upstairs, guessed her mother would be down any minute. Needing time to digest her father's words she poured herself a cup of tea and took it into the sitting room. Now she was more confused than ever. She sent a text to Connor, suddenly anxious to feel his arms around her.

For years she'd imagined her parents were grateful for her and Adam taking Toby off their hands from time to time. But maybe we were just being selfish, she thought, and we've confused and unsettled him. A familiar ache settled in her heart so she concentrated on Auntie Maureen's revelations instead.

'I'm going to see if I can get on a flight tomorrow.' In the kitchen her parents were preparing lunch.

'I was hoping you'd stay longer.' Her mum put down the cauliflower she was separating into florets.

'Well, I think it's a good idea, Lovie.' Natalie caught her dad's eye then he turned away, adding milk to the cheese sauce.

'What about your job, your house?'

'I'll ring Glenda tomorrow. I'm not going back to the vets. I know it sounds ungrateful after all she tried to do for me but … I've got to do something new. I don't know what. Adam's selling the house so that's a bit irrelevant anyway.'

'Toby will be upset.'

'I know but … I sometimes think … I mean … it might confuse Toby, me being here.'

Her mother frowned but didn't look up, 'Confuse him?'

'Maybe that's not the right word. When I'm gone he'll have your undivided attention and vice versa.' She gabbled on. 'If things work out with Connor maybe you could all come to Salzburg in the summer. Stay at the hotel where Glenda and I were last year.'

'Another good idea,' her dad said. 'It would be nice to see

some mountains wouldn't it, Chris?'

'I suppose so.' Her mother had resumed cutting florets. 'It would have to get a lot warmer, though. I'm used to hot sunshine holidays.'

Natalie met Toby from school and she didn't get the tears she'd expected. Instead he seemed resigned to her going. 'Is Dad cross with me?' he asked as they approached the house.

'Nobody's cross with you. I talked to Dad and he's sorry you were upset, and they've said you might all come to Salzburg in the summer.'

'What about Italy?' His eyes were wide and she hoped he didn't see through her reassuring smile.

'They won't make you go if you don't want to.' She prayed it was true, especially as Toby's face relaxed into a smile.

When her suitcase was packed Natalie took Grandma's photos out of the plastic bag. Starting with the wedding one she prised up the little metal flaps that held the backing in place. She slid out the picture saw there was nothing behind it and replaced it in its frame.

She tried two more but nothing was hidden. When she removed the back from a picture of her and Toby a small square photo with wavy edges slid from behind it, onto the floor, face down. Her pulse quickening Natalie hesitated picking it up, suspecting she would be looking into the face of her real grandfather. But turning it over she sagged with disappointment. The image was feint and blurry. Instead of a face it seemed to be some rural scene, a barn with trees behind and a backdrop of grey clouds. On the slope up to the barn stood a tractor with a small boy at the wheel. The other frames yielded nothing. Pushing the blurry snap into her handbag she zipped up her case and carried it downstairs.

Toby handed her a drawing he'd done of her skiing. She seemed to be accompanied by Homer Simpson. When she asked for a hug he pressed himself against her till she thought her heart would break. He smelled of baked beans and clean hair. Her mother burst into tears, clinging on to Natalie's hand at the door while her dad took her case to the car.

'Please come and see me in Salzburg,' she said, her own chin unsteady. 'Come soon.'

On the way to the airport her dad was quiet. Natalie broke the tension. 'About Italy, you will talk to Tobes won't you?'

He nodded and cleared his throat. 'I took on board what you said, Lovie. Don't think I didn't.

'He's such a little star, Dad. For Heaven's sake enjoy him while he's young. Give him more of your time.' She paused and took a deep breath. 'You're so lucky to have him.'

He laid his hand over hers for a second then nodded again. 'Italy would give us more chance to be with him, don't you see? Your mum would give up work and…'

'And you'd be able to relax, maybe write a crime novel, look after that heart of yours.'

'Yes, that too.' He smiled at her then. 'When did you get to be so smart, Natalie? It doesn't seem five minutes since you were his age and I was telling you what to do.'

Outside Departures he kissed the top of her head and held her close for a moment. 'I hope this American knows how lucky he is.'

She called over her shoulder as she pushed open the door. 'If he doesn't I'll just have to tell him.'

Before she boarded the plane she tried to ring Connor but his phone was switched off. She sent another text giving him her flight details and wondered if he might meet her at the airport. Then she remembered he'd be doing his shift at the restaurant.

Touching down in Salzburg she felt the old pull of the city she'd experienced all those months ago with Glenda. The sun turned the mountain tops to glitter and the air was bitingly fresh. If she was going to stay she'd need to get a work permit or whatever was needed. Connor would help her with that. She was tempted to take a taxi to the restaurant but wanted to wash her hair and change her clothes so she waited for the bus, loving the sound of German chatter and thought about her newly discovered German roots.

As soon as the lift doors opened she heard the music: Connor's retro collection. She glanced at the ever present pushchair on the landing and wondered how much the noise was disturbing the neighbours. She turned her key in the lock and the first thing she saw was Rachel wearing just a tee-shirt and underwear. A stab of shock made her gasp but then she saw Robbie on the sofa, lying back taking a long drag on a cigarette. Connor hated anyone smoking in the apartment. He'd be furious when he got home.

'Hi Sweetie,' Rachel said, and gave Natalie a sweaty hug. Robbie raised a hand.

Natalie saw now they were both stoned. She was too angry to speak as she took her bag through to the bedroom. The duvet was crumpled on the floor, Rachel's jeans and Robbie's jumper on the bed.

'You two not working today, then?'

'We took a day off.' Rachel flopped down next to Robbie on the sofa and took the joint from his mouth.

Natalie went into the bathroom. She was desperate for a shower but there was a row of Rachel's bras and pants drying over the shower rail.

'Connor get hold of you yesterday?'

'No. Is he OK?'

'Oh. He'll be real sorry he missed you, then.'

'Missed me?'

It was then she saw it wasn't Connor's cologne on the glass shelf. His battery toothbrush was gone. Panic swirled in her chest. She opened the door. 'Is he at the restaurant?'

Rachel squinted through the smoke. 'Hey, keep up, Sweetie,' she broke into laughter. 'His mom sent a ticket. He left for home yesterday.'

Chapter Twenty-Eight

'It isn't a deep cut and doesn't need stitches but I'd like to bind it up.' The vet let go of Max's paw and reached a box down from a shelf. 'I'll give him a long lasting antibiotic and a painkiller.'

Cursing whoever smashed a bottle on the footpath, Leo lifted the dog into the back of the car. 'No walks for a few days, Boy.'

At home Max sniffed at the bandage and refused to put his foot to the floor until tempted with a biscuit. Leo changed into his running gear and tried not to look at Max's reproachful face as he left the house.

He had bought a stopwatch and began timing the circuit he ran each day. Steadily the time grew shorter. He paused in Elsbethen for a long draught of water thinking it would only add a few seconds. Setting off again he sidestepped a dog walker and took the path behind Hotel Friesen. As he approached the gate leading into the hotel garden he saw a mop of dark hair. Someone was leaning against the railings but clearly not taking in the view of the mountain.

As he drew level he saw Otto at her feet. Leo stopped; the woman was crying. When she looked up he felt a jolt somewhere in his stomach. The jolt became a ripple of excitement but he could only stare.

She leaped away from the gate.

'Sorry if I made you jump,' he said. But she can't have understood because she simply gave him a greeting. When he felt he couldn't stare into her face any longer he dropped a dog biscuit through the gate for Otto and moved on. He kept his pace steady until he was past the cemetery; stopped on the bridge that crossed the stream.

It was her, he was sure of it; the girl who, all those months ago, had understood his urge to escape her friend's questions in the Mozarteum. And then he'd seen her again in the hotel a few nights later. He slipped his earphones out so that they hung around his neck; Mozart's serenade for winds became a tinny echo until he turned it off.

She'd looked terrible; distraught. Her wide grey eyes were red, the skin around them swollen. He wondered where her friend was. Maybe she was travelling alone this time. Leo's mind set off along a tangent. Maybe they had quarrelled and were no longer friends. Maybe she was gay. Would it matter to him if she was?

He watched low cloud creep down the mountain, swallowing the clearing where smoke curled from a farmhouse chimney. He found it did matter.

Jogging to a trot his pace advanced to a run. His arms pumped; he blew out his breath in sharp bursts. At home he checked his watch. Even with the two stops he noted his time was faster than the day before.

Max hadn't nibbled the bandage so Leo gave him a biscuit and let him out into the garden. When the weather improved he was going to dig his dog a sandpit in the hope he'd stop excavating the flower borders. Wind blew the branches of the apple tree; next door Gerde's blankets flapped on the washing line. Leo had the sudden sensation of being part of the world again – not just working towards it, not making the best of things, but feeling it. He went back into the house, picked up his phone and dialled the hotel's number.

Chapter Twenty-Nine

Natalie stumbled out of the flat caught the wheels of her suitcase on a chair leg and knocked it over. She didn't wait for the lift. As she struggled down the stairs Rachel's voice followed her. 'Come back, we'll sleep on the couch tonight.'

Patches of snow remained on the grass beside the river but roads and pavements were dry. On Makartsteg bridge she was overwhelmed with panic and stopped to lean against the rail. Hundreds of engraved padlocks clung to the wire mesh bearing lovers' names. Connor had talked about buying one but now …

Gulping cold air she wept until a woman put a hand on her shoulder.

'Sind Sie okay?'

Natalie nodded, wiped her face on the back of her hand and moved on. She arrived at the bus stop her face stinging, searched for the euro coins she'd inadvertently mixed up with English money.

She concentrated her thoughts on the times she was in Salzburg with Glenda, the lovely evening of the dinner concert, lunchtimes they'd eaten under the horse chestnut trees at the hotel. Anything to push away the terrible reality that Connor had run out on her.

Getting off at Valkenauerstrasse she tried to calm herself but shock made her teeth chatter and her heart knocked against her ribs. From the corner of the road she saw the hotel was busy, cars parked outside and along the lane. Dreading a crowd she almost turned back but where could she go other than the airport?

Reception was empty but voices came from the bar. Leaving her case to one side she found Karin talking to guests. When she saw Natalie her face broke into a grin.

'Hey, look who's here.'

But then her smile faltered as Natalie couldn't hold back tears. The guests melted away.

Karin sat beside her in reception but Natalie couldn't speak. She sobbed into her hands aware Karin's brother had appeared and quickly disappeared, returning with a small glass of Schnapps. It seared Natalie's throat but the warmth, as it seeped down, helped her breathe slower and she managed a smile of thanks.

'I'm sorry about … this … I didn't know where to …'

'Let's go to the garden. Less busy.'

'So you were living in Salzburg this winter?' Karin didn't seem to feel the cold wind that made Natalie huddle into her scarf.

'Only for a few weeks. I wasn't sure what was going to happen. Then my grandmother …' she turned away for a second, blew her nose. 'My whole life seems to be … I mean … wherever I look there's a problem. I thought Connor and I were … well, obviously I was wrong about that.'

'You want a room? You can rest then we could talk again?'

'I can't afford it. I'd love to stay but …'

'I think you can stay with my aunt. I'll go in and see her. You stay here with Otto?'

In the far corner of the garden was a large traditional chalet house, Karin tapped on the back door and went in. The Dachshund barked a couple of times then waddled to the gate that led to the footpath. Natalie followed him, wound her fingers into the wrought iron rail and watched a woman pushing a pram, a little dog on a leash beside her. That should have been me, she thought. More tears came; sadness mingled with gratitude for Karin's kindness. With luck she could spend another night in Salzburg before facing the flight home; her parent's astonishment, and Toby. She'd left hoping her parents would bond with him more but her reappearance might now hinder that. She closed her eyes; let her forehead sink down onto her hands.

When Otto began to whine and shuffle Natalie looked up then leapt back, startled. On the path a jogger had stopped to stare at her. She stared back. He was tall and blond. He muttered something that she took to be an apology for making her jump. Natalie swept her hair from her face, knowing she looked a wreck. She met his eye and felt at ease even though he made no attempt to move on. There was kindness in his face. He looked familiar. Had she seen him last year? She cleared her throat and gave the local greeting, 'Grüß Gott.'

He nodded, returned the greeting then he looked down at Otto, fished a small dog biscuit from his tracksuit pocket and flicked it through the bars of the gate. Then he moved away, picking up his jogging pace.

Natalie watched him until he reached the cemetery and then he was lost from sight.

Fifteen minutes later she was sitting on the bed in a pretty room overlooking the fields and the mountain beyond. Karin's elderly Aunt Lexi had shaken her hand and insisted on carrying her case up two flights of stairs. The scent of wood smoke hung in the air and the house was warm; the furniture heavy, solid wood; the double bed covered with a white quilt. In the bathroom Natalie looked in the mirror. Her face was blotched red and her hair tangled. No wonder the jogger had stared but then maybe they had met before. She couldn't remember where.

She ran a bath. Peeling off her clothes exhaustion took hold and she sank into the water, grateful for its comforting warmth. Afterwards she lay on the bed watching the afternoon light fading to dusk. She forced herself to concentrate on the sound of the strengthening wind moving in the trees, the creak of old wood, and the cool, starched pillow against her cheek.

Chapter Thirty

If Karin noticed Leo was more smartly dressed than usual she didn't pass comment.

In the bar was a group of men attending a seminar. From their conversation he gathered they were opticians. He perched on a stool beside the group and ordered a beer. There was no sign of the English girl. When Karin had a spare moment he told her about Max's foot.

'So I went running alone,' he said, 'and on the way back I saw one of your guests crying near the gate.' He adopted what he hoped was a concerned but not overly-so expression. Then before Karin could reply, 'Actually I think I've met her before, at the Mozarteum. Was she here last year, with a friend?'

'Yes. Her friend was a little crazy, but Natalie is nice. She's at Aunt Lexi's.'

Natalie. Leo turned the name over in his mind. Karin was called into reception and it was a frustrating fifteen minutes before she walked back into the bar, this time with Otto.

'So are they both staying here again, the English girls?'

Karin raised her eyebrows. Leo rushed on. 'That friend was really quite rude to me when we met last year.'

'She's not here this time. Natalie has been living in the city for a few weeks.'

She cupped her hand around her mouth and whispered; a gesture he remembered from their childhood. 'She was with a guy but he's run out on her, gone back to the States. I think she'll return to England now.'

'Poor girl,' Leo said, his emotions in a muddle. Why was he even here? This girl was of no consequence to him and it sounded as though her life was very complicated. But his stomach had done summersaults when he saw her at the gate. He wanted to talk to her, just once, thank her for her kindness last year. Of course the odds were she wouldn't remember him and he'd look an idiot. It was a second or two before he saw the mischievous look on Karin's face.

'I need to ask her if she's eating tonight,' she said, and walked back to reception. Otto sat at his feet, staring up at him, his expression saying, *biscuit.*

'She's coming soon,' Karin said, shall I get you another beer?'

Leo said no to the beer but ordered a bottle of mineral water. He adjusted the position of his stool so that he could watch the door to the garden. The opticians were getting ready to go into dinner. Pretty soon he'd be there alone with only Otto for company. He was pleased when another group from the seminar came in and ordered drinks. He could see from their hair they'd been in the swimming pool.

Minutes passed, the door to the garden showed nothing but the reflection of people in the bar. Leo heard his heartbeat in his ear. He took a swig of water and over the heads of the seminar delegates he saw Karin en route to the kitchen. Briefly her head inclined towards a table by the window. The pulse in Leo's ear quickened as he turned and saw her.

Her hair was curly, reaching her shoulders and fastened with some kind of slide. There was a glass of beer on the table and he watched as she raised it to her lips. No make-up. Her eyes closed as she drank. For Leo the world slipped into slow motion, he saw the fingers of her right hand curled around the glass, her neat little nails. The movement of her throat as she swallowed made him want to caress the pale skin. It seemed an eternity before the glass was lowered and her tongue slid to catch the foam on her lip. Her eyes opened. For Leo they opened slowly, the lashes, dark as her hair, parted and as they parted she met his gaze. He knew in that instant that everything had changed.

Sofia had stepped into the shadows.

Chapter Thirty-One

When she woke, disorientated, the room was dark and she heard gentle tapping on the door. Pulling on her jeans and tee-shirt she rushed to open it.

Aunt Lexi smiled. 'Karin has telephoned and asked if you'd like to have dinner. You can eat in the bar if you can't face the restaurant. Or you could always bring something back here.'

'You're all being so kind.' She felt a waver in her voice. 'I could walk up and take a look at the menu.' Suddenly she wanted the bustle of the hotel, something to distract her. She'd left a message on Connor's phone. Just one. She wasn't going to humiliate herself with multiple pleas for him to get in touch.

She changed into her smart leggings and a long jumper, knowing she'd have to go back to Connor's apartment for the rest of her clothes. Turning on her phone she steeled herself to look at her messages. Nothing from Connor but a short text from Toby: *Markus said I'm his best friend. Shall I say he's mine too?*

'Bless his sweet little heart,' she said aloud, and texted back, *Yes, tell him he's the best friend you've ever had.*

It was raining so she put on knee-length boots. Her hair was in tight curls but now that it was longer she was able to clip it back. There wasn't much she could do about her sore eyes but at least the blotchiness had left her skin.

She wasn't sure of her footing in the garden so she went out into the lane which led to the hotel entrance. A tiny ripple of the old Salzburg magic ran through her as she approached the door, the aroma of food, the chatter of German voices. The language her grandfather spoke?

'I think you were asleep?' Karin gave her a grin. 'You want

to eat?'

'I'm starving, but I want to say thank you for finding me a room. It's so …'

'It's no problem. Come through, I bring a menu.'

Otto was in the bar sniffing under stools. A group of men were talking and Natalie felt a little shy sitting down at one of the tables. Karin appeared with the menu. 'You need help with translation?'

'Definitely.'

She was talked through the dishes which all sounded delicious. If she were going to get a flight tomorrow she thought she deserved something nice. She ordered baked chicken and a large glass of Stieglbier.

Karin disappeared into the kitchen. Otto came to sit by her feet and she stroked his ears. When her beer arrived she took a long sip, feeling the bite at the back of her throat. When she lowered her glass she found herself staring into the face of a man at the bar. He gave her a quick smile then looked away. For a second or two she studied him and realised he was the jogger she'd seen earlier; the man with the kind eyes. His hair was now swept back and he wore the traditional collar-less jacket. He joked with Karin as she walked by. He was local, then, lucky man.

Listening to the hubbub of conversation she tried to pick out words, but the Salzburg dialect was hard to follow. She went to the loo, looked again at her phone but still nothing from Connor. Anger rose in her chest. Why hadn't he called to explain? She wanted shout at him, demand answers. It was like a bizarre nightmare she hoped to wake from, except that here in the hotel she felt soothed.

Returning to her table she saw the jogger hovering by her chair. The day was getting weirder by the minute but the beer had lifted her mood a fraction.

'Forgive me for disturbing you,' he said. 'Karin told me you were dining alone.'

'Yes … but …'

'I have a table booked. You are welcome to join me.'

'Oh. That's kind of you but I'm … I'm fine here thanks.'

'Of course. I'm sorry.'

He seemed about to move away when Karin brought her a small hors d'oeuvre.

'This is a present from the kitchen,' she said, but she didn't put it down on the table. 'Leo and I have been friends since school.' She stood beside the jogger. 'Since we were this high.'

She stooped to hold her hand a ludicrous few inches from the floor. 'Leo is a little older. I was like his sister's age. We used to play tricks on him.'

Leo rolled his eyes and smiled. Natalie had to smile too.

'You are eating with him?' Karin was already on the move with the hors d'oeuvre. Leo looked apologetic but Natalie picked up her beer and followed them out of the bar.

The dining room was busy but Karin showed them to a table near the window. Through the thick, woven curtains Natalie could hear the wind buffeting rain against the glass. As soon as they were seated the jogger reached his hand across the table.

'Leo Meier,' he said, 'pleased to meet you.'

'Natalie Grey.' His hand was soft and warm. 'I'm sorry if Karin asked you to sit with me. I'm fine really.' She thought that sounded a little rude and added, 'but it's nice to meet you too.'

He seemed to struggle for something to say. This was going to be a long night. How weird that this morning she'd woken in her mother's house, bade a tearful farewell to Toby all in anticipation of a romantic reunion. Now here she was trying to keep Connor's face out of her thoughts and having dinner with a total stranger who was staring at the table cloth.

'So you live in Salzburg?'

'Yes. I live here in Aigen,' he inclined his head towards the window. 'Beyond the church. And you are from England?'

'Yes. I live right in the centre of the country, as far from the sea as you can get.' Now she was gabbling. She took another sip of her beer.

'But you've been in Salzburg for a while?'

How much had Karin told him? 'Not that long really. I went home … my grandmother died and …'

'So you're sad and maybe want to talk of other things?'

Before she could answer a waiter returned placing an hors d'oeuvre in front of Leo. They ate in silence until the slivers of smoked salmon were gone.

'Natalie,' he gave her a hesitant smile, 'this isn't the first time we have met.'

He raised his fingertips to his forehead, swept his hand through his hair and in that moment, before he spoke again, she knew.

'We met at the Mozarteum,' he said.

Natalie gaped at him, trying to superimpose the hollow cheeks, the rough stubble, the aura of pain onto this shy but cheerful man.

'Your friend asked me questions. I fear I was not too helpful.' He looked down again, the fingers of both hands around the base of his glass. 'I should apologise for my rudeness.'

'No. I mean … we didn't ... Glenda thought you worked there and …'

He smiled again. 'So you remember?'

'I remember that day yes, but …'

'You don't recognise me.'

Natalie felt heat creeping up from her neck, infusing her cheeks. 'Well, no. I …'

'I was not at my best back then.'

She wanted to say she'd seen him again on the bus; that on

their last evening, after the concert, he'd been in the hotel with his family. He'd looked happy that night and she remembered thinking if he'd been so ill and could laugh then maybe she could survive the hurt Adam had inflicted. Now she stayed silent and let her gaze flick to his left hand, to the mark where a ring used to be.

Their main course arrived and Leo asked if she'd like to share some wine. Why not, she thought. There was more silence as the bottle arrived and the waiter poured them each a glass of deep red Zweigelt. Natalie took a sip, feeling the smoothness on her tongue; then took another. How could this be the same man? She looked at the healthy shine on his hair, his lovely smile. There was the faint hint of expensive cologne and he had the glow of someone who exercised regularly. Most surprising of all she found he was helping her to relax.

'I found out, after my grandmother died …' she spoke between mouthfuls of chicken and salad, 'I might be part German. Actually it's almost certain I am.' She told him about Grandma's affair. He didn't look bored, in fact he seemed relieved just to listen, this man who had entered her thoughts many times during the winter. Had he been seriously ill and recovered? He was smiling as she described opening up Grandma's photo frames and finding the faded picture of the barn, the boy on the tractor.

'You don't know his full name?'

'No, nor where he came from. I just know he was a prisoner of war in Leicestershire.'

Natalie had cleared her plate. Talking and eating were good distractions from wondering if Connor would call.

'There must be records of those prisoners,' Leo said. 'The authority in that city might be a good place to start if you want to find him … or his family.'

Find him. What a project that would be. Her mother would

kill her.

'I do speak a little German.' Natalie was enjoying the wine. She dabbed at her face with her napkin in case she had red streaks at the corners of her mouth. 'I went to lessons until I came out here but …' she wasn't sure how to finish the sentence. She'd abandoned the class and her new found friends, had all but abandoned her job and Glenda who'd shown her nothing but kindness. Now she'd torn herself away from Toby and it had all been for nothing. Oh God, what a mess.

'The best way to learn a language is to live among the people who speak it,' Leo said.

'You're right,' Natalie swallowed the lump in her throat that heralded tears. 'I learned a lot of vocabulary when I was … living here with a friend.'

'You are at a crossroads?'

Leo poured a little more wine into her glass. For a ludicrous second she thought he wanted her to translate the sentence. She felt a tiny bit drunk but still took a sip before replying.

'Yes. That's where I am, a crossroads.' She met his gaze and saw sympathy. What was his story? Was he divorced too? Is that why he looked so ghastly last year?

'With a number of possible roads to take you should try to be excited. If you choose a wrong one you can retrace your steps, try another.'

'Trouble is I think I've been down them all and found they were dead ends. Oh, I'm sorry that sounded a bit dramatic.' She laughed, finished her wine, noting that the carafe was empty but not daring to ask for more.

'There is not just one crossroad in our life,' Leo said. 'They appear all the time. One of the most important ones is what to choose for dessert.'

His expression was serious but then she saw a tiny twitch of his lips and she laughed again, suddenly not needing more wine, not needing to anaesthetise away the pain Connor had caused. She would deal with it. She had dealt with worse.

Leo recommended the filled pancakes. While Natalie watched ice cream melt and mingle with the apricot sauce she listened as Leo told her about his work.

Looking at his long, slim fingers she could imagine him playing the piano. He must be a very patient teacher she thought; after all he'd listened to her ramblings.

As they drank coffee she felt a depressing sense of the evening coming to an end, of having to face ringing the airport, flying back to try and pick up the frayed threads of her life again.

When it was time to pay Leo placed a credit card on top of the bill. Natalie moved it to see the amount and reached for her purse. Leo put his hand over hers. The gesture was gentle and somehow comforting.

'Please let me pay,' he said. 'It has been so nice to meet you.'

'No. I can't let you do that.' Her voice sounded harsher than she'd intended and she turned away, unzipping her purse only to find she had no euro notes at all. Amid the confusion of the day she'd forgotten to draw some out. Instead she dropped her card on top of Leo's. 'I'll ask them to take half from mine.'

Looking up she saw he was embarrassed, his lower lip caught between his teeth.

'I would much rather … after all it was I who asked you to join me.'

Natalie wondered if she'd made some huge cultural gaffe. Was it still tradition for a man to pay here? She and Connor had always split the bill. What was she thinking? This wasn't a date. 'Let me at least pay for the wine then,' she said, her cheeks burning.

The easiness of their earlier conversation was gone and she was pleased when the waiter returned with the receipts. Leo stepped aside for her to walk out of the dining room ahead of him. It was a relief to see Otto sprawled on the carpet in reception. Leo stooped to tickle the dog behind the ears and Natalie felt a memory nudge her. 'You have a dog, don't you?'

'I do. How did you know?'

She thought of the sack of puppy food on his knee, his thin frame seeming to sag under the weight of it when he got off the bus.

'You had dog biscuits in your pocket when you were jogging.'

'Ah yes.' He seemed a little awkward then; fishing his umbrella from the stand by the door and returning to her side. 'Are you walking back to Lexi' house? We could walk along the road together.'

'Oh, that's kind but I … I need to speak to Karin and …' she gestured to the desk where a guest was checking in.

'Of course. Well, it was a pleasant evening, thank you. I hope you find the path you want to take, Natalie.' He turned and strode out of the door, a blast of cold air replacing the warmth of his handshake.

Chapter Thirty-Two

'Scheiß! Scheiß!' Leo strode along the lane. When he reached the footpath he continued across a track between the fields. It was only when he reached the other end he realised rain was running down his neck, his umbrella still furled in his right hand.

Under the shelter of a tree he put it up but still didn't head for home. He turned towards Elsbethen.

How did that go so wrong? She seemed to be fine up until … 'I scared her off,' he said, aloud.

I shouldn't have offered to pay. She's young. Women are more independent these days. But we got off to such a good start and she was … what was she? Sweet, that's what she was. None of the falseness of Julia Weber; not even any make up but her legs looked gorgeous in those boots. Okay, I could only see the bit where her long jumper finished and the boots began but still. And she was taller than I'd imagined.

His thoughts continued to tumble as he splashed through puddles, taking a lane that would lead him to the main road. What were you expecting from this escapade anyway? She'll probably be on a plane tomorrow; you'll never see her again. What impression has she taken away?

He reached the junction, walked past the school where Sofia had taught. He wondered what she would make of his evening. Her voice in his head '*You were just being you, Leo, no more, no less.*' Yes, he would always offer to pay. If she had a problem with that then … except maybe she'd thought he wanted something in return and … Oh God, I offered to walk her home. No wonder she said, no.

The rain was easing off, the wind lessening. He could see the distant beacon on top of the fortress, the summit of the

Untersberg emerging into moonlight. Should I go back, explain to Karin or … no. Just go home Leo. He took a longer route avoiding passing the hotel. Somewhere in the kitchen there was a bottle of Schnapps he'd bought in Vienna. He quickened his pace, thought about Max waiting at home; hoped he hadn't chewed the bandage off his foot. Maybe he'd just have hot chocolate and watch a film. You're forty, Leo. He chided himself. You're too old for bright young women.

Chapter Thirty-Three

Natalie lingered in reception. She ordered a coffee, found a magazine in English and sat on one of the sofas just as she and Glenda had done. Karin was busy, checking in more seminar delegates, answering questions about free wi-fi, but each time there was a lull Natalie explained a little more about Connor. She even told her about the accident, her mother's anger, the aborted interview for promotion.

Karin was a good listener and when it came time for her to walk Otto she asked if Natalie wanted to go along.

The rain had stopped. Otto made slow progress along the lane, sniffing at car wheels, gate posts, lifting his leg a dozen times.

'Did you enjoy dinner with Leo?' Karin waited for her dog to catch them up.

'Yes, he was … very kind.' Natalie felt awkward, remembering the man's embarrassment. 'I did see him last year and …'

'Yes, he told me you met him at the Mozart institute.'

'Glenda mistook him for a member of staff, poor man. But also … I think I saw him in the hotel last year too. Does he have a little boy?'

Karin looked away for a second, called to Otto before she answered. 'No, why would you think that?'

'He was in the restaurant with a child.'

'No. He has no … small boy.'

The air was cold and the freshness made Natalie feel dizzy for a second. 'Oh, it must have been someone else's then.' She breathed out, felt her shoulders sag. 'I'll go online when I get back, check flights.'

'You want me to do that for you? We can go back to

Reception after walking.'

'No, thank you. You've helped me so much already. I have my laptop.'

At a bridge over a gushing stream they turned back. Karin stopped and looked at her. 'It must have been Florian in the hotel with Leo, last year. I should have remembered. He comes sometimes from Vienna. He is the son of Leo's sister.'

'Oh. I see.'

Karin dropped her voice. 'I shouldn't say this but last year Leo was sad for a long time.'

'He did look … different last year, certainly not how he was this evening.'

'His wife died, last spring. She was my age but always sick. Her heart was never strong.'

Natalie stopped walking. She wasn't expecting that. All these months she'd been convinced he was ill. She stared at the ground for a moment. 'How horrible for him.'

Now she felt even worse for having embarrassed him. He was probably lonely and she'd hurt his feelings.

'For a long time he didn't look after himself, not eating, sometimes not washing his clothes. His sister bought him a puppy so he had to come out of the house.'

And it all falls into place, Natalie thought. Funny how you can take a look into a stranger's life and jump to the wrong conclusions.

'Have you told your family you're coming home?' Karin walked with her to Aunt Lexi's gate.

'No. They're going to be very surprised when I turn up tomorrow.'

'So maybe you stay a little longer. Sounds like you should relax.'

Natalie imagined a couple of days in the cosy room at the top of the house, walks in the hotel garden, maybe a trip into the old town just to drink coffee and eat cake.

'Would your aunt mind, do you think?'

Karin gave the dismissive shrug Natalie remembered from the previous year.

'Maybe just a day or two, then.'

She climbed the stairs to her room. The house was silent but Lexi had left lights on so she didn't stumble. A note on the bed invited her to make herself a drink in the kitchen across the landing. Puzzled Natalie pushed open a door opposite her room and found a lounge, a sofa with heavy wooden arms and windows that looked out over the garden. The next room along was a tiny kitchen, its décor rooted in the seventies, but she found milk in the fridge, a jar of cocoa next to a kettle and a plate of homemade biscuits. The top floor must once have been a self-contained apartment. What I'd give to live here she thought, carrying her mug of cocoa back to the bedroom. She picked up her phone. No new messages.

Sitting on the bed and powering up her laptop she found there was a hot water bottle under the duvet. It made her think of nights spent at her Gran's when she was little. Sentimental tears welled. Gran was someone worth crying over, she thought, fishing a tissue from her pocket and blowing her nose. Why cry over a feckless man who's too scared to tell the truth. Two feckless men if she included Adam, although she felt her days of shedding tears for him were over.

There were no seats available on flights for the next couple of days. It's a sign, she thought, I'm meant to stay a little longer. Then it struck her, there was nobody she needed to call, text or email. Nobody at home, not Connor nor his friends knew where she was. It should have felt frightening but it was exhilarating instead.

She brushed her teeth and got into bed, hugging the hot water bottle and listening to the night sounds of the unfamiliar house, wood settling, wind finding a casement that didn't fit snugly. But sleep wouldn't come. With no distractions thoughts of Connor wouldn't go away. She couldn't fathom why he'd been so cruel; and what about Toby? Could she stay away from him once she was home? She had to try if it meant her parents wouldn't feel pushed out. She tried to tuck her worries into compartments, tell her overactive brain that it wasn't the time for solving problems. Then she thought about Leo and their evening together. He was kind and interesting to talk to and she was pleased, after last year, to know he was alright. But he's carrying more baggage than I am, she thought as her eyelids finally began to feel heavy. No matter how lonely he might be she wasn't in a rush to meet him again.

Chapter Thirty-Four

From her room at Aunt Lexi's Natalie saw the clouds had retreated from the mountain; the rounded summit now visible. She began to understand the local people's love of their mountains. They were like faithful friends. She had been to Connor's apartment to collect her clothes, grateful nobody was there. She left her key on the hook in his tiny kitchen and closed the apartment door without a second glance.

I always seem to be leaving somewhere, she thought as she made herself a cup of tea and carried it to the bedroom. She was just folding her jumpers into a drawer when Aunt Lexi called up the stairs.

'Could you ring Karin? She wants to ask you something.'

Natalie thought how perfect it would be if Karin wanted to offer her a job. But then her phone rang and she saw her father's number on the screen.

'Hello Lovie, how are things?'

'It's great here, Dad. Looks like spring's on the way.'

'And what about you? Everything alright with whatsisname?'

'His name's Connor,' she said, stalling for time. 'Can you just hang on a sec?'

Dad was the one person she could tell about Connor's departure and know he'd say all the right things but suddenly she couldn't say it. She took deep breaths, stared at the mountain for a second. 'Sorry about that. Yes, everything's fine.' A whopping lie. It was a good job they weren't face to face or he'd have seen right through it.

'Well that's good because we've been thinking about what you said when you left the other day.'

'Have you changed your minds about Italy?' She imagined

Toby's relieved little face.

'No. Well, the jury's still out on that, Natalie. It's what you said about us coming out to see you.'

'Oh. Yes. I …' She took a sip of tea, scalded her lip. 'When are you thinking of coming?'

'During the Easter holidays, maybe for a week. What do you think?'

'Won't it still be a bit cold for Mum then?' She stifled a nervous laugh.

'She'll just have to put a cardi on.'

'How's Toby, Dad?'

'Alright. I've signed him up for some cycling proficiency classes.'

'But he doesn't have a bike.'

'Well, we're going to see about that. An early birthday present maybe. And what do you reckon to this idea, Lovie? I'm thinking of having him home for his lunches. That German friend of his goes home so it's not like I'd be splitting them up at dinnertime.'

'That would be brilliant, but don't go giving him chips every day.'

'I'm not allowed chips myself so I'm sure as hell not making them for him. Anyway, I'll need details of that hotel you stayed at last year. Is it very far from where you are?'

Natalie screwed up her face. 'Not that far.'

'Okay, well you text me the email address and we'll get it sorted.'

'Dad. I've given Glenda my notice; I'm going to find something here.'

There was a beat of silence and then he cleared his throat. 'I think you're doing the right thing. I'm proud of you, Natalie. To pick yourself up like this after what's happened. More so now Adam's having a kiddie with … her. There's only one thing worrying me.'

She bit her lip, felt her chin wobble. 'What's that?'

'That you'll disappear off to America with this Connor and we'll never see you.'

'There's no chance of that, Dad.'

As she rang off a few minutes later she heard Karin coming up the stairs. 'Hallo, Natalie.'

'Hi, sorry I was on the phone and …'

'Do you want to come up the mountain with my brother and me? Lukas wants to hang-glide before he has to work.'

'I couldn't do that, I'd be terrified.'

'No. He hang-glides, we drive down. Are you coming? We'll wait for you outside the hotel. Five minutes?'

There was no time to dwell on lying to her dad, no time to think about anything. She pulled on her walking shoes, grabbed her warmest jacket, took another sip of tea then abandoned the mug on the work surface.

Lukas heaved the hang-glider into the back of the hotel van. Karin bundled Otto onto the front seat. 'He can sit on our knees,' she said.

Natalie was happy to be swept along. It was easier than sitting in her room wondering what on earth she was going to do about her family's visit. Squashed into the passenger seat with the safety belt around both of them was less uncomfortable than she imagined. Lukas steered the van out of the village onto the main road and headed for Elsbethen then swung up a steep, narrow road which plunged into a forest. Soon they emerged into pretty meadows where picturesque farmsteads and houses dotted the hillsides. Turning off onto an even narrower lane they climbed higher, once again driving between banks of tall fir trees so dense no light seemed to penetrate to the ground. Then they broke free of the woods and Natalie couldn't help a loud gasp when she saw how high they were.

There were mountain peaks as far as she could see; the wide valley below them; the mighty Salzburg fortress reduced to an insignificant toy.

Once out of the car she saw others had the same idea. Groups of men and girls her age were chatting, unfolding paragliders, some, like Lukas, pulling covers from fibreglass and components that would make up their hang-gliders.

'What do I do?' She asked. 'Can I help?'

'No, Lukas does it all. You haven't been up here before?'

Natalie shook her head. 'I didn't even know you could drive up here.'

They walked to the edge of the mountain where the ground sloped gently, the tops of trees way below them now.

'This is a great place to watch the sunset,' Karin said.

Natalie felt the sun had gone down on too much of her life lately. 'What about the sunrise?' she asked, 'is that good too?'

'Never been up here that early.' Karin pointed down into the valley. 'See, the hotel is there.'

Despite her friend's best efforts to show her landmarks the only one she recognised was the little church. *I live beyond the church,* Leo had said and she looked at the clusters of houses tucked up against the foot of the mountain and thought that despite his loss and sorrow, it must be wonderful to live there. Across the valley the higher mountains were silhouetted by the afternoon sun. They haven't changed for thousands of years, she thought and something about their permanence raised her mood.

Karin introduced her to some of the paragliders and friends who had been walking on the mountain. Natalie found her confidence and tried out her German. They seemed to understand most of what she said and were friendly, shaking her hand and encouraging her to try a tandem paraglide descent, laughing at her exclamations of horror.

Congregating at the point where the hang-gliders left the mountain Natalie felt a thrill of admiration as Lukas, his glider now assembled, was putting on the flying suit he would wear for the ride. A paraglider nearby, his parachute and strings spread out on the ground behind him, began to run down the slope; the breeze caught the fabric, billowing it into shape. Stripes and multi-coloured patterns glistened in the sun. Then his legs were running in air and he lifted, sailed away from the mountain and rose until his body was indistinct against the sky. Natalie whooped with excitement along with others who had come to watch.

When it was Lukas's turn Natalie felt a twist of anxiety in her stomach but Karin seemed unconcerned, holding on to Otto's collar to stop him following down the slope. As Lukas left the edge he swung his legs up behind him into what looked to Natalie like a sleeping bag attached to the underside of the glider and as he too rose in the warm air, he looked like a bright, giant insect.

'Now we drive down,' Karin said, 'but he will take some time so we can have a drink.'

Natalie hadn't noticed the wooden cafe behind the trees. Crowds of flyers and friends were drinking at tables, enjoying the sunshine. Karin pushed open the door and went in, ordered mugs of hot chocolate for them both and wouldn't let Natalie pay.

Later, in the fields behind the hotel, as Lukas glided to a perfect landing, Natalie felt her real life settle around her shoulders like a damp coat. She had five weeks to find a job, somewhere to live and admit to her family that another of her relationships had gone sour.

Chapter Thirty-Five

'She's staying?' Leo ignored Karin's raised eyebrows and the mischievous twist to her mouth. But he couldn't ignore the surge of pleasure that rose straight to his face in a blush. He turned to watch Max rolling on the grass with Otto, his blue bandage waving in the air.

'She likes it here and she's free to do whatever she wants now.'

'But what will she do? I know she can speak a little German but … and is she still with Tante Lexi?'

'For now. She's trying for some jobs. She doesn't mind what she does. Too bad *we* have nothing for her here.'

Leo wanted to ask more questions but Karin's eager expression told him she longed to hear what he had to say, might even repeat it. 'Wish her all the best from me. I hope she finds something soon.' He called Max over and clipped on his lead, muttered about having a pupil and said goodbye.

'Laters!' Karin called after him.

'What?' He turned back and she was grinning.

'It's something English people say.'

All through Alex Buhringer's piano lesson Leo's mind wandered. What was he to do now he knew Natalie was staying in Salzburg? He mustn't rush to the hotel in the hope of seeing her. What would he say? They'd parted on an embarrassing note and besides, in less than a week he was going to Vienna to stay with Marina. He might have postponed the trip but Andreas was joining them. For the first time his son would meet his aunt and young cousin. It would be an emotional few days. For months sorrow had consumed him but now he was assailed by a variety of feelings, the most surprising of which was attraction to Natalie. It was a moment or two before he realised the piano was silent and his pupil was waiting for further instructions.

Chapter Thirty-Six

'This one looks interesting.' Karin drew a red line under an advertisement in the newspaper. 'It's for a shop assistant and knowledge of English is an advantage.'

'What are the hours?'

'Just says part-time. You want me to call him?'

'Where is it? Maybe I could call in today.'

'It's in the old town.' Karin wrote down the address. Much as Natalie wanted to crawl upstairs to her cosy room and sleep she knew if there were a chance of another job she should go for it.

After three days working mornings as a chambermaid at a hotel in the city her back ached and her hands were sore, but she was teamed up with a lovely Indian girl called Binita who spoke excellent English and was very patient when Natalie put duvet covers on inside out and forgot to empty waste bins.

'I'll go and get changed then.' She folded the piece of paper and thanked Karin and in return received the now familiar shrug that meant, *no problem*.

On the bus into town Natalie thought about Toby. Everything she was doing reinforced her distance from him, made seeing him more difficult. But hadn't her dad hinted that distance was needed?

She took deep breaths as she crossed Mozartsteg bridge and concentrated on phrases of German she knew well.

The shop was in a quiet part of the old town, below the fortress. Peeping in the window she saw it sold a variety of tourist gifts such as china, jewellery and paintings. A man around her dad's age was behind the counter. A couple of tourists were browsing. Natalie waited till the women left then went inside.

'Good morning,' the man said.

How come Austrians could always sense you were English? She returned the greeting. 'I've come to enquire about the job you have advertised.'

'I see. And do you also speak German?' He smiled and she felt a little less nervous.

'I'm not yet fluent but I speak it quite well.' Wild exaggeration, she knew.

He told her his name was Karl and they shook hands.

'Have you worked in a shop before?'

She decided to stretch the truth. 'In England; a long time ago.' Saturday girl in a florist didn't really qualify her for this but she pushed the guilt aside.

'Okay, tell me about yourself, in German of course.'

She drew a deep breath and although she wanted to stare at the wall or the floor she forced herself to meet his gaze. Halting at first she soon got into her stride and talked about her family and her job at the vets. Thank heavens for Gabi's class and hours of role play, she thought.

It was when he began to ask her questions she struggled. He spoke quickly in the local accent. Thinking she'd gathered the gist of his enquiry she blundered through her replies, hoping for the best.

A few people came in and she stood aside while he served them. Hoping it might ingratiate her with Karl she admired one customer's choice of vase and when the woman replied Natalie added a few more comments.

Once they were alone again he gestured for her to sit on a chair close to the counter. He asked her about her work at the vets which was difficult to translate, but hoped she'd said enough to impress. 'Do you have references?' he asked in English.

'Yes. My manager would fax or email them to you.'

'Why do you want to work in Salzburg? You see I worry you might just want a few week's work and then you move on.'

Natalie shook her head. 'I'm staying. It was a big decision to come here and I'm not going back.'

'Do you have an address?'

'I'm living with friends, in Aigen.'

Karl nodded. 'Well, I like you, Natalie, but I have someone else to see today. I will take your number and call you tomorrow.' He scribbled it down. 'You know the job is only for three afternoons?'

'That suits me. I could study my German on the other days.'

He laughed at that and walked with her to the door. He folded up the slip of paper with her number on and put it into his pocket. They shook hands again and she walked out into the cold wind.

It was hard not to get excited. On the bus she looked at other passengers, imagined herself travelling with them each day. Back at the hotel Karin explained she must register her intention to live in Salzburg, with the local government. 'Tante Lexi needs to sign a residence form,' she said.

Panic swirled in Natalie's stomach. It was becoming very real now.

Next morning Karl from the shop telephoned. He was apologetic but explained he'd given the job to the other applicant. Smothering her disappointment Natalie asked if he'd tell her the reason she'd been turned down.

'The other girl has lots of experience and,' he hesitated, 'still I am a little worried that you will not stay long. I'm sorry for this. I hope you understand.'

'Of course. Thank you for seeing me, anyway.' There seemed little point in saying anything else. She shook her head when Binita gave her an enquiring look.

'You should come with me and learn to drive taxis,' her new friend said. 'But don't tell the boss here.'

After work, a few days later, Natalie took her residence form to the council building then picked up a copy of Salzburger Nachrichten to scan the jobs column. She tried to read it on the bus but the sun was breaking through clouds and burnishing the mountain tops. It was hard to pull her gaze away.

Arriving home at Aunt Lexi's she spotted Karin across the fields with Otto. She was standing talking to someone and then, when she saw a black Labrador emerge from the undergrowth, she realised it was Leo with his dog, Max. Karin raised a hand and waved. Feeling she really should get over the embarrassment of her and Leo's parting she began to walk along the path towards them but when she looked up she saw Leo had moved away and was leading Max in the opposite direction.

She felt an involuntary thud of disappointment and then thought he was probably embarrassed too. Otto ambled up, tail wagging, twigs trailing from his undercarriage.

Karin seemed distracted.

'Is Leo avoiding me?' The words were out.

'Why would you think that?'

'It was a bit awkward that night after the meal. He wanted to pay and I think I offended him.'

Karin shook her head, called to Otto then turned to face her. 'Leo would not be offended. He's very easy going.'

'OK. Well that's good then.'

They walked into the garden, Natalie branching off to Aunt Lexi's back door. 'I'll nip up for something to eat later,' she called over her shoulder.

'What time will you come?'

'Maybe seven o'clock?'

'That sounds good. We might have a talk.'

Running a bath and then tugging off her jeans Natalie felt uneasy. What could *having a talk* mean. It wasn't said in Karin's usual friendly tone. Maybe they needed Aunt Lexi's room for someone else. She thought about staying in, buttering some of the lovely bread she'd bought in the city; but a plate of spinach dumplings and tomato salsa was calling her up the garden.

Karin was in the kitchen with Luisa and Lukas. As she passed the door Natalie noticed they were in a huddle, whispering. She sat down at the bar, ordered her food and felt the vibration of her phone in her pocket. Imagining it to be her dad or Toby she was puzzled to see a local number on her screen.

'Frau Grey?' Here is Karl Kogler.

'Sorry?' Natalie couldn't place the voice and wondered if it was some kind of official matter. With Karin's help she was gradually sorting out her tax and insurance details.

'I am Karl, from the shop. You were asking about the job. Can you call by again?'

She smiled into the phone. 'I can come in tomorrow, just after lunch.'

'Can you guess why I telephoned?'

'Is there still a vacancy?' She found her hand was shaking.

'Yes. I was wrong and I apologise. The girl who started here did not stay. Yesterday she said she is going to Wien and she just is gone. Do you now have another job?'

'I work each morning at a hotel across the river, but I'd very much like to work at the shop as well.'

'And you finish what time? One o'clock?'

'Yes.'

'I really need you from two o'clock. Can you do that?'

She told him she could.

'Do you eat your lunch fast? I wouldn't want you to have indigestion.' He laughed very loudly before continuing. 'This would just be on Thursday, Friday and Saturday. I'm sorry I don't need more than that. Sometime perhaps more days, but not now.'

'That would be fine.'

'I'll see you tomorrow then. Tschüs!'

Her first reaction was to tell Karin but now she hesitated. It wasn't until her food had arrived that her friend walked by, Otto at her heels.

'The man at the shop wants to see me again.' She blurted out the story of the unreliable girl he'd taken on.'

It was a huge relief to see Karin's wide grin. 'That's great and you know what? We might have some good news for you too.'

Natalie felt a warm and comforting happiness flood through her. 'What news? What do you mean?'

Karin tapped the side of her nose. 'I tell you tomorrow.' Her smile grew mischievous and she hurried away.

Chapter Thirty-Seven

Lovely as Binita was Natalie couldn't wait to get away from her morning shift the next day. She took the bus to Hanuschplatz and hurried through the maze of alleys and streets of the old town. At Café Tomaselli she slipped through the side door and upstairs to the ladies loo.

In a cramped cubicle she struggled out of her jeans and into a smart skirt and thick tights. Pulling on boots and bashing her elbows on the partition, she knew she'd have to think of somewhere else to get changed each day. She left a tip for the somewhat bemused toilet attendant and ran back downstairs, stuffing her other clothes into her bag.

Arriving at the shop, with her most business-like face on, she was taken aback to find Karl sitting at the counter with a woman about his own age beside him. Both were eating doughnuts and when Karl stood up to greet her he had icing sugar on the end of his nose.

'Here is our new girl.' He wiped his hand and thrust it out to Natalie. It still felt sticky. 'And this is Mariette, my girlfriend. She has a shop too but mostly she runs a Sound of Music tour.'

Natalie couldn't help grinning and thinking how impressed Glenda would be.

It was a great tension breaker and Mariette was charming, shaking her hand and making them all a cup of coffee. 'There is a cake for your afternoon break,' she said.

When she had gone Karl set about explaining the workings of the electronic till and credit card machine, then she was let loose on a customer. She almost cried with relief when the first man turned out to be American. Too churned up to eat her cake she stuffed it into the bag with her jeans and sweatshirt.

Only once did she have to call Karl from the tiny office to answer a query about a brand of pottery, and at five-thirty he said she'd done well. He gave her the security code for the burglar alarm and showed her how to throw the bolts in the ancient front door. As she headed towards the river to catch the bus she remembered walking the same route with Glenda on the last evening of their holiday. *Then* she had been so gormless she hadn't even carried money most of the time. Now she was working a German till and counting out wads of Euro notes to rich Americans.

On the bus she pulled out the cake Mariette had given her. It was a rich iced fancy, moist and delicious. She licked icing from her fingers and laughed when a woman across the aisle caught her eye.

Back in her comfy jeans Natalie walked up the garden to the hotel. The sun had set but it wasn't entirely dark. She saw the buds on the fruit trees and remembered the apples lying on the ground the previous autumn. Time moves on and everything changes. Guiltily she thought about Connor, realising that her feelings for him could not have been as deep as she imagined when they were together. She was still angry at him for not contacting her but as her new life unfolded he came into her head less and less. She felt something approaching contentment as she pushed open the door to the bar and walked in.

Karin was in Reception, typing. When she saw Natalie she called, 'Come and tell me everything, then I'll say the news I was going to tell you.'

Scooping Otto into her arms she described her day, ran through her duties and mentioned Mariette.

'I know her,' Karin said. 'Some of our guests go with her tours.'

'Tell me this news.' Natalie couldn't wait any longer.

Karin beckoned her behind the desk. She busied herself for

few seconds saving the document she was working on. 'You know we own a few apartments?

'I remember you said you, Luisa and Lukas each had one close by.'

Karin glanced towards the bar as though checking no one was listening. Natalie felt the stirrings of excitement. Her friend drew a deep breath and looked at her computer screen. 'There is a free apartment near the river. It was to be taken by a writer for the whole season but now the writer isn't coming.'

'Okay.'

'It's on Ignaz Rieder Kai. Do you think you would want to live there? It's not very big, just one room and a bathroom. I think you say a bedsitter.'

A tangle of emotions gripped Natalie. . A place of her own would be amazing but … she loved living at Lexi's; almost felt part of the family. She was pleased when Karin got up to book in a guest, leaving her to pull her thoughts together.

'This is brilliant,' she said when the guest had taken his key and disappeared upstairs, 'I don't know what to say. But could I afford it?'

'I think so now you have two jobs.'

'Is it far from here?' She almost bit her lip. That sounded ungrateful. She should be turning cartwheels.

Karin picked up a tourist map a guest had abandoned on the desk. 'Two stops on the bus or about walking twenty minutes. You want to see it tomorrow? We could go early before your work.'

'Yes. That would be fantastic but could you tell me the rent so I don't get too excited if I can't afford it?'

Karin looked down at her feet. 'I have to check but I don't think you will worry.'

Natalie wanted to ask a million questions. She knew the road by the river. It stretched from the city down past Aigen and petered out into a footpath which continued for miles. When she'd walked along it with Glenda they'd commented on how smart the area was. How could she possibly afford …?

'I must finish typing accounts. You eating tonight?' They stood aside as Otto trundled past and settled on his bed behind Karin's chair.

'Yes, give me a few minutes, though.' Natalie walked through the bar and out into the garden. She looked up at the mountain, the summit just visible in the moonlight. This was an amazing turn of events. When her parents came at Easter she could truthfully say her life here was working out. There was, after all, no shame in admitting Connor had upped and left. There'd be sarcasm from her mother but she'd be able to take them to her apartment and …

Her phone buzzed in her pocket and drawing it out she smiled as Toby's number lit up the screen.

'Nat, Dad's bought me a bike and it isn't Christmas or anything. It's white and Mum said Dad was stupid and should have bought black, but it's great and I let Markus have a go on it.'

Natalie's smile was wide. It was wonderful to hear his excited breaths between descriptions of handlebars and chunky tyres.

'That's fantastic, Sweetheart. Dad must think you've been really good to give you such a treat.'

Her brother was silent for a moment. A moment that lengthened until she glanced at the screen to make sure they were still connected.

'I want you to see the bike, Nat. You can have a ride on it if you like … when you come home. Will you be coming home soon? I hope so because I really want you to.'

Chapter Thirty-Eight

Leo had immersed himself in family life for the whole weekend, sitting for hours with his father discussing everything from politics to computer games; helping Marina prepare food and watching Andreas and Florian become acquainted over Star Wars Lego. Now, heading back along the autobahn his precious son was beside him. Andreas would stay overnight in Salzburg then take the train home in the morning.

They hadn't been travelling long when Andreas told him the orchestra would be performing in New York in the winter and he'd be going with them.

'That's fantastic,' Leo said. 'How long will you be there for?'

'Only a few days but … I was wondering if you'd come.'

'To see you play in New York? Try stopping me. But you kept this to yourself all weekend. Why didn't you tell us all at dinner?'

'I wanted to tell you when we were alone. We didn't get much chance to talk, did we?'

Leo was shot through with pride. His life was opening up in ways he couldn't have imagined. 'I've never been to the US so that will be an exciting trip for me.'

Before they could say more Max sat up in the back seat and whined. Leo glanced at the satnav and left the autobahn at the next exit.

When Max had watered every tree for half a kilometre they looked for somewhere to get a drink. In a small Konditorei Leo sipped his coffee and unfurled a pastry swirl. 'Your mother must be very excited about New York. Will she be going?' He tried to keep a note of negativity from his voice. He didn't want responsibility for Britte while he was there.

'Ah.' Andreas put down his cup. 'This is something else I was going to tell you. Mama and … Ulrich are …'

'You can call him, *Papa*. I don't mind. He's the one who has raised this fine musician.'

'Well, they are back together.'

Leo almost choked on his pastry. He whipped out his handkerchief and wiped flakes from his face. 'That is wonderful news, too.'

'It's only been a couple of weeks,' Andreas crossed his fingers, 'but the aromatherapist is no longer on the scene. I don't think that was ever a serious thing.'

'I'm very pleased for them both.' Leo's smile was mainly one of relief.

Back in the car Andreas told him that at his step-father's insistence his mother was playing the flute again. 'I don't know how far she'll take it but it's good to see her enthusiastic about her music. She's been very lonely these last few months.'

Leo dragged his thoughts from the night in Wurzburg when Britte had blamed Andreas for curtailing her career.

'Anyway, Papa. What about you? How is your social life? Do you have … anyone special?'

'Oh. I …' Leo felt a blush start somewhere under his collar and creep up to his hair roots.

'Sorry. I shouldn't have asked. It's probably too soon and …' Andreas' voice trailed off and he turned towards the window.

'No. You can ask. There isn't anyone. I mean there is … someone I …like.' Leo pressed the indicator, pulled out and shot past a lorry. 'But … what does everyone say these days? It's complicated?'

His son had turned to look at him but Leo stared ahead, hoping the colour in his face was receding.

'Why complicated? Is she married?'

He decided on a half-truth. 'Not any more. But she's English and she will probably return home and … anyway, tell me more about New York.'

'We can talk about that later.'

Leo heard the smile in his son's voice and couldn't help his own expression softening. 'She's a friend of Karin, at the Hotel Friesen where I like to eat sometimes. We had an un-planned meal together but that's all. Her life is a bit of a mess so it wouldn't be fair to … suggest anything more.'

'Is she pretty?' Andreas had shuffled round in the passenger seat and when Leo glanced at him he was still smiling.

'She is pretty, yes, but she's much too young for me and …'

'Can I meet her?'

'No. She'd take one look at you and fall in love.' He put a laugh into his voice but there was more honesty in the statement than he cared to admit.

'So, what's the problem?'

Leo felt himself sag. 'I saw her very briefly last autumn when I was … a mess. She was kind. I never thought I'd see her again but suddenly she turned up at the Friesen.' It felt good to say it. 'She's got herself a job but who knows how long she'll stay in Austria?'

'You said she's younger. Do you know how old?'

'Karin said she's thirty.'

'Okay, so she's too young for you and too old for me.'

'I guess so.'

'Except I'm joking, Papa. What do ten years matter? It's nothing.'

'It might matter to her.'

'Does she have children?'

'I don't think so.'

'Well I can't see why you don't just ask her out on a date. What do you have to lose if she says, no?'

And that, Leo thought, was the crucial question. This weekend he'd put her out of his mind; delighted in seeing his father embrace Andreas after all these years and enjoyed the closeness of the family, even shared a joke with his aloof brother-in-law.

But now his thoughts were turning to Natalie again. Part of what he had to lose if she said, no, was the tiny green shoot of hope he nurtured, secretly. Apart from his feelings of attraction he wanted to help heal the wounds her husband and the American had inflicted. 'There must be a million men her own age who could make her happy,' he said aloud.

'Don't throw away an opportunity for happiness, Papa.'

'Now you sound like your grandfather.'

Andreas turned back to the window. It was a moment or two before he spoke. 'I regret not contacting you years ago,' he said.

Leo's throat tightened. 'But you've been happy. Ulrich has loved you like his own son.' His voice made it a statement but it was the question he'd wanted to ask since that first meeting with Andreas in Salzburg.

'He does love me and I ... I love him. But he's never been interested in music. He's supported me and given me all the opportunities but music isn't … in his heart.'

Traffic was slowing behind a lorry with a wide load. When they came to a halt Leo turned to look at his son. 'It wasn't your responsibility to make contact. I could have telephoned your mother, begged her to let me see you. Sofia suggested it many times.' He clamped his jaw, trying to take hold of the emotions, long dormant, that were trying to surface. The casual ease of the journey had evaporated. 'Oh, I could say that my wife's health was not good, that it was hard for me to leave her. But that wasn't always true.' Leo thumped the steering wheel with his knuckles. 'I was a coward. I was terrified of … being rejected … of letting my feelings show in case they couldn't be returned.' He ran a hand through his hair. 'If there are regrets to be had they're all mine.'

Max wriggled to his feet and pushed his head between the front seats. Andreas stroked the dog's muzzle. 'I'm looking forward to seeing your house,' he said. 'Is it close to the city?'

Leo, grateful for a change of subject, let out a long breath. 'About four kilometres. It's at the foot of the Gaisberg with great walks everywhere. You must come and stay longer some time.'

The traffic was moving again. For the rest of the journey they talked about the orchestra and the difficult pieces they were to play.

It wasn't till they pulled up outside his house that Leo saw his son's wide smile again.

'Wow, this place is fantastic.' Andreas walked from room to room, Max at his heels. He ran his fingers over the keys of the grand piano, rushed upstairs to see the view from the balcony and finally pulled open the back door to explore the garden.

Leo listened to his messages. One of his students was down with flu and wanted to reschedule a lesson. His ordered life began to settle back round him.

He cooked lasagne – one of the few dishes he knew would turn out OK. They watched TV, checked emails and rang Marina to let her know they'd arrived safely.

Later, after his shower, Andreas came down in joggers and a long tee-shirt. 'I'm really sorry if I upset you on the way home.'

Leo poured them both a beer and sat at the kitchen table, gesturing for Andreas to sit opposite. 'You didn't upset me. I've always had feelings of regret but I've buried them. It was good to give them an airing.' He smiled hoping to lift the tension.

'When you said you were scared of … you know … being rejected, I think I used to feel that too. Maybe there wasn't room for me in your life.'

Leo ran his fingers across his forehead, closed his eyes. 'I … no, Sofia and I would have loved to have you in our lives. But I don't think we should dwell on regrets. You have good things ahead of you now and we'll all be here to support you. You can be proud you made the first move, asked your mother to call me. I bless the day that call came.'

Andreas sipped his beer, wiped moisture from the glass. 'Maybe we did do it at the right time then. We couldn't have talked like this when I was a kid.'

Leo nodded, not trusting himself to speak. He got up to let Max in from the garden and when he turned back Andreas was on his feet, arms wide, folding Leo into a hug. The boy held tight and Leo felt his son's heart beat thudding against his own chest. They clung together until Max nudged his way between them and they laughed, patted each other's shoulders and Andreas went up to bed.

Unable to sleep Leo pulled his laptop from his briefcase, sat up against the bed head, pulled his dressing gown round his shoulders and tucked Max's blanket over the dog's back. The tiny seed of an idea had come to him and he spent an hour turning up pages on Google. When he dozed off and came to, still hunched over the laptop he knew it was time to turn out the light.

Next morning he saw Andreas off at Aigen station. They shook hands and Leo promised to call him for details of the orchestra tour. A feeling of peace engulfed him as he walked home. Last night's seed of an idea was growing. It might come to nothing but he felt compelled to give it a shot. At home he made coffee and picked up the phone, took a sheet from the printer and ran his finger down it. The call was answered on the second ring.

'Hello,' he said. 'I'd like to talk to someone about German prisoners of war.'

Chapter Thirty-Nine

'On a nice day you'll see the Gaisberg from this window.' Karin stood at the sink in Natalie's new apartment. Luisa was opening pizza boxes and putting bottles of Radler shandy onto the scrubbed pine table.

'I can't quite take it all in,' Natalie said, taking three plates from the rack. 'I'll wake up tomorrow in this gorgeous room and see the fortress from my bed, if this fog ever lifts.'

Karin had been right; it was more of a bedsit but a huge one with everything she needed including a separate airy bathroom.

Her case wasn't yet unpacked but she'd booked the following morning off work so she could get everything straight before going into Karl's shop at lunchtime.

Despite her excitement a few butterflies were batting around in her stomach too. She'd now moved three times in almost as many months and wondered if she'd ever be settled.

'It will feel strange at first,' Luisa said, 'but we're only ten minutes away if you need us.'

Natalie felt the press of tears. 'You've been so kind and I'm sure you're not charging me enough rent.'

Karin waved a dismissive slice of pizza.

'What do your family think about you getting this place?' Luisa asked.

'I haven't told them yet.' Natalie pulled a face. 'I'll call them in the morning.'

Accepting the offer of this flat she'd lit a torch under her bridges. 'My little brother isn't going to like it. He … he really wanted me to go home.'

'But you cannot live life for your brother,' Karin said, flicking olives into the pizza box. 'He is very young and will make his own decisions when he grows, just like you must.'

'I know. But … we've always been very close and … I don't always think …' It was hard to find the words. She didn't want to be disloyal but … 'I don't think my mother copes that well. Since I was ten she's worked full-time and when Toby came along at such a … late stage she hated being at home. Even though she adored him she was used to … being confident in everything she did. She was always stressed. I guess Adam and I thought we were helping, taking care of Toby so much, giving her a break.'

Drawing in a deep breath she knew she was on dangerous ground and might say more than she wanted to. 'My dad thinks it's good that I'm away from my brother now. I think Toby was …'

'Thinking you are his mother instead?' Karin, as always, straight to the point.

'Maybe. I hope not. I miss him, though.'

'You will see him in a few weeks when they come to the hotel. We all look forward to meeting your family.'

It was weird trying to imagine them here in Salzburg. She prayed for good weather so that her mother didn't harp on about Italy and how much warmer it was.

'Karin tells me you have German ancestors too.' Luisa opened another bottle of Radler. Evening had closed in and it was cosy sitting at the table, a pull-down lamp spreading a soft light around them, subtle aromas of herbs and garlic wafting from the food.

'You should try to find your grandfather,' Karin said.

'If he's still alive he'll be very old, but there's no way I could trace him. I only know his first name and that he was in Leicester.'

'Shame. And you said there was a photo of a farm?'

Natalie reached over to the sofa, lifted her laptop case and unzipped it. 'I scanned it into the computer,' she said. 'Don't know why really. I suppose it's all I've got of him and don't want to risk losing it.' She brought up the photo, its grainy condition worsened by pixels. Details of the boy at the wheel of the tractor were indistinct. She couldn't even guess his age.

'Maybe I could Photoshop it for you,' Karin said. 'Make it a little clearer.' She peered at the photo. 'You know those clouds are not clouds, they are mountains.' She turned the laptop around for Luisa to see.

'Mountains? Let me see.' A flutter of excitement spread through Natalie's stomach.

'I've seen tractors like that here, getting rust in barns,' Luisa said. 'But I guess they have them everywhere.'

Karin drew out her phone and pointed it at the screen.

'Hang on,' Natalie said. 'Use the original.' She pulled her purse from her bag and drew out the flimsy snap.

Karin took pictures from a couple of angles then handed it back. 'I'll see what I can make. Your mother might be pleased.'

'No! She doesn't know anything about this.' Natalie grabbed the photo, pushing it back into her purse. 'Auntie Maureen made me promise never to tell her.'

'She doesn't know?' Luisa looked shocked. 'Your grandmother was very good at keeping secrets. In our family we could not do that. Someone would tell. Probably Karin.'

Her joke lightened the mood and they ate in silence for a few moments. Natalie relaxed, allowing the pleasure of moving into the apartment to surface again.

'I nearly forgot.' Karin slammed the flat of her hand down onto the table making the others jump. 'You remember Leo?'

'Yes.'

'He is going with some of his students to a concert in the city next Saturday and one of them cannot go. He asked if you'd like to take the place.'

'Why would he ask me?' There was no denying a flutter in her stomach.

'He remembered you like Mozart.'

'Wouldn't you like to go instead?'

Luisa laughed. 'Not really Karin's … thing. Or mine.'

Feeling her face grow hot Natalie said, 'Can you tell him, thank you, but no?'

'Sure. But you should go. You might make new friends.'

'How old are his students?'

'Not his children students, his older ones. Maybe early twenty-something.'

Both Karin and Luisa were staring at her, their expressions encouraging. She turned her attention back to her pizza. 'Alright. Tell him I will but I must pay for my concert ticket.'

When the sisters had gone Natalie unzipped her case, piled clothes onto the bed and opened the wardrobe. There was a high shelf and before stashing her clothes away she opened her laptop case and took out the brown A4 envelope and pushed it to the back of the shelf. Covered with knitwear she could almost forget it was there.

Having thought she might be nervous on her first night in the flat her mind was now working overtime wondering why she'd agreed to go to a concert with Leo. At least with others there it shouldn't be too awkward.

She made tea and picked up her phone. There was a voicemail and a missed call. She could hardly believe it when she saw the voicemail was from Connor. Finally he'd decided to get in touch. His message simply said, *Sorry for everything, Sweetie. Call me, please.*

'I don't think so,' she said aloud and deleted the message. 'What a nerve.'

Checking the missed call her pulse picked up to a gallop when she saw it had been Adam trying to ring her. She sat down at the table; put her hands around the mug of tea, staring at his name on the screen. Hating herself for doing so she glanced at the clock: five past ten. In England it was an hour earlier. She ran her finger over the call button then dropped the phone onto the table. What could he possibly want after all this time? She'd told him to contact her through the solicitor but what if something was wrong? What if the house had burned down? She took a gulp of scalding tea, winced and picked up the phone.

A silky voice said, 'Adam Grey's phone.'

Natalie held her breath for a couple of beats. 'This is Natalie Grey returning his call.' I sound like Glenda, she thought.

'Oh, Natalie. I'll just get him for you.'

How civilised we are. There was a time when I'd have screamed abuse at her.

'Hi.' He sounded like the old Adam.

'You rang me.'

'Yes. I wouldn't mind a chat.'

'Go ahead.'

'It's about the house.'

'Keep going.'

'Err … well … we have a buyer.'

'Oh.' Another bridge about to ignite. 'A serious buyer? Already?'

'Very. She works for Barclays and just transferred here. She's not in a chain so …'

'So … what Adam?'

'Well, we can go ahead. Are you okay with that?'

'Of course.' She ran her finger along the edge of the table, picturing her tiny house; the drab garden. She wouldn't see any of it again now.

'It's just that you seemed … gutted when I came round and suggested selling.' He lowered his voice. 'You know when I told you about …'

'Things have changed.'

'I saw Maureen in town. She said you're in Austria.'

Natalie made a sound that might suffice as confirmation.

'When are you coming back?'

'I'm not.'

'You're not? I can't believe you'd stay there. What about Toby?'

She only missed a beat. 'I don't think you need to worry about Toby, Adam. Was there anything else?'

'I'll need to clear the house out and I wondered if …'

'Go ahead. All I want are my German books and some clothes. Dad will collect those for me. There's some rubbish in the loft you might want to get rid of.' Their wedding album in the darkest corner.

'Right, well, I'll talk to her solicitor in the morning. You haven't asked what her offer is, Natalie. It's more than I thought we'd …'

'Let my solicitor know, Adam. You've got her number. She can send me whatever I need to sign.'

'But …'

She ended the call but felt no satisfaction in doing so. Of course she wanted to know what the offer was but she didn't want to continue talking to him. It was unsettling. She'd consigned him to the past and then suddenly his voice was in her new apartment.

Her tea was cooling on the table but she drank it and dug into the box of food Luisa had brought as a moving in present. She peeled the cling film off a plate of home-made biscuits and took a fistful but then ate them too quickly and choked on the crumbs, coughing until her eyes ran. This wasn't how her first night was supposed to be. In the space of an hour three different men had managed to cause her stress.

Sitting up in bed with the lights turned off she pulled the

curtain back a fraction. The fog had cleared; lights on the far river bank now visible. A bell chimed way off in the city, then another. She wriggled down; the duvet cover was crisp and fresh smelling, the down-filled pillow, caressing her neck. She heard a door close in the apartment below, a child's voice and then nothing but the river rushing over rocks and the swift beat of her heart.

Chapter Forty

By Saturday lunchtime Natalie still had no idea what she might wear to the concert. She didn't even know the venue.

'What if it's really smart and I look out of place?' She asked Binita's advice as they changed out of their cleaning overalls.

'Wear black. It always looks good. But you'll look nice whatever you wear.' Her friend smiled. 'And it's not like it's a date.'

'No. It certainly isn't that, but all the same I want to make an effort. It's ages since I've had an occasion to dress up for.'

On the way to Karl's shop she nipped into a department store near the river. With no time to try anything on she grabbed a black, knee-length puffball skirt in her size, some black tights and a white blouse with long sleeves. As she sprinted across the bridge into the old town it began to rain. Great, she thought, now I'll have to wash my hair again.

Karl was unpacking new stock in the back room when she arrived. He called a cheery greeting and didn't seem to notice she was five minutes late. Customers came in to buy souvenirs and shelter from the rain. Serving them wasn't a problem for Natalie but trying to return their small talk was a challenge. She hoped lots of smiles made up for any missed responses on her part.

Towards the end of the afternoon an American family came in. They bought a couple of large paintings and several items of china that they wanted shipping back to the States. Desperate to leave on time, Natalie ended up staying late to finish packing the boxes.

Arriving home at five-thirty she had just over an hour to shower, do her hair and be ready. No time to eat. Karin told her Leo would pick her up; Natalie wondered if he thought she was still living at Aunt Lexi's.

Now that her hair was longer she thought of putting it up but after ten minutes of struggling to pin it in place she let it drop back, fingered some styling wax through it and hoped for the best. She pulled on her new tights being careful not to snag them then cut the tags from her new skirt and blouse.

'Natalie, you look like a waitress,' she said to her reflection. The skirt fitted beautifully and the blouse looked nice but she didn't want people asking her if they could order interval drinks so she threw it off and searched her wardrobe for something else. Only her long, crimson jumper looked right with the skirt so it would have to do. Her black jacket was shorter than the jumper so she decided to carry it and put it round her shoulders if needed. Out of the habit of wearing heels she pulled on her black boots. There wasn't time for full make up so she applied some mascara and as she heard a car drawing up outside she smoothed on lipstick in swift strokes.

Leo must have been about to ring the bell because opening the door she made him jump. They both laughed and he stood aside to let her walk down the path to the large BMW. She could see three youngsters on the back seat and as she approached they smiled and waved. Maybe this wouldn't be so much of an ordeal after all. Leo held open the passenger door for her. She saw he was wearing black jeans and a dark green traditional trachten jacket with no collar.

'Here are Melanie, Julius and Claudia,' he said. They took turns to thrust a hand between the front seats so they could greet Natalie in the formal way.

'They want to talk to you in English. Is that OK?'

'Of course.' That was a relief. She really ought to practice more conversational German but maybe not when she was quite so nervous. *Why am I nervous?* The thought struck her. A Mozart concert was a great thing to attend in Salzburg. The rain had abated and a watery sun shimmered on the mountain tops as they reached the main road. This was certainly the most luxurious trip into town she'd ever made. She relaxed into the soft leather seat, tried not to stare at Leo's long legs, and allowed the three students to grill her on English fashion, films and boy bands.

Leo parked in an underground car park close to Mirabelgarten. Tourists were taking a pre-dinner stroll. It was apparent Julius and Melanie were an item as they walked ahead, holding hands. Claudia was extremely tall, almost Leo's height. Natalie thought what a striking couple they made and the thought irked her.

'Do you know the pieces we will hear tonight?' Claudia asked Natalie.

Before she could answer Leo touched her shoulder for a brief moment. 'I'm so sorry, I haven't told you. It is Mozart's last piano concerto. Number twenty-seven. There are some pieces by other composers too.

Natalie was certain most of the music would be unfamiliar to her.

Leo continued, 'Twenty-seven is quite a playful piece but the second movement is divine. You will like it.'

She smiled but thought, how does he know I'll like it? He doesn't know me at all. She turned away, watched a man take a photo of his wife beside an ornamental pond and wondered why peevishness was creeping into her mood. Claudia was now talking into her phone in such an accented tone that made Natalie despair of ever being able to speak German in this city. They were approaching the Landestheater and she assumed that was the venue but she saw Melanie and Julius walk past the doors and disappear round the corner.

'Where is tonight's concert?'

Claudia was putting her phone away. 'At the Mozarteum.'

As Natalie glanced across to thank her she caught Leo's eye for a second and saw his discomfort.

The foyer was crowded; many people smartly dressed in traditional jackets, women in dark satin dirndls. Leo became surrounded by teenagers. He tried to introduce them all but Natalie couldn't catch their names. Some of them had come with parents and there was much handshaking.

'May I buy you a glass of wine?' Leo asked and there was the tiniest hint of teasing in his voice. Natalie was about to say she'd buy one herself but then he smiled and she thought of the last time the two of them had stood in this foyer when a smile had seemed impossible for him.

'You may. But please let me pay for my ticket.'

'Our tickets are complimentary this evening, so no need to worry. This is why I have so many of my students here.'

He gestured to the chattering youngsters and she saw pleasure in his expression.

'You seem to be a popular teacher.' Natalie shifted her jacket on her arm and looked at his students.

'I have a bottomless treat jar and they love my dog. Shall I take your jacket to the cloakroom?'

'Please.' She handed it over and he disappeared into the crowd. Melanie and Julius came to stand with her. They talked about Mozart for a few moments although Natalie could add little to the conversation.

'So are you Herr Maier's new girlfriend?' Melanie asked, seeming to ignore a glare from Julius.

Natalie was about to say an emphatic *no* when Leo arrived back with two glasses of wine.

'None for us?' Julius asked.

'And have your parents after me?' Leo smiled at Natalie who was still recovering from the girl's question. She sipped her wine slowly aware she'd eaten nothing since a quick sandwich at lunchtime and hoped her stomach wouldn't rumble during the performance.

She wasn't prepared for the beauty of the concert hall. Like much of the town it was decorated in the Baroque style with ornate plaster friezes on the walls and ceiling. Leo placed a gentle hand on her shoulder and led her to the second row from the front. The stage was low giving an excellent view of the individual musicians. Leo sat to her right. On her other side were Claudia and a couple of students she recognised from the foyer. Julius and Melanie and several others filed into the row behind them.

'This is a wonderful place,' she whispered.

'Next time you must see the Großer Saal, it's even better.'

Next time. He thought there'd be a next time, did he?

A glance at her programme told her the Mozart concerto would be played after the interval. The first pieces were nice enough but she didn't feel terribly drawn in. Instead she took surreptitious glances at the people around her. Claudia, sitting forward in her seat seemed to devour the music. She heard an intake of breath from one of the students in the row behind when a clarinettist began a complicated solo.

The seating was comfortable, the chairs individual and large. Leo was able to straighten his legs under the vacant chair in front. Natalie thought of Adam's shorter, stockier legs that, if she was honest, were not terribly attractive. At her side Leo seemed relaxed. For a moment she tried to conjure up her first impression of him, the hollow cheeks, hair unkempt, but it was difficult to sustain the image. He'd had his hair cut since she saw him at the Friesen but he still wore it collar length. She thought this gave him a pleasing eccentric air. He was wearing cologne, a very subtle one she didn't recognise. It was when she breathed it in, trying to place the citrus notes that she realised her surreptitious glance had turned into a full-blown stare. She turned to watch the musicians but then Leo leaned towards her and she felt his breath against her ear, whispering that the

Shostakovich was a piece Julius played well. She prayed he hadn't seen her watching him.

At the interval she turned down another drink and escaped to the loo. Now so hungry that her stomach gurgled every few moments she wondered if Mozart's concerto had slow, quiet passages in which people would hear her insides protesting. Apart from the hunger she was enjoying the evening. Karin was right, it was good to get out and meet people although apart from Leo they were all much younger than her. Fancy staring at him like that, she thought as she made her way back to her seat. I hope he doesn't get the wrong idea.

Leo was right about the Mozart. She liked it very much. The first movement was swift and jolly but even so she sensed other emotions in the music which she couldn't articulate even to herself. She thought back to that long ago conversation with Manu at the dinner concert when he said Mozart understood the fragility of humans and expressed it in his music. The second movement was indeed beautiful, the pianist's fingers rolling over the keys like gentle waves. Now she did allow herself to sink into the music, let her eyes close and think about how nice it was to be in Mozart's city with people who were friendly and kind.

She was disappointed when the final movement came to its close and the applause began. Some of the students rose to their feet and, caught up in the moment, Natalie did too. When it was time to leave Leo touched her arm. 'So you liked it?'

'I loved it. Thank you so much for …thinking of me. I mean … when you had a spare ticket.'

'My pleasure,' he said, then turned away as a young student and her parents approached him. Natalie didn't know whether to wait in the foyer or stay until Leo had finished talking but then he turned and introduced her to his student. 'This is Lucy, she plays piano very well indeed.'

Natalie held out her hand but was suddenly tongue-tied and

beyond *Grüß Gott* didn't know what to say to them in German.

Leo came to her rescue, explaining she was from England.

Lucy's mother seemed to look Natalie up and down and find her lacking in some way. She steered the child away while her father said their goodbyes.

In the foyer the others were waiting. They exchanged a few words and Leo said they were getting a lift home with Claudia's brother. 'They're probably going to fib their way into a night-club,' he said.

By the time Leo had retrieved Natalie's jacket from the cloak-room the crowd had all but dispersed. He held the jacket for her to put on. 'Would you like to eat somewhere?'

'Oh.' The question hung between them for a few seconds.

'You can pay if you like,' he added, his expression solemn at first and then he smiled.

'Yes. I'd like that.' There was no denying she needed to eat and maybe this would dispel the awkwardness of their previous dinner together.

As they descended the steps to the pavement Leo offered her his arm. For a second she could only gape. It was a simple, old fashioned gesture that nobody had ever made to her before. She slid her hand into the crook of his elbow and they fell into step.

'We can get the car now or walk into the old town. Which would you prefer?'

'I'm happy to walk if you are,' Natalie said, feeling the wool of his jacket soft beneath her fingers, the scent of his cologne fragrant on the evening air. Winter was definitely receding, the air warmer now.

They crossed the footbridge. The fortress, illuminated on its hill was, as always, a glorious, comforting sight. Tourists returning to their hotels had stopped to photograph it. Somewhere, Natalie thought, there is a photo of me standing here, grinning into Glenda's camera. But that was in her tourist days.

She didn't ask where they were going; happy enough to drift along. They navigated the courtyards and brightly lit shopping alleys emerging into Getreidegasse. Passing Mozart's birthplace Natalie gave the composer a silent thank you for the wonderful music.

At the top of Judengasse Leo pushed open the door of a small bistro, exchanged a few words with a waitress and they took a corner table.

Ravenous, now, Natalie ordered a large spaghetti dish hoping she'd be able to eat it without splattering sauce everywhere. She was relieved when Leo asked for the same.

'So now I know you are a real Mozart lover,' he said as the wine arrived.

'How can you tell?' Natalie fingered the stem of her glass.

'I studied your face. The music had taken you to another place.'

She felt her cheeks flush. When had he looked at her so intently and how did she not notice?

'There is something … other worldly about him, yes.'

'But you didn't sense it in the other pieces?'

'No. Every minute was enjoyable but there's something about Mozart.' She smiled, again remembering Manu's words. 'I think I feel it in my heart.'

She kept her eyes on her wine glass, feeling foolish. Was this a date or another accidental dinner? There was no denying he was a nice man with whom she felt safe and, this evening, increasingly comfortable.

The food arrived. Natalie twirled a heap of herb scented pasta around her fork.

'Have you read much about Mozart's life?' Leo asked.

'Not really. I've learned a little from cd covers.'

'Read the family letters. You can learn a lot about him from those. My copy is only German and I think you would need the English translation.'

'I can't imagine my private letters being read a couple of hundred years from now.'

'Some of Mozart's are … quite intimate. Today we email and nobody keeps those.'

'I keep a few,' Natalie said, thinking of Toby and his funny little messages.

'You must miss your family.'

'I do, especially my brother, but … '

'Our families play a part in our lives but they cannot live them for us.' For a brief second Leo stared at a point some way above her head. Then he smiled. 'So are you still at that crossroad?'

For a moment she was puzzled but then remembered their conversation at the Friesen.

'No. I've started to move along one of the roads.' She smiled. 'If it's not the right one I'll do as you said before, go back and try another.'

'Well I hope you don't have to turn back just yet.' He poured them some more wine. 'And have you thought any more about finding your German grandfather?'

Goodness me, she thought, a man who really listens and remembers what you've said. 'No. I've had so much else to think about lately. Maybe one day I'll get round to it.'

'You like your new apartment?'

'I love it.' She sipped her wine. 'But I don't think Karin is charging me enough rent. It must be mate's rates.' She laughed when she saw his frown. 'A special rent for friends.'

'Maybe,' he said.

'My family is coming to visit at Easter. Maybe you'll meet them at the hotel.'

He didn't look entirely surprised. Karin strikes again, she

thought.

'I'd love to meet them. Should I bring Max?'

'My brother, Toby would love that. He's keen to have a dog himself, but my mother won't let him.'

When the waiter had taken their dessert orders Natalie felt the conversation had centred around her for too long. While she tried to think of something to ask him she noticed how neat and clean his fingernails were and that below the cuffs of his white shirt he had pale hairs on his wrist. Finally she asked, 'So do you have family in Salzburg?'

'No longer. My sister lives in Vienna. Also my father but I have ...'

She waited. Felt tension in her stomach without knowing why.

'Did Karin tell you I have a son?'

'No. She didn't tell me that.' The tension eased.

He smiled. 'She can keep secrets sometimes. He lives in Germany with his mother. He wasn't the child of … of my late wife. Someone else.'

Now she was puzzled, how many times had he been married?

'I was young. She was too. It was … one of those things. Last September he came to see me.'

'Had you not … I mean …'

'I did not see him since he was three years old. He is twenty-two and plays viola in an orchestra. We are friends now.'

Wow, she thought. That's a revelation. 'So he has inherited your talent for music.'

'His mother's too. She plays flute.'

Natalie's questions dried up. They ate Apfelstrudel, drank coffee and talked about the city, Mozart and her job at Karl's shop. On the long walk back to the car she took his arm again, feeling like a character from an old movie, their footsteps echoing in the quiet streets.

In the car she wanted to ask more about his son, the boy's mother but found she was nervous about what his answers might be. You've had too much wine, she thought, her emotions were muddled. She tried to concentrate on the music she'd heard but couldn't conjure up a single note.

When they pulled up outside her house Leo didn't turn off the engine. He leaned towards her then slid his arm between the seats and drew something from a rear pocket. The scent of his cologne wafted close to her face. 'I found this today.' He handed her a CD. 'It's the concerto we heard this evening, and another besides. I thought, if you enjoyed it, you might like to hear it again.'

She held the CD, stared at it while her heart beat slowed. 'Oh, that's brilliant. Thank you …'

He got out of the car, came round to her side and opened the passenger door. 'I'll wait till you're inside,' he said.

Her knees felt unsteady as she walked up the path, fumbled for her key and slid it into the lock. Leo followed. The door swung open but she didn't reach for the light switch. In the dim glow from the street lamp she saw Leo hold out his hand. She did the same and his grip was firm but brief. 'Thank you for a lovely evening,' he said. He smiled, gave her the polite nod that Austrians gave to strangers, then turned away and walked to the car.

Natalie ran up the stairs, let herself into her apartment. Peeped through the blinds but the BMW was gone. She flopped down onto the bed still holding the CD in one hand, her bag in the other. Staring into the darkness she tried to pull her thoughts together. Eventually they drew in, gelled into a feeling, a word. Disappointment.

Chapter Forty-One

'You took her out on a date?'

Leo hesitated. He had heard a smile in his son's voice.

'Not really a date. There were students with us. But the two of us went for dinner alone afterwards.'

'And?'

'There is no *and*. I drove her home.'

'But you're seeing her again?'

Leo lay back against the sofa cushions. Over and over he'd relived every minute of Saturday evening, from his first sight of her legs in that black skirt to the moment in the car when she thanked him for the cd but her eyes told him she'd expected a kiss. 'I don't know. Anyway, this is a strange conversation to be having with my son.'

'You rang *me*, Papa.'

I just needed to say her name to someone. 'Is it a bad time?'

'No. Mama is shopping. Ulrich is at work. So tell me more. Did you kiss her goodnight?'

Down the phone Leo could hear crockery chinking, a cereal box being shaken. Andreas was having a late breakfast whereas he was unable to eat so much as a croissant this morning. 'No. But I wouldn't tell you if I had.' He laughed, played with Max's ears as his dog, tired from his walk, sat beside him.

'What is your plan, Papa? You ought to have one.' Leo heard a refrigerator door open and close.

'I'll give it some thought. Now you must eat your breakfast before the cereal goes soggy.'

'How did …?'

Leo said, *Tschüs* and hung up. He leapt off the sofa, gave Max a biscuit and turned on the coffee maker. He should go jogging but he'd been pacing the house and smiling for so long there wasn't time now before his first student.

The weather was getting warmer. He'd seen wild garlic carpeting the wood at the foot of the Gaisberg. Just a few weeks and Natalie's family would be here. The thought made him uneasy. To be introduced as a friend might seem odd. Her father might think he had designs on her, which he had, but only good ones. It would be great to meet the little brother. He was Florian's age. Should he ask his family to come at Easter? Maybe they could all eat together. No, too much, too soon.

On the kitchen table he had a notebook, a pile of scrappy jottings about POW camps, his laptop and a list of phone numbers. So far enquiries in Austria and Germany had yielded little. Without her grandfather's last name they could tell him nothing but simply confirmed that soldiers were held in prisoner of war camps all over England. Last week he'd typed L-E-S-T-E-R into Google but had come up with nothing but people's names. He was certain that was the place Natalie had said in reply to Karin's *innocent* questioning.

He poured himself a mug of coffee, sat down in front of his laptop and tried again, typing *town* after *Lester.* This time it brought up details of a city but the spelling was entirely different. Of course, English was not phonetic. He spent the next half hour discovering that there had been dozens of camps in the area but none of the sites he explored gave details of individual prisoners. The phone rang and Leo stifled a groan when he heard Julia Weber's voice.

'Lucy has a dental appointment this week, Leo.'

How he hated her using his Christian name but, thank goodness, she'd never referred to the ghastly night of her husband's party.

'Can we change her lesson to eleven o'clock?'

'I'll check my diary.' He could hear her squawking as he laid the phone on the worktop. 'Yes, that will be fine. I hope Lucy doesn't have to have a filling.'

'We so enjoyed meeting you at the concert on Saturday,' she said.

Get off the phone, he thought.

'Who on earth was that nervous-looking English woman?'

'I've no idea who you mean.'

'But you introduced us, Leo.'

'Oh yes. Then I must have told you who she was when I introduced you so you can't have forgotten.'

'But I have. Poor girl looked like a fish out of water.'

'She's friendly with the family at the Friesen. Perhaps they could give you more details if you need them.' He stared through the window at a bird taking nuts from the feeder.

'Oh don't be coy, Leo. If there's a new woman in your life we're all thrilled for you.'

Who are *we*? he wondered as he walked to the front door, opened it quietly and pressed the doorbell. Max began barking and skidding up and down the polished floor. 'My next student is here. I'll see Lucy at eleven on Wednesday.' He rang off, praying Herr Weber would accompany his daughter to the lesson.

Even the woman's over familiarity couldn't upset Leo for long. Andreas said he should have a plan and in a way he had. The *long game* was risky but for now it seemed the right one to play. He went back to the table, drank the rest of his coffee and continued perusing English websites, occasionally letting his thoughts stray to the way Natalie's red sweater had caressed the curve of her breast.

Chapter Forty-Two

Natalie watched the sun catching the top of the Gaisberg, the late dusting of snow like frosting on a cake. She sipped coffee and watched a para-glider above the mountain making slow sweeps around the summit. She felt something of the glider's freedom. The house was sold and it wouldn't be long before her share of the money was in her account. She had an apartment she loved and friends who were kind and generous. At the shop she was gaining confidence all the time and soon she'd see Toby. So why was she feeling … restless?

She was certain it was her flagging ego that had made her wish Leo had kissed her after the concert. It might have been nice to feel … desirable. But like her he was dealing with stuff and she wasn't really interested in anything more than friendship.

At seven o'clock she put on her trainers and walked up to the Friesen. Karin and Luisa were having to work even though it was Monday and their rest day. As usual a seminar was in residence but Karin said they could all eat later and take Otto for a walk.

Chatter and laughter drifted from one of the dining rooms as Natalie walked through the bar looking for Karin. She found her in the kitchen piling plates into the dishwasher. She looked up and smiled. 'Hallo, go and sit in the bar. I'll come soon.'

She sat at one of the tables and Otto ambled up to lean against her legs. She pulled a twig from the long hair on his ear.

'I hope you don't mind if I am nosey,' Karin said, flopping down into the seat opposite.

Natalie wondered what on earth was coming.

'Your German grandfather story is interesting so I made some …some …'

'Enquiries?

'Enquiries. Yes. It might have been difficult for you to say everything in German.' She leaned across the table and spoke quietly even though the bar was almost empty. 'The archive in Koblenz can only help if you have a last name or an army number.'

'Which we don't have,' Natalie said.

'But in Leicester there is an office of records and we emailed them. Did we do wrong?'

'We?'

Karin gestured vaguely towards the kitchen.

'No. Of course you didn't do wrong. Wow, I can't believe it. I mean I often think about it but with all that's been happening I keep forgetting. So what did the record office say?'

Sometimes the prisoners were taken into houses for a meal or a party. They told us that many times they were in the newspaper with a photo, especially at Christmas. They will look at the photos and see if there is an Adolf. If it gives his name we can talk to Koblenz again.'

Natalie sat back in her chair, thoughts racing. An image of Grandma whispering Adolf's name made her bite her lip. 'This is amazing. But what on earth would I do if I found his details? He may have died, possibly years ago.'

'But he had a family. Wouldn't you want to find them?'

'I don't know. I mean, yes, I would but … what if they didn't react well? I couldn't just write to them and pour out the story.'

'You could just say you knew he was a prisoner; that your grandmother worked with him. Was friends.'

Natalie pulled Otto up onto her knee, kissed the top of his head; buried her fingers in his fur. 'This is all a bit scary. I mean it's wonderful that you've started the search for me but … well … for one thing I couldn't tell my mother.'

Karin shrugged. 'Doesn't stop you seeing them.'

Luisa came to join them. 'Let's eat,' she said.

Natalie thought Karin would fill Luisa in on their conversation about her grandma but instead she changed the subject, describing a walk they could all do near the Golling waterfalls.

In the kitchen they ate at the family table. Lukas grabbed a few minutes to sit with them before rushing back to check on food for the seminar delegates. Natalie drank a bottle of lemon radler and thanked her lucky stars that Glenda chose this hotel with its warm and generous family. Could she really search for her grandfather's family? How amazing would it be to discover German cousins?

At ten o'clock the last of the delegates had eaten and many of them congregated in the bar. Karin put on her jacket and coaxed Otto out from under the table. Lukas came over, pointing to the back door. 'You have seen the stars? Amazing tonight. Shooting ones, too.'

'It's so clear,' Luisa said. 'Maybe we haven't finished with snow yet.'

Out in the lane they made for the fields. It was a warm evening and Natalie was suddenly aware how much further south she now lived. As the street lights ended and they set off along the grassy path towards the Gaisberg, the brightness of the stars intensified. 'There's hardly a gap between them,' she said, her face upturned. 'We'd never see it like this in Coventry. Way too much light pollution.' Otto, unimpressed, trotted ahead and soon disappeared.

'Was that a shooting star or a satellite?' Karin asked. Natalie didn't know where she was pointing but then she too saw an arc of light that disappeared in seconds.

'Another.' Luisa's voice drifting from somewhere ahead.

The spangled sky was mesmerising. Natalie began to feel light-headed. She looked down for a few seconds and massaged her neck, then Otto, rustling far off in the grass, began to bark.

'I hope he hasn't found a hedgehog,' Karin said. 'He eats

them.'

But there was a deeper barking too, another dog. Luisa went forward to investigate. 'Oh. It's Max.'

Natalie's pulse quickened, probably due to the light-headedness, she thought. But the sensation moved to her stomach and then places she didn't realise you could feel a pulse. She held her breath as Leo and his dog approached. There was much greeting and trying to quieten the dogs.

'Natalie. How are you?'

'I'm … umm … fine. Fine, thank you.'

They walked back, Leo falling into step beside her.

'Karin and I were talking the other day about your German heritage.'

'Yes, I can't believe she's been to all this trouble for me.'

Leo mumbled something she didn't catch then said, 'I think it has captured our imagination.'

'Well, I'm a bit nervous about it all. I'd love to find them but how would they feel if I turned up out of the blue?'

'Another crossroads,' Leo said and he gave a laugh that was very low-pitched. Why had she not noticed before how deep his voice was?

'If I were you I would take one step at a time. If this lady at the record office comes back with nothing then you cannot proceed and you may have to let it go.'

Wow, he really did know all the facts. For a second she wondered just how close Leo and Karin were and the thought was discomfiting.

'You're right. I'll wait and see.'

Then Leo and Luisa both let out a gasp. He put his hand on Natalie's shoulder and left it there. 'Look,' he said, bringing his head close to hers, 'that shooting star is going on forever.'

She looked to where he pointed and saw the arc of light, then it was gone but the joy of it remained. When she closed her eyes she saw it again as though the beam travelled into her body, radiating to the tips of her fingers, intensifying on her shoulder where Leo's hand had rested.

'You have to make a wish,' he said.

They had reached the path which led them back to the Friesen. They chatted for a few moments but the dogs grew impatient, Max whining, Otto trotting off on his own towards home. There was no delaying their goodbyes.

'See you again, soon,' Leo said. In the glow of the streetlight moisture glistened in his hair. With a final wave he walked away.

Later, back in her apartment, Natalie pulled off her trainers and lay down on the bed, staring at the ceiling, reliving the moment of the shooting star, thinking about her wish. *Please let him kiss me. Please let him kiss me, even if it's only once.*

Chapter Forty-Three

'Hello. Is that Natalie speaking?'

'Yes, it is.'

'Good. Here is Leo Meier … Natalie? Are you there?'

'I am. Yes, umm …'

'Are you working? Is it difficult to talk?'

'Not at all. I'm just walking back from the post office.'

Leo stood up, glanced across the square. She'd been here seconds ago. He sank back onto the bench. 'You know Karin is on a little … vacation and …'

'Yes. Lucky thing. She texted from Spain and said it's very hot.'

She sounded flustered. Was that good or bad, he wondered.

'Well I am left with the research for your grandfather and I have found something.'

'Really? Is he alive?'

'I cannot yet say if he is alive but I have something to show you which I think you will like.'

'What is it?'

'Could we … meet when you have finished working?'

'Yes. Yes of course. Where?'

'Do you know MozArts under the Glockenspiel?'

'I do. I can … be there at just after half past five.'

'I will be waiting there.'

'Alright. I'll see you later.'

'Yes. Tschüs!'

Leo ended the call then realised he hadn't said he would be inside the cafe, not at one of the pavement tables. Surely she would know to come in. Of course she would, she wasn't stupid. If he took a table near the window he could watch her approach and …

He stood up, a group of tourists hovered clearly wanting to take the weight off their feet. Leo moved away. Glancing at his watch he saw there were forty minutes until she could join him. He crossed the square heading for St Peter's. It would be cool and calm in the cemetery garden. He had almost reached the gate when he thought that her boss might let her off early if she was excited to see what he'd found. He turned back.

In MozArts he had the choice of a corner table or one by the window. He chose the one tucked away in the corner and ordered a coffee. As the waitress walked away he called her back and asked for peppermint tea instead. He didn't want to risk coffee-breath. With his jacket on the chair back and his tea cooling he went through to the toilet and checked his antiperspirant was working. He wet his comb and ran it through his hair; made sure his fingernails were clean, smiled at himself in the mirror then felt a complete idiot and went back to his table, grabbing a magazine from the rack on the way. It wasn't until he sat down he saw he'd picked up *Die Salzburgerin*, the magazine for local women. Still twenty minutes to go. He almost laughed. You could read a lot about business women and which cars they liked to drive, in that time.

Chapter Forty-Four

It was impossible to apply eye-liner when your hands were shaking. Natalie wiped it off and settled for a sweep of mascara and some lippy instead.

Karl had left early so it was her job to set the burglar alarm. Twice she punched in the wrong number. She locked up the shop, grateful there were no last minute customers.

Dodging round tourists on the pavement she arrived at MozArts, her heart dancing a jig. Umbrellas were up, shading customers from the late afternoon sun. Not wanting to peer under each parasol she marched up to the door and went inside.

He was there, in the corner, smiling and waving her over. Had he been watching the door? As she approached he stood up like a gentleman in a Jane Austen novel. They shook hands. Oh, for a good old British hug, she thought.

'Thank you for meeting me,' Leo said. 'And what would you like to drink?'

'What are you having?'

'I have peppermint tea.'

The waitress hovered.

'I'll have the same, please.'

Natalie glanced around the room. It was that time of day when some people were still eating cake and others were ordering an early dinner.

'So you will want to know what I have discovered,' Leo said.

His smile dispelled any doubts Natalie might have had about her attraction to him. She liked him and that very fact caused a knot of anxiety in her stomach. She couldn't bear another let down.

As she swirled the teabag in her cup she watched Leo open

an envelope and slide out a sheet of paper. Tantalisingly he left it face down.

'You remember the girl at the record office said sometimes prisoners were invited to join local families for meals?'

Natalie nodded, her gaze now fixed on the paper.

'She kindly looked through newspaper photographs for me and found something that might … or might not be significant. I don't want to disappoint you so …' he touched her arm for a second. 'Please try not to get too … hopeful.'

He pushed the paper towards her and she held her breath, met Leo's gaze for a second then turned the sheet over. It was a photocopy of a newspaper article. People were grouped together in front of a doorway, a collie dog sitting at their feet. Natalie searched the faces, a middle-aged couple, a boy about Toby's age, a girl, maybe twelve years old. Two young women, one much taller than the other, stood on the right of the picture their hair pinned and curled like girls in war films. Behind them was a young man whose face was slightly hidden.

Leo whispered, 'Natalie, read the names.'

Her gasp was so loud people at neighbouring tables turned to stare. Tears took her by surprise and she covered her face with her hands.

'Mein Gott, I've upset you.'

'No. No you've been so … I mean … finding this.' She gulped for breath and stared at the photo. The farmer was called Wheatley; the reporter had listed the names of his wife and children. The two young women, happy and smiling into the camera lens were Florence and Maureen Siddons. The young man's name she could hardly read for her tears, *Adolf Lindner.*

'It's him. That's my grandfather. This is … beyond belief that you should …'

'You are sure? Are these women …?

'Yes.' She was aware of her tear-stained face, the mascara

heading south. Leo leapt up and found her a paper napkin. She buried her face in it. 'Florence is … was my grandma who died and … the other is Auntie Maureen. I don't … exactly recognise their faces as they were then but … how could it not be?'

'I'm so pleased for you,' Leo said. 'With his last name I can telephone the archive at Koblenz. We might just find where he lived. But again don't anticipate too much.'

On an impulse she took hold of his hand across the table. His fingers were cool and dry. Hers she knew were hot and damp with tears but she didn't care.

'Leo, how can I ever thank you and Karin for doing this for me? You've all been so kind since I came here and I feel … so … at home now. Even if we don't find him at least I'll have this.' She looked down at the picture. 'It brings the whole story to life.'

The waitress came to take their empty cups. Natalie let go of Leo's hand, feeling the loss of his warmth.

'Are you … in a rush to get home?' He asked. 'If not we could have a bite to eat, talk for longer.'

'Yes. I mean no, I'm not in a rush. Something to eat would be great.' Anything to extend her time with him was good.

It was hard to concentrate on the menu but she selected a Greek salad dish and Leo asked for the wine list. This was their third meal together. She wondered if he was counting too.

'Do you know what you will do if we get an address from Koblenz?' He poured her some wine.

'No. I didn't let myself believe Karin would find anything but this …' She studied every bit of her grandmother's dress with its puffed sleeves and sprigged pattern. She wore white ankle socks and Auntie Maureen, with a ribbon in her hair looked about twelve but must have been sixteen. It was incredible to see their youthful faces. She could see Adolf's blond hair swept back from his forehead and one side of his face, no smile but not an anxious face either. Grandma was as tall as he, her hair shading his other cheek.

'What must it have been like for them,' Leo said, 'in love but unable to tell anyone. He, so far from home, she, knowing he would leave eventually.'

'It would be … oh, what's it called?' Natalie stared at her wine glass for a second. 'Bittersweet. That's it, a bittersweet romance.'

'I never heard that word but it works for this. When are your parents visiting? It must be soon.'

'Next week. I'm longing to see my brother. Do you think we might know more by then?'

'Maybe. What will you do?'

'I should tell my mother but I think she'd freak.'

'You said Adolf returned to England in 1955. Do you know if he had children by then?'

'Boys, I think Auntie Maureen said. I wish I'd written it all down now.'

'You see Karin told me there were mountains in that picture he gave your grandmother. In Bavaria a farm will be passed down to son and grandson. They might still be there.'

'But when he came to England that second time it was for work, something to do with selling tractors.'

Leo stared at a point somewhere above her head then lowered his gaze and their eyes locked for a second or two. He smiled. 'Maybe we must make one step and then another. I'll ring the archive tomorrow and then let you know. Is it alright to send you a text message?'

You can send me any kind of message, she thought, the wine stealing down. Semaphore, smoke signals, just keep in touch. 'Yes, text is fine.'

After they'd eaten she was surprised to hear he'd come into town on the bus.

'My car is in the garage today and Max hates the bus. He

howls and makes everyone angry.'

'I love riding the number seven,' Natalie said, 'It reminds me of the holiday when I fell in love with the city.'

Minutes later it was nice sitting beside him, their legs touching, their shoulder's moving together with the rhythm of the bus.

When they reached Leo's stop he seemed a little embarrassed just getting up and leaving her. 'I'll call you as soon as I have some news.' After crossing the road he turned and waved. Natalie waved back and thought of that other time on the bus, his gaunt frame and sorrow-etched face.

Walking down Salzachstrasse, the photocopy clutched to her chest it was hard to know what she was most excited about, finding her grandfather's family or the prospect of meeting up with Leo again. 'Oh, Natalie, what are you doing?' She said aloud as she unlocked her door, kicked off her shoes and felt the cool tiles beneath her feet. It was impossible to guess how Leo felt about her. Was he just helping a friend of Karin's or did he like her? It sometimes felt as though he did. She thought of his hand in hers for those few brief moments in the cafe. Please, please don't let me fall in love, she prayed to nobody in particular.

Chapter Forty-Five

Natalie clicked on her parents' Skype address and adjusted her new webcam. She sat back, taking a sip of coffee as the call went out. It was two o'clock at home. Toby would be at school. She half hoped her dad would answer so that she could run all this past him first, but it was her mother's face that appeared on the screen and greeted her. She turned the volume down as her mother's delighted screech made her jump.

'Natalie. We can't wait to see you at the weekend. I've been looking at the weather temperatures, you did say the hotel has a pool?'

'It has one inside and one in the garden. Both are lovely. Are you on your own?'

'Yes, your dad's gone into town. I told him he needed new trousers so he's gone to M&S. God knows what he'll come back with but at least he can exchange them. He's picking up the Euros too.'

The copy of the newspaper photo was just out of the camera view. Natalie pressed her fingers on it as though touching wood. 'I'm glad there's just us. I wanted to talk to you.'

'Sounds serious. Are you okay'

'Yes. I'm fine. I wanted to talk to you about Grandma.'

Her mother's frown came after the slight satellite delay. 'Grandma? What do you want to know?'

'I don't want to know anything … I mean …' she took a deep breath and smiled, wishing she'd telephoned instead. 'You know when Auntie Maureen and I cleared her things from her room I brought home a photo of Toby and me.'

Silence. Her mother stared at the screen.

'Only, when I opened up the back there was another picture,

a little boy on a tractor. Have you ever seen it?'

'Why did you open the frame?'

'I … well … I wanted to bring the photo of us with me and it was easier out of the frame.'

'Goodness knows what the other one was,' her mum said, reaching across the desk. She picked up a tube of hand cream and squeezed some onto her palm.

'Thing is, Mum, I've been doing a bit of digging and …'

'Digging about what?' The friendly tone was gone.

'When … Grandma died Auntie Maureen told me they worked on a farm during the war.'

'That must be it then … the child on the tractor. He must have been one of the children there. Sweet of her to keep it.' Her mother's smile looked nailed on.

'No, Mum. A … German prisoner of war gave Grandma the photo. There are mountains behind the tractor and …'

'So it was the German's child then.' The hand cream was rubbed in vigorously.

'I guess so but Auntie Maureen told me something else.'

The hands became still.

She said Grandma was in love and …'

'Natalie. Can you cut to the chase?' Now her mother turned her face to the side as though she was looking out of the window.

'What? Well it's not easy to say. I don't want to upset you and …'

'Go on.'

'Gran must have been in love with the German and she saw him after the war when he …'

Her mother sat forward, her face close to the camera. 'Let me guess. Maureen told you this man was my father?'

Stunned, Natalie could only gape.

'Well it's not true so get that ridiculous idea out of your head.'

'You already knew?'

'I'm not talking about it, Natalie. It's ridiculous. I'm furious with Maureen for saying this and I'll be having a few words with her I can tell you.'

'No! I promised her I'd never tell you but … something amazing has happened and I've got to tell you about it.'

'Whatever it is I don't want to hear. I'm turning this off now.'

'Mum, don't. This affects me and Toby too. Please listen.'

'No it doesn't. It's a stupid notion your grandmother got into her head. How do you think I felt when she told me? It wasn't long after your Grandpa died and … I … loved him… he was a saint of a man and …'

'I know he was and … oh, Mum, don't cry … let me tell you what I've …'

'I don't care if she had a fling with a German, Natalie. It's trying to make out he was … well, he wasn't. I don't want this raking up, especially now she's gone.'

'Mum, I'm going to email you a web link. Please promise me you'll look at it. I'm so sorry I've upset you I …' she wiped her own tears away. She could see her mum reaching for tissues. 'Will you promise me that?'

'What is it?'

'Just a link to a website. I'll send it now from my phone.'

'Alright but I'm closing this Skype thing.'

The screen went blank. Natalie leaned forward and rested her head on the table. This had gone horribly wrong. She'd been in an agony of indecision before making the call but Leo's discovery was so great she knew she couldn't just pour it out while the family were at the Friesen. She needed to prepare the way a little but now she'd be lucky if her mother ever spoke to her again.

She wished Leo was at home. The day after their meeting at MozArts he was called away to Vienna, his father had taken a tumble and broken his leg. Even so he'd called Natalie with the news that the Lindner farm in Bavaria *was* still run by the family. 'They have a Gasthaus on the property too,' he'd said. Most important was the news from Koblenz: Adolf Lindner's address when joining the army was the farm. 'They couldn't tell me if he was alive or not.' Leo was apologetic. 'I think you will have to go there.'

With Karin not back until the day before her family arrived Natalie felt bereft of someone to discuss it with. She looked at the clock, not much of her afternoon off remaining. She could go for a run but prayed her mother would call back once she'd looked at the website.

It was tea time before the Skype ring tone sounded and it was her dad's face she saw on the screen. 'Natalie, you've stirred up a proper hornet's nest. Good job Toby's at Markus's.'

'Is Mum okay? I'm so sorry I upset her. I was going to wait until you were …'

'Hang on, Lovie. She's sort of alright. That picture on the website's a bit of a shocker, though. I was as gobsmacked as she was.'

Natalie had the link up on her screen. The family at Gasthaus Lindner were photographed, grouped around the door. Frau Huber, clad in dirndl and spotless apron stared out of the picture with Natalie's mother's face. The short, bleached hair was almost an identical style and they looked similar in age.

When she'd first seen the link Natalie thought she might faint. It had taken her a full half hour before she could ring Leo and tell him of the resemblance.

'How on earth did you come up with this, Lovie?' Her dad said. 'Where did you even start?'

It seemed sensible to play down Leo and Karin's part in the discovery. 'The record office in Leicester was brilliant,' she said. 'I've even got a newspaper photo of Grandma and Maureen at the farm.' She hesitated for a second. 'He's in the picture too. So … you knew about it then, Dad?'

'Not till recently, it was when you started your German classes. I guess you remember she was less than thrilled about it. '

'I do but why is she so …'

'Hang on, she's coming downstairs.'

Natalie was appalled to see her mother's tear stained face and swollen eyes. 'Mum, I'm so sorry, if I'd known …'

'I'm okay.' The voice was calm now. 'Tell me everything.'

Chapter Forty-Six

Natalie looked at her father's Panama hat and suppressed a laugh. It can't have been his idea to buy it but after the initial surprise she thought he looked rather good in it. All he needed now was a pale linen suit and he'd really look the part.

'Make a note of today's date,' he said. 'Your mother loves *everything*!' She's already been in both pools, examined the sauna and given it the thumbs up and said the scrambled egg at breakfast was the best she's ever tasted.'

Toby, swinging on Natalie's hand, asked if he could walk to the bottom of the garden. He'd become Karin's new best friend when she said he could go with her to take Otto for a walk. The dog was rootling in the undergrowth as Toby reached him. Natalie could hear her brother's stream of chatter.

She turned back to her dad. 'Is Mum nervous about tomorrow?'

'She didn't sleep well last night. I heard her go out onto the balcony at one point; thought for a minute she'd taken up smoking.'

'I'm anxious about it too,' she said, and he put a comforting arm round her shoulder.

After much discussion they'd decided not to telephone Gasthaus Lindner ahead of their visit. They would simply turn up and see what happened, with Leo going along to be interpreter. Karin had to work which was just as well as Leo's car would be pretty full as it was.

'She'll be down in a minute,' her father continued, 'she's just changing out of her swimming stuff. By the way, all Toby knows is we're visiting someone Grandma used to know.'

'If Adolf is still alive what's she going to tell him then?'

'One bridge at a time, Lovie. It may not even be the right farm.'

From the moment her family walked into the airport arrivals hall Natalie had been struck by how much she'd missed them. Toby was constantly in her thoughts and it was a joy to have him close, but seeing her parents bewildered by the German signs and language she'd felt a sudden need to protect them and had taken charge, helping them buy a map of the city, speaking to the taxi driver and giving their destination. Karin had given them a great room with an extra bed for Toby.

Their balcony overlooked the pool and beyond, the mountains. Only her jumbled feelings for Leo prevented Natalie from happiness

'That Leo's a nice chap,' her father said, as though reading her thoughts. 'He came in this morning to say hello. Are he and that receptionist an item?'

Natalie felt a jolt in her stomach but managed a nervous laugh. 'I don't think so. They've been friends since they were children.'

'Well, they had their heads together. He's joining us for dinner. That's okay isn't it? Thought it was the least I could do as he's driving us over there tomorrow.'

'And Mum agreed did she?' Another meal with Leo, all they seemed to do was eat together. She wondered if they could ever progress to anything more.

'Haven't told her yet.' Her dad winked, pulled the brim of his hat further over his eyes and set off after Toby.

It was warm enough to eat on the terrace. Natalie sat with her back to the view so that her mother could enjoy it. The ever present paragliders circled the summit of the Gaisberg and Toby, struggling to hold his father's heavy binoculars, gave a running commentary on their progress, getting more and more excited when he realised they were landing in the field beyond the hotel garden.

Leo arrived precisely on time. He wore his green trachten jacket and black jeans. Natalie tried not to stare at him.

'How is your papa's leg?' she asked.

'In a cast and he cannot walk but his spirits are good. Thank you for asking.'

He gave her the little incline of the head that she was trying to perfect herself.

She wanted to look like a local as well as sound like one.

Leo shook hands with her parents and then with Toby who looked shy but put down the binoculars and thrust out a grubby hand. When Max ambled up with Otto in tow Toby slid off his chair and tried to embrace both dogs. Natalie saw her mother's disapproving glance, and whispered that it was perfectly normal to bring your dogs to dinner in Austria.

Karin treated them to Birnsekt and presented Toby with a fizzy soft drink, almost indistinguishable in colour from the adults' Champagne. His eyes grew wide until his mother said it was okay. As he settled Max under the table Leo smiled at Natalie and she felt a blush steal up from her neck. She buried her face in the menu.

When Rosina came to take their order Natalie couldn't help showing off a little by speaking German.

'That's just what Markus's mum sounds like when she talks to his dad.' Toby looked impressed.

'Natalie's German is very good,' Leo said, 'considering she has not been speaking it long. She is even deciphering our dialect.'

'Could be those German genes?' Her dad raised his eyebrows.

Natalie held her breath expecting her mother to throw him a warning frown but instead she smiled across the table. 'When she finally comes home she'll be able to get a job as a bilingual secretary or something. Great for her CV.'

Natalie's gaze darted to Leo. Their eyes met for a lingering moment but she couldn't read his expression.

'When *are* you coming home, Nat?'

'Not for a while, Tobes.' For a second she felt panic rise in her chest and took deep breaths to slow her quickening pulse. Leaving Salzburg was unthinkable now but the thought of not seeing Toby growing up was equally unbearable. Until now she hadn't let these thoughts crystallise and she couldn't face them today. There was enough to deal with. Tomorrow would be emotional no matter how it turned out.

She was grateful when Luisa popped out of the kitchen to say a quick hello and to wish them luck in Bavaria.

'How long will it take to get there?' Natalie's mother directed her question to Leo.

'If we take the autobahn the route is longer but quicker maybe an hour or just over. There is a route through the mountains but because there will be much anticipation, we should perhaps go the quickest route and take the mountain road to come back. Does that sound good?'

They all agreed it did then conversation turned to places the family might visit while they were in Salzburg.

'Christine would be happy to sit by the pool, I reckon.' Natalie's father gave an exaggerated wink. 'She prefers soaking up the sun to soaking up culture.' He laughed at his own joke and was given a stony stare but Natalie noticed her mother beginning to relax. Leo had ordered wine, insisting on paying for it and suggesting they make a toast to the future, whatever it might hold. As her glass clinked against Leo's his fingers brushed hers and it was as though a current passed through her skin.

'The future,' she said.

Leo left as soon as dessert was eaten, thanking Natalie's father for his generosity and shaking everyone's hand again. She wondered why he didn't stay for coffee but a few moments later she saw him with Karin, heading off down the garden with the dogs.

She hated the jealous pang that ran through her.

'Big day tomorrow,' her dad said. 'We'd better all hit the hay. Will you be okay getting back to your flat on your own, Lovie?'

'I'll hop on the bus,' she said, giving them all a kiss and hugging Toby who was almost asleep on his feet.

As she walked through to reception Rosina called to her. 'Your mother left this on her chair.'

'Her pashmina. She'll worry if she thinks she's lost it. Thanks, Rosi.' Natalie rushed back to the stairwell intending to call up to her parents before they reached their room but then she heard them talking and stopped to listen.

'Don't know if I'm imagining it,' she heard her father say, 'but I reckon Leo's got a bit of a thing for our Natalie.'

'Do you, John?' her mother's voice was strident. 'I rather think it's the other way around.'

Chapter Forty-Seven

The weather was cloudy and a breeze rippled the awning as Natalie waited outside the Spar shop. Leo had offered to pick her up at her apartment but she knew that would delay them. Her mother would surely want to go in and criticise it.

Despite the early hour Spar was doing a good trade, Salzburgers buying cigarettes and sandwiches on their way to work. Natalie nipped in and bought a couple of bottles of mineral water and a Kinder egg for Toby. As Leo's car pulled into the car park she felt a thud of disappointment when she saw her father in the passenger seat. Her mother got out of a rear door and enveloped her in a hug. 'This is going to be a strange day,' she said. 'I'm half hoping it's not the right place and we can just come back and have a nice lunch in the hotel.'

'Have you got the photos?' Natalie still felt the touch of her mother's cheek as she got into the car.

'Of course I have.' The brisk tone was back.

'Morgen, Natalie.' Leo caught her eye in the rear view mirror.

She returned his smile.

Toby was staring out of the window, a frown creasing his face.

'What's up, Tobes? I got you this.' She fished the Kinder egg out of her bag.

He took it and thanked her but continued to keep his face averted.

'He's peeved because Leo didn't bring Max,' her mother said. 'Just where he thought the poor dog would sit I really don't know. In the boot?'

'Max will have a nice day with Gerde, my neighbour.' Leo's voice was soothing. 'I promise I'll bring him to the hotel tomorrow.'

Natalie stroked Toby's cheek. Whispered it was impolite to ignore someone.

'Alright then.' He turned from the window and concentrated on unwrapping the chocolate egg.

They headed south to pick up the Autobahn. Natalie, sandwiched in the back seat stared at the road ahead but found her gaze shifting to the mirror; to Leo's expression of concentration. The mountains looked dark and brooding, the clouds lowering. She'd hoped for fine weather so that her parents could enjoy the scenery but a while later, as they crossed the border into Germany, torrential rain beat down on the car. The road surface was awash and traffic slowed. Natalie saw her mother's hands clenched tight in her lap.

'Someone told me when it rains here it *really* rains,' her dad said. 'And they weren't joking. Did we bring umbrellas?'

Leo caught Natalie's eye and winked. 'Toby,' he said, 'there is something for you in the pocket beside your seat.'

Toby drew out a disposable camera. 'Oh cool.'

'You are in charge of it, is that okay? You can take pictures whenever you want. Maybe you'd like to photograph this rain?'

'Yes, 'cos it's jumping back off the road,' Toby said, squinting through the viewfinder and pressing the button. 'How many can I take?'

'It says twenty-four but you know, I brought another couple of cameras along in case.'

Toby took pictures of the car interior, the Toy Story model from his Kinder egg and a few more of the rain which was beginning to ease.

'Save some for later,' his mother said as the bunched traffic flowed more freely.

'Up ahead there is sun,' Leo said and sure enough there was a defined edge to the weather front. The mountains began to appear out of the mist and the mood in the car lifted.

'Shall we stop somewhere for coffee?' Leo asked as he steered the car into the slip road. 'Ruhpolding is a nice little town, we could find a Konditorei.'

The aroma of fresh baked bread and cakes greeted them as they filed into the cafe. They sat at a circular table; Toby hung about at the counter checking out the cakes.

'Mum, can I have a look at your photos?' Natalie asked, pushing her plate aside to avoid getting icing sugar on the pictures. Her mother delved in her bag and pulled out a brown envelope. The first snapshot was of Grandma and Auntie Maureen standing either side of a man's bike. Both had ribbons in their hair.

'Maureen reckons she was twelve there so Gran must have been fifteen. I doubt she'd have looked that much different at nineteen, a bit taller of course.'

Another photo showed Gran young and smiling. Dad had scanned her wedding photo into the computer and printed off just her face. It seemed inappropriate to bring one with Grandpa standing beside her. Natalie slid them back into the envelope along with the one she'd found secreted in the photo frame.

'I'm so nervous I can't eat.' Her mother wrapped up her cake in a paper napkin. Toby, with only crumbs on his plate eyed the napkin. Natalie put her arm round his shoulders and dropped a kiss on the top of his head. She whispered to her mother, 'I think we've got to be prepared for the fact that he might have died. He'd be over ninety now and …'

'I know. I'm not even letting myself think he'll be there. It's just … pitching up at someone's home with an unbelievable story. What if they throw us out?'

Leo glanced at Natalie as though asking her permission to chip in. She smiled and then wondered, did he just catch his breath or had she imagined that?

'If your story did not have some foundation why would you

choose their farm out of every one in Germany? I'm sure they will listen and of course, you do … resemble Frau Huber quite strongly.'

'That's another thing,' her mother said, 'it's going to be freaky seeing her.'

'I'll have to remember she's the one in the fancy dress and pinny,' her dad said, a wicked grin on his face.

Natalie couldn't look at Leo. 'Dad, it's called a *Dirndl*.'

They emerged to bright sunshine; steam rising from the wet street, flower-filled meadows rose to rocky peaks. Toby dawdled on the way back to the car, photographing a Fiaker carriage as it rolled by, the horses still wearing their waterproofs.

'We go south along this road for a few miles,' Leo said. 'The farm comes on the right side and there should be a sign.'

Natalie gripped her mother's hand for a few seconds and felt the pressure returned.

Back in the car she tried not to let Toby see she was stressed. She encouraged him to take pictures of the cattle with bells round their necks. She saw her father point to a turning ahead and Leo slowed the car. An ornately painted wooden sign beside a gateway announced Gasthaus Lindner where Familie Huber waited to greet visitors.

'Christine, Sweetheart,' Natalie's dad turned in his seat and spoke softly, 'you'll let Leo do the talking won't you?'

Her mother nodded, bit her lip and stared straight ahead as they turned into a track with grass growing down the middle. The large traditional chalet was visible now.

Two other cars were parked in front of the house. To the side Natalie saw a trampoline encased in netting and a child's bike.

In the reception area a man in full-length lederhosen and waistcoat greeted them in English.

'Herr and Frau Grey are staying in Salzburg, Leo said, 'but they have come today because a Lindner family member was in England years ago. We might have the wrong house but we hope not.'

Herr Huber's smile of greeting stayed in place although his brow furrowed.

'Is it possible to speak to Frau Huber?' Leo added.

'Yes, of course. Well, this is interesting. I am Horst Huber, my wife is in the garden. Please come through.' He gestured for them to follow but then his hand fell to his side as he stared past Natalie to where her mother was standing. 'Oh. I … yes. Please follow me to the … '

Frau Huber was hanging snow white pillow cases on the washing line. She had a peg in her mouth but quickly removed it when her husband called her name. Natalie found herself gawping. The woman was slimmer than her mother but facially the similarity was startling.

Before Leo could speak the man rushed forward, whispered to his wife. Natalie held her breath, couldn't make her mouth work to give the German greeting she'd planned.

'This is my wife, Sabine.' Herr Huber said.

She walked forward, smoothing down her apron then stopped in front of Natalie's mother and the two women stared at each other. Natalie wanted to be by her mother's side but was unable to move. Sabine's hand came forward, found Christine's and held it; then she let go, covered her face, her head dropped forward.

In fascinated horror Natalie watched the woman sink to her knees. Both her mother and Herr Huber reached to help her as Sabine let out a wailing sob.

Leo, clearly horrified, spoke so quickly to Herr Huber Natalie couldn't catch a word of it. Both men crouched over the sobbing woman. Taking her arms they helped her to stand but the tears still came. Leo pulled a handkerchief from his pocket, as white as the linen billowing on the line. Sabine took it, turned away for a few seconds and as she faced them again she had found her composure. A silence lengthened broken only by the click of Toby's camera.

'So,' she said. 'I didn't … ever … want it to be real, but here is the truth in front of me and I … I don't know what to say.'

Natalie saw her mother was weeping. Her dad seemed as unable to move as she was.

'Leo, please tell them how sorry we are for upsetting them,' she said. 'This is terrible. We shouldn't have come.'

'No!' Sabine looked at her for the first time. 'No. It is right that you are here. There is much we must say.'

'You knew.' Christine spoke, her voice flat.

'My father said things to me but I … there are photographs and …'

'Come inside. We must all drink something, I think.' Herr Huber, considerably paler than when they'd arrived, walked to the door, waved for them to follow.

Natalie found that Leo's hand was on her shoulder. Her mother and Sabine, each wiping away tears, didn't move.

'Adolf …' Natalie's mother finally spoke. 'So Adolf was your father? Is he … I mean I wondered if …'

'Adolf Lindner is my father.'

Natalie felt a shiver start in her scalp and shoot down through her body. 'Does that mean … is he …'

Sabine drew in a shuddering breath, turned to face her. 'My father, he … yes, he is alive.'

Chapter Forty-Eight

Sitting in the gasthof's tiny bar Natalie watched her mother knock back a glass of Schnapps. Sabine Huber blew her nose; waved the bottle away.

Through the window Natalie saw Leo holding Toby's trainers while her brother struggled up through the trampoline netting then did a few tentative bounces. Despite the unfolding drama indoors it was difficult to tear her gaze away.

'My father lives in a Seniorenheim,' Sabine said, 'for old people, you know? It is close, we can go there … if you …'

Fresh tears poured down her mother's cheeks. Natalie passed her some tissues. 'Is his health good?' she asked in German.

'Yes. He is a little forgetful but still strong in his body. Here he always tried to do too much; wanted to work still at ninety-one. Once he broke his …' she gestured to her own collarbone, 'and once his leg. It is safer for him to be there, but he comes home on Sunday and stays a few hours. We visit often.'

'What year … were you born?' Natalie's mother had her tears under control and was gulping deep breaths.

'Nineteen fifty-four,' Sabine said. 'And you?'

'Fifty-five. Did he … I hardly dare ask but did he mention my … my mother, ever?'

'Not until after … my mother was dead.'

The stark sentence sat in the air. Natalie cleared her throat. 'I know this is a shock, us turning up like this. But once we uncovered a little of the story we had to know more.'

'I understand that. In your place I would do the same and of course,' she glanced through the window, 'you want your little boy to meet his great-grandfather.'

Natalie felt the usual jab of pain. Her mother touched her

arm and said, 'Toby's my son.' She smiled at Sabine still with her fingers resting on Natalie's jacket sleeve. 'This is my second marriage. Natalie's father died when she was very young.'

'Oh I'm sorry.' The German woman's cheeks flushed.

'Do you have children?' Natalie rushed to fill the embarrassed silence.

'My son lives in Wiesbaden. He has two girls. My daughter lives very close by. My grandson, Milo, is usually here to eat after school but he is gone to friends. He must be a close age to Toby.

'He's ten this summer.' Natalie looked out of the window then laughed out loud. Toby was taking photographs of Leo who was on the trampoline in stocking-feet, looking less than confident.

Her dad caught her eye; smiled then he took hold of her mother's hand and spoke to Sabine. 'I'm sure I speak for all of us when I say we're delighted to hear your father is still in good health. We're only in Salzburg for a week … would it be possible to visit him … today? Would he be up to it if he knows who we are?'

She exchanged a long look with her husband.

Horst smiled. 'Maybe if Sabine prepares him a little?'

'Of course.' Her mother's voice was wobbly. 'And if you're not sure then we'll … leave it … and …'

'No. We won't leave it.' Sabine stood up. 'He's ninety-two next week. You don't leave things when someone is ninety-two. I'll just make a phone call to the home and then we will go.'

'There are too many of you,' the care home manager said. 'He will be overwhelmed.'

Sabine rattled off a few sentences and the woman turned to look at the family. They all stared back except for Toby who was photographing a man in a wheel chair.

'Toby' Natalie whispered, 'don't take someone's picture

without asking.'

'Durr! I don't speak German.' He rolled his eyes.

Leo crouched down next to Toby; Natalie heard him whispering a German phrase for Toby to repeat to the man.

Sabine was still negotiating with the manager. 'Christine and Natalie, you come with me. She is right we mustn't confuse him with lots of people.' She gave Natalie's dad an apologetic smile.

'No probs,' he said.

At the door to the day room her mother paused.

'You alright, Mum?'

'No. Are you?' She gave a little laugh.

Sabine smiled. 'He is a lovely man. All will be well.'

The room was large; floor to ceiling windows gave onto a view of Linden trees, a sweep of lawn and the mountains beyond. Sabine stopped at a high-backed chair, bent to kiss the cheek of the white-haired man who put down his newspaper and magnifying glass. His frame was slight but it was easy to see he'd once been tall.

'Papa. You're looking well. Today I have some very special visitors for you.'

'Grüß Gott, Herr Lindner.' Natalie thrust out her hand. His grip was startlingly firm and he returned her greeting, his voice deep and gravelly. He gave Sabine an enquiring look.

Natalie pulled up chairs and Sabine sat close to her father, took his hand. He gave her a smile that made Natalie's heart constrict.

'You remember how to speak English, Papa? These people are from England.'

'England? Beautiful … countryside,' he said, treating everyone to the smile. 'Hedgerows. I was … in England … I …'

'Yes and do you remember you … told me a long time ago about a girl. I know it might be difficult to talk about but …'

He frowned, his lips pursing then relaxing as though he

wanted to speak but couldn't find the words. He glanced at Natalie and her mother then concentrated on Sabine's halting questions.

'A girl at the farm, Papa. You told me … she was a … a very special girl?'

'Yes. I remember. Of course I remember but …'

He broke into German, his accent so strong Natalie could only glean that it was a question he'd asked.

'Because … this lady …is her daughter.'

Adolf stared at his knees. Natalie held her breath. Did he really remember? But then he fixed his gaze, the dark blue of his eyes magnified by rimless glasses, on her mother.

'This cannot be Flore.' His tone was flat. 'She is too young.'

Sabine laced her fingers through his. 'No.' With her free hand she delved into her handbag, pulled out a dog-eared, black and white photograph, turned it round for them all to see. A small blonde girl smiling, sitting on a cushion, a teddy bear in her lap. Natalie's mother gasped, covered her mouth with her hands.

'This is Florrie's daughter, Papa. This is Christine.'

Chapter Forty-Nine

Of the four of them only Adolf was not weeping. He gazed at the photograph of the infant Christine, nodded slowly and whispered to Sabine.

'He kept this in his desk at work, looked at it every day,' she said. 'You can see where his thumb lies, the picture is all worn.'

He passed the photo to Natalie who ran her own finger over the spot where he had held it and noticed with a jolt, as she handed it back, that his fingernails were wide and short like hers and her mother's. He put the picture down on the arm of the chair, shuffled to lean forward and took hold of Natalie's hand, reached for her mother's, held them both. 'Flore … Florrie …?'

Natalie braced herself, looked at Sabine.

'She is gone,' Adolf said, 'why else would you be here, I am right?'

Sabine nodded. 'Yes, Papa. But look at the gift she has left behind.'

'I never thought this day would come. Long ago I … told myself I must … I must forget but …' he gripped their hands tighter. 'Some things you cannot forget, especially children.'

Natalie bit her lip, took a shuddering breath but it wasn't enough, she needed air. Gently sliding her hand from her grandfather's she stood. 'I'll be back in a bit, Mum.'

In the corridor her dad was having a stilted conversation with an elderly lady. Toby sipped from a can of Coke.

'Take Toby in to see him, Dad. Where's Leo?'

'In the garden I think, are you okay, Lovie?'

She nodded, turned and headed for the door.

He was sitting on a bench under a Linden tree. Natalie ran across the grass, saw him catch sight of her and stand up. She wasn't sure who opened their arms first but she clung to him, sobbing into his shoulder. He didn't ask what the matter was, didn't say anything but her name, whispered into her hair, over and over. When she couldn't cry anymore she sat beside him and pulled tissues from her pocket. 'What a messy family we are today, all tears and hankies.'

'It is a most emotional time.' He put his arm round her shoulders and it seemed the most natural thing in the world to lean against him.

'Adolf is so sweet and so old and he … he was talking about children and … how we must never … forget. He had a photo. Grandma must have sent it and Sabine found it and …'

'But that is not he what is making you cry.'

She turned to face him, sun dappled through the leaves making patterns on his hair. 'No.'

'Do you want to tell me?'

She shook her head. 'Not today but … maybe …'

'Nat!'

They both rose from the bench. Toby was running across the grass.

'That man's my Grandpa. How cool is that? Did you already know because you ought to have told me.'

Natalie wiped her eyes. 'I only found out recently, Tobes. It's a nice surprise though, isn't it?'

He stopped to take a picture of a delivery van making slow progress up the drive. 'So did Grandma live here then?'

'No, Sweetheart, it's a long story. We'll tell you all about it, I promise.'

'Can I go back and see him again?'

'Course you can. I'll be there in a minute.'

She turned back to Leo; he didn't move but gazed into her eyes for a long moment and it was as though everything inside her melted. She took a step forward, closed her eyes, felt his hand touch her hair then his lips brushed hers and the whole world fell into place. The kiss lengthened, she reached to wind her arms around his neck. She was on tiptoe or floating, she didn't know which. When they came up for air he rested his chin on the top of her head, let out a breathy sigh.

'You could not guess how long I've wanted to do that,' he said.

'Tell me then.' She sat down on the bench and patted the wooden slats. But they heard her mother calling.

'We must go,' Leo said. 'But we won't forget to talk later, I hope.'

They all went for a late lunch at a hotel in Ruhpolding. Sabine asked them to stay overnight at the Gasthaus. Natalie felt a pang of guilty pleasure knowing she had to get back to Salzburg. 'I have to work in the morning. But I'll come over again very soon.'

'I too cannot stay,' Leo told them, 'but I'd be happy to come back tomorrow to collect you.'

'So kind, Leo but I will drive them,' Sabine said. 'I have not been to Salzburg for many years. It will be a treat for me.'

After another short visit to the home, when Grandpa showed them his room and let Toby play with his coin collection, they headed back to Haus Lindner. Sabine scanned and printed off photographs of the family for Natalie to take back to Salzburg. It was after five when she kissed them all goodbye and climbed into the BMW.

Now they were alone again she felt shy, staring ahead at the rush hour traffic as they approached the autobahn.

'That's quite a day you have had,' Leo said.

'It isn't over yet, is it?'

He glanced at her and she felt her face burn. Had she really just said that?

'Would you like to stop somewhere for dinner or wait until

we get back.'

'I could cook you something.' Where had this bold Natalie sprung from?

He looked straight ahead but he was smiling. 'You've had an exhausting day. I should cook for you.'

'I'm not tired at all,' she said, keeping her eyes on the car in front.

Leo slid a cd into the player and the strains of a Mozart aria filled the car. 'We should see a performance at the festival this year. If you'd like that.'

'I *would* like that, I'd love to go … with you.'

'Then I'll take a look at the programme tomorrow.'

He laid his hand on hers for a second; excitement rippled through her and then all manner of possibilities entered her mind. Would he kiss her goodnight? Of course he would, that kiss under the tree told her all she needed to know about his attraction to her. But this had happened so quickly, should she really invite him into the apartment or wait till next time? A longing she hadn't felt since the last time with Adam stole through her. This wouldn't be a fling to make her feel better. Leo was … something special.

They pulled off the slip road at Salzburg Süd, drove along roads she knew well but which had never been bathed in such a rosy glow. When they passed the turning for the Friesen Natalie thought of how much she would have to tell Karin tomorrow and maybe there'd be some things she wouldn't tell.

Feeling bolder than ever she took his hand as they climbed the stairs to her apartment and once inside held him close, felt the urgency of his kiss and his hands caressing her back. Finally she pulled away. She must at least make him coffee and he seemed to understand. He gave her a smile that almost stopped her heart and moved over to the window while she filled the kettle.

'Do your parents like this apartment?'

'They haven't been here yet. But there's plenty of time, they don't leave till the fourteenth. Please say you don't mind instant coffee, it's all I have. I feel very decadent asking you back here.'

'The fourteenth?'

She went to him, slid her arms around his waist, leaned her cheek against his back. But he didn't yield, he moved slowly from her embrace, turned to face her and she saw his expression of … what? Anger? No it was more like disbelief.

'Natalie, I have to go.'

'Go? Now?' Her heart began to race. She took hold of his hand but he snatched it away as though she'd burned him. 'Leo?'

'I'm sorry.'

He went to the door and opened it. She reached to touch his shoulder. 'Leo, what's wrong. What have I done?'

'You've done nothing wrong. I shouldn't be here, I …please forgive me.'

She opened her mouth to beg him to explain but then shrank back; she was in the living room at home again, all dignity gone, pleading with Adam. She would not do that again.

Then he was gone, the door shut, no sound but his feet on the stairs and the heartless click of the kettle.

Chapter Fifty

Leo felt the rain seep through his jacket, it dripped from his hair to cheeks already streaked with tears. He wiped blood from his hand where he'd grazed it scrambling over the cemetery railings. The Pfingstrosen he'd brought two weeks ago were wilted and colourless on Sofia's grave. There should be camellias, he thought, her favourite flowers. He'd planned to cut them for her. What sort of man am I, he asked himself, who gets so taken up with someone who is almost a stranger that he forgets the day his wife died? He knelt down and, in the dim light of the memorial lamp, removed the dead flowers and brushed away twigs that had blown onto the soil in front of the headstone. He'd chosen not to have a photograph on her grave and tonight he was grateful for that. He couldn't bear to see her sweet, heart-shaped face, her dark eyes always so full of love. He leaned forward, let his forehead rest against the wet marble, felt the contours of the engraving.

'Leo.' A whisper.

He didn't look up until he heard Max's whine, his paw scratching at the stones of the path. Silhouetted against the distant street light was his neighbour, a heavy blanket over her arm.

'Leave me, Gerde. Please.'

'Come back with me. Max is here, look, he wants to greet you.'

'Take him home. Feed him would you? I'll be along soon.'

But she came closer and soon Max's comforting bulk leaned against him.

'Put this round your shoulders Leo and we'll walk together.'

He let her drape the blanket around him but he didn't move. 'Please Go. You can see I want to be alone here.'

'I can see you're dripping wet.'

He ignored her.

'Let's go. 'We'll raise a glass of Schnapps and you can come back in the morning. She won't think any less of you.'

'She couldn't think less of me than I do myself. I forgot. Can you believe that?' The cold marble against his forehead was making his head ache. 'After months of counting the days when it came to the anniversary I missed it.'

'You haven't missed it, you're here now.'

'But if it wasn't for … Just leave me, Gerde.'

She scooped up the dead flowers and he heard her walk away but she only went as far as the compost bins and soon she was back beside him.

'I was in Bayern today,' he said. 'I should have been here. Today I should have been thinking of nothing but her.'

'Is this what she'd want for you, this wallowing in misery?'

He looked up. 'I haven't been miserable for a long time now. Maybe … maybe that's the point. I've been selfish.'

'Leo Maier, I've known you since you were ten years old. You're the least selfish man I know. So it's guilt. We've all been there.'

'Sorry. I know you've been through it too.'

'But you're barely forty, a young man and if I'm honest you haven't had much of a life for a few years now.'

'There's a girl,' he said. 'A young woman, I've let her down too. Humiliated her.' He thought of Natalie's eyes, bewildered; the touch of her hand on his shoulder at the door of her apartment. 'It was too soon. I'm not ready.'

'Enough, now.' Gerde's hand beneath his elbow was surprisingly strong and he allowed himself to be pulled up. He felt the chill of the wind as Gerde locked the cemetery gate.

'You have a key?'

'I borrowed it once and got a copy but don't tell anyone,'

Gerde said.

At home she fed Max, let him out into the garden and made coffee. Leo went upstairs, peeled off his wet clothes; pulled on joggers and a tee-shirt. The agony of those early days without Sofia settled in his chest. He wanted to sleep.

'I found this in the cupboard.' Gerde had poured a measure of Berentzen for them both.

He raised his glass but said nothing; knocked it back in one gulp. The alcohol burned but the blackcurrant taste was soothing. He poured another.

'You need to eat something. Let me make you an omelette.'

'No.' He set down his glass, took Gerde's face in his hands and kissed her forehead. 'I really need to be alone but thank you … thank you for everything.'

She looked him in the eye for a long moment.

He tried to smile. 'Don't worry, my dear friend. I'll be alright.'

'Go somewhere, Leo. Go to Vienna, stay a while.'

'I've just returned from there.'

'Go somewhere else then.'

She let Max back into the kitchen, touched Leo's cheek and picked up the damp blanket. He knew he should offer to wash and dry it but he didn't. Upstairs in the bedroom drawer he found the sleeping tablets the doctor prescribed a year ago. He'd never taken any of them but now he pressed two into the palm of his hand, swallowed them with water from the bathroom tap and crawled into bed. It wasn't until he heard Max stretch and sigh in his basket that he closed his eyes and let the drug do its job.

The telephone woke him. He dived for his mobile then realised it was the land line ringing. A father cancelling a child's lesson. He stood on the landing trying to rub some life into his face. The disappointment that it wasn't Natalie calling fought with the guilt that gnawed at his stomach. He might have gone back to bed were it not for Max's claws pattering on the tiles downstairs.

He put the coffee machine on, watched his dog sniffing round the lawn where the pine martens had probably left their scent. Beyond the lawn the camellias were an array of perfect blooms.

The coffee stirred his brain and he looked at the clock. Natalie would be working at the hotel in town. He paced the floor, phone in hand, took a deep breath and keyed her number. It went straight to voice mail as he guessed it would. 'Natalie. I want to apologise … for leaving you like that. The fault is all mine. I don't think I'm … You are a wonderful girl and you deserve … more. I'm leaving Salzburg for a while. I'm so very sorry I upset you.' He ended the call, threw the phone at the sofa. Upstairs he packed underwear and shirts into an overnight bag. When he'd fed Max he retrieved his phone and scrolled through his contacts.

'Raimund, Leo here. How are you both?'

'We're well, Leo. What about you? Haven't seen you for a long time.'

'I know we must put that right but first I confess I'm asking a favour. Is Barbara there?'

'Hold on.'

Leo grabbed his appointments diary and moved the phone to the other ear.

'Barbara, I'm so sorry to drop this on you but could you cover my lessons for a couple of weeks?'

'Are you ill, Leo? Of course I'll cover but …'

'No. I just need … a holiday … I mean I …'

'How many lessons? Are they all piano? You know my guitar playing is terrible.'

He read her the names of his pupils. 'I'll call them and let them know. Thank you for doing this at such short …'

'Go and enjoy your holiday, Leo. We must meet up soon.'

He made the other calls, fielded questions about his health, closed the diary. In the garden rain had mottled the camellia leaves. He wiped them on his sleeve until they shone. He supported the flowers with one hand and cut long stems with the other. 'They're an English variety,' Sofia had once told him. 'Think of those lovely gardens in British magazines.' But he didn't want to think about anything English right now. He slid the flowers into a supermarket bag, placed them on the car's passenger seat and threw his bag into the boot. Once Max was attached to his safety harness in the back seat Leo slid a thank you note into Gerde's mailbox. He drove to the cemetery, arranged the camellias as best he could in the vase beneath Sofia's name and stared at the gravestone until his vision blurred. He couldn't find words to say aloud or silently. Sorry was pitifully inadequate when she deserved so much more. In the car he started the engine, reversed out of the space and accelerated away. He had no idea where he was going.

Chapter Fifty-One

'I've got to say, Lovie, you're well set up here.' Natalie's dad was standing at the window looking at her view of the river and the sky streaked red behind distant fortress. The sun was going down on yet another failed romance, she thought. The rest of the family were seated at the table, drinking coffee. Toby on the sofa, earphones in, clutched his mp3 and kept up a tuneless hum. Surprisingly her mother found nothing in the apartment to criticise and even said how cosy she'd made it. Maybe it was because Sabine was there.

'I've got great friends, Dad. They've made it easy for me.' She hoped her smile looked genuine.

'So it didn't work out with the Yank then. He's back in the States now?'

'I don't know and I don't care. I'm off men at the moment.'

'You looked quite chummy with Leo yesterday.' He nudged her arm.

'I think we all got caught up in the moment. Don't read anything into that.' She turned away, felt for the phone in her pocket, saw there were no texts, no further messages. She'd had one call that morning from her boss, Karl, saying he had something important to ask her and wondered if he could interrupt her evening by calling again later.

Why couldn't he just say what it was then, she wondered. She wasn't in the mood for guessing games. She wasn't in the mood for anything right now and it was all Leo Maier's fault. How dare he lead her on like that only to run off with no explanation? For the third time in the space of a year she'd been made to look ridiculous. It wasn't going to happen again. But still …

'Natalie come and look at these pictures of Milo as a baby. He looks just like Toby.' Her mother held up a snap for her to see.

Right now she should be happy, relishing this time with her new-found family, practising her German with Tante Sabine. Leo had spoiled that too. She didn't let herself dwell on the part he'd played in finding them all. She needed the anger, it kept heartache at bay.

'Now you live here you must see us again,' Sabine said. 'We'd love you to come and stay. You can meet all your cousins.'

'She might not be living here forever,' her mother leapt in. 'I mean … she left the chance of a good job to come here.'

'It wasn't a job I wanted, though.'

'But it's better than serving in a shop or being a chambermaid.'

'I like serving.' Sabine came to her rescue. 'You meet all kinds of lovely people. Cleaning rooms keeps me fit.' She winked. 'What was it made you leave England and come to Salzburg?'

Natalie was gratified to see her mother blush but had no intention of dragging up that ghastly day, the accident, Adam and Sigourney, the harsh words her mother had meted out. 'I came here on holiday with a friend last year and fell in love with the city,' she said. 'Later someone offered me a bed for a while and I decided to come back; get a job. I like what I do.'

'It was brave to come but I can see why you want to stay.' She gestured to the room, the views of the Gaisberg.

Natalie jumped as her phone rang and she turned away.

'Sorry to disturb you.' It was Karl again. 'Can you talk for a few minutes?'

'Natürlich,' she said, edging down the room.

'How would you feel about working more hours? I mean to say mornings too. You would of course have to give up your other job but I think my pay is better and no toilets to clean.' He barked his loud laugh and she held the phone at arm's length for a second.

'Oh. Yes … I mean I'd love to do that.' Not having to get up early to make beds *was* an attractive thought. She would miss Binita, though.

'There is a … snag?' Karl drew out the word. 'Or maybe not, see what you think. I am opening another shop in St Gilgen. It wasn't finalised when I rang earlier. Could you work there for a few weeks, then you come back to town?'

'Yes! It sounds great. It will be … an opportunity.'

'Okay, we talk tomorrow on money and things.' He ended the call.

'That was my boss,' she said, thankful to have something new to think about. 'He's opening another shop and wants me there for a few weeks. It's on the shore of Lake Wolfgang.'

'That sounds wonderful.' Sabine clapped her hands. 'There you see you must stay after all.'

Natalie couldn't look at her mother.

They took Sabine to the Friesen for an early dinner then said goodbye with lots of hugs and promises to see each other again before too long. Sabine embraced Toby who looked less than impressed. Natalie pressed a small box containing Gran's edelweiss brooch into Sabine's hand. 'You should have this,' she said. 'It was your grandmother's.'

As they gathered in the lane to wave her off Toby sidled up to Natalie.

'Leo promised he'd bring Max here today and he didn't. Can we go to his house and see him?'

She was surprised how much it hurt to hear his name. 'He's had to go away, Tobes. I'm sorry I should have told you. I think his father's ill or something.' It was all she could think of on the spur of the moment.

'People shouldn't say *promise* and then they don't.'

'You're right. But sometimes things come up unexpectedly.' What, she wondered, had come up last night in the couple of minutes it took her to fill the kettle and put coffee into cups?

When Toby went into the garden to find Otto she walked through to reception. 'Any idea where Leo has gone?' She hoped she sounded casual enough.

'No.' Karin looked up from her keyboard. 'He sent me an email saying he'd be gone for two weeks. I thought you'd know. Hey, your aunt is nice. When are you going to tell me all about yesterday?'

'I'll come by tomorrow. Sorry to sound distracted,' she tried to smile, 'my boss just called and wants me to work full time. I'd have to go to St Gilgen for a few weeks.'

'Great. Why are you frowning? No dirty linen.'

'He only rang this afternoon. Lots to think about.'

She found her parents by the pool. Toby was throwing a ball for Otto.

'I hope you don't mind if I get off now. I think I need an early night.'

'You've not got a date, then?' He dad's grin was teasing.

'Definitely not.'

She walked back to her apartment; the air was warm. Until yesterday she'd looked forward to the summer. Karin and Luisa had promised all sorts of get-togethers with friends. She'd imagined Leo might be included but now there didn't seem any way they could be friends. They'd crossed a line but he'd retreated behind it.

Lying in bed she focused her thoughts on Karl and the shop. St Gilgen was a lovely little town. She'd have to take two buses each day but the scenic journey out to the lakes would hardly be a chore. Inevitably Leo stole into her mind, his strong, warm embrace, the kisses that had made her feel her life was complete, the delicious anticipation on the drive back from Bavaria. '*You could not guess how long I've wanted to do that*,' he'd said. He must have found me disappointing, or boring like Adam did. She turned on her side. Through the open blinds she watched stars appearing and disappearing behind clouds while tears seeped into her pillow.

Chapter Fifty-Two

Leo's mood sagged when he saw that his sister's car was not on the drive. His brother-in-law answered the door, neither man greeting the other with much enthusiasm.

'Marina has gone out for the day with a friend so I'm babysitting your father,' Michael said, giving Max a less than welcoming glance.

'So you're not working today?' Leo resented the word *babysitting*. He hoped his father wasn't within earshot.

'No. Marina arranged this some time ago and it couldn't be changed. Anyway, back so soon, Leo. Is something wrong?'

When he didn't answer Michael waved a hand towards the annexe.

'Go and say hello to Papa, I'll make you a coffee. Does the dog want a drink?'

'Some water would be good, thank you.'

His father was pleased to see him. 'I thought I heard your voice. But of course I couldn't get up to see.' He tapped his plastered leg with a walking stick. 'Are you in Vienna for music?'

'No. I …' Leo glanced towards the door. 'I need some down time, I think. It seemed an opportunity to come back and spend some time with you.' He bent to kiss his father's cheek which smelled of soap and made him want to weep.

'I thought last week you were looking much better, Leo' his father narrowed his eyes. 'But you're looking peaky again.'

Michael brought two cups of coffee and a bowl of water on a tray. 'I've a few phone calls to make if you'll excuse me.' His smiled snapped on and snapped off again. He went out and closed the door.

'He's a good man, Leo so don't pull that face. He adores your sister and she him.'

'Well, that's ... good.' He picked up his coffee cup and stared into it. It was a good blend if the aroma was anything to go by and for a few seconds it soothed him.

'You need down time?'

His father's words hung between them. Leo continued to study the cup. 'I've made a mess of things, Papa. A big mess.' Max came to lean against his legs.

'Are you referring to money or feelings?

'Leo smiled. 'Feelings would cover it.'

'I know a year has gone by. It's not like we don't think about them every day but these anniversaries are always difficult. Twenty-eight years since we lost your mama but the date we always remember.'

'That's just it, I didn't remember. I was consumed with ... thinking of someone else.'

'Ah, your sister was right. She thought there was a new ... spark about you. So there is a lady?'

'I thought there might be. I mean yes, I know she likes me but I'm not ready, Papa. The worst thing is I didn't explain and I left her not knowing what was wrong.'

His father picked up his coffee and sipped it. Leo stood up and took off his jacket, folded it over the back of a chair. He walked to the window. Blossoms covered the horse chestnut tree across the lane. Florian would be home from school soon and there'd be no more time for quiet talking.

'You came ... what is it, a week, ten days ago when I stupidly fell down the steps outside? You were worried, I could tell that. You sat with me in the hospital. You said all the right things and I loved that you came so quickly.'

Leo turned away from the view, sat back down opposite his father. 'Of course I came. What else would I do when you fall?'

'Don't speak. Just listen. I hadn't seen you since the winter when you were thin and tired and looking as though you didn't care about anything. Last week you looked as though you cared very much. Your precious wife was still gone, but you had come back to us. You know what I mean by that?' You looked as if you *were* ready.

It seemed as if something were lodged in Leo's throat. He swallowed but it was still there. He nodded unable to look at his father.

'I guess this transformation was because of this woman? But what has that to do with Sofia?'

The words hit Leo in the chest. How could Papa say such a callous thing?

'Ah. You're angry now but I still ask the question. Sofia is safe in her grave. Your life with her was finite. Nothing that has happened to you since the day she died takes anything from your life together. Surely you see that?' If it turns out that this new woman is not the one you must be with, then okay. But if she is,' his father wagged a gnarled finger in Leo's direction, 'don't let her go. Your mama is in a safe place in my heart. There was a time when I would have liked a new companion but nobody came along and maybe I didn't look hard enough. Don't make that mistake, my dear, good son.'

Leo closed his eyes; saw the camellias on Sofia's grave; the hurt in Natalie's eyes. The back of his nose tingled and tears followed. When he opened his eyes his father was hooking a tissue box with his walking stick. He swung it round to Leo and they both laughed.

'Papa I need to lie down. I'm so sorry but …'

'My bed is not yet made but help yourself.'

'He stood, his legs leaden, dropped a kiss on his father's forehead, whispered his thanks.

He showered in his father's tiny bathroom, dragged on jogging bottoms and lay on the bed. It bore his father's comforting masculine scent. Max, he noticed, had stayed in the sitting room.

When he woke the sun was going down. There was an eiderdown over him, Max perched on one corner. Leo pulled on a sweatshirt and walked through the house to the kitchen. Marina was back, his father, sitting at the table, gave a nod of greeting. Michael was cooking. 'Have a glass of wine, Leo. Dinner's a little behind schedule.'

Marina came to kiss his cheek. Florian and a friend were in the throes of a game in the conservatory. He sipped the wine and let his breathing slow. The comforting mantle of family settled around him.

Chapter Fifty-Three

Although the shop was set back from the shore in a narrow lane, it had a storeroom upstairs with tall windows through which Natalie could see the glittering lake, and mountains beyond. Karl's partner Mariette was working with her while interviews were held for a permanent manager. Natalie wished she were fluent enough in German to apply for the post herself.

Two weeks had gone by since she received an email from Leo and three weeks since that terrible night in her apartment when he'd left her with no explanation. She knew the message by heart. *Please forgive my terrible behaving,* he'd written, '*I want so much to explain. Could we meet for a coffee in your lunch time?*' But she didn't want to meet up and hear the "we can just be friends" speech. That day in Bavaria had crystallised her feelings for him and it was terrifying to think she'd be hurt all over again.

Here by the lake the tourist season was underway and she was serving a growing number of tourists while Mariette set up the stock systems. During the day she had little time to dwell on what happened, but it was her bus journeys that allowed her time to confront them. Added to the humiliation of Leo's rejection were worries about Toby. Twice during the last few days of her family's visit he'd asked if he could stay in Salzburg and live with her.

'You'd miss all your friends,' she'd said. 'And Mum and Dad would be lost without you.' Her mother had told her Markus and his family were leaving Coventry within the year. Her heart ached for Toby who didn't know about this yet. At the airport he had cried so much she almost bought a ticket to back with them.

Karin ceased to mention Leo. Instead she, Lukas and Luisa invited her to go hiking with them in the mountains most weekends. In her unsubtle way Karin resumed matchmaking, this time with a man called Paul who was a fireman from Grödig. If the group of walkers was large Karin always seemed to allocate Natalie a place in Paul's car. He was nice; as tall as Leo but broader in the shoulders. His hair was white-blond and cut very short.

'I wonder what he looks like in his uniform,' Luisa once said.

Natalie found him easy to talk to on their walks but Leo occupied her heart and it was impossible to evict him.

One Sunday evening Karin and Luisa asked her to go out for a meal at a local Chinese restaurant. Natalie was pleased money wasn't so much of an issue for her now. Although selling the house in Coventry was breaking another tie to her old life she was grateful for the security the money would bring.

When Karin went to speak to a friend at a nearby table Luisa lowered her voice and asked, 'Have you and Leo quarrelled? I thought you two were getting close.'

Natalie felt a jolt at the unexpected mention of his name. 'He and I … well, we … kissed a couple of times but that's all and nothing else is going to happen.'

'My sister is a little disappointed. I think she wanted to match make you both.'

While she forced herself to smile Natalie couldn't help thinking back to that first meal she and Leo had at the Friesen, Karin had done a pretty good job that night. She'd been upset and anxious that night but Leo had been easy to talk to, kind and thoughtful. *You're at a crossroads*, he'd said. Well, she'd set off along a path and now she was back-tracking. When would her life ever be settled? When would the sun rise instead of setting all the bloody time?

Karin re-joined them. 'I nearly forgot. Lukas is planning a barbecue before the festival starts,' she said. 'The friends we walk with are coming. I think Paul will be there.'

Luisa glanced at Natalie and rolled her eyes. Natalie put on the brightest smile she could muster. 'Sounds great.'

Back at her apartment she took in her washing from the garden, folded it and added it to the pile of ironing on the table. She stared at the laptop for a few seconds then turned it on. After a few false starts she wrote: *Dear Leo, I can never thank you enough for all the help you gave us regarding my German family. One day, no doubt, I would have looked for them but I might have been too late to meet my lovely grandfather.* She paused, got up to make herself a mug of hot chocolate, looked out at the stars above the Gaisberg then continued. *Please don't worry about rushing off that night. I think we both became caught up in the emotion of the day and one of us needed to be sensible. So thank you for that.* She sat back, sipped at the foam on her chocolate and wondered how she could type one thing and mean the opposite. *I hope your father has recovered from his fall and you have a good summer. Regards, Natalie.*

She pressed send before she could make any additions or alterations.

Although she'd never seen his house she imagined him sitting watching TV, hearing the beep of the laptop and getting up to read her message. Would he be relieved? Embarrassed? Unhappy? It didn't matter. She had lots of other things to think about; Toby, her job.

Her bookshelves needed clearing of the old, German novels so she could start a collection of her own. She sat on the sofa, the television muted so that if, just maybe, Leo replied, she'd hear the message come in.

Half an hour of a Rosamund Pilcher drama crawled by. She turned off the TV, the lights and finally the laptop. So maybe he's relieved now and will forget it, she thought, and that's what I must do.

Her days fell into a pattern. The early start and long bus ride enabled her to listen to an on-line German course through headphones. At lunchtimes she walked to the lakeside to eat her semmel rolls under a tree by the Mozart museum, took a stroll round the village, often buying a little something to send to Toby, then back to the shop. The first round of interviews didn't yield a manager so Karl advertised again and Natalie's secondment was extended. 'I must find someone soon,' he said. 'With festival approaching I need you back in town.'

The weather turned hot in mid-June and she was glad of the breeze that rippled the lake and lifted the awning of the cafe next door. She didn't have much time for jogging now so she joined an aerobics class at a fitness centre in the city. Sunday afternoons were spent walking with Karin and Luisa who treated her pretty much like a sister.

Leaving work one afternoon she saw Paul from the walking group get off the small ferry boat. He shuffled along the wooden pier surrounded by tourists. She wasn't sure if he'd seen her and she could have kept walking but it seemed rude to ignore him so she waited until he reached the promenade.

'Natalie.' He ran his hand over his cropped hair and slid his rucksack from his shoulder, pushing sun cream and a crumpled map further into the side pocket. Natalie wished she hadn't changed into her trainers.

'I walked from here to St Wolfgang this morning. I was going to walk back but …' he waved a hand towards the blazing sun.

'Are you parked here or …' she hoped he didn't think she was hankering after a lift back to Salzburg.

'No. I came on the bus. My car's in the paint shop.'

'There's a bus in ten minutes,' Natalie said. 'I'm just on my way to catch it.'

They fell into step and Paul told her how steep the paths had been between Furberg and Ried. 'But the view over the lake was worth it. Maybe we could walk there sometime,' he said.

Natalie chose to misunderstand him. 'I'll suggest it to Karin,' she said and was grateful to see the bus approaching.

It was good having someone to talk to on the way back and when they arrived at Schloss Mirabel Salzburg looked its best with late afternoon sun on the cathedral and tourists strolling back to their hotels.

'You want to get a drink somewhere?' Paul asked hitching his bag onto his shoulder.

'Aren't you on duty this evening?'

'Not till ten.' He gave her an encouraging smile.

Natalie wavered. Did she really want to give him the wrong impression? 'Just one then,' she said.

The tables outside MozArts were full so they went inside. I sat over there with Leo, she thought, when he told me about finding my German family. That day all things had seemed possible.

She asked Paul about his job, content to let him relate anecdotes about fires and rescues. She sipped her drink and looked at his handsome face. He must be about my age, she thought. Unmarried.

'Are you going to Lukas's barbecue at the weekend?' he asked.

She was about to say, yes, when voices called to them from the door. Two girls she recognised from their Sunday walks flopped down into the seats beside them. Natalie thought the one called Isabella didn't seem too pleased to see her but the other girl wedged several bags between herself and Natalie and said her feet were about to drop off.

'We've had a shopping day,' she said, beckoning the waitress. 'I have no money left till pay day, so Paul, you'll have to buy me a drink.'

If he was frustrated by the interruption he hid it well. When he spoke to Isabella she blushed to her hair roots. So that's the way the wind blows, Natalie thought. No wonder she looked less than thrilled to see us together.

'You'll have to excuse me,' Natalie said, draining her drink and standing up. Paul opened his mouth to speak.

Natalie glanced at her watch. 'I need to run across for the bus.' With a quick wave to them all she escaped out into the early evening. Long shadows reached across the square while swallows swooped and screeched around the cathedral. Her head was a little woozy as she crossed the river and she'd just missed the bus. It wouldn't be too long till the next one but she turned into Ignaz Rieder Kai and began the four kilometre walk home. She quickened her pace, took deep breaths and kept her eyes front. Halfway along the lane her phone rang. It was tempting to ignore it but pulling it from her pocket she saw her dad's number on the screen.

'Guess what,' he said. 'we've decided to drive down to Tuscany next month instead of flying and we thought we'd detour to see you and Sabine. What do you reckon?'

She didn't know why she burst into tears. Maybe it was Dad's voice injecting a little touch of home into her day.

'Hey, we'll not bother if it upsets you that much,' he said, his voice half teasing - half concerned. 'What's up? You're alright aren't you?'

'I'm fine Dad, just a bit tired with all the extra travelling. I'll be counting the days till you get here.'

She set Toby's eager little face in her mind's eye as she jogged along the lane.

Chapter Fifty-Four

'She makes it quite clear in her email.'

Leo thought it must be alright to put his feet up on Gerde's balcony rail because she had put hers up there too.

'But she hasn't given you the chance to explain. I'm sure she'd feel differently if you talked to her.' She leaned over and poured him more lemonade.

'I asked for the chance to explain and she side-stepped it. Anyway, I'm *moving on* as they say in the movies. I had a nice meal with some old friends last week and I enjoyed myself.'

He *had* enjoyed the evening at Barbara and Raimund's apartment. He'd met some interesting people: a musicologist from Vienna who said they should get together for a beer next time Leo was in the capital, and he'd caught up with another couple he and Sofia had known for years. It was only when he was en route to the bathroom and saw Barbara and Raimund embracing in the kitchen, that he felt a tug at his heart. He wanted to feel that sort of intimate closeness again, the kind he and Natalie had fleetingly shared.

Gerde passed him a piece of cherry pie. 'No, my dear Leo. You don't fool me. You moved on when you fell for this girl.'

Her words gave Leo a jolt. He had meant he was moving on from Natalie or trying to, at least. Gerde assumed he was referring to Sofia. He felt a stab of guilt but it only lasted a second. Those feelings were now reconciled thanks to much soul-searching and the wisdom of his old papa.

'Why don't you send her a message, or a letter explaining why you acted that way,' Gerde said. She settled back in her seat, her plate resting on her chest. 'At least she would know your reasons and then if she doesn't respond well … maybe she doesn't deserve you.'

'I'll think about it.' In fact he'd thought of it a dozen times but each time he sat down to write to her he couldn't find the words. He could read her humiliation between the lines of her email. *I think we both became caught up in the emotion of the day and one of us needed to be sensible.* Her kisses had been anything but sensible but he carried the words around in his head, analysed them, dissected them looking for a trace of hope but found none.

'As much as I'd love to stay here all afternoon eating pastry I need to walk Max,' Leo said. He could see his dog in the garden next door, staring up at them.

'Go quickly then.' Gerde took his plate from him. 'It looks like rain coming in.'

In his kitchen Leo opened the laptop and typed Natalie's email address. He stared at the blank screen wondering how he could describe to her his feelings that night in her apartment, the searing guilt, the need to rush to the graveside. What if I bear my soul and she still rejects me? I would have no cards left to play. Finally he began to type, hoping she would understand, hoping she'd see through the words to his unspoken plea.

He sent the message and took Max's lead from its hook. The dog danced around him, picking up toys and a sock that Leo had dropped by the washing machine. He knew today was Ruhetag and the family at the Friesen would more than likely be in the garden. Would Natalie join them? He knew she often did. After a few minutes hesitation he set off, turned left at the church so that he followed the path at the foot of the mountain.

At the dog park Max strained on the lead, wanting to go inside and play with the pack that ran up and down the grassy enclosure but Leo urged him on along the path. The clouds were darkening as he skirted the field behind the Friesen. Through the wrought-iron gates by Aunt Lexi's house he saw figures beside the pool, others walking across the lawn.

Leo slowed. He could hear voices now. Hidden by the wall and the trees he was safe to take a peek. They were having a party. Lukas was loading steaks onto a barbecue and Otto was barking. There was lots of laughter and then he heard Natalie's voice. '*My turn.*' She sounded happy. He looked away, leaned against the wall; closed his eyes. A male voice called out, 'Natalie, you're doing brilliantly.' Then there was a roar of what sounded like disappointment. Leo turned and saw her on the lawn between two of the trees, a tall man folding her into a hug. The spasm of pain was like a punch to Leo's stomach. He backed away grasping Max's lead and retreated back along the path. You stupid man, he thought, made even more foolish for having sent that email. Whatever will she think of you now?

Chapter Fifty-Five

Natalie loved the Friesen when the restaurant was closed for rest days. Guests would disappear in search of a place to eat and the garden became a family space. Lukas fired up the barbecue on the lawn and although the sky looked threatening with blue clouds gathering beyond the Untersberg, it was still warm enough for them to swim and lie by the pool.

She greeted her new friends from the walking group and they said her German had improved. Paul still spoke to her in English.

He'd arrived with the two girls who had joined them that evening in MozArts but he left them and made his way over to Natalie.

'You didn't come walking last Sunday,' he said.

'No. I was a bit busy.' It was a lie. She had sat in her apartment for most of the day, ignoring the housework and finally going out for a run.

'Still working in St Gilgen?'

'Only for another week. They've found a new manager at last so I'll be back in town. I'll miss the lake.'

'So we should do that walk to St Wolfgang some time,' he said.

He looked good in knee length cargoes and a short sleeved shirt and Natalie tried to dispel the image of Leo in black jeans.

Karin and her father were greeted with cheers when they came out of the hotel carrying trays of venison steaks. Paul went into the bar and brought back two large beers. Natalie wished Luisa would join them but she had put on her chef's whites and was unwrapping sausages. Rosina the waitress brought bowls of herb-scented salad.

'Do you think you'll stay in Salzburg forever now you have a job you like?' Paul asked her.

'I hope so. It feels like home now.'

'I'm glad to hear that.' He held her gaze for a second.

The aromas of sizzling steaks and wood smoke mingled. Otto paced around the barbecue, whining. Aunt Lexi took a quick dip in the pool before going inside to get changed. She looked up at the darkening sky. 'Not good,' she said.

'Let's grab a place at the table.' Paul took Natalie's drink and set it down next to his. 'Have you been to the Trattberg mountain?' He cut into his venison.

Natalie noticed the muscles working in his forearms and wondered what it would be like to be carried from a burning building by this handsome man.

She looked down at her plate. 'No, but I've heard it mentioned.'

'We were talking of going there, perhaps next week. You want to come?'

Where was the harm? She had to stop thinking of Leo. 'Yes. Why not.'

When they'd eaten someone produced a tightrope and attached it between two trees. One of the men was first to give it a go. Much laughter accompanied his efforts to stay on the rope. Karin made it almost the whole way across as Otto barked below her. Natalie leapt up. 'My turn,' she said, and scrambled up onto the rope clinging to the tree for support. Luisa came to hold one of her hands, Paul took the other. 'Don't look at your feet,' someone shouted so she stared at the tree ahead, but about half way she began to wobble and there was nothing for it but to jump down. Paul caught her, his arms folding round her just for a moment.

When everyone had humiliated themselves on the tightrope it was taken down and a volleyball net put up in its place. Natalie had another beer and felt light-headed so she piled her plate with more food and ate as much as she could while the girl who liked Paul chose teams. Unsurprisingly she found herself on the opposite team to him. She hadn't played volleyball since school but she was taller than some of the others and found it easy leaping into the air to return the ball over the net. It wasn't long before her team was in the lead.

Moments later she walked onto the terrace to retrieve the ball; a breeze was tugging at the surface of the pool. Aunt Lexi's towel blew off the back of her deck chair and into the water. Luisa ran to retrieve it. Natalie, standing still after the exertion of the game, noticed the temperature had dropped.

'There is thunder, I think,' Karin said, taking her position by the volleyball net. Otto, his ears back had wriggled under a sun lounger. The players facing the hotel became distracted, one of them pointing to the sky. Natalie and Karin turned to see that the clouds behind the Untersberg were almost black. They all walked down the garden to get a wider view. Paul was beside her. 'This will be good.'

The breeze strengthened. It began in one corner of the garden, swaying the shrubs, moving the branches of the fir trees. Sweeping around behind them it rattled Aunt Lexi's shutters, tipped over the enamel pail beside her door and sent it rolling. Luisa, Otto in her arms, shouted from the terrace, 'You're all mad, come inside.'

Lukas had dampened the barbecue and wheeled it under the eaves. Now the hairs began to rise on Natalie's forearms. The sensation crept up her neck and prickled her scalp.

'Static,' Paul said, putting an arm around her shoulders as the wind tore at his shirt, rippling it against his solid chest. Garden chairs fell sideways and tumbled across the grass. A flash and a fizzing sound made everyone jump. Lightning had touched the earth in the field behind them. Shrieking, one girl ran and they all followed, fear and shock making their laughter hysterical. The crack of thunder was loud enough to make Natalie gasp; Paul took her hand as the first heavy drops of rain splashed into the pool. Most of her friends ran indoors but there was shelter under the balconies. Below the room where she and Glenda had stayed Natalie huddled against the wall, Paul shielding her from the downpour with his body.

She had never seen anything like this. *String rain* they called it and now she knew why. Thick grey threads hung from the sky. As it hit the ground it bounced back into the air. Overwhelming the guttering rain poured in torrents down the hotel walls. When she shivered Paul pulled her closer. The others were in the breakfast room, laughing, calling to them to edge their way along the wall to the door. Water cascaded from the balconies above and stung their legs.

Reaching a point where the rhododendron bushes hid them from view Paul stopped, took her face in his hands and kissed her on the lips. The kiss was long but heartbreakingly tentative; his gaze afterwards, questioning. Natalie looked into his eyes, wishing she could give him the answer he wanted. Seconds ticked by. Finally he gave her a wistful smile and slid his arm around her waist as they made a dash for the door. Luisa was waiting with towels, Otto barked, scampering round Natalie's feet. Karin was counting the seconds between lightning and thunder. The fleeting tender moment was gone.

In the bar Lukas made coffee for everyone. Natalie, returning from changing into her jeans found Paul watching her. He gave a tiny shrug and smiled. He's so kind, she thought, kind and sweet and very good looking. I must be mad or obsessed or something. She smiled back, making her expression as apologetic as she could.

When they were all ready to leave he came over to say goodbye. 'Your heart is somewhere else, I think.'

Natalie wanted to cry. 'Is it that obvious?'

He whispered in her ear, 'Is it Lukas?'

'No. It's … not Lukas.' She smiled but her chin didn't feel very steady. Paul unlocked his seven seater and a few people piled in including Isabella and her friend. They all waved as he pulled away from the hotel.

'Do you want more coffee?' Luisa asked as Natalie buttoned up her jacket.

'I'll help you clear up and then get off if that's alright.'

'Festival is coming,' Karin said as they carried plates into the kitchen. 'We will be asleep on our feet for three weeks.'

What a weird day, Natalie thought as she dodged the puddles along Salzachstrasse. The storm had passed as suddenly as it arrived. Steam rose from the trees on the Gaisberg, filtering upward, curling like smoke. I must be insane turning Paul down, she thought. But when she remembered Leo's kisses an ache rose in her chest. So much for putting him out of my mind, she thought. How simple life would be without men, except for Toby of course and, thank goodness, it wouldn't be long before she saw him.

Chapter Fifty-Six

'This is very strange.' Natalie spoke aloud the next morning. She hadn't looked at her emails when she arrived home after the barbecue but now she was staring at the screen when she should have been getting ready for work. *Dear Natalie,* Leo had written, *I remember you were hoping to build up a collection of Mozart CDs and I thought I would make these recommendations.* He had listed two recordings by the Scottish Chamber Orchestra. *The tempo of these pieces is perfect and, I imagine, just the way Wolfie would want to hear them. Sir Charles Mackerras was a fine conductor.*

She went into the bathroom and brushed her teeth; saw in the mirror that she was still frowning. He'd made no reference to her email and she found this mildly irritating. What was she hoping for? That he'd beg her to meet up and talk? Then she reminded herself that weeks ago he'd asked to do that and she'd ignored his request. She rinsed her mouth, tried to smooth away the crease between her eyebrows with her finger, but it stayed in place. His closing line had been that if she couldn't get hold of the CDs she could borrow his. Was that a hint to get in touch? It certainly sounded like it.

On her way to St Gilgen she tried to remain affronted but a tiny flame of hope ignited. She pulled out her phone and typed a message: *Dear Leo, thank you for the recommendations. I'll take a look on Amazon this evening.* Should she say more? No. She pressed Send. The ball was back in his court.

Leo didn't expect her to reply so soon. She hadn't signed her name and kept her words to a minimum. He thought of the tall blond man who had his arms around her in the garden, someone her own age, unburdened by emotional baggage, no doubt. Why did I send that stupid email? Imagining he could play the long game and strengthen their friendship before hoping for more, he'd misjudged the speed at which she might move on. She was lovely; more attractive than she realised herself. He was a fool not to realise someone else would step in. He dialled his sister's number. 'Marina, how is Papa's leg?'

'It still gives him some pain but it's improving quickly considering his age.'

'I thought I'd come over for a few days, would that be convenient?'

'You're always welcome, Leo. You know that.'

Maybe he could look up that musicologist he'd met at Barbara and Raimund's house. It was time he widened his circle of friends.

'How is Andreas?' She asked. 'Have you heard from him lately?

'I email and text him often. He's passed his test and has a car.'

'He must be such a joy to you, Leo.'

'He is.'

But despite their frequent communications Leo was aware just how grown up his son was now. He was fond of his new-found papa but the bottom line was Andreas didn't need him. Nobody needed him now. It was a terrifying thought.

'Are you still there, Leo?'

He thanked his sister, ended the call and deleted Natalie's email. Further attempts to contact her would only bring humiliation.

Chapter Fifty-Seven

The famous festival blew into the city on a wave of torrential rain. Natalie saw street musicians huddling under umbrellas and tourists donning their emergency rain ponchos. Even so, the television and radio stations had reporters on the streets and it was impossible not to be caught up in the excitement. Now back in the shop in the city she was impressed when Karl told her Anna Netrebko was in town. The beautiful soprano's face was on the cover of a CD she had just bought. There'd been no more emails or recommendations from Leo and she was doing her best to put him out of her head, but a few days before the festival began she'd taken a walk with Luisa.

'Karin saw Leo's neighbour,' her friend had said. 'And you know Karin, she asked why he was not friends anymore with you.'

Natalie braced herself.

'Gerde wouldn't say much but it's something to do with his wife. Maybe he can't get over her.'

Natalie had felt an uncomfortable finality settle in her heart. There was no competing with a dead wife.

Now, with the hotel packed with guests Karin and Luisa were working flat out and could only communicate by a few hurried texts and emails. Natalie missed them and with the rain disrupting their walking and her solo jogging, she went regularly to aerobics classes.

Every day her German improved and although Karl grumbled when he had to emerge from the tiny office to help in the shop she felt as though her working life was finally falling into place. Helping customers was fun and Karl was teaching her how to order stock on the computer, so her tasks were varied.

One lunchtime her solicitor telephoned to say her share of the money from the house sale was ready to be paid into her bank. She dismissed negative thoughts. It was the end of an era but one that had turned sour and painful. She was pleased to feel some financial security at last. Buoyed up by this she decided to buy a ticket to a performance at the festival but found the opera events were sold out. She managed to grab one of the last seats at a concert at the Mozarteum and was relieved to note it was in a different hall to the one she'd attended with Leo. How long ago that felt now. She wasn't sure she'd had feelings for him at that time, but during the meal in the bistro afterwards she'd felt the first stirrings of attraction. She was sure he'd felt the same.

'Where can I get something special to wear?' she asked one evening when Mariette called into the shop.

The older woman grinned. 'Ooh, I love spending other people's money.' She recommended an exclusive boutique on Wiener Philharmoniker Gasse and after work they went to take a look.

In the window pastel linens nestled against silks and taffeta. There were no prices on the clothes.

'My mother always says if you have to ask the price you can't afford it,' Natalie said, her nose pressed up against the glass.

'But you must ask if you try something on.' Mariette too was up close to the window, peering towards the back of the shop. They both jumped when they saw a woman inside, carrying an exquisite black dress which she hung on a rail. She turned and smiled at them.

'I thought they'd be closed.' Natalie was embarrassed.

'Lots of people stay open for the festival crowds. Let's go in.' Mariette linked her arm then pushed open the shop door.

Natalie tried on a long, narrow skirt in old rose silk and a cream jacket which was lined in the same pink shade.

'You're so slim now you exercise all the time,' Mariette

said. 'It's not fair, you could wear anything in the shop.' She smoothed down her own skirt and sat up a little straighter.

The assistant was helpful but discreet, allowing Natalie lots of time to decide. When she was sure no one could see she took a swift glance at the price tag on the jacket. It was €300. With the skirt she'd be spending over €450, a ludicrous amount.

'You know you could dress the jacket down for another occasion,' the woman said, 'and you could wear a different top with the skirt. It's very …' she seemed to struggle for the right English word,

'Versatile?' Mariette suggested.

'Yes, that is the word but I'm not saying it.'

They all laughed and Natalie broke into German to show she wasn't a tourist.

With Mariette nodding encouragement she decided to buy the outfit even though she had no shoes to go with it.

She took a taxi home. It was a day of extravagances and her credit card had taken a battering. She hung the skirt and jacket, in its protective cover, on her wardrobe door and took peeks at it every now and then. Her excitement waned a little when she remembered she'd be alone at the concert with no one to compliment her on the stunning clothes. Turning the negative thoughts to positive ones she tackled the bookcase she'd been putting off for ages but once her own books were arranged on the shelves she had nowhere to store the German ones so she heaped them up onto the table and wished she hadn't started the job in the first place.

On the evening of the concert she put her hair up and managed to tame all the springy curls with an armoury of pins. If she kept her head reasonably still throughout the performance they might stay in place. Her cream sandals weren't a great match for the suit but she'd run out of time and they sort of went with the jacket so they'd have to do. The rainy weather had gone leaving a gorgeous balmy evening but even so she booked a taxi to take her into town. The taxi driver's English wasn't great but he greeted her with a wide grin and told her she looked a hundred dollars.

As they reached the town she saw glamorous groups of concert-goers emerging from cabs. Outside the Sacher hotel a television crew was filming someone in the doorway but a crowd of photographers hid the celebrities from view. A wave of loneliness hit and she wished she'd asked Mariette to go with her. She focused for a moment on Toby and the family's forthcoming visit. When they drew up outside the Mozarteum she booked Anton to pick her up afterwards.

The foyer was a clamour of beautifully dressed people and she was pleased she had bought the fabulous suit. In the bar she had a glass of wine and ordered one for the interval.

Not wanting to be late finding her seat she mingled with a group of Austrians heading into the Grosser saal. The room was breathtaking, the walls and ceiling decorated with classical figures and musicians. Garlands and Greek urns were picked out in gold. More than a dozen chandeliers glittered on long chains. She was still gawping as she took her place at the end of a row in the rear stalls.

'Wonderful, isn't it?' A woman in the next seat touched Natalie's arm. 'We're so excited to be here.'

With the friendliness she'd grown used to from American tourists she was introduced to the woman's husband and soon learned they were from Maryland on a tour of Europe.

'I love it so much here I don't really want to go home.'

'That's what happened to me,' Natalie said. 'I fell in love with Salzburg and can't imagine leaving now.'

'Really? Honey, did you hear that?'

They chatted as the room began to fill. Above their heads a u-shaped balcony reached around the back and sides of the hall.

The Mozart pieces were to be played at the beginning and end of the programme. As soon as the viola player drew her bow across the strings Natalie sat back and let the music soothe her. When I think what I might have missed, she thought, if I'd never gone to that concert with Glenda. Lost in the beauty of the performance it was easy to forget she was alone, but back out in the bar for the interval, she felt self-conscious. The American couple had not followed her out and once she'd been to the ladies and to the bar to collect her drink, she felt awkward.

From a corner she studied the assembled groups. It was easy to tell who were the experienced concert goers, the women were relaxed, clutch bags tucked under their arms, chattering ceaselessly. The tourists and those like her who weren't used to such occasions stood silently, looking around, drinks glasses clenched in their fingers, glancing at their watches.

Across the room a tall woman in a lovely black skirt and silver top was deep in conversation with her friends. When her pashmina fell from her shoulders to the floor she was so busy talking she barely noticed but her partner did and he bent to retrieve it. Natalie's glass stopped on the way to her mouth. The man draping the scarf around the woman's shoulders was Leo.

Chapter Fifty-Eight

Unable to look away Natalie studied the woman; older than herself, sophisticated and very at ease. Now Leo had his back to Natalie and she moved, clattering her wine glass down onto the nearest table, ducking behind a group of Italian youngsters. They gave her cover until she could slip back into the auditorium.

She thought of running from the building but a masochistic curiosity made her want to take another look. She thought Leo would have seats at the front but when the audience returned she scanned the heads of those nearest the stage and couldn't see his dark blonde hair. Hurt battled with anger. So much for the grieving widower. He'd seemed perfectly happy in the foyer with his … friend. But then why had he kissed *her* so passionately that day in Bavaria, said he'd always longed to do it. It didn't make sense. Since that night her anger had evaporated but now she fought to get it back.

For the next twenty minutes she found herself staring along the rows of seats, craning her neck to catch sight of him. It was a pointless exercise in the darkened hall and she felt ridiculous. It was when the final Mozart piece began that she spotted them. Up on the side balcony, illuminated by the glow from the stage they were on the front row. The woman was to his right, her pashmina discarded now on the balcony rail. They looked a perfect couple and it tore at Natalie's heart. She couldn't access any joy in the music and prayed for the concert to end. When finally everyone was applauding she watched him, his head close to that of his companion, both of them smiling.

Natalie stared at them for so long the American couple gently asked her if she'd let them pass. Mumbling apologies she moved into the aisle. The audience was milling towards the doors but

Leo and the woman remained seated. Finally, when there was just the two of them they stood. Down in the stalls Natalie was at the back of the moving crowd, the house lights up. Desperate now to blend into the mêlée of people she joined a queue at another exit. Glancing up again she saw him staring down at her, his expression one of astonishment. She turned away, edging through the crowd, into the foyer. Unsure which way he would leave the balcony she shrank against the wall behind groups of people who were planning where to eat; laughing, arranging to meet up soon. Reaching the door and the cool air she prayed Anton was waiting. She hurried along the row of cars but couldn't see him, then he was waving from further down the pavement. She would have to walk back past the doors of the Mozarteum. Barely two strides along she saw Leo rush down the steps and catch sight of her.

'Natalie.' He ran forward but something in her face must have warned him to stop a few yards away.

'Leo, I have to go my taxi is waiting.' She tried to walk past him but he touched her arm. 'Please.' His hand rested on her shoulder for a second, his gaze travelling over her.

'You look beautiful.'

For a second she hesitated but then she saw his partner, at the top of the steps, a worried expression on her face.

'I'm sorry.' Again she attempted to pass him but he walked beside her.

'We must talk, Natalie. I have to say things.'

She stopped. People moved round them; taxi doors were opening and closing; friends bade farewell to each other.

'Leo … that day … you made me think something … well, that we had a future and …' she couldn't look him in the eye, 'then you … humiliated me. I just want you to leave me alone.'

'Then let me explain, please.'

The elegant woman stood by the steps, her head turned away

but she must have heard every word.

'Do you know what?' Natalie found her anger. 'I'm sick of being in bits over someone. I just can't do this anymore.'

She saw puzzlement on his face so she spoke again in German. 'I'm fed up of being unhappy, Leo.'

Turning then and giving him no time to say more, she hitched up the narrow skirt to her knees and began to run. She knew she must look foolish among the sophisticated crowd but she didn't care. In the taxi she glanced back. He was standing as she'd left him, alone.

'Sind Sie OK?' Anton's face was worried in the rear view mirror.

'Ja, ja.' She turned away.

Her beloved city flashed by the open window as tears cooled her hot cheeks. He's probably on his way to Saran Bar now. She tortured herself with the thought. Maybe he has a regular table for after the concert and the only variable is the woman.

At home she kicked off her sandals; took off the suit, threw it over the arm of the sofa and pulled on joggers and a t-shirt. In this mood she knew she'd never sleep.

'I look beautiful do I?' She said aloud to her reflection in the bathroom mirror. She dragged a make-up remover pad across her eye-lids, making them sore, snatched all the pins from her hair and watched it tumble down over her face. She needed a drink.

There was only radler in the fridge but shandy was better than nothing, she thought, levering off the top and taking hasty glugs that gave her hiccoughs. Sitting at the kitchen table she pulled the pile of German books towards her and flicked through one or two. There were novels, biographies of people she'd never heard of and some poetry. She dragged a cardboard box from behind the sofa and stacked the books inside. There was a collection of Goethe's poetry. After opening another bottle of radler she turned the pages of the poetry book. She knew he was incredibly famous but the old German words and abbreviations were too baffling. Wondering when it was printed she turned to the title page where a single phrase was written in green ink in a spidery hand, *To Leo, Happy Birthday from your Papa.*

Chapter Fifty-Nine

Does Leo own my apartment? Natalie texted Karin at eight o'clock the following morning. She had left far too early for work and strode along beside the river. With every footstep she grew angrier. How could her friends lie to her like that? After ten minutes her phone rang.

'Sorry,' Karin said. 'Leo telled us not to say he owned it. How did you find out? Have you seen him?'

'I found a book with his name inside. I want to know why everyone lied to me.'

It was a second or two before Karin spoke. 'Some of it is the truth. A writer had booked it for the summer and then didn't come. He thought it would be an answer for you because he knew you wanted to stay.'

'So why didn't you all just tell me it was his apartment?'

'He … well, he thought it was best this way.'

'Can't you see how difficult this is for me? Leo and I had … a … a falling out. I can't stay there now.'

'Yes you can. We all love you being there and … oh, I have to go. I'll ring soon. Don't be angry.'

Natalie knew a lot of her anger was rooted in hurt. Since the festival started and they'd been so busy she realised just how much she relied on Karin and Luisa. She loved her job and Karl was a great boss but the weekends were long without her friends to meet up with. Now they'd betrayed her. She glanced at her watch and decided to go for a coffee before work.

The city was awake and busy. Natalie walked past the horse carriages in Residenzplatz. It was already hot and the drivers held pails of water for their horses to drink. Unable to face MozArts cafe she went into Altermarkt and took a seat at the Tomaselli kiosk. When her phone rang she answered quickly thinking it was Karin.

'Natalie, here is Leo.'

She sagged in her seat, every bit of her anger filtered away leaving a weight of exhaustion. 'Why are you calling me?'

'I felt terrible when you ran away. Maybe we …'

'I meant what I said, Leo. I can't cope with … all this … emotion.'

'I will leave you alone but I just want to tell you one thing. At last night's concert was Christe, one of my oldest friends come from England. Her husband Erik …well, he prefers Wagner to Mozart. Often we see concerts together. That is all.'

She felt a wash of relief but still said, 'It's really none of my business.'

'I wanted to tell you anyway.'

A silence lengthened then she said, 'we do need to talk, Leo, about my … *your* apartment.'

'My what? Oh … oh, I see.'

'But I can't face that right now. Can I ring you?'

'Of course, yes. When …?'

She ended the call. So, he and the elegant woman were just friends. It didn't explain why he rejected her so horribly, though. She sipped her coffee, watched tourists gathering for an early guided walk and wondered why her heartache was fading when Leo might still want only friendship.

Chapter Sixty

Christe was trying to be kind but Leo just wanted to be left alone. He'd walked Max at the crack of dawn after a sleepless night and made the call to Natalie which had thrown him into turmoil. Now his dear old friend was on the phone wanting him to go for lunch with her and Erik.

'I have lessons,' he said. In fact he only had one all day but he needed time to think.

'But you were so upset last night, Leo. Why didn't you tell us you'd met someone? She looked lovely, what went wrong?'

'It's a long story.' He looked down at Max who had his breakfast bowl in his mouth. 'I will tell you but I need to get things straight in my head first.'

'Alright. Well, we're here if you want to talk.'

It was so clear to Leo now. Papa was right. The story of his marriage had come to an end but it was still a beautiful story and one he'd treasure forever. It was time for a new chapter in his life and he wasn't going to let the chance slip away again. It was just the matter of seeing her with the young blond guy that plagued him.

'But why would she run from the Mozarteum like that if she had no feelings for me and why wasn't the blonde man with her?' he asked Max as his dog vacuumed up his breakfast. 'And she said she'd ring me.' He thought of the heat in her kisses that night in her apartment; the way she had slid her arms up around his neck, pressed against him. 'Sorry boy,' he said to Max, clipping on the dog's lead again. 'But I'm sure you won't say no to another walk.'

At the Friesen the family were having breakfast in the corner of the hotel kitchen. Leo felt guilty interrupting their private time. 'Karin, do you have a minute?'

She brought her coffee out into the bar and they sat down.

He took a deep breath. 'A few weeks ago you had a barbecue here on a Sunday. I was passing, I saw Natalie and …'

'I know we should have invited you but I thought …'

'No. That's fine. I just wanted to ask …does Natalie have a boyfriend now?'

Karin took a sip of coffee and Leo felt his mood sinking. The answer he least wanted to hear must be coming.

'Why haven't you asked her this?'

'So she *is* seeing someone.' His hands felt damp around Max's lead.

'No. But she's very upset. She called just now asking if you own the apartment.'

'She doesn't have a boyfriend? Because I saw her here with a tall, blond guy and it looked like …'

'That was Paul. He liked her but it wasn't reciprocated. He's just a friend and anyway he's with someone else now.'

'Alright.' He sat for a moment while his pulse slowed to normal. Otto trailed in from the garden with a long strand of grass in his tail; within seconds the dogs were play fighting on the floor. Karin grabbed at the strand of grass but missed it.

'For Heaven's sake, Leo, try and sort this out with Natalie. She's miserable, you're miserable. It's her birthday soon and we could all have such a great time if you two were together.'

'Her birthday? When is that?'

'Last day of this month. Her family are coming. I can only fit them into Tante Lexi's house. I hope that will suit her mother.'

'Does she have plans for her birthday?'

'I don't think she has any plans at all but if her brother is here she'll be happier. I know that for sure.'

'Okay. I will see her and talk but I think she needs time.'

Karin rolled her eyes. 'Time for what?'

Leo got to his feet, untangled Max from Otto's huge paws. 'Promise me you won't tell her we've spoken.'

'Can I tell Luisa?'

'Yes,' he said. 'I know she keeps secrets better than you.'

How strange human nature is, he thought on the walk back. He relaxed his shoulders, settled into a slower stride. We're relieved to find that those we love are unhappy. He alternated between guilt and elation and prayed it wouldn't be long before Natalie called.

Chapter Sixty-One

The apartment had never looked as wonderful as it did now she might have to leave. There was money in the bank so she could offer Leo more rent instead of the meagre amount she gave to Karin each month.

At least that way I could stay here with some dignity, she thought. It was seven o'clock, twelve hours since he had called her to explain about the woman at the concert. She should ring him back and get it over with but what if the conversation left her upset? It was her weekend off and with no chance of seeing her friends the time would drag. She poured herself a glass of wine, fished her phone out of her bag and dialled her parents' number but when Toby answered he sounded distracted and passed the phone to her dad.

'Hi Lovie, everything okay?'

'Fine, Dad. Just wanted to say hello.'

'That's great but … the thing is, we're just on our way out.'

She heard her mother's voice calling for him to hurry.

'Natalie, can I call you on hands-free in the car? I'll only be five minutes.' He rang off.

She went over to the CD rack and found a recording of The Magic Flute. For ages she'd intended to listen to the whole opera. Half way through the overture her dad rang back.

'Sorry about that. We're just … well, we're just off to the ferry. We're going to Tuscany a week early. Thought we might as well have a bit longer there before we come to you.'

A sudden desire to see them all made her want to cry. 'Will you be here for my birthday?'

'Course we will. Wouldn't miss it, would we? Karin's already booked us in. We're really looking forward to seeing you.'

Toby called something to her from the back seat but she didn't catch it.

'Are you going to a hotel in Florence, or an apartment?'

There was a brief silence then her mum said, 'we're not sure yet. We'll see what's available when we get there.'

'That's brave in high season.' Natalie said.

'Well … we know a few people now who might …'

'Don't you worry about us, Lovie,' her Dad interrupted. 'We'll find something.'

'Can we go to … Salzburg on the way … there … as well, Dad?' Toby sounded as though he was chewing something. 'Then we can see Nat twice.'

She held her breath, imagined the exchange of glances between her mum and dad.

'Not this time,' her mother said, her voice drifting away as though she'd turned her head.

'Won't be long till we see you.' Her dad's cheerfulness sounded forced. 'Signal's on the blink here, Natalie; might lose you in a minute.'

'Okay. Have a lovely time in Italy. Love you all.'

There was a chorus of goodbyes then her dad said they'd ring her as soon as they reached Florence.

She restarted the CD, lay down on the sofa and thought of them all in the car, Toby's excitement when they boarded the ferry. Why am I feeling like this, she wondered. If I was in England I probably wouldn't be going with them anyway.

She wasn't sure of the plot of the Magic Flute but the arias were beautiful. As she picked up the CD booklet she heard the ring of the intercom bell. Knowing it couldn't be Karin or Luisa she leapt up, glanced in the mirror and smoothed down her hair. Don't be daft, she told herself. It's not going to be Leo. At the window she peeped through the blinds then jerked her head back in disbelief. Adam was standing at the gate.

Chapter Sixty-Two

Natalie stood in her apartment staring at the wall afraid to look back through the window in case he was still there. The insistent buzz of the intercom jarred with Tamino's aria. Eventually she opened the door and walked downstairs to the gate.

'Natalie.' He grinned as though there was nothing unusual going on at all. 'I thought you must be out. This is some place you live in.' He gestured to the river. In the distance the fortress was catching the evening sun.

She wanted to speak but her tongue had welded itself to the roof of her mouth.

'Are you going to let me in then?'

With an effort she managed to make her fingers work, opened the gate and stood aside then walked ahead of him, up the stairs and into her precious sanctuary; a place entirely unrelated to all the hurt that this man had caused her.

Tamino had finished singing. The recitatives were playing. Adam frowned. 'What on earth are you listening to?'

It was enough to anger her. 'What the hell are you doing here?'

He put his hands in his pockets. He was wearing a suit he might wear for work. Natalie could see he was trying to look nonchalant.

'Well, obviously I came to see you.'

'How did you … who gave you my address?'

He had the good grace to look sheepish. 'I asked Auntie Maureen for it. She always had a soft spot for me.' He flashed a quick smile.

She wondered if she might wake up from this nightmare any moment now and it would be morning; time to get up, wash, dress, grab some toast and go for a jog. But when she bit down hard on her lip she didn't wake up. Adam was there, hair gelled, shirt slightly rumpled and, good grief, an earring.

On the CD Papageno had begun to sing about finding a wife. It was one of her favourite arias; it reminded her of the dinner concert and the sweet old Frenchman, Manu. It was that night she realised how passionately she loved Salzburg. The thought gave her strength. She folded her arms. 'Tell me why you're here and then go.'

'I got the divorce papers through.'

'And?'

'It just felt weird not to talk to you about it.'

Natalie remembered how empty she had felt when she finally signed them and sent them back to Irene.

'You could have phoned.'

'I know.' He stared at the floor. His face reddened. 'Now the house is sold. I just … I suppose I just wanted to see you.'

She could have thrown all the nasty things he'd said back at him; reminded him he'd called her *boring as hell*; asked him why he'd refused to talk when she'd begged him to do so on at least two heartbreaking occasions. But the words wouldn't come. Instead she took another wine glass from the cupboard and poured him some. 'Does your girlfriend know you're here?'

'God, no!' He gulped at the wine. His hand was shaking. 'She thinks I'm going to a weekend course in London.'

He's already lying.to her, Natalie thought. Pregnant Sigourney sitting at home in her smart flat. She almost felt sorry for her.

'Adam what on earth can there be for us to talk about? We're … living new lives now and …'

'I said things … I shouldn't have. I feel bad when I think about it.'

'Are you here looking for my forgiveness?' He really was unbelievable.

'Natalie, have you eaten yet?'

'What?'

'Can I take you out to dinner one last time?'

They both jumped when her mobile rang. It was Karin saying Lukas had taken pity and given her Sunday afternoon off. 'You want to go somewhere?'

Natalie replied in German, saying that her husband had turned up. She wondered if Adam could hear Karin's shriek of disbelief.

'Do you want me to come round? Shall I bring Otto?'

She laughed then. The idea of sloppy old Otto intimidating anyone was hilarious. 'Nein Danke. Ich bin okay. Tschüs.'

'I'm impressed.' Adam raised his glass. 'You really speak the lingo.'

'Alright we'll go for dinner. Where are you staying?' She wanted him out of her apartment.

'I can't pronounce it.' He pulled a card from his pocket to show her.

'The Weisse Taube.' She passed it every day. Now it would always be the place where he had stayed.

'I bet you know somewhere nice to eat?'

He was being so pleasant it confused her. She glanced at her watch, picked up her phone again, and punched in a number. A minute later she told him she'd booked a table for eight o'clock. It was seven fifteen. Taking her best jeans into the bathroom she changed out of her leggings. Her initial shock had worn off but her stomach was still in knots. Anger and resentment fought with curiosity and, confusingly, a feeling of wanting to show him what he was missing.

Back in the living room he had drained his wine. Natalie, too churned up to finish hers, stood in front of the mirror and worked her hair into a neat plait then pulled a thin, linen jacket from the back of a chair. 'We'll take the bus,' she said when

Adam asked if they needed a taxi.

They got off at Mozartsteg footbridge and walked across the river. Natalie strode out at a fast pace; Adam, took off his suit jacket and panted along at her side.

'This city's a bit of alright,' he said. 'Pity I'm not here for longer.'

She didn't encourage his small talk but she was proud the old town looked so beautiful. 'This is where I work,' she said as they passed the shop. Adam paused to look in the window but she pressed on, turning up the tiny, narrow lane in the direction of the funicular station.

Stieglkeller was busy and there were no tables available on the terrace. Perhaps it was just as well; it might be too weird to sit where she had enjoyed lunch with Connor.

Instead they were shown to a table by the window in one of the large dining halls. Adam looked suitably impressed as he took in the view of the domes and rooftops of the old city. Once they'd ordered their food and each had a large glass of beer in front of them Natalie felt strong enough to ask Adam what on earth was going on.

'Like I said. I wanted to see you. Coming here seemed the only way.'

'I don't understand *why* though, Adam. Things have gone the way you wanted. Why are you looking back?'

'I suppose it was seeing it in black and white on those papers.' He stared out over the city; a warm breeze blew in, moving the petals of flowers on the window sill. 'It was you initiated the divorce, Natalie.'

'I just got in first. It was always going to happen.'

'Was it?'

'Adam, you're living with a woman who's expecting your child. What other outcome could there be?'

'You left your ring behind.'

'I have no use for a wedding ring,' she said, 'and neither, it seems, do you.'

'Are you with anyone?'

The dull pain she was becoming used to nudged her heart. 'No. I mean … there is someone but I'm not going to talk about him.'

'The American?'

Auntie Maureen must have been working overtime. 'No. Not the American.'

Their food arrived. Natalie found she was hungry and tucked in.

'I have to say you're looking amazing,' he said. 'That long hair really suits you.'

She recalled his compliment about her hair, shortly before he devastated her with news of Sigourney's pregnancy.

He put down his knife and fork. 'You're looking really fit too. I mean in every way. Do you work out or something?'

'Yes I do, and I walk a lot with friends.'

'It's weird to think I don't know who your friends are.'

For some reason it was this remark that made her feel sorry for him.

'Are you alright, Adam?'

Again he looked out of the window. A flock of swallows swooped down to the rooftops then veered away towards the dome of the cathedral.

'Yeah. I'm fine.' He gave a smile that confirmed to Natalie he wasn't fine at all.

As he began to eat she studied his face looking for something of the Adam she'd loved for more than ten years. His eyes were just as blue, the lashes dark, a sprinkling of freckles over his nose. But there was nothing of the old Adam in any of his expressions.

'I can see why you like this place,' he said. 'But what made you want to come and live here? It just seems so … unlike something you'd do.'

'Maybe I'm not the same person, Adam, or perhaps you never really knew me properly.'

'I thought I did.'

'You thought I was boring.'

'Well, I got that wrong, didn't I?'

It dawned on her then that he had been the one always holding them back. He wouldn't spend money on the house or think about moving.

'I came here because it makes me feel more alive. It began on my holiday a year ago. I don't know if it's the mountains or the city or the people. Things just seemed to click into place for me.

Despite the conviviality she couldn't ask him about his new life. He seemed to sense this and offered nothing on the subject himself.

They didn't order dessert and over coffee Adam became quiet. He stirred sugar into his cup and fiddled with the spoon. Natalie sat back in her seat trying to appear more relaxed than she felt.

Eventually he spoke. 'Do you ever … do you think about him?'

'Every day.'

'Even here?'

'Location makes no difference, Adam. Time does a bit, but not that much.'

'I was wondering what had happened to the envelope. It wasn't in the house and …'

'It's here in my apartment.'

The waiter brought their bill. Adam took a credit card from his pocket and Natalie thought he'd need to keep his statement well hidden.

They bought ice creams from a kiosk and sat on a bench in Mozartplatz. Passers-by, she thought, would assume they were a couple.

Long after they'd finished eating they continued to sit. Despite the awkwardness Natalie was reluctant to say goodbye.

'I was wondering,' Adam said, 'I mean say no if you're not comfy with it but …'

'What?'

'Could I see it again? You know … the envelope? It's my last chance.'

She hadn't expected that. She looked across the square at tourists gathering at the foot of Mozart's statue. 'You'll take a taxi back straight afterwards?'

He nodded.

As they got off the bus Natalie felt the weight of her old sadness descending. She knew it would lift again, as it always did, but Adam's request had sharpened its edges.

In the kitchen cupboard was half a bottle of cheap brandy she'd bought at the supermarket. She poured them both a glass. Adam sat at the kitchen table, the glow of the lamp picking out the lines of sorrow in his face. She walked slowly to the wardrobe, felt behind the box of German novels and slid the envelope out, placing it unopened, on the table in front of Adam. He began to cry before he even touched it.

Sitting on the bed she listened to him weeping. The brandy swirled around her glass. She didn't really want to drink it but took a sip, felt the comforting warmth and took another. After a while she went to the table, sat opposite him. He had cradled his arms around the sheet of paper; fallen tears were blurring the outlines of the images imprinted on it. Natalie drew the paper across the table, traced her finger around the tiny toes, so perfectly formed.

'Natalie.' Adam searched in his jacket pocket for tissues. 'Do you think things might have been different? You know, if he'd lived?'

She kept her voice even. 'Our entire lives would have been

different, obviously.'

'No, I mean … I mean with us.'

A huge weariness gripped her. 'It's pointless thinking about it.' She picked up the envelope and looked at Adam. He nodded and she slid the paper back inside watching first the left and then the right foot disappear from sight.

Adam reached across the table and gripped her hand. She tried to pull it away but he clung on. 'Let me stay? Let me stay tonight.'

'What?' No. Don't be stupid.' She wrenched her hand free and stood up. He came round the table, tried to stroke her hair but she dodged away.

He was crying again now. He put his hands over his mouth, his voice muffled behind them. Natalie picked up her phone to call for a taxi. Adam grabbed it and threw it across to the sofa. 'Please, let's just talk. Don't send me away.'

'No! For God's sake, Adam.' She retrieved the phone.

'What if I came back?'

She sank down onto a chair. Adam knelt on the floor beside her, grasping at her hand. 'I could even come here. I could get a job.'

Horrified, she tried to get up but he laid his head across her knees, forcing his arms around her waist, clinging to her. 'Please … let me stay.' His tears soaked into her jeans and the fight went out of her. Finally she laid her hand on his hair, the alien touch of the gel sticky under her fingers.

'Adam I … I can't begin to think why you're saying all this.'

He lifted his head and looked into her eyes and there was the Adam she knew.

'I still want you, Natalie.'

Gently she pushed him away and stood up. 'Your girlfriend is waiting at home. You're going to be a father.' She glanced at the envelope. 'You've got another chance.' She picked up her glass and finished the brandy. 'I'm sorry.' She faced him. 'There's nothing I can do to help you.'

He stood. 'Do you really mean it? I can wait, I can …'

'No. It's too late, Adam and yes, I mean it.'

She made the call while he was in the bathroom. Walking down to the gate she saw his shoulders sag in resignation. When head lights approached she leaned to hug him. He held her more fiercely than she could ever remember. Then he was in the car, his eyes never leaving her face until the taxi sped away.

For a long time she sat at the table, staring at the wall, waiting for the tears to come. When they did she moved to the sofa, burying her face in the cushion to stifle her sobs. She wept for her little boy who wasn't strong enough to live, for Adam's new baby, praying it would thrive, for all the times she'd longed for Adam to look at her the way he had tonight and for the realisation that pity was all she could ever feel for him now.

Head throbbing she lifted the envelope from the table and pushed it back behind the box in the wardrobe. It would be a long time now before she opened it again. Closing the doors she whispered, 'Sleep tight, Georgie.

Chapter Sixty-Three

The next morning a steady rain set in. Still she didn't ring Leo. Instead she tidied her apartment, hung washing to dry in the bathroom then walked up to the cosmetics and toiletries supermarket. The shop always soothed her and she spent a long time looking at sweet-smelling candles, perfumes and bath oils eventually buying new eye liner and foundation. She thought about Adam. A year ago his words would have filled her joy and hope. Now she felt sad but relieved he was out of her life forever.

She walked outside and pushed up her umbrella. Across the car park, outside Billa supermarket, Max was sitting tied to a handrail. Natalie bit her lip, breathed in to try and slow her quickening heartbeat. Then Max stood and wagged his tail as Leo emerged, a bag of shopping in each hand. Placing them on the floor he untied Max, straightened up and met her gaze.

Moments passed. She didn't move and neither did he. Her pulse slowed, a gentle warmth filling her body, the discomfort of the rain receding. I love him. I really love him. Why have I wasted all this time?

Finally Leo's lips parted and he said something. It didn't matter what the words were. She walked towards him and he came to meet her. Beneath her umbrella their lips touched and she, on tiptoe, relaxed into the long dreamy kiss and knew her life would never be the same again.

Still not speaking they walked to her apartment, he carrying the bags, she holding Max's lead. The rain had never looked so beautiful. A watery sun caught droplets on her gate and turned them to jewels. Flowers on the lower balconies spilled their scent as she opened the door. Upstairs she went to him, stroking his cheek. He breathed into her hair, 'My darling Natalie,' and then more kisses until she gently pulled away. She shrugged out of her wet jacket, brought a towel from the bathroom for Leo's hair but then his hands were around her waist, drawing her towards him, his lips moving over her eyelids, softly whispered words she didn't recognise.

It was she who sank down onto the bed, reached for him and when he lay beside her wrapped her arms around his body.

'I thought I'd lost you,' she said.

'And I thought I'd thrown you away.'

His smile was slow, his eyes searching hers. 'You are happy for me to be here with you … like this?'

'Very happy.'

Then the time for talking was over. He kissed her throat, her fingers tugged at his shirt, there was an ecstasy of peeling away, caressing, arms enfolding. Natalie lay back on her cool, soft duvet, eyes closed. Where his fingertips trailed his mouth followed until there wasn't an inch of her skin that his lips had not explored. She had imagined making love with him but the reality dissolved those thoughts to nothing. Gripping the solid muscles of his shoulders as he moved inside her she found herself smiling, dizzy with excitement until the moment her joy exploded and his mouth against her lips whispered, 'I love you, Natalie.'

The sun was setting over the fortress, the evening sultry with steam rising from the pavement. Leo, barefoot in jeans, his shirt buttoned loosely was in the garden with Max. From the window Natalie stared at him hardly able to believe that she could now picture him naked, know that the fine hairs on his body were silky soft and a tiny scar on his chest, where he'd fallen as a child, was feathery white against the darker skin. He looked up and smiled. Hands in his pockets he looked relaxed, the anxiety she'd seen in his face that morning had faded as surely as her own sadness. A frisson of desire shot through her as he walked back to the door, Max following.

'Will you stay tonight?' She poured him a glass of wine.'

'As long as you let me cook you something.' He stroked her fingers as he took the glass. His discarded shopping bags were still on the table. He rummaged inside and drew out eggs, milk and a loaf of granary bread. 'I still need to say things to you,' he said, 'explanations and so on.'

'There's lots of time for that.' She slid her arms around his waist, pressed her hips against him and felt the thrill of his response.

Much later he cooked omelettes; Natalie threw a salad together and cut chunks of bread. Sitting at the table she couldn't stop looking at him. Under scrutiny he was shy, colouring when he met her gaze. After eating they moved to the sofa. She snuggled into his shoulder as he put his arm around her and she felt the warmth of his body comforting against her own.

'I'm so sorry for running away that night,' he said. 'It was unforgivable.'

'Leo you don't have to explain. Not now.'

He reached for her hand, stroked her wrist. 'But I will explain, soon. I'll tell you why and make you see that it wasn't because I didn't love you.'

Shivers of pleasure ran along her skin where he touched it. 'I thought I'd disappointed you. I seem to have disappointed … everyone during the last year.'

'You could never disappoint me.' He kissed the top of her head, his warm breath made her scalp tingle. 'You know, a week after we first met at the Mozarteum my father and sister were here from Vienna and we ate at the Friesen. I saw you for a second as you passed the restaurant door.' He let go of her hand and lifted a strand of her hair, let it run through his fingers, 'there was a storm, your hair was wet, the dogs were barking.'

She remembered the moment but didn't want to interrupt him.

'That night it was … a shock to me that someone could move me so soon after …' He closed his eyes for a second. 'When I saw you here again early this year I thought I was dreaming. But I never thought you could feel the same, Natalie. I said to myself, yes, we can be friends and perhaps see concerts but never …' He glanced towards her bed and Natalie felt heat creep up her face.

'I don't know when I started loving you.' she said, thinking of him on the bus a year ago but didn't want to remind him of his sadness. 'I remember coming back to Aunt Lexi's a few months ago. I'd just had an interview and I saw you with Karin in the lane. I came up to speak but you hurried away and …'

Leo's arm tightened around her. 'That was when I … I told Karin you could rent this place and … I'm sorry we didn't say the truth but …'

Natalie turned to face him, smiled to let him know she wasn't angry. 'So why didn't you tell me?'

'Maybe you'd think I was … trying to make you like me or be grateful to me. Karin and the others own a few apartments so I thought it was best that way.'

She thought about it for a few seconds, could see his logic. 'Okay, but maybe you should have taken the books away.'

'There was a big selfish reason too. I didn't want you to go back to England.'

'I'm not going anywhere.' She kissed him then and felt the last remnants of tension dissolve. Adam's face as his taxi left, drifted away, and baby George settled back into the folds of her mind; cocooned in her memories, safe, and for the first time she felt no guilt at leaving him there.

Chapter Sixty-Four

Leo rummaged in his bedside drawer until his fingers closed over the credit card he hadn't used since its renewal. He signed it on the back and stuffed it into his wallet. Today he was going shopping. The thought was exhilarating and terrifying at the same time.

'Sorry, Boy,' he said to Max,' but you wouldn't like this trip. Gerde will come and walk you soon.' He stroked the dog's ears and dropped a biscuit into his bowl.

His phone beeped. A text from Natalie. It wasn't yet twenty-four hours since he'd seen her but already he missed the taste of her mouth, the way her body curved against his as they lay in bed. *Haven't stopped thinking about you since I woke up.* She had written. He texted back, *Me too.*

Modern love affairs, he discovered, benefited from all the advances of technology. Natalie had sent messages several times during her walk with Karin the previous afternoon, even sending a photo of Karin's face when she learned he and Natalie were now together. But Karin's smile could never be as wide as the one he saw on his own face every time he passed a mirror. Not only did Natalie desire him as much as he wanted her but she loved him too. She had said so over and over as they lay in her bed, their faces so close his eyes became unfocused and he'd allowed his lips to explore the soft contours of her eyelids, her chin, the hollow of her throat …

'Concentrate on your driving, Leo' he said aloud as he took the slip road to the autobahn.

He'd never been to the Designer Outlet centre before, on the sprawling site of hotels and mega stores at the airport. He drove up the car park ramp and surrendered himself to what the

English called *retail therapy*.

But after twenty minutes of walking up and down the smart walkways he was mesmerised. Normally he bought his clothes at Moser, the traditional outfitters where Karin, Lukas and Luisa bought their trachten wear. Here there was a massive array of men's underwear. Always having worn boxers he now wondered what style of thing Natalie liked to see.

In Calvin Klein a large wall-mounted photograph of a couple in their underwear told him sex definitely played a part when making a choice. Baffled by descriptions of low rise, concept micro, woven and contrast waistband he grabbed four packs of stretch boxer trunks, two in black, two in grey. It wasn't until he paid he realised there were three pairs in each pack. If Natalie didn't like them it would cost him a fortune to replace them all.

After a while he began to relax. He bought a snack and drank coffee at a small cafe then continued to stroll in and out of the shops. Natalie had said she loved his black jeans so he bought two more pairs and some shirts which, the assistant told him, he could wear either buttoned up or open with a t-shirt underneath. A new word entered his vocabulary - *layering*.

No sooner had he expressed interest in a pullover than he was handed a shirt to go underneath it, a scarf to put over it and an expensive leather jacket to drape around his shoulders. 'It would all look excellent with these trousers,' the female assistant said, handing him some brown Dockers which she described as *Dark Pebble*. 'You're nice and tall so I've given you the slim fit design,' she said, smiling and showing perfect teeth. Leo went into the changing room. Despite the air conditioning he was hot pulling the sweater on and throwing the scarf round his neck. Removing his own trousers he thought of Saturday at Natalie's apartment, the glorious excitement of taking off each other's clothes and abandoning them where they fell. But then he thought of Natalie naked on the bed, her legs entwined with his and it became impossible for him to zip up the slim fit Dockers.

'How are you getting on,' the assistant called.

'Erm, alright, I think.' He stared at the wall trying to conjure up bland images, the burly decorator who might have painted the cubicle, rows of paint tins in the DIY store. Eventually it was safe for him to emerge and find a mirror.

'Oh dear, you've got the scarf all wrong.' The young woman reached up teasing and tugging the thick wool into a position she liked. Leo almost laughed as he saw himself muffled up in sweater and scarf in the middle of August and despite the jacket looking pretty good when she slid it onto his shoulders he declined it having seen the €680 price tag.

He took all his bags back to the car but returned to find something to buy for Natalie. I mustn't look as though I'm coming on too strong, he thought, and chose an extension bracelet which the jeweller told him he could buy pieces to add in the future. He asked for a rich green peridot to be set into it as it was her birthstone.

It was mid-afternoon as he headed home. It would be so easy to stop off in the city and nip into Karl's shop to say hello, but again he didn't want to crowd her. I'm so out of practice at this he thought. Back at home he took all the tags and labels from his clothes and hung them in the wardrobe. He could smell their newness. His life felt renewed. He was smiling again.

He took Max out for a walk. The afternoon was still hot so he walked at the foot of the Gaisberg where the trees gave cool shade. He took out his phone to send a text to Natalie but it rang before he could press a key.

'Hi,' she said.

He loved the note of shyness in her voice. She was feeling her way just like him.

'What are you up to this evening,' he asked.

'Nothing much. You?'

'Want to do nothing together?' He held his breath.

'I doubt we'd do nothing, Leo.'

Ripples of desire made sweat break out on his forehead. Suddenly he didn't know how to respond.

'Leo?'

'I'm tongue-tied,' he said. 'I need a refresher course on talking to … to someone I love.'

Silence. He wondered what she was thinking.

'I'll be home at six.' There was a smile in her voice. 'I'm going for a run but I can be ready to do nothing by about seven.'

When the call ended he looked at his watch, time to finish his walk and have a shower. He whistled Max and they headed for home. In his bedroom, rubbing a towel over his wet hair, he opened a drawer and stared at the Calvin Klein trunks. Black or grey? His life was now full of deliciously trivial decisions.

If only she could see Toby more often, Natalie thought, life would be perfect. He would be in Salzburg with her parents in a couple of days but each time she saw him it made saying goodbye harder. Now she was with Leo, and if their relationship lasted as she prayed it would, it was likely she'd never return to live in England.

She couldn't think about Leo without tingling from head to foot. Returning from her jog she found he was early. His car parked in the lane, Leo leaning against the passenger door

He opened his arms for a hug.

'Oh God,' she said, pulling the scrunchie out of her hair. 'I'm all hot and sweaty.'

'I like you hot and sweaty,' he said, pulling her closer. 'You want to come to my house for dinner?'

'Can I get changed first?'

'No.' He gave her a teasing smile and opened the car door.

'I have something for you,' he said, as he edged around parked cars on Salzachstrasse. 'It's there on the parcel shelf.'

She lifted the gift-wrapped box and tore it open. 'Oh Leo, it's beautiful.' She slid the bracelet onto her wrist. 'I love early birthday presents.' She leaned across and kissed the side of his face.

'It isn't a birthday present,' he said, keeping his eyes on the road. 'It's a … *I love you* present.'

At his house, with Max skittering about on the polished wood floor, he led her into the kitchen. There was a covered bowl of salad on the table and lasagne ready for the oven, pushed to the back of the worktop where the dog couldn't reach it.

'Dinner isn't quite ready then?' She smiled and raised her eyebrows.

'We have a few minutes.' Leo kissed her on the mouth and she stood on tiptoe to slide her fingers into his hair. The kiss lengthened, his hand stroking her back, moving down to her bottom. 'You look wonderful in Lycra,' he whispered.

'And you look great in those jeans,' she said, moving her hands down to the waistband of his 501s. 'But you'd look so much nicer out of them …'

Chapter Sixty-Five

They ate side by side at the kitchen table, Natalie dressed in one of Leo's t-shirts and a pair of his shorts. Ladling salad onto their plates he said, 'It's great that your family will be here soon.'

'I can't wait to see them, especially Toby. I ring him a lot but … it's not the same as seeing him. I miss his quirky smile and the way his eyebrows seem to have a life of their own. He must have grown loads since I last saw him.' She bit her lip for a second, ran her fingers over the peridot stone in her bracelet. 'They want to buy me dinner on my birthday. I hope … well, it would be lovely if you came too.'

'Oh.' He touched her hand. 'I think this is a time you should spend with just family. You see them so seldom.'

'But it will more than likely be at the Friesen … and …' She hid her disappointment. 'Yes, maybe you're right.' She didn't want to seem pushy.

'I'll see you beforehand,' he said. 'We have many days … at least I hope we do … to be together.'

A rush of happiness made her smile. 'I hope so too.'

'It took a long time to be with you, Natalie. I wonder, is it okay with you that I have such strong feelings?'

There was uncertainty in his eyes. She put down her knife and fork, turned to embrace him. 'That's exactly what I want to hear. I couldn't be more in love with you.'

'And I've loved you for so long now.' He kissed her forehead. 'I loved you even when I … when it seemed to you that I didn't. When I made you so unhappy.' He ran a gentle finger down the side of her face. 'I need to tell you things. They must be said because you're in my house and I don't want you to feel uncomfortable.'

'There are things I need to say too.' She swallowed a sliver of pasta and wondered where on earth she would begin to tell him about Adam's visit.

She loved his house, the traditional pale wood panelling on the walls and tiled floors. It was large but cosy at the same time.

They finished eating and Leo poured them both another glass of wine and took it over to the sofa. He drew a deep breath and Natalie, settling down beside him, felt a ripple of anxiety.

He held his glass in both hands and stared into it. 'Just after my … after Sofia died I couldn't bear to lie in the bed we always shared. 'Even the bedroom, I did not want to go in. It was not in this house that she … I mean she died in hospital but even so …'

'Leo, don't say things that will upset you. Really it doesn't matter …'

'But I think this does and I want to say it.' He sipped his wine. 'Lukas was having some work done at the hotel and he said the builders were very good. I asked them here. To make the story short they builded the new kitchen and over it my bedroom. I got new furniture, sold the old ones. Nobody but I have slept in the room or the bed. I thought you'd like to know this.'

She nodded. He had sensed her reticence to explore the house even before she'd fully formed it in her mind.

'The night we came back from Bavaria,' he turned to face her, 'you said the date your parents were going home. It made me remember … that day … that night. It was just one year since she died.'

'And you were kissing me.'

'I know it shouldn't have mattered.'

'Of course it mattered. I do understand, Leo'

'I wanted to come back the next day to explain, but I'd hurt you so badly.'

Abandoning the wine he took her hand and led her upstairs. In his bedroom they undressed in silence and slid under the duvet. She'd taken a major leap into his world.

Through the cheval mirror Leo could see their reflection. After hours of love making he'd gone down to the kitchen and made her a mug of hot chocolate. She was blowing across the surface to cool it, her lips a little swollen from all the kissing.

'You know I met Andreas' mother when I was eighteen.' It seemed strange to be telling the story in detail after all those years. Little by little he related it all, being cut out of his son's life, not seeing him grow up. He stopped short of telling her about Britte's outpourings in Wurzburg last winter. It was irrelevant now.

'I hope I can meet Andreas soon.' Natalie wiped chocolate foam from her lip.

'No. Because he's very nice looking and you might like him better.'

'Maybe, but can he make me hot chocolate as good as this?' Their eyes met in the mirror.

'I hope not.'

He told her about Sophia, of her love of teaching and how devastated she was when her heart grew too weak for her to work anymore.

'She was so lucky to have you, Leo.'

'But I was lucky too.' He kissed the top of her head. 'We were happy but … there was always a … shadow. She was thirty-six when she died.'

Knowing she was struggling to find something to say Leo took the empty mug from her hands, turned off the lamp and wriggled down in the bed until his face was level with hers. When he kissed her she tasted of chocolate. 'I'm sorry but you're going to be late for work tomorrow,' he said.

Exhausted they lay entwined and after a few minutes he knew she was asleep. There was no sound but Max dreaming, his paws nudging the side of his basket. Leo breathed in the scent of Natalie's hair. 'If you let me,' he whispered, 'I'll try to make you happy for ever.' She didn't stir, her breathing now deep and warm against his neck. Just one thought formed a knot in his stomach and kept him awake for a further hour. He knew how much she adored Toby. She spoke of him this evening with such tenderness. Could she really stay in Salzburg, as he desperately wanted her to do, and not see that dear little boy grow up?

Chapter Sixty-Six

'Aren't we going to the Friesen?' Natalie asked as her dad drove past the turning and continued towards Elsbethen. She was sitting in the back of the car with Toby who was surprisingly quiet but kept giving her a wide, closed-mouth smile. She ruffled his hair. 'Where are we going if not to the hotel?'

'Karin recommended a place at Fush … Fush …'

'Fuschl am See?'

'Yes. That's it. A nice restaurant by the lake.'

She'd really hoped to see Karin and Luisa on her birthday but although it was Ruhetag they said they had to work. Leo had stopped by that morning with a lovely card, covered in hearts, and a gift-wrapped boxed set of Mozart's complete works. There were so many CDs she was sure she wouldn't live long enough to play them all. He'd also said he would take her into town so that she could choose a new piece for her bracelet. She touched it now, running her finger over the tiny stone and hoped he might call later.

'Anyway,' her mother said, 'I'm glad to get away from the place for a bit. What Karin was thinking of sticking us in that house down the garden I don't know.'

'Chris.' Her dad's tone was embarrassed. 'It's alright. Best she could do at such short notice.'

'Rooms for the festival time get booked up months in advance,' Natalie said. 'Anyway, what's wrong with Aunt Lexie's? You get loads more space than in a hotel room. I loved living there.'

'I like Aunt Lepsie,' Toby said. 'She gives me gingery biscuits with icing on.'

'Which will rot your teeth.' Her mother stared ahead, her

shoulders rigid.

'Let's not bicker on Natalie's birthday,' her dad said. 'Look at this lovely countryside.' They had left Elsbethen and were following the narrow lane that climbed steeply then broke through trees into endless meadows. Natalie pointed mountains out to Toby and told him their names.

'He'll never remember them. You're wasting your time.' Her mother glanced round at them for a second. Natalie felt as though she were twelve years old. As she settled back in her seat she felt Toby's sweaty little hand slide into hers and squeeze her fingers. She returned the pressure and flashed him a smile.

Even her mother thawed out as they drove alongside Fuschlsee. The lake was cobalt blue, the sun catching the eastern shore and stretching the shadows of trees and farmsteads.

'We should have stayed here, John,' her mum said as they parked the car at the Seerose Hotel.

A waiter led them to a long table on the terrace at the lakeside. 'Do you have a smaller table?' Natalie asked in German.

'Leider nicht.' He shook his head.

'You sit on the end,' her dad said, 'as you're the guest of honour.'

Natalie led Toby by the hand so that he could sit next to her, still wearing his strange smiley face. The same waiter appeared with an ice bucket and bottle of Champagne. Two more waiters arrived, one with another bottle, the other with a tray of glasses. She was about to ask her dad how many bottles he'd ordered when she saw Karin and Luisa appear round the side of the hotel followed by Paul and other friends from the walking group.

Karin gave her a bear hug. The walkers gathered round, patting her on the back. Paul, holding hands with Isabella, pecked Natalie's cheek.

'This is wonderful, thank you so much.' She turned to her dad but he held his hands up and shook his head. He was grinning though and even her mother flashed her a smile.

'I wasn't allowed to tell you, Nat,' Toby said, giving her an awkward hug.

Before she could answer Karl and Mariette appeared. Mariette bustled up, gave her a kiss on the cheek and thrust a card and gift box into her hand. 'You look all in shock,' she said. 'I hope you have a wonderful evening.'

Natalie, still stunned to see her friends all seated and chattering, noticed further empty seats then stared at the corner of the hotel. A second later Sabine appeared, a wide grin on her face, a boy of around ten at her side looking slightly bewildered. He made a bee-line for Toby and held out his hand. Natalie struggled not to cry as Toby solemnly shook hands with Milo and said, 'Grüß Gott.'

She hugged her aunt and didn't want to let her go. 'Thank you so much for coming all this way. I can't believe you're here … how is …'

'Your grandfather is fine.' Sabine smiled into her eyes. 'He has sent you something.' She handed her a small wrapped parcel. 'Open it later.'

When she looked up from the parcel Leo was standing a few feet away. She drew in a long breath. He didn't move; seemed uncertain. Natalie couldn't take her eyes off him. In a dark grey trachten jacket, and full length suede trousers, he looked fabulous. Desire shot through her, her heartbeat speeding up. He walked forward, gave her the smile that turned her knees to jelly and kissed her cheek; whispered in her ear. 'Surely you didn't think I would just give you CDs and say a quick hello.'

Guiltily she met his eye and smiled, knowing that colour must be flooding her face. 'I'm so glad you're here.'

'Your friend Binita wanted to come but she is now driving a taxi and cannot take time off. She sends her love and this.' He put a card on the mounting pile and then walked away to take a seat half way down the table. Natalie, still reeling from the surprise of seeing everyone sat down with Mariette to her left. Toby's seat was empty and she saw him hurling chunks of bread into the lake, Milo beside him.

'Toby,' her dad shouted, 'you're supposed to throw bread *for* the ducks not *at* them.'

Then he stood and she realised the Champagne had been poured.

'Thank you to Leo for getting everyone here and Happy Birthday to my beautiful daughter, Natalie.'

She smiled at her mother and caught a wink from her dad.

'Thanks so much, everyone, for coming. This is …' she didn't want to say her best birthday ever in case it hurt her mother's feelings. '… the most wonderful surprise and …' she dried up, gulped back tears.

Glasses were raised, cries of Happy Birthday and Alles Gute echoed along the table.

As food orders were being given she opened her cards. There was one from Auntie Maureen which she'd signed from herself and Bernard. It took Natalie a minute or two to remember he was the poodle fancier they'd met at the care home.

Karin came to top up her Champagne glass. 'Leo did everything,' she whispered. 'He just asked from me a little help with names. He paid for a bus to bring us all; he's paying for everyone's meal too. I've never seen him like this.'

Natalie caught Leo's eye and he held her gaze for a long moment. She hoped she conveyed as much love to him as she saw in his eyes.

'I thought you were all working,' she said to Karin. 'I really wanted to see you and …'

'I know. It was hard to keep the secret. Your brother was so funny we had to give him a bribe not to tell.'

'What bribe?' Natalie turned to watch Toby and Milo

wielding sticks, trying to knock conkers out of the young horse chestnut trees in the car park.

'We have to let him have a little Champagne. He doesn't know but again he has lemonade in his glass.'

Between the main course and dessert she opened her presents. Karl and Mariette had bought her a small, limited print of the fortress that she'd admired in the shop. Knowing the price she was touched by their generosity. The others had clubbed together and bought her a day sack for her walking trips. It was ultra-light and very stylish.

'Wow. This is fantastic.' She leapt up and slid it onto her back.

'Always you have either a too big rucksack or carry some little bag that is no good. We thought you must have the right equipment,' Paul said.

As the waiter brought plates of freshly made strudel Natalie explored all the pockets on her bag. From time to time she caught Leo's eye and shared a private smile, her thoughts straying to Leo's bed and a night of lovemaking. Then her dad led her over to the car park and opened the car boot. There was a set of luggage in a rich mauve colour. As she hugged him he said, 'You'll be sure to spot these at baggage reclaim.'

Leo was standing a few feet away.

'I have something for you too,' he said.

'You mean apart from bringing my friends and family together and surprising me with this wonderful evening?'

Her father grinned, patted Leo's shoulder and headed back to the terrace.

Beneath a tree, the sun sinking towards the lake behind them, Leo drew a square flat box from his pocket. Natalie's fingers were a little unsteady as she flicked the clasp. Inside, nestling in black satin, lay a heart shaped pendant on a chain. At first she thought it was silver but in the warm light she realised it was white gold. The reverse was smooth but the front was a cushion of tiny stones in every colour she could name.

At first she couldn't speak, simply laid it on the palm of her hand and stared at it. 'It's … it's completely … gorgeous … I …'

'Like you are.' Leo lifted it from her hand and slid it around her neck. The touch of his fingers sent shivers of pleasure across her skin. She turned and kissed him attracting a chorus of *oohs* and *ahhs* from her friends.

'I'm going to see what it looks like,' she whispered to Leo and headed into the hotel, and followed the sign for the toilet.

She leaned close to the mirror, seeing the light catch the stones then she saw the sparkle in her own eyes and smiled at herself. How long was it since she'd done that? The door opened and her mother walked in.

'Mum, look at this.' She lifted the pendant from her throat.

'That must have cost a pretty penny.' Her mother's mouth set into its firm line.

'Couldn't you just say it's nice?'

'It is nice,' she peered at it. 'Looks expensive. But try and keep a sense of proportion, Natalie.'

'I have absolutely no idea what you mean by that, Mum.' She turned back to the mirror, saw two spots of red high on her cheeks.

'I'm just worried you're going to get very hurt again. The more you get attached to him the worse you'll feel when you come home.'

Natalie stared at the hand basin, watched water drip from one of the taps. She tightened it so that the dripping stopped. 'Mum. I am home. Salzburg is where I live and where I intend to stay.'

'But Toby misses you.'

Wham. She knew just where to strike. 'And I miss him but it was you who … you and dad said it was better for Toby if I was …'

'We're not the only ones who miss you. I … wasn't going to tell you this but your dad bumped into Ruth in town before we came away.'

The mention of Adam's mother made Natalie's stomach turn over. She opened the door and went out into reception.

'Don't run off, Natalie.' Her mother caught her up. 'This is important. She said Adam's in bits. He says leaving you was ….'

'I don't want to hear any more.' She tried to walk away but her mother grabbed her arm.

'He wants you, Natalie. Think about it, you could have your old life back.'

She pulled her arm free. 'After all he said and did to me you want me to … to be with him again?'

'He's wiser now. Got whatever it was out of his system, and think about it …' her mother looked hard into her eyes. 'That girl's a career woman. What if she let him have custody of the baby?'

Natalie felt nausea rise. She held up her hands wanting to ward off the horror of what her mother was suggesting. She backed up against a sofa and sat down. 'You … you'd want to …' Tears came now, she wiped them away, smearing mascara across the back of her hand. 'you want *me* to deprive that woman of her baby after … what I went through? That's … unbelievable, Mum, even for you.'

'I just … I want …' Her mother started to cry, she turned and went back into the Ladies. Natalie didn't follow. Her own tears were replaced by shock and anger. When Luisa walked by, heading for the toilet, Natalie stopped her. 'Have I got make- up smeared all over my face?'

'Just a little but … what has happened?'

'Nothing. I think I've just had a little too much Champagne.' She smiled and walked outside to their table. The sun was touching the lake now. Karin was taking photographs with her friends silhouetted against the view. Natalie caught her father's eye, nodded slightly towards the hotel entrance. His face told her he understood. She knew Leo was trying to catch her eye but she avoided his gaze and sat down at the table. 'You can have my strudel if you like, Tobes,' she said, 'but don't tell Mum.'

Chapter Sixty-Seven

Leo spent all of September in a haze of happiness. He could never have imagined the excitement or joy of their lovemaking; and if he ever worried that being older than Natalie would be a problem then every touch of her mouth and fingertips on his body told him otherwise.

'Being with you is like coming home,' she told him one night as they lay entwined, reluctant to move warm skin from warm skin, and he knew in that instant what she meant. Their lives had synchronised and every day his love for her grew.

They spent the occasional night apart but more often than not he slept with her beside him, her dark hair wild and curly on the pillow until she woke and tamed it. He loved to watch her dress, sliding underwear up her slim, smooth legs, fastening her bra at the front and swivelling it round to put her arms through the straps, seeing the movement of her beautiful breasts.

'Stop watching me,' she often teased, throwing a towel or a pillow at him. But he saw pleasure in her eyes too, as though she'd gone too long without being admired.

He never asked her what had happened the night of her birthday party. He guessed she'd had a spat with her mother. John had offered apologies saying Christine felt unwell and he was taking her back to the hotel. Toby had sulked at being wrenched away from his cousin and Natalie sat beside him on the bus that night as they all returned to Salzburg, her head resting on his shoulder, eyes closed. There'd been flecks of black on her cheeks and faint streaks in her make up where tears must have flowed.

Two nagging thoughts stopped life being perfect. The first was his trip to New York. Andreas had sent his concert ticket several weeks before, unaware Leo might need more than one. When he enquired after another he discovered the concert was sold out.

'Don't worry,' Natalie said. 'It'll be a wonderful chance for you to spend time together.' But he thought he saw a hint of wistfulness in her eyes and although he longed to see Andreas he cursed the timing.

The other worry was her brother. Natalie seemed to avoid talking about him now.

'How about asking Toby to come and stay during half term,' he suggested.

'Mum and Dad will probably have something planned,' she said, but didn't, as far as he knew, ring to find out.

In late October, three weeks before he was due to fly to the states, he drove Natalie into Bavaria to see her grandfather. For her birthday the old man had carved her a tiny whistle out of a wooden dowel. Leo noticed she'd had it made into a key ring and carried it in her handbag. Often he saw her take it out and stroke the smooth wood.

'Stay the night with us,' Sabine had said to him on the phone. 'We've just closed for a month and it would be lovely to see you. It's a shame Christine and John are in Italy or I'd invite them over too.'

So Natalie was right about them going away for half-term, Leo thought.

He picked her up on Saturday morning and headed out to the autobahn. He couldn't help thinking of the last time they'd made this journey, more particularly the car drive home and the terrible end to the evening. If she thought about it too she didn't say.

'There's something I haven't told you,' Natalie said as they sped towards the border.

Leo felt a jolt of anxiety.

'I mean it's not that I deliberately didn't tell you, it's just that we … got together the next day and so it was pushed from my mind and then … I …'

He bit his lip.

'Adam came to see me. He came to Salzburg, to my apartment. I couldn't believe it when I saw him standing at the gate.'

Leo's grip on the steering wheel tightened. 'He came … why?'

She touched his arm. 'He wanted to talk, so we did and then he left. We had a meal in the city and …'

A flame of jealousy ignited in Leo's chest. He glanced at her but she was staring ahead. His breathing quickened. He thought, obtusely, of Britte, the old attraction that initially surfaced that first night in Wurzburg. He battled to keep his voice level, 'So you had a meal …'

'I didn't want him in my apartment,' she said. 'It was just after the divorce papers were signed. He had this … mad idea that we could … somehow … get back together. He must have been insane.' She touched his arm again, her fingers caressing. 'I mean, his girlfriend was about to have a baby and … anyway, I told him there was no way and he went home. I wish I'd told you ages ago. I'm sorry.'

Feeling his pulse slowing Leo smiled. But will it always be like this, he wondered. Younger men might come along, lay down challenges. 'Thanks for telling me.' He smiled, took his hand from the wheel and held hers for a moment hoping she couldn't hear the tension in his voice.

Sabine had prepared lunch for them. After dumping their overnight bags in one of the guest rooms Leo folded Natalie into a hug and held her so tightly she gasped for breath.

'Sorry,' he said, stepping back. 'Didn't want to let you go, then.'

'I don't ever want you to let me go.' She took his hand as Max scampered down the stairs ahead of them.

After lunch Sabine drove them to the care home. The trees in the garden burned gold and red in the sun. The mountains cast longer shadows now and the breeze was keen.

Adolf was dozing in the lounge, a copy of Sueddeutsche Zeitung open across his lap. Sabine kissed the top of his head and he opened his eyes.

'I wasn't asleep,' he said.

'Doesn't matter if you were.' Sabine folded the newspaper and tucked it down the side of his chair. 'Look who's here to see you.'

Natalie kissed her grandfather's cheek and thanked him for the whistle. She told him it was now her key ring and he turned it over and over in his swollen fingers, nodding. 'Eine gute Idee,' he said.

When the old man looked up at Leo Sabine introduced him. They shook hands and Leo gave him the box of lebkuchen they'd bought in Ruhpolding. Adolf held the box to his nose and sniffed. 'Ahh, gingerbread. The scent of Christmas.'

'A little early,' Natalie said,' but we thought you'd like it.' She pulled her chair close to him and slid some photographs of her birthday celebration out of her bag. She pointed out her mother on each picture and managed to keep her smile in place.

'But where is your handsome, little boy today?' he asked.

Natalie felt her cheeks grow hot. Sabine spoke quickly. 'Toby is at school, Papa.' She avoided Natalie's eye.

She knows, Natalie thought. My mother has told her everything. A feeling of vulnerability rippled through her. What if Sabine wanted to talk about baby George at some stage? For months she'd been with people who knew nothing of his existence, he'd been her precious secret. Glancing up she met Leo's gaze and saw surprise and concern in his eyes. Then his expression turned to something she couldn't read at all and he looked away.

'It was Leo's detective work that helped Natalie and Christine find us, Papa.' Sabine said. 'He teaches piano in Salzburg.'

'Well then he must play for us.' He waved a hand in the direction of a piano in the corner.

Before Leo could object Adolf had summoned a member of staff. 'Could this young man play for us, just for a little while?'

The woman smiled and gave Leo a look that said, *Are you sure you want to do this?* But he winked at Natalie and said if nobody objected he'd be happy to oblige.

He'd only played to her a few times but she was still in awe of his talent. Those slim, cool fingers that stroked their way down her back in the mornings danced over the keys in a Mozart minuet then he did a medley of what she guessed were traditional folk songs as several residents sang along. Natalie wished she knew the words and felt a sudden surge of love and for these people who had become her family. As if she felt the same Sabine linked arms with her. 'He is a lovely man, your Leo. You must keep him.'

'I will,' she whispered back.

After fifteen minutes Leo played a strident, marching song which had staff and residents stamping their feet, clapping and singing. He took a bow at the end and everyone cheered. This time last year, Natalie thought, I was miserable and sending half-hearted, flirty emails to Connor. Now I'm in love with a wonderful man; sitting with a grandfather I didn't even know I had, and speaking German. Life is strange. Strange and wonderful.

In the back of Sabine's car Leo held Natalie's hand, their fingers interlaced.

'Sabine, would you drop us off at the top of the lane? I think Max should take a walk after being in the car for so long.'

'Of course, poor boy. I didn't think about that.'

She stopped at a layby. 'Take your time and have a nice walk.'

She waved and drove away.

Natalie took Max's lead, steering him onto the safety of a grassy bank. Leo grasped her free hand and raised it to his lips.

'Your grandfather was a little confused about Toby,' he said. 'Did that upset you?'

'No. It didn't … upset me.'

'I thought … you know, from your face …'

Natalie wanted to brush his concern away but she met his gaze for a fraction too long.

Leo whispered, 'Do you want to talk?'

'About what?' She wound Max's lead around her wrist, stared at the floor.

'I have to ask you and I hope you won't be angry but … Toby … is he your son?'

Chapter Sixty-Eight

'*My* son? No, of course not. Natalie strode ahead, Max trotting beside her, his tail wagging against her legs. She turned and saw that Leo hadn't moved.

'Please don't go away,' he said. For a few moments they stood, ten metres apart, staring at each other. Finally he walked towards her. 'I don't want to upset you but I saw in your face … something when Adolf said …'

'He's not my son, Leo. Can we leave it at that for now?'

He nodded and they walked back to the Gasthaus. Sabine and Horst were in reception talking to some tourists.

'Sorry about this,' her aunt said, 'we're closed but they want to make a large booking for December.' She touched Natalie's arm. 'Something wrong, Liebchen?'

'No. I'm fine. I'll come down and help you with dinner in a bit.'

In their room Natalie threw open the window, breathed in the crisp cold air; watched smoke rise from a farmhouse chimney part way up a mountain. Leo's arms slid round her waist and he kissed the top of her head. She leaned against him.

'Toby's my half-brother. My real father died when I was very little. An accident in his van. I don't really remember him but Mum said they were very happy.'

Gently Leo drew her away from the window and while she sat on the bed he poured two glasses of the wine Sabine had left for them.

'She married John when I was six and I loved him from day one. I took his name and he's been … the best dad ever.'

She didn't want to cry; didn't actually feel any sadness but still a single tear rolled down her cheek. Leo sat beside her and stroked it away.

'When Adam and I had been married a few months Mum got pregnant.' She smiled. 'She was so shocked she couldn't speak for about half an hour after the doctor told her. I didn't tell her we'd been trying for a baby but a couple of days later I found I was expecting too.'

She felt Leo's body stiffen, his hand found hers and grasped it.

'Auntie Maureen - at least we think it was her - rang the local newspaper and a reporter came to interview us. Mother and daughter due to give birth on the same day.' She took a sip of wine. 'Mum was anxious because of her age and worried … things might go wrong but …'

Setting her wine glass on the table she wriggled up the bed so that she could lean against the pillows, her knees tucked up against her chest.

Leo turned to look at her. 'Natalie. I have asked questions and made you unhappy with my mistake.'

'No. I need to tell you this.' She pushed one foot down towards him and he stroked her ankle. 'The scans told us we were both having boys. I was a school secretary then and I used to watch the children in the playground, wonder which type of boy he'd be. The bold one taking charge of the games or the shy one waiting to be chosen. The newspapers loved it all. One baby would be uncle to the other.' She remembered painting the tiny second bedroom and knew that beneath three coats of cream emulsion stencilled rabbits and teddies still frolicked across the walls. The drawers had been full of tiny blue clothes folded in tissue that she and her mother had bought.

'Everything went … really well. I was hardly sick. Poor Mum was throwing up all day, every day.'

Leo put down his glass, moved up beside her and she laid her head against his chest. The rapid beat of his heart told her how anxious he was.

'He was always so active … my baby … that when I'd had a whole night's sleep I woke up feeling great. There was just … just a week to go. By the time I'd had my breakfast I got panicky and rang the midwife. She said she was sure he'd be kicking the life out of me any minute now … but she still wanted us to go to the hospital. I went to call Adam but he'd already got the car running.'

Natalie lifted her head and hugged her knees, rested her chin on them and stared at the window. Leo's hand was warm on her back. 'I was staring at the nurse, looking for her reaction but she was really good at keeping her face … blank. Then she said she'd just ask the doctor to pop in. He couldn't find a heartbeat.'

She turned then, to look at Leo and saw tears on his cheeks. His lips tight. She stood and paced the room not wanting his comforting embrace. 'They put a mask on my face … oxygen. It was so … claustrophobic I kept pulling it off. Adam was saying, "try again, try again" and I was thinking over and over, *breathe, George, breathe.*'

For a moment she focused on the view outside, the last rays of sun were catching a window high on the mountain. It looked like a star. 'Mum and Dad came to the hospital. Mum was huge and could hardly walk. They wanted to stay for the … inducement, but I wouldn't let them. And it was quick, thank goodness.

Afterwards they gave me a sedative and I know I slept for hours. Adam and his mum went home and dismantled the … nursery. Put everything away in boxes, painted the walls. I never saw any of it again.'

'Toby was born sometime while I was asleep. When I was back at home I begged Mum to bring him to see me and when she did she couldn't look at me. She went out into the garden. Dad sat with me for hours. Adam had fallen apart. I should have told you all this before,' she said. When Leo didn't reply she asked what he was thinking.

'I'm thinking, how could he leave you? After all that you shared why did he …?'

'It was a long time ago, Leo. He didn't want to try … for another baby. We looked after Toby so often, as the years went by he sort of … filled a need.'

'Now I can see why you're so very attached to your brother.' Leo's voice was a whisper. 'Please forgive me for thinking he was your child. Although I won't forgive myself for opening up your sorrow.'

'We had to have this conversation sometime, Leo.'

'So your little boy is … he is buried in England.'

'No. We didn't … couldn't do anything for ages after the funeral, but in the end Adam and I took his ashes out into the countryside, to a shallow stream we used to see when we were out walking. It was really early in the morning.' She turned back to the view, looked up at the window on the mountain that was now glowing red. 'When we emptied the jar the sun was on the water. It was like … every tiny fragment of him was twinkling, swirling round the rocks and then … he was gone.'

Leo came to her then, wrapped his arms round her but he didn't speak. She realised she was shivering and let his warmth seep into her. 'When Adam came to Salzburg to see me he … he wanted to see George's footprints one last time. That's what they do, did you know that? They coat the baby's feet with ink and make a …'

'I understand.' Leo kissed the top of her head, left his lips there.

'I can't believe I'm not crying,' Natalie said.

'You must have cried a lifetime of tears already.'

She looked up into his eyes. 'I won't ever love you more than I do right now,' she said.

Chapter Sixty-Nine

Leo was leaving and the Friesen was closed for a month. Karin and Luisa had flown to South Africa for a horse riding holiday.

'If you get lonely,' Aunt Lexi said, 'come and drink coffee with me.'

Leo offered to buy her a ticket to New York even though she'd be unable to attend the concert.

'I'd love to come but I've had so much time off work this year I'd feel awful asking Karl for another week. Anyway, I'm looking forward to having Max all to myself.'

Leo was flying from Munich so he took the train from Salzburg on a grey, drizzly November day. Natalie clung to him on the platform, choking back tears.

'Have a wonderful time with Andreas,' she said. 'Ring me when you land. I don't care what time it is.'

'This is so hard, Natalie. I am torn with wanting to go and coming back home with you.'

But the train had arrived so she gave him one last kiss and hugged the breath out of him. He blew her a kiss from the window and then he was gone.

Over the weekend she walked Max for miles along the river and at night settled him onto her sofa, avoiding his reproachful, *where have you hidden my dad*, looks.

She loved the sound of Leo's voice on the phone and tried to imagine he was at his house rather than thousands of miles away.

The concert in New York was on Monday night. Leo said he'd call her the minute it was over.

On Monday morning she took a call from Binita. She hadn't seen her since one day in the summer when she had brought a number of visiting cousins into the shop anxious for souvenirs.

'Will you and Leo come to our party? My parents are here from India and we're having a big get together.'

'Leo's away but … yes, I'd love to come. When is it?'

'It's tonight. We only decided this morning. We have so much food it's madness here. We're ringing everyone. Please come.'

'Love to.' It would distract her from missing Leo. 'What should I bring?'

'Anything but food.' Binita laughed. 'No. Seriously don't bring anything. Can't wait to see you.'

At lunchtime Natalie went out to buy flowers from the Market. Walking across Residenzplatz she saw that the horse fountain was encased in its wooden covering for the winter. Another few days and the Christmas Markets would be setting up. She remembered watching them on the webcams last winter in her tiny spare bedroom. It was still a thrill to be a resident and know she could visit them as often as she liked. She put aside thoughts of home, particularly of her mother who had astonished her beyond measure the night of her birthday. It was strange to admit Sigourney had unwittingly done her a huge favour by enticing Adam away. She knew they now had a baby girl. Her dad had texted the news and asked if she was okay.

'I wish them well, Dad,' she said, and meant it.

That night a frost covered the city and on the Untersberg the snow line crept lower. Natalie dropped Max off at Leo's house then stood at the bus stop, stamping her feet to keep them warm.

Binita and Prakash lived in Gnigl, a suburb not too far from Aigen; their apartment in a quiet, tree-lined street. Natalie changed buses in the city and alighted almost at their door. Binita waved her in with a beautifully henna-painted hand. She hugged her, thanked her for the flowers and dragged her through to the kitchen.

'Some cousins are here from Leicester if you want to speak

English,' Binita said. 'Although they never shut up about their cars so maybe not.'

Natalie laughed and found herself relaxing. Just five more days and Leo would be home. No need to feel depressed.

The apartment was heaving with people and Indian music pulsed through the rooms. Natalie was introduced to a succession of relatives and knew she would never remember anyone's name. Food covered every flat surface and the scents mingled and wafted through the apartment. Natalie, mouth-watering, tried to pace herself, restricting the number of samosas in anticipation of the vegetable biryani Binita told her was to die for.

Later, while Natalie was in deep conversation with one an off-duty taxi driver, Binita brought her some tea. 'Chai, a little taste of England.' They escaped out onto the balcony where the cold air was welcome.

'It seems a long time since we were making beds and cleaning bathrooms,' Binita said.

Natalie took a sip of the hot, strong tea. 'We were a great team. I bet they missed us when we left. You must be enjoying driving, though.'

'Yes. I'm sorry I didn't make it to your birthday party. Leo was so sweet when he telephoned. I think he loves you.' She drew out the word *loves* and rolled her eyes, making Natalie blush.

Together they leaned against the balcony rail and drank their tea then Binita said she'd better get back to see if her nephew was smoking in the bathroom.

Left alone Natalie turned on her phone to see if Leo had left a message or text. She discovered several missed calls from a mobile number she didn't recognise. Frowning over the phone for a second she jumped when it rang.

'Hello?' Hello?' A woman's voice, high pitched.

'Yes. Who's ...?'

'Natalie? I can't hear you properly, Lovie.'

She pulled the balcony door closed. 'Auntie Maureen?' A sour taste rose in her mouth.

'Yes. Yes it's me. Oh Natalie, thank goodness. I've been trying to get …'

'What's wrong?' Her breath was short puffs of white in the freezing air. 'Is Toby ill?'

'No, it's not … Oh Natalie, can you come home?'

'What's wrong? Impatience made her shout. She gripped the balcony rail.

'Your mum asked me to ring you. She's at the hospital and 'it's your dad, Lovie. He's had a heart attack.'

Chapter Seventy

Somehow Natalie crossed the crowded room, found Benita and was helped to the door, her coat trailing, her mind alternating between numbness and panic.

Benita manoeuvred her car out of the narrow street and turned towards the main road. Natalie, hands trembling, punched out her mother's mobile number but it went to the messaging service. 'Mum, call me please. Tell me what's happened.'

Tears began and then whimpering. 'Dad, be okay, please be okay.'

By the time they reached Leo's house Prakash's voice was coming over the radio. Binita spoke English, 'There are three seats on the Stansted flight in the morning but you'll need to hurry if you want to take one of them.'

Natalie rummaged in her bag. 'Credit card, where's my bloody purse?'

'Let's get inside. Two minutes won't make a difference.'

Max ran to greet them, bringing one of Leo's socks. 'I need to catch Gerde before she goes to bed,' Natalie said.

'Let's book that seat first.' Binita gently took the bag from her and lifted out her purse. 'Is it in here?'

'Yes. Can you … ring them …?' she began to tremble and buried her fingers in Max's fur, desperate for something familiar to cling to.

Binita held up a Visa card. Natalie nodded.

It took only a couple of minutes to call the airport and book the seat; her friend speaking calmly into the phone. 'I said you'd just take hand luggage. Am I right?'

Leo's neighbour was ready for bed but pulled on a heavy dressing gown, calling them into the warmth of her kitchen.

Natalie stumbled out her words, Binita holding tight to her hand. Gerde said she would have Max for as long as was needed.

'Please d…don't let Leo know. I don't want … him rushing back.' She could hardly breathe.

'But what will you say when he rings you on your Handy?'

'I don't know yet. But … this is … his chance to spend time with Andreas. '

Gerde enveloped her in a hug. 'And what news of your father?'

She bit hard on her quivering lip. 'Just that he's in hospital.'

At Natalie's apartment Binita made tea and stayed until she had packed her bag. Now instead of longing to speak to Leo Natalie dreaded his call, hated the idea of lying to him, wondering how on earth she would hold it together once she heard his voice. Binita promised to speak to Karl in the morning.

'Tell him I'll ring when I know what's happening.'

Every five minutes she tried her mother's mobile but it was still turned off. She rang international directory enquiries and found the number of University Hospital. When the English voice confirmed that her father had been admitted it all became horribly real. He was still being assessed, she was told. Perhaps she could call back later.

'He's alive,' Binita said. 'Hold on to that thought.'

When her friend had gone Natalie paced the room, phone in hand. Still shaking she pressed out a text to Leo, tears dripping from her chin onto her fingers. *Hi you, I hope you don't mind but I'm off to bed. I'm really tired and have a headache. Hope the concert is fantastic. Talk tomorrow. All my love, A.*

A few moments later her mother finally answered. Natalie bombarded her with questions but an angry voice stunned her to silence.

'For God's sake shut up for a minute, Natalie. Don't you think I've enough to think about?

She stared at the wall waiting for her mother to speak.

'I'm sorry but I'm just about at the end of my rope. Toby's hysterical. Maureen's taken him to her place.'

'But Dad … how bad is it?'

'He's in the coronary care unit and they're doing things with monitors and tubes and there are screens bleeping and all sorts. He's awake and they say that's a good sign.

'But how did it happen, where was he?'

'He was … he was running along beside Toby's bike. He just keeled over. They'd only been out ten minutes. Are you coming home?'

'I can't get a flight till the morning. Are you alright, Mum?'

'I've come home to try and sleep but I don't suppose there's a chance in hell I'll be able to.'

'Try though, Mum. I'll be there as soon as I can.'

Walking to the window she suddenly found the apartment cold and unfriendly. She longed for Leo's voice, the patter of Max's claws on the floor, but the only sounds were the wind in the trees along the river bank and the ceaseless rushing of the water.

Chapter Seventy-One

Sleep eluded Natalie and she was wide awake when Anton arrived to drive her to the airport. For a few minutes on the plane she drifted into a doze but waking, nerves jangling, she'd forced herself to stay alert. Even during the interminable train journey from Stansted she didn't nod off.

Arriving at Coventry she took a taxi straight to the hospital. At the sink in the toilets she washed her face and plaited her hair. She checked her mobile and saw there was a missed call from Leo.

Her mother was in the corridor outside the CCU, on her phone. 'Maureen, give him whatever he wants to eat,' she was saying, her voice impatient. She rang off as Natalie approached. 'No change, but they say he's stable,' she said, then pulled Natalie into a tight hug. 'Don't be frightened of all the machines and he looks much worse than he is, apparently. He's awake but a bit groggy.

At her father's bedside Natalie took hold of his hand, bent to kiss it. She hadn't intended to let him see her cry but tears slid down her face anyway. After rehearsing all that she wanted to say to him the words evaporated and she just stared into his face, trying to smile, when all she wanted to be was his little Lovie and for to him to make everything right. The pressure she felt when she squeezed his hand was weak and it frightened her.

'Natalie,' her mother's whisper was barely audible, 'this is the last straw.'

'Last … what do you mean?'

'We're not staying here now. When John's … when he's well enough we're moving.'

A cold, panicky sensation made Natalie swallow her next

question. A nurse arrived to look at the monitors. She smiled in a distracted sort of way.

'I think the main thing now is being here for Dad,' Natalie said, not wanting to hear more. 'Why don't you go for a coffee or something, Mum? I'll sit with him now.'

'Alright, but I won't be long.'

Her father had drifted off to sleep and Natalie found herself watching the rise and fall of his chest, matching her breathing to his. Feeling her mother's hand on her arm she realised she'd fallen asleep, her forehead resting on the bedclothes.

'Get yourself home and sleep. I'll call you if … if anything changes.'

Reluctantly she agreed but took a long time putting on her coat, not wanting to turn away from her dad.

In the taxi home her phone rang. Leo's number. Tempted to decline the call she stared out at the drab streets but then answered, biting her lip against the temptation to tell him where she was.

'How was the concert? Was he fabulous? Tell me everything.' She prayed the taxi driver's radio wouldn't burst into life.

'He was indeed fabulous but oh, Natalie, I wish you were here. It's snowing and it's beautiful. I miss you so much.'

'I miss you too.' The words were inadequate to describe her longing.

In her mother's spare room she didn't even take off her shoes but sank onto the bed, pulled the duvet over her body and gave in to exhaustion.

When her phone rang she woke disorientated and groggy. It was dark outside. She leapt up, answered without noting the caller.

'No change. But the doctor has been by. He says it wasn't a severe attack. It's been a sort of … warning to make changes, I suppose.' Her mother's voice was flat.

'Is that all they could tell you?'

'Don't harp on, Natalie. I'll be a long in a bit and I'll pick up Toby from Maureen's.'

'I'll come in and sit with Dad then, shall I?'

'No. They think it's best we conserve our strength or something.'

'But that sounds ominous. Why should we …'

'Look. Let's just all get a night's sleep and go in first thing tomorrow.'

In the kitchen, fighting down her annoyance and worry, she found baking potatoes and put three into the microwave. I should ring Leo, she thought but instead opened a large tin of tuna and mixed it in a bowl with mayonnaise. Despite everything she was excited about seeing Toby. There was a drawing of a wizard stuck to the fridge door and she wondered if Dr Who had given way to Harry Potter.

She didn't hear them come in but was aware of Toby's stamping tread on the stairs and landing above. He hadn't come to greet her.

'Is Toby alright?'

'No. But I'd leave him be for now.'

'I haven't seen him since August.' She walked past her mother and up the stairs, tapping on Toby's door. 'Hi Sweetie, can I come in?'

'Don't call me Sweetie it's babyish and stupid.'

'Alright.'

'You can come in if you want but don't say stupid things.'

He was sitting on his bed, feet not reaching the floor. Natalie resisted the urge to hug him.

'Why did Dad have to get ill? Nobody else's dad gets ill.'

Natalie closed her eyes, took a deep breath and let it out slowly. 'Nobody has a heart attack intentionally, Tobes.'

'Don't call me Tobes either. My name is Toby George Grey.'

'Well, Toby George Grey I've done jackets with tuna-mayo. Do you want some?'

He shook his head. 'Now you've come home you won't be going away again, will you?'

'But you know I have a job in Salzburg and … well, that's where I live now.'

'But Mum said you'd be staying.' Tears welled and spilled down his face. She sat on the bed but he wriggled out of her hug.

'I'll stay for a while, of course I will. But I'll be going back.'

'I want you to stay here. Mum's always cross and Dad's in his shed all the time and only takes me to Markus's house when Mum reminds him.'

'Dad probably won't be spending so much time in the shed now, though.' She didn't want to say more and her thoughts were snagged on his comment, *Mum said you'd be staying.*

They had their food in front of the TV, something her mother had never allowed when she was a child. Toby ate very little and begged to go back up to his room. Natalie looked at her mother's exhausted face and knew now wasn't the time for questions. Her phone buzzed a few times in her pocket. When she took a look there was no message from Leo but astonishingly one from Glenda with the heading, *How is your Dad!*

Chapter Seventy-Two

Upstairs in the bathroom Natalie read the text. One of your Dad's neighbours was in the surgery today. Is he okay? Have you come home? If so would love to meet up.

Glenda, her funny, kind friend without whom she'd never have gone to Salzburg and met Leo. She glanced at her watch. Eight-fifteen. Was it too late to ring?

Another text was from Binita asking how things were. Nothing from Leo. She called Glenda.

The minute she heard her friend's voice Natalie dissolved into tears.

'Come round if you like,' Glenda said, 'or I can come to you.'

She imagined her mother's face if Glenda appeared at the door. 'I can come over to you but are you sure it's not too late?'

'No.' There were a few seconds silence. 'No, please come. I'd love to see you.'

In the sitting room her mother was asleep on the sofa. Natalie scribbled a quick note, picked up her mother's car keys and tip-toed out of the house. A thick fog had blanketed the cul-de-sac and she nearly turned back but the draw of Glenda's unswerving sensible attitude forced her on.

Once on the main roads where shops were decked with early Christmas lights, it was easier to navigate. Her tears dried on her cheeks and she knew she looked a wreck. Her head ached and now there was the added worry of why Leo had gone quiet. Before going to the door she sat in the car and sent a quick text to Binita giving her an update. I have the best friends in the world, she thought.

Martin opened the door and gave her a wide smile. 'Glenda's in the kitchen,' he said. 'Go on through. Would you excuse me if I leave you to it? I've some marking to do and a Christmas panto half written.'

Natalie had forgotten he was a teacher. Her old life seemed light years away now.

Behind the sparkling clean kitchen island Glenda was pouring a small glass of wine. Natalie went to hug her and then stopped. As her friend moved away from the worktop Natalie saw her huge belly. Glenda burst into tears.

'I'm so sorry I didn't tell you. I really wanted to but …'

Natalie enveloped her in a hug, holding herself away so as not to press on the baby.

Now they were both crying. 'I saw into your dad not long after we knew I was …' Glenda looked away for a second. 'He told me what had happened … to you. I just bottled out of telling you.'

'It's fine. Really. I'm thrilled for you.'

Glenda thrust the glass of wine into her hand and poured mineral water for herself. 'It's only a small one as you're driving but you look as though you need it,' she said. 'And I insist you eat this cheese sandwich. It'll soak up the alcohol.'

After a few minutes the wine eased her stress but a mind numbing tiredness was taking over.

'Tell me about Salzburg,' Glenda said. 'You've a job and a flat, your dad said.'

It was soothing bliss to talk about normal things. 'I should have emailed you ages ago. I'm with someone now. His name's Leo. He's a music teacher.'

'Wow! So your life really is sorted. I guess you won't be coming back?'

'My mother seems to think I am.' She didn't really want to visit those thoughts now. 'Leo and I don't live together … yet. I mean, we've only been together since the late summer but … it's going well. He's in New York seeing his son perform in a concert.

I haven't told him what's happened, he was so looking forward to seeing Andreas and …' She glanced at her phone, a text from Sabine asking for news. Mum must have rung her, she thought.

Natalie told Glenda about Leo discovering her Bavarian family. She was just flicking through the photos on her phone when the door opened and two fluffy cats walked in.

'Is that Mr Woo?' One cat was enormous, his long fur accentuating his size. The other, smaller and a slightly different colour, hung back a little.

'Yes. Woosie is a huge gorgeous boy.' Glenda swept him up and draped him round her neck. 'And that's Pandora. She's from the same breeder. Martin thought Woo would be a bit jealous of the baby so we got him a playmate. She's neutered of course. Don't want any of that funny business.'

'So how are things at the vets?'

'Well. They don't know yet,' Glenda lowered her voice as though someone from the practice might be in the next room, 'but I'm not going back after the baby's born. It's not finalised yet but we're buying a boarding cattery near Warwick.'

'How fantastic.' Natalie imagined her running it with military precision, bullying pet owners about the importance of worming and grooming.

'It's a bit of a commute for Martin but hopefully he'll find something closer. So, it seems like you and I are finally settled.' She touched Natalie's arm. 'You didn't say where you met Leo …'

Chapter Seventy-Three

Despite her anxiety Natalie found herself smiling as she let herself back into her parent's house. For once Glenda had been lost for words when she explained that Leo was the man from the Mozarteum. To show that he was no longer the pale ghost he'd been that day she showed Glenda some photos on her phone: Leo in the garden at the Friesen, up the ladder picking apples; the two of them at Sabine's, sitting on a bench in the late afternoon sun. 'You make a very … interesting couple,' Glenda had said, scrutinising the pictures at very close range.

Her mother was still asleep but while Natalie debated whether to wake her or bring a duvet downstairs her she stirred, squinted at the clock and ran her hands through her hair. 'Any news?'

Natalie shook her head. 'Want some tea?'

'I'd rather have whiskey. Do you want one?'

'I'll pass.' Instead she made herself some hot chocolate and wished she were sitting up against Leo's pillows. As she poured hot milk into her mug her phone rang.

'I was just thinking about you,' she said, relief making her speak too loudly.

'I have been at lunch with Andreas and his … parents. 'My phone is flat. I'm calling from my room telephone.'

'It's so nice to hear your voice. What are you doing this evening?' The mention of Britte gave her a pang of jealousy.

'I will sleep. Nobody seems to sleep here. Natalie, are you okay?'

'I wish I was with you, that's all.'

When she heard her mother turn on the TV she rushed outside into the back garden. The fog hadn't lifted and moisture formed a halo around the security light.

'I'll call you in the morning, Leo. I love you so much … I miss you.'

When her mother walked into the kitchen Natalie ended the call and went indoors.

'This fog's set to stay for a while according to the news. Have you been out?'

'Glenda's. I left you a note.'

Natalie picked up her chocolate. It was still too hot.

'How is the weird friend?'

'She's not weird, Mum. She's expecting and she's buying a cattery?'

'Well you don't get much weirder that that. How's a pregnant woman going to run a cattery?'

'If I know Glenda, very well indeed.' She swallowed her annoyance, needed to sleep.

'Maybe you could help her out. Do the business side of it or something.'

'I work in a shop in Salzburg, Mum.'

'I mean when you come home.' Pouring herself another whiskey her mother looked defiant.

'Salzburg is my home.' They were on dangerous ground and Natalie's anger mounted. 'And can I remind you that you and Dad wanted me gone from Toby's life so that you could have him to yourselves more.'

Standing by the fireplace her mother tapped her foot on the carpet. 'Yes, I know but …we thought you'd be back after a few weeks.'

'So you only wanted to spend time with him for a few …'

'Don't twist words, My Girl.'

'My Girl?' Natalie wanted to laugh. 'I'm thirty-one and haven't lived at home since I was twenty?' Her hand shook so she put down her drink. 'And why are you permanently in a bad mood, Mum? Toby mentioned it tonight. You don't have a good word for any of us. I've picked my life up out of the ruins and started again. Everyone tells me I've been brave. Why not you? Can't you say something nice about it instead of harping on about me coming home?'

'Natalie, I've got so much in my head you wouldn't believe.'

'What then? Let's talk now. Let's clear the air.'

'We're buying a house in Italy. It was only going to be a holiday home at first but I've been trying to get John out of this … cycle of restlessness and boredom he's been on since he left the job.'

Natalie stared at the carpet, forced herself to speak calmly. 'But Toby doesn't like Italy. He's told me loads of times.'

'Which is why you should come home!' Her mother was almost screaming now.

Natalie closed the door to the hall and whispered, 'I'm with Leo and that's the way it's going to stay.'

'Wake up. Leo might be having fun with you now. Don't you think I had boyfriends after your father died? But when he's finally over his wife he'll choose someone his own age, from his own … country.'

'You sound like a loony racist, Mum. Leo loves me. He's told me a thousand times.'

'Toby needs you more.'

'What?' It wasn't just her hands shaking now. Tremors shook her body.

'You can have this house, Natalie. We'll give it to you. You can live here with Toby. You'd both be happy and you'd be set up forever.'

It took a few moments for the words to sink in. 'You … you'd give up your child to swan off to Italy? Is that what you're saying?' She sat down on the sofa, her hands gripping the fabric of the cushions. 'On my birthday you were trying to get me back with Adam, encouraging me to wrench Sigourney's baby away

…' Before she could say more the house phone rang. They stared at each other for a second, both of them weeping.

Her mother snatched up the phone, mumbled something; put it down again. 'Your Dad's asking for us,' she said.

Chapter Seventy-Four

Toby cried in the taxi. Natalie hugged him to her. 'No need for tears, Sweetie. We'll soon see Dad and I'm sure he's going to be fine now.' Her mother was tight-lipped in the front seat.

On the ward staff nurse said they could only see him one at a time but after a withering look from Natalie's mother she said they could stay two minutes then take it in turns. Her dad dissolved into tears as they approached his bed. It looked as though Toby might turn and run until his father reached out a hand, still with a tube in the back of it, to touch his arm.

From his pocket Toby pulled a folded piece of paper and smoothed it out on the covers. It was a drawing of Harry Potter pointing his wand at a man she took to be their dad.

'Natalie. Sorry you've had to come all … this way, Lovie.'

Her mother sat on the chair, took Dad's hand in hers, bent to kiss it and spoke to him in a soft, gentle voice Natalie hadn't heard in years. Her father didn't answer but Natalie saw him squeeze her mother's hand before picking up Toby's drawing and giving him a thumbs up.

The staff nurse was hovering so Natalie took Toby for a drink then sat on a bench outside the ward.

'Dad liked your picture,' she said. 'Are you reading the Harry Potter books now?'

'Yes, I had to read through ever so quickly to find a *get-better* spell.'

Natalie tried to listen to his subdued chatter but the row she'd had with her mother was replaying over and over and clouding her thoughts. *Give me the house?* What were they thinking? Surely Dad wouldn't agree to this. Above all she knew Toby would be devastated if he were hauled off to Italy. But would it be so bad? He'd soon adjust. But it depended where the house was. Knowing her mother it would be on a hill in Tuscany with a swimming pool, miles from anywhere. Her head ached with tiredness, she longed for Leo but her brother's anxious face was her priority. 'The doctors said Dad's illness isn't too serious so when he comes home everything will be fine.'

He looked up at her then with an expression that made her sadder than she could have imagined. He knew what would happen. He knew he'd be going to Italy.

Natalie couldn't look her mother in the eye when she came out to join them.

'I know they say he's going to be fine but I want to talk to the doctor in the morning. We should go home and sleep if we're to be back here early.

It was one-thirty. Natalie spent a few minutes at her dad's bedside but he was drifting in and out of sleep. She kissed his forehead and noticed for the first time how lined his face was now. She began to see her mother's point. He needed to be away from his old life. But what was the cost going to be?

She slept late and found a note blu-tacked to the bathroom door. Her mother had left for the hospital, dropping Toby off at school and arranging for Auntie Maureen to pick him up.

Soaking in the bath her mind was still a turmoil of worry.

She was certain her mother was wrong about Leo. It was impossible to imagine he'd drop her for someone else. There were two texts from him telling her how much he loved her. But Toby … what could she do to make him happy? She couldn't bear to think of her mother's solution.

At eleven she caught the bus to the hospital. The fog had melted away and the sun shone. She looked out of the grimy bus windows at rows of terraced houses and longed to see a backdrop of mountains.

Dad was sitting up, some of the tubes removed but they were still monitoring his heart.

'He's had quite a good sleep,' her mother said, as though her dad was incapable of speaking.

When her mother went to get a drink her dad watched her go.

'I've let her down, Natalie. What am I going to do?'

'Nothing but lie here and get better.' Her heartbeat racked up a notch.

'I've neglected her, you know. I've been wrapped up in my own thoughts for months. I've got so much to make up for.' A tear threatened to spill down his cheek.

Natalie was shocked to feel anger forming in her chest. He hadn't said he'd neglected Toby too. Was her precious brother so far down the list of priorities?

The doctor, a nurse and an entourage of students arrived and pulled the curtains round the bed. Natalie met her mother at the door to the ward. 'Mum, you go in and see what they have to say then you can tell me later.' She took her coffee and stood at the window, sent a text to Leo and knew that she'd have to tell him the whole story when he next rang. Now the New York concert was over and he'd had a few days with Andreas it seemed wrong to let him think she was still in Salzburg.

It was over half an hour before her mother emerged from the ward. Some of the lines of tension were gone from her face. 'They're really pleased with him. He'll be in for a couple more days but he'll be home at the weekend.' She sank down onto a chair. I can't believe it, Natalie. I thought I'd lost him.'

'I'll ring the school. Get someone to let Toby know,' Natalie said, scrawling through her contacts list.'

'That's a good idea.' Her mother stood up. 'I feel I could eat something now. There's a cafe in here somewhere.'

Natalie felt the weight of un-said words. After they'd had some sandwiches and endless cups of coffee she took a deep breath. 'I'd better go on-line and look for flights back home. Karl's been very patient about everything but I'm needed at the shop.' She stared out of the window. The sun had gone and the fog was creeping back with the dusk.

'This is home and you're needed here. You know that, don't you?'

'Not this again, Mum. Things will be different for you now … after what's happened. Dad will have to take it easy.'

Her mother stared into her cup, tapped the spoon against the saucer. 'I meant what I said. John and I have talked about it. You can stay here. There's no mortgage. You can get shop work if you like it so much. We'll still pay some of the bills and …'

'Mum! Listen to yourself.' Natalie dropped her voice to a whisper. 'How do you imagine Toby's going to feel if you tell him you're leaving him behind? You can't do this to him. For God's sake don't you love him at all?'

She'd gone too far.

Her mother leapt up from her chair and strode across the cafe, leaving her phone behind. Natalie grabbed it and hurried after her. She caught her up at the lift doors.

'Don't ever question my love, Natalie. Don't you *dare* do that.'

There was a tone to her voice Natalie had never heard before. The lift doors opened, a porter with an empty wheelchair came out. Natalie went to go in but her sleeve was pulled back. Her mother crossed her arms over her chest. 'When you look at me all you see is a grumpy, menopausal bitch. We'll that's not the full picture at all. Do you know there are times when I can't even look at you? When the sight of you makes me want to run and hide.'

'What?' Shock made Natalie shrink away. She turned, saw an alcove by the window and headed for it and leaned against the wall, letting it take the weight her wobbly legs could no longer hold.

'It all went wrong, didn't it? Her mother was beside her now, her voice low. 'It shouldn't have happened at all. Not to me. I had to watch you … carry a … tiny coffin into a church. You, my lovely girl, my precious, beautiful daughter….' Tears poured down both their faces.

'No, Mum. Don't say this … please …'

'I saw you broken and wretched and … all the while I had … everything you wanted and I didn't even …' her mother's voice was a strangled scream, 'I never wanted another baby. I never wanted him.'

'No. No. Stop.' Natalie put her hands over her ears, slid down the wall until she was sitting on the floor.

'Of course I love, him … but he should be yours. You lost … everything and I … I had a new … life I never bargained for.' Her mother drew in great heaving sobs of air then sat down beside her. 'Toby ad … adores you, Natalie. He always has. I look at you together and it … it breaks my heart … for so many reasons.

'Please go away, Mum. I can't handle this … I really can't.'

'Think about it … please.' Her mother kissed the side of her face, their tears mingling. 'Promise me that.'

Natalie went back to the cafe. It was hard to know how long she sat with a mug of tea in front of her but when she took a sip it was cold. Snatches of memory flitted across her mind: Toby staying over with her and Adam so regularly they had some of his clothes in drawers. Toby refusing to tell anyone but her when he had a horrible rash. Her mum at Fuschl encouraging her to go back to Adam; to challenge Sigourney for custody of their baby. When she focused her eyes on the window it was dark outside. Toby would be at Auntie Maureen's. She should go to him.

She rang for a taxi and saw there were no texts or messages on her phone. The hospital foyer was a buzz of voices, the lights too bright for her throbbing head. She pushed the door open and went outside. The fog was so thick she couldn't see across the road but a line of taxis was visible against the kerb. Wondering which was hers she stepped forward and saw one of the drivers walk towards her. She went to meet him but recognition made her stop. She stared, uncomprehending, legs weakening as he approached. It wasn't the taxi driver. It was Leo.

Chapter Seventy-Five

His arms were around her, holding against his body, whispering into her hair, stroking her cheek until she had no more tears to cry.

'Why are you …here? How did …'

'Shhh Liebchen, not now, not now. I will tell you, soon. But your father, he is not …?'

'No. He'll be OK. '

The taxi took them to his hotel in Birmingham. After sending a message to Auntie Maureen - she couldn't even bear to text her mother - Natalie clung to him throughout the journey drawing strength from his closeness.

Once in his room he kissed the breath from her body, holding her tight. 'You should have told me, Natalie. I should have been here with you.'

'I didn't want you to miss the concert. I … it was so important.'

Stroking her hair he whispered, 'But Andreas will always be there to visit. This is where I should have been.'

'How did you even know?' She stared into his eyes.

'Binita rang Gerde to ask how you were. Gerde rang Lukas who rang Karin.'

'And Karin rang you.'

'I'm so glad she did. And believe it or not I spoke to your friend. The one who thought I was so rude last year.' He smiled. 'She told me where to find you. Lukas looked up her details, passed them to Karin. Telephones have been hot all over the world, although Karin and Luisa are back now, I think.'

Natalie thought of her friends, suntanned, greeting their parents, Otto going wild with excitement. Her throat ached as more tears came.

'What is it, Natalie? Tell me everything.'

'I don't know where to start, Leo it's … it's so awful.' But out it came, the whole sorry business. Toby's distress, her mother's suggestion that she stay in England. Her voice drained away. Leo, still holding both her hands stared down at them. It was a long time before he spoke.

'They will leave their child and go to Italy?'

'I can't believe it either.' She moved away from him as though some distance might make what she had to say easier. 'Dad needs a complete break from his old life. Mum says she has to get him away. But Toby… he … he doesn't want to go. Oh God, I feel torn apart by this.'

He walked towards her but she dodged away, stood by the window. The fog was clearing, the lights of the city glittered below.

'I think … I'm … I'm going to have to stay with him. What else can I do? I can't abandon him.'

Leo was silent, she turned to see him, head down, sitting on the bed.

'I'm so sorry, Leo. I'm so sorry … I just …'

'No. This is not good.' He looked up. The pain in his eyes was indescribable.

She sank onto a chair. 'I know, it's terrible but Toby is in the middle of all this. He doesn't deserve to be hurt.'

Now he was beside her, lifting her from the chair, wrapping his arms around her, holding her so close she could hardly breathe.

'Then I will come here too.' His voice was calm. 'I can give piano lessons here as well as in Salzburg. I don't want to lose you, Natalie. Not now. Not after all these months of loving you.'

Slowly she shook her head. 'No, Leo. I can't … tear you away from your life, your … h … home.' Sobs wracked through her again. He took her hand, brought it to his lips. She felt the tremble in his kiss. There were tears on his cheeks.

'Let me do this. I can't live without you now. Let us go and eat or have a drink and talk.'

Despite her exhaustion she agreed. She texted her mother then turned her phone off. They walked through the Bull Ring centre. It was packed with late night Christmas shoppers. Leo clung to her hand.

They pushed open the door to a small restaurant. It was already busy but the waiter found them a table. Leo said, *Good Evening*, to the couples at neighbouring tables. Nobody acknowledged him except for one man who gave him a hostile stare.

Leo smiled at Natalie. 'Did I not say it right?'

'You said it perfectly.' She felt her heart might break into brittle pieces. 'It's just that in restaurants here we don't … usually greet people … we don't know.'

'Ah. I see.' He took the menu from the waiter's outstretched hand and smiled but said nothing.

They ordered pizza. Natalie thought of the meal after the concert at the Mozarteum, the hope she'd had that he might kiss her; the night of her birthday when he brought all her friends together at the restaurant beside the lake. Not in her wildest dreams could she imagine him living here.

But she let him talk and she forced food into her mouth and swallowed it over the lump in her throat. He would rent out his house, he said, and when they visited they could use her apartment. She nodded and smiled through her tears.

Back in his room they undressed and got into bed, clinging together for comfort.

He whispered into her hair, 'You don't want me to do this. To live here.'

She couldn't answer for a long time. Wrapping her arms round his neck she whispered into his ear, 'Living here would destroy you.'

'But I would have you and Toby … and Max. We'd be a family.'

'You'd end up resenting me, Leo.'

They didn't make love. Instead they held each other until sleep pushed the pain to the edges of her mind.

When grey light fringed the blinds Natalie opened her eyes. The room was silent, she was alone in the bed but she didn't call his name. His case was gone. A letter lay on her handbag.

My Darling Natalie, when I bought you the pendant for your birthday I had a ring made to match it. In the weeks that followed I was more and more certain you would wear the ring if I asked you to be my wife. I say this only for you to know how serious is my love for you. Call me if you want me to come to you and I will do this in a heartbeat. I truly believe we must be together. Your Leo.

She could shed no more tears. Instead she was consumed by pain. The *unreal* Natalie beckoned. Leo had paid the bill and she wandered out into the grey morning in the direction of New Street Station. It was a miracle she got on the right train. She heard nothing, not the chatter of passengers nor the rumble of the train. Everything was drowned by his voice against her ear, murmuring his love.

Chapter Seventy-Six

Leo watched the fields and villages recede as the outskirts of London approached. The train was busy and he spent a lot of time with his eyes closed trying to formulate a plan. He must contact a rental agency about the house; enquire about a pet passport for Max. But he kept seeing Natalie's face, stripped of all happiness, pain etched into her features. She didn't want him to leave his home. He couldn't let himself believe that she no longer felt the same about him but what if that were the case? He'd left that desperate note.

She'd be back in Coventry now but he wouldn't look at his phone. He couldn't bear to see more bad news. If she loved him she would let him know and he would come to her.

At Euston he took a cab to Hampstead, asking the driver to drop him off on East Heath Road. He walked across onto the heath where the cold wind ripped through his hair. He saw the city laid out below. Standing there he could almost imagine he was part way up a mountain.

In Heathside Erik's car was on the drive. He felt a fragment of relief but still he should have phoned ahead.

Through the window he could see Christe's grand piano covered with a sheet to protect it from the sun. What uncomplicated lives my friends lead, he thought, so sure of their love and happiness. After he rang the bell he tried to gather his features into a smile of greeting. When Erik opened the door his head jerked back in astonishment.

'Leo. My good friend. Christe, come and see who's here. You won't believe it.'

When Erik put out his hand it was all Leo could do to respond to the handshake. Christe looked up into his face, reached out and took his arm.

'Get him some coffee,' she said, 'and maybe something strong to go with it.' She tugged at Leo's sleeve. 'Come in, you poor man. Whatever it is you're with friends now.'

Chapter Seventy-Seven

The house was empty. Natalie sank into a hot bath but she'd been seized by panic and even in the warm water her limbs shook. Her new life was crumbling and all she could see in her mind's eye was the hurt in Leo's eyes. She tried to focus on Toby. How would it affect him knowing his mother and father abandoned him, and how was she to get over Leo? She thought of her mother's astonishing outburst. Could it really be guilt that had made her so anxious and irritable all this time? Could they ever be friends again?

She washed her hair, wrapped a towel round her head and went down to the kitchen. A text from her mother told her she was at the hospital. Her father had slept well. When the doorbell rang she leapt up, pulled the towel from her head in the sudden hope of seeing Leo.

It was Auntie Maureen.

Natalie hardly recognised her. Gone was the comfy anorak and tweedy skirt. In its place a black duvet jacket and sheepskin boots. She looked furious.

'I'm not staying long. Bernard's in the car.'

'Ask him in then, Auntie.' Entertaining was the last thing she needed.

'I'll not if you don't mind. We're off to Woodlands Garden Centre for Christmas knick-knacks, but I had to come and have a word.'

Her great aunt perched on a stool. 'I've been to the hospital to see your dad this morning and I have to say apart from the tubes and what-have-you he looks right as ninepence. He's been moved out of that coronary care, now. He's on one of them wards with bays and curtains.

'Thank goodness. How did he seem to …?'

'And your mother told me all about this scheme for going to Italy and leaving Toby here with you.'

'Oh God.' Natalie leaned against the breakfast bar. Her head throbbing again. 'Mum said some very weird things to me yesterday, about … George and …'

'I know all about it, Natalie, her feeling guilty from day-one and all that. I saw her sobbing in Florrie's front room enough times.'

'Why did she never say anything to me? Why has she just been horrible and aggressive?'

'She don't cope well, your mother. She's alright with work and such but she never knew how to deal with feelings. I think she should have given up that job of hers and stayed at home. Anyway …' Auntie Maureen wriggled off the stool. 'What I want to know is what you're going to do.'

'I don't think I've got any choice. I've got to do the right thing for Toby. I'll have to stay here.'

'What about this Leo? You said in your message he'd turned up.'

'He wants to stay here with me. But I can't let him do that.' She felt so weary she wanted to slide to the floor like she'd done in the hospital.

'Well I'm not going to ask you why you can't let him do that, but I'm here to tell you this ...'

Her tone was so sharp Natalie struggled to hold back tears.

'Natalie, your dad's helped you out of all sorts of situations over the years, especially since Adam went. He's always been strong but he's not going to be after this. He'll be shipped off to Italy to sit in the sun and wear that stupid hat. You've got to be the strong one now.'

'I've already said I'll stay with Toby and …'

'I don't mean that, Natalie. I mean take control of your life again like you did over there in Austria. Don't be told what you're going to do. Do it to suit yourself and if that means Leo coming over here then that's that.'

She turned to go. 'Look at me,' she said. 'I'm seventy-nine and engaged to be married. You've got to grab happiness, Natalie, it don't blow by that often.' She put on smart black gloves, pushing the fingers over her arthritic knuckles. 'I was supposed to pick Toby up this afternoon but I've rung the school and said you'll do it. Is that alright?'

'Yes. Yes of course I'll pick him up.'

She was engulfed in an Estee Lauder-scented hug and then Auntie Maureen was gone.

She made herself tea, sat on the stool her aunt had vacated and looked at her watch. There was an hour before school ended. For a long time she emptied her head of painful thoughts, stared at a point on the kitchen tiles until her vision blurred. Then she leapt up, grabbed her coat and bag and ran to the bus stop.

There was a crowd of mothers at the gate. Natalie nudged her way gently to the front. Toby was walking towards her with Markus and a teacher. She waved and he waved back, his little face still creased with uncertainty. The teacher introduced herself, asked after her father, but Natalie was in a hurry, just keeping within the bounds of politeness as she lifted Toby's school bag and put it on her shoulder. 'You fancy a walk, Tobes?' She smiled at Markus and his mother and said *Tschüs,* as they waved goodbye.

In the park they sat on a bench. She gave him a chocolate fudge bar and watched him unwrap it. 'I want to ask you something, Toby. It's not Mum's idea or Dad's. It's all mine.'

He looked up at her, his expression guarded as he took his first bite of chocolate. But gradually, as she spoke, his eyes grew wide and his funny, straight eyebrows lifted. When she finished speaking he offered her the last half inch of the fudge bar. She declined it and watched him stuff it into his mouth, thrust the empty wrapper into her hand. He slid off the bench and begin to run doing a circuit of the large flowerbed of winter pansies. His arms were thrust out at the sides and she could just hear the strains of aircraft noise as he wheeled towards the bandstand.

'Come on, Toby. I need to make a phone call.' They just made it to the stop as the bus pulled up.

At her father's computer in the summerhouse Natalie brought up Google, clicked on a link and noted down a telephone number. Glancing at her watch she knew she might just catch someone before they left for the evening.

'*Sprechen Sie Englisch, bitte?*' she asked. This was a call she couldn't trust to her limited German vocabulary.

Chapter Seventy-Eight

'Auntie Maureen, it's Natalie. Did you have a nice time at Woodlands?'

'Yes. We got a tree that actually snows.'

Natalie frowned. 'I have to go to the hospital would you have Toby for a couple of hours.'

'Is your dad alright? He's not had a relapse?'

'No. I'm being strong, Auntie, like you suggested.'

She dropped a grumbling Toby off; held him in a long hug until he struggled and called her an emo. Handing Maureen a bunch of white roses in a glass container she didn't wait for the kiss on the cheek but gave her a smile and headed back to the bus stop.

'You shouldn't spend all day here,' she told her mother as she met her at the coffee machine outside the ward. 'You need some time away now Dad's doing alright.'

Her mother gave her a sheepish smile. 'Where's Toby?'

'Auntie Maureen's.'

'And Leo?'

Natalie bit her lip. 'Back in Salzburg I expect.'

For once her mother didn't seem to have anything to say.

In the ward she kissed her father on the forehead. He was out of bed and sitting in a chair looking more like himself.

'I know the timing is awful for this but I have to tell you something.'

'Are you pregnant?' Her mother clutched her coffee cup with both hands.

'No, I'm not. But I'm going back to Salzburg.'

Red patches appeared on her mother's cheeks and her mouth turned down. 'I really thought you'd stay. That's …'

'Toby's coming with me. I don't mean immediately, but after Christmas, and he'll live with Leo and me.'

'No. Not a chance.' Her mother spilled coffee on her shoe, grabbed a paper tissue and mopped at it. 'I'll never agree to that.'

'He'll go to the English school, I've already spoken to them. They have vacancies and I'm going to see them next week.'

'Don't be ridiculous. You think I'd let my son live with someone we don't even know?'

'He'll be living with me! You wanted me to care for him and I will, forever if need be, but it will be in Salzburg, with Leo.'

'He's talked you into this.'

'No. He knows nothing about it. He doesn't even know I'm going back to him.'

'This is not going to happen. Toby needs to stay here. He's part way through his school year and …'

'And his only friend is leaving in January. He's ten. It's not like he's at high school. And he loves Salzburg, he'll be fine.'

'This is his home. I'm not having you dictate to me …'

'Shut up, Christine.' Her dad spoke very softly. 'Natalie's a thirty-one year old woman offering her brother a home in a place other kids could only dream of and weren't we intending to take him to Italy?'

Her mother blushed to her hair roots. 'John, you're not telling me you think this is a good idea?'

'No. But I think Toby will.'

'Let me finish what I was saying.' Natalie gave her Dad a grateful glance. 'We'll try it for six months and if he isn't happy I promise I'll bring him home. If that happens then we'll think again but …'

'Aren't we forgetting something here?' Her mother put down her coffee and folded her arms. 'We haven't heard what Toby has to say. Why are you so confident he'll want to go?'

'Because I've already asked him. I've told him it's entirely my idea, not yours.'

Her mother's chin began to wobble. 'He said yes? He … he really did? Oh Toby. Toby, my little man.' Her head went down. She covered her face with her hands. Natalie tried to hand her a tissue but was pushed away.

A staff nurse came to the foot of the bed. 'Is everything alright? John, are you feeling okay?'

'I'm alright, Love, it's everyone else at the moment.'

She turned to Natalie. 'I'm not sure this upset is really what your father needs.'

'Please give us a few moments.'

Her mother sobbed for a full minute then she stood up and walked out of the ward.

'Go after her, Natalie. She's about exhausted.'

'No, Dad. I've said all I want to say.'

'It was half an hour before her mother returned. She'd combed her hair, dried her tears and put some lipstick on.

'Sorry, Natalie but what you've said is not going to happen.'

She opened her mouth to speak but her mother's expression silenced her.

'John, if our son wants to live in Austria then we'll all live in Austria.'

'Chris, what are you saying? You've been dreaming of Italy for donkey's years.'

Natalie was speechless. She clasped her hands together to stop them shaking.

'I thought I could do it but I can't. I can't lose him, I …' Her mother sat on the side of the bed, stroked her father's cheek. 'Let's rent a house at that Fuschl place on the lake. It's not far from Salzburg.' She touched Natalie's arm. 'He can still go to that school. We can rent out the house in Italy, maybe go there for a few weeks in the summer. Sell the one here. What do you say?'

Natalie and her father stared at each other. Finally she found her tongue. 'I can't believe you'd do this, Mum. After all you've …'

'I know what I've said, don't remind me. We'd be close enough to see you but not be in your pocket. Not too far from Sabine and … my Papa.'

Mention of her grandfather was the last straw for Natalie. She reached for her mother and they wept together until the staff nurse returned.

'They're about done now,' her dad said.

'I have to go. I've a taxi booked to Stansted. He'll be on his way here now.'

'You're going tonight?' Her mother took hold of her hand.

'I am. I've just about broken Leo. I need to talk to him.' She pulled on her jacket, kissed her father's cheek. 'If Dad is well enough will you all come to Salzburg for Christmas? You can stay with us or in my apartment or even the hotel if you'd rather. Get to know Leo a little better.'

'If they'll let me fly then we will, Lovie.' Her father said. 'Of course we will.'

'Take care, Dad,' she whispered, 'and when you get home tear up that horrible newspaper cutting.'

'If he doesn't I will.' Tears were pouring down her mother's cheeks. 'I'll wait with you for the taxi.'

On the pavement they hugged.

'Natalie. I love you so much and I'm more … proud than I … can ever tell you.'

They held hands until the taxi arrived. She gazed into her mother's eyes as it pulled away then the traffic hid her from view.

Chapter Seventy-Nine

She wept most of the way to Stansted, a long slow release of tension. The taxi cost a fortune but she'd booked a seat on a flight early the following morning and couldn't risk being late.

At the airport she curled up and fell asleep across seats in the baggage-drop hall, her head on her rucksack. When the alarm on her phone went off she stared at the upholstery of the chair, unable to make sense of her surroundings. Troubles crowded in, her dad's health, Toby, Leo's sorrow and then waves of relief when she remembered she was going back to Salzburg.

The airport had filled as she slept; a group of girls, heading to warmer climes wore cut-off jeans, T-shirts and sandals. Natalie, in her fleece and boots didn't envy them a bit.

During the flight she dozed and it hardly seemed any time at all before they began their descent. As the plane sank down into cloud she stared out of the window, anxious for her first glimpse of the mountains.

She saw the three peaks of the Stauffen on the German border, the solid bulk of the Europark shopping mall and the Red Bull's stadium. They'll be Toby's local soccer team, she thought. When the wheels touched the tarmac she let out a sigh loud enough to make the woman at her side turn and smile.

In the arrivals hall she searched the sea of expectant faces for Binita but saw instead Karin, brown as chocolate from her holiday, a wide smile on her face.

'Binita telephoned me. She had to do another trip and Prakash does not work today.'

She held Natalie in a fierce hug. 'You've had a lot of worry. Your Papa is okay?'

'He will be. There's so much I have to tell you.'

As they walked to the car park Natalie breathed in the cold, clear air and held it in her lungs for as long as she could. She saw the Untersberg, like a friendly giant, now wearing a cloak of snow around his shoulders.

'Have you seen anything of Leo?' she asked as Karin steered the mini expertly through the airport complex.

'No. I thought he would be on the flight with you.'

Disappointment seared through Natalie. 'Surely he's back here in Salzburg though?'

'I saw Gerde walking Max this morning so maybe not,' Karin said. 'You know we don't open the hotel for a few more days. You want to meet tonight and go into the city? The Christkindlmarkt has started now.'

'Yes. I'd love that.' It might take her mind off her worries.

'You and Leo, you are still together, yes?' Karin sped down the slip road to the autobahn and Natalie gripped her seatbelt.

'I hope so.'

At her apartment she tried to sleep but an endless trail of events and emotions were on a loop in her head. Even a long soak in the bath couldn't help her relax. She knew she should call Leo, tell him she was in Salzburg, but some things just had to be said face to face. Also she worried he might be angry or re-thinking his feelings.

Standing by the window she saw clouds enveloping the top of the Untersberg. Her fingers strayed to the jewelled heart on its chain and she thought of the ring he said was made to match it. Things had to work out after all they'd been through, the misunderstandings, each of them pulled different ways by their emotions. What a year it had been. She saw rays of sun catching the clouds. Beyond those mountains was her precious, newly discovered family. Soon, not far off to the east, her parents would be living and surely now her mother would find some peace.

Toby would be at school in the city, she could see him whenever she wanted.

At five o'clock she put on clean jeans and a sweatshirt; pulled on boots and her waterproof jacket and walked up to the main road. She headed down one of the quiet lanes which led to the fields and the foot of the Gaisberg. Gerde was at the corner of Leo's road, returning from a walk with Max. The dog danced excitedly, whining a greeting.

'How is your poor Papa?' Gerda kissed Natalie on both cheeks. They stood for a few moments in the cold evening air, catching up on news.

'You and Leo must sort things out and be together.'

'I'm sure we will but … Gerde, I don't know where he is. Has he been in touch?'

'He's in London. He stayed last night with some friends.' The older woman unlatched Leo's gate and led Max to the door. 'He's coming home tomorrow morning.'

Natalie sagged with relief. 'If you speak to him before tomorrow, don't let him know I'm here. I want to surprise him.'

'I won't say a word. Are you staying here tonight? I've put the heating on and groceries in the kitchen.'

'No. I'm just popping in for a moment then I'll take Max to my apartment if that's alright.'

'Yes, you can see he is happy now you are home.'

Thanking Gerde for the supplies Natalie slid her key into the lock. The house was welcoming but still she felt like an intruder moving through to the kitchen and filling Max's water dish. The dog skittered around on the polished floor, nuzzling at her hand.

She fed him, made herself some coffee and sat at the kitchen table. She turned on her phone and rang Karl, explaining she'd be at work on Monday.

Upstairs she ran her hand over Leo's side of the bed, hugged his pillow to her face but the linen was clean and there was no trace of him.

Back down in the hall she was ready to leave but Max pushed open the door to the darkened music room. Natalie watched him barge in, sniffing around the desk before loping back out into the hall.

'Not long now till we see him, boy,' she said, stooping to stroke his head.

Moonlight slanted into the room, illuminating the piano and the piles of sheet music. She walked in, sat down on the stool, switching on a small lamp, pressing a few of the keys, the sound discordant and harsh in the silence. At right angles to the piano was Leo's desk. Was the ring box in there, she wondered. She knew where he kept the key, had seen him lock some lesson fees in there. If she stole a look, then she would know for certain that Leo meant it when he said he wanted her to be his wife. Staring at the drawer until her vision blurred she sat up with a jolt.

'What on earth am I thinking?' She asked Max. 'I don't do that sort of sneaking around. Come on boy.' She stood up, turned to switch off the lamp and that was when she saw it.

Sofia's photograph.

He had placed it on a shelf behind the door, between books on the theory of music. Leo's first wife smiled out of the frame and Natalie, unable to move her legs, smiled back. 'I promise I'll take care of him,' she said. 'And I will always love him.'

Chapter Eighty

Max sat in the back of Karin's mini, leaning into the bends as they hurtled into town.

Crossing the river Natalie saw Makartsteg footbridge ablaze with Christmas lights. In Mozartplatz the composer's statue looked down on the skating rink where children glided expertly around the ice, their parents watching from the sides.

The city was packed with people. She heard English, Italian and American voices as they walked through to Residenzplatz and there was the tree, as tall as the ones on the Gaisberg, shimmering with lights from top to bottom. The Christkindlmarkt stalls lined the square selling every kind of decoration, gifts, jewellery, toys and crafts.

'You like Gluhwein?' Karin gestured to a stall. The scent of the wine was pungent with spices.

'I've never had any.'

Karin opted for coffee but Natalie perched on a high stool and accepted a large steaming mug of wine, sipping it hesitantly. Within seconds the warmth seeped down through her body. 'Wow, this is potent. I need something to eat.'

They ate at a tiny restaurant with Max lying on their feet. Natalie, giddy and excited about seeing Leo in a few hours, talked to her friend about her parents coming to live in Fuschl.

'It's great that they will be here,' Karin said, 'and already they have many friends.'

Later, as they made slow progress through Domplatz Natalie noticed a stall selling giant cookies with personal greetings iced onto the surface. She called to Karin, 'Take Max. I'll see you in a minute, at the Dom steps.'

Fingers shaking she scribbled three words onto a piece of

paper and handed it to the cheerful woman on the cookie stall. Minutes later she wove her way through the crowd, holding the bag aloft to avoid it getting crushed.

'If we wait five minutes we can hear the advent singers.' Karin pointed to a group of people, in traditional clothes, taking position at the entrance to the cathedral. A couple of children walked into the crowd handing out hymn sheets.

When the first voices rose into the frosty night Natalie's skin tingled and sentimental tears sprang to her eyes. She linked her arm through Karin's and they sang, *Stille Nacht, Heilige Nacht.* This time last year she had longed to be in this city. Now it's my home and I'm not that passive, meek little woman any more. Finally I'm the *real* Natalie Grey.

Anton looked a little bleary eyed when he came to her door the next morning but Natalie was wide awake.

'You're sure you want to go up there so early?' he said, holding the taxi door open for her.

'Absolutely. And can you look after this?' She handed him a large flat box which he placed on the passenger seat.

Max, picking up on her mood danced around on his lead but he soon settled next to her as they set off.

It was dark, but already people were gathering at bus stops on the main road. Anton turned away from the city towards Elsbethen then took the lane that zig-zagged into the trees and changed down gears as the road grew steeper. They passed homesteads, windows a-glow, Christmas lights strung along balconies.

'There is snow here,' Anton said, 'but no problem on the road, I think.'

In the light of the headlamps Natalie saw trees sparkling and a thin layer of snow covered the fields. They drove through patches of valley fog and she prayed the summit would be clear.

As they reached an open valley the mountains were silhouetted against a ribbon of pale blue sky. Natalie smiled, hugged Max closer, resisting the urge to ask Anton to drive faster.

They broke the treeline. Ahead was the tiny Gasthaus where she had sat with Karin while Lukas put his hang-glider together. A lifetime ago. The place was closed and the summit carpark deserted.

'Tell me you are not going to walk down the mountain,' Anton said, turning in his seat, an anxious expression on his face.

'Nein. Ich will die Sonnenaufgang sehen.'

Anton looked to the east and nodded. 'Okay, but I think you've gone a little crazy.'

He kept the car engine running and the heater turned up high. Natalie's nose was pressed against the glass watching the strip of blue sky widen then she gripped the door handle as a brushstroke of pink fringed the distant clouds.

She swung open the door and Max bounded out, snuffling through the covering of snow. 'Come on,' she called to Anton. 'You can't miss this.'

Pink spread across patches of cloud, growing closer, a hint of it echoed in the snow at her feet. The colour transformed to yellow and then, cradled between two distant peaks, a bubble of gold. Natalie held her breath as the jewel of sun grew, the mountains edged with orange and the snow-laden trees burnished so bright she had to shade her eyes.

'Wow. It's a new day,' Anton said, coming to stand beside her, his jacket zipped up to his chin and a hat pulled down over his ears.

Natalie barely felt the cold. 'Not just a new day. A new life. A new life for me and for my family too.'

Now the whole sky was streaked with orange. Fans of sunlight reached towards them, the snow glittered like shards of amber.

Natalie drank in the scene, knew at that moment that everything would be alright. More than alright it would be wonderful.

Anton stamped his feet. The blissful moment was over. Natalie picked up Max's lead and walked back to the car.

'So now I take you home?' Anton started the engine.

'Now you take me to the airport,' Natalie said.

With the box under her arm she led Max into Arrivals. Passengers were filing through from the Zurich flight. Natalie saw there was half an hour before the first plane from Gatwick was expected. She bought a takeaway tea and went back out into the sunshine, walking past the taxi rank so that Max could lift his leg against the shrubs. With every step she grew more nervous. Once she nearly dumped the decorated cookie in a waste bin but as the minutes ticked away she went back to arrivals to ensure a place by the barrier.

Max was restless, turning in circles before finally sitting on her feet and giving the biscuit box a sniff. Behind her Natalie heard an English voice. A tour guide had a plastic sign on a stick ready to display to Skiway passengers. An Austrian man in a smart suit had scribbled "George Capewell" on a sheet of A4.

'Gatwick flight's just landed.' She heard someone say. Now her stomach was doing a series of back flips and if Max hadn't been leaning against her legs she was sure they'd have given way. She slid the cookie from its box, holding it with the words hidden against her chest.

Within ten minutes people began to file through; businessmen with just a briefcase; single travellers with hand luggage. Up went some of the handmade signs. People greeted each other, shook hands then the trickle of passengers dried up.

Natalie knew if Leo was on this flight he'd be waiting for his suitcase to come round on the carousel. Her mouth was dry and she could hardly breathe as once again travellers began to appear - youngsters carrying skis and snowboards, middle-aged couples wearing rucksacks, trundling larger bags on wheels.

Natalie thought she might faint.

But there he was, eyes cast down, a newspaper under his arm, wheeling his case towards her. She wanted to call out his name but her mouth couldn't form the word. He was nearly beside her, his head still down, shoulders drooping. Max barked and tugged on his lead. As Leo looked up she let the lead go and held the cookie aloft. Leo's eyes met hers; a look of astonishment at first then his gaze moved up to the iced message and she saw his lips move as he read the words: *Marry me, Leo.*

Then he was round the barrier, his case discarded, holding her, kissing her face, her hair, her lips. The cookie had slipped from her grasp, skidding to the feet of the English tour guide who whooped and clapped, then others joined in. Max leapt against their legs, scattering crumbs and icing, gobbling up the broken pieces.

Natalie clung to Leo, burying her fingers in his hair, breathing in the scent of the man she loved. Arms entwined, blushing from the attention and trail of biscuit crumbs, they moved outside. Leo reined Max in as a taxi moved forward.

Natalie stopped, touched his cheek with her fingertips. 'Leo, my family are coming to live here. Not Salzburg itself, but …'

'That's wonderful,' he said. 'And Natalie …' a wide smile lit up his face as he opened the car door, 'the message on the cookie; the answer is *yes*.'

The End.

Acknowledgements

This novel has been a joy to write. When you can immerse your thoughts, for months on end, in a location you love it makes the writing much easier.

I must first thank the Schnöll family for their enduring friendship and their glorious hotel that was the inspiration for the Hotel Friesen. Members of Leicester Writers' Club and Just Write have given me masses of writing advice and patiently listened to the novel from raw first draft to polished version. Thanks go to the RNA Leicester chapter especially Lizzie Lamb for author publishing advice, to Alison May for pointing me in the right genre direction and Tel Asiado for her unstinting encouragement. Most of all I thank Nigel Ringrose for believing in me and my writing and for hours spent researching author-published material in order to produce this beautiful paperback.

Also by Liz Ringrose

Favourite Things

12936157R00240

Printed in Great Britain
by Amazon.co.uk, Ltd.,
Marston Gate.